BE SURE TO DISCOVER THE FIRST FOUR BOOKS OF
THE MONARCHIES OF GOD

HAWKWOOD'S VOYAGE

THE HERETIC KINGS

THE IRON WARS

THE SECOND EMPIRE

D0365842

SHIPS FROM THE
WEST

BOOK FIVE OF THE MONARCHIES OF GOD

PAUL KEARNEY

ACE BOOKS, NEW YORK

This is a work of fiction. Names, characters, places, and incidents either are the product of the author's imagination or are used fictitiously, and any resemblance to actual persons, living or dead, business establishments, events, or locales is entirely coincidental.

SHIPS FROM THE WEST

An Ace Book / published by arrangement with
Orion Publishing Group

PRINTING HISTORY
Victor Gollancz hardcover edition / 2001
Ace mass-market edition / January 2003

Copyright © 2001 by Paul Kearney.
Cover art by Steve Crisp.
Cover design by Rita Frangie.

Visit our website at
www.penguinputnam.com
Check out the ACE Science Fiction & Fantasy newsletter!

ISBN: 0-441-00929-8

ACE®
Ace Books are published by The Berkley Publishing Group,
a division of Penguin Putnam Inc.,
375 Hudson Street, New York, New York 10014.
ACE and the "A" design
are trademarks belonging to Penguin Putnam Inc.

PRINTED IN THE UNITED STATES OF AMERICA

10 9 8 7 6 5 4 3 2 1

For Dr. Peter Talbot

Acknowledgments to:

John McLaughlin and Jo Fletcher,
for their enormous patience.

PROLOGUE

YEAR OF THE SAINT 561

RICHARD Hawkwood hauled himself out of the gutter whence the crowds had deposited him, and viciously shoved his way through the cheering throng, stamping on feet, elbowing right and left and glaring wildly at all who met his eye.

Cattle. God-damned cattle.

He found a backwater of sorts, an eddy of calm in the lee of a tall house, and there paused to catch his breath. The cheering was deafening, and en masse the humble folk of Abrusio were none too fragrant. He wiped sweat from his eyelids. The crowd erupted into a roar and now from the cobbled roadway there came the clatter of hooves. A blast of trumpets and the cadence of booted feet marching in time. Hawkwood ran his fingers through his beard. God's blood, but he needed a drink.

Some enthusiastic fools were throwing rose petals from upper windows. Hawkwood could just glimpse the open barouche through the crowds, the glint of silver on the grey head within, and beside it a brief blaze of glorious russet hair shot through with amber beads. That was it. The soldiers tramped on in the raucous heat, the barouche trundled away, and the crowd's frenzy winked out like a pinched candle flame. The broad street seemed to unclench itself as men and women dispersed, and the usual street cries of Abrusio's Lower City began again. Hawkwood felt for his purse—still there, although as withered as an old woman's dugs. A lonely pair of coins twisted and clinked under his fingers. Enough for a bottle of the Narboskim at any rate. He was due at the Helmsman soon. They knew him there. He wiped his mouth and set off, a spare, haggard figure in a longshoreman's jerkin and sailor's breeks, his face nut-brown above the grizzled beard. He was forty-eight years old.

"SEVENTEEN years," Milo, the innkeeper, said. "Who'd have thought he'd last so long? God bless him, I say."

A rumble of slurred but cheerful assent from the men gathered about the Helmsman's tables. Hawkwood sipped his brandy in silence. Was it really that long? The years winked past so quickly now, and yet this time he had on his hands here, in places like this—the present—it seemed to stretch out unendingly. Bleary voices, dust dancing in the sunlight. The glare of the day fettered in the burning heart of a wineglass.

Abeleyn IV, son of Bleyn, King of Hebrion by the Grace of God. Where had Hawkwood been the day the boy-king was crowned? Ah, of course. At sea. Those had been the years of the Macassar Run, when he and Julius Albak and Billerand and Haukal had made a tidy sum in the Malacars. He remembered sailing into Rovenan of the Corsairs as bold as brass, all the guns run out and the slow-match smoking about the deck. The tense haggling, giving way to a roaring good fellowship when the Corsairs had finally agreed upon their percentage. Honourable men, in their own way.

That, Hawkwood told himself, had been living, the only true life for a man. The heave and creak of a living ship under one's feet—answerable to no one, with the whole wide world to roam.

Except that he no longer had that hankering to roam. The

life of a mariner had lost much of its shine in the past decade, something he found hard to admit, even to himself, but which he knew to be true. Like an amputated limb which had finally ceased its phantom itching.

Which reminded him why he was here. He swallowed back the foul brandy and poured himself some more, wincing. Narboskim gut-rot. The first thing he would do after— after today would be to buy a bottle of Fimbrian.

What to do with the money? It could be a tidy sum. Maybe he'd ask Galliardo about investing it. Or maybe he'd just buy himself a brisk, well-found cutter, and take off to the Levangore. Or join the damned Corsairs, why not.

He knew he would do none of these things. It was a bitter gift of middle age, self-knowledge. It withered away the damn fool dreams and ambitions of youth leaving so-called wisdom in its wake. To a soul tired of making mistakes it sometimes seemed to close every door and shutter every window in the mind's eye. Hawkwood gazed into his glass, and smiled. I am become a sodden philosopher, he thought, the brandy loosening up his brain at last.

"Hawkwood? It is Captain Hawkwood, is it not?" A plump, sweaty hand thrust itself into Hawkwood's vision. He shook it automatically, grimacing at the slimy perspiration which sucked at his palm.

"That's me. You, I take it, are Grobus."

A fat man sat down opposite him. He reeked of perfume, and gold rings dragged down his earlobes. A yard behind him stood another, this one broad-shouldered and thuggish, watchful.

"You've no need of a bodyguard here, Grobus. No one who asks for me has any trouble."

"One cannot be too careful." The fat man clicked his fingers at the frowning innkeeper. "A bottle of Candelarian, my man, and two glasses—clean ones, mind." He dabbed his temples with a lace handkerchief.

"Well, Captain, I believe we may come to an arrangement. I have spoken to my partner and we have hit upon a suitable

sum." A coil of paper was produced from Grobus's sleeve.
"I trust you will find it satisfactory."

Hawkwood looked at the number written thereon, and his
face did not change.

"You're in jest, of course."

"Oh no, I assure you. This is a fair price. After all—"

"It might be a fair price for a worm-eaten rowboat, not
for a high-seas carrack."

"If you will allow me, Captain, I must point out that the
Osprey has been nowhere near the high seas for some eight
years now. Her entire hull is bored through and through with
teredo, and most of her masts and yards are long since gone.
We are talking of a harbour hulk here, a mere shell of a
ship."

"What do you intend to do with her?" Hawkwood asked,
staring into his glass again. He sounded tired. The coil of
paper he left untouched on the table between them.

"There is nothing for it but the breaker's yard. Her interior
timbers are still whole, her ribs, knees and suchlike sound as
a bell. But she is not worth refitting. The navy yard has
already expressed an interest."

Hawkwood raised his head, but his eyes were blank and
sightless. The innkeeper arrived with the Candelarian,
popped the cork and poured two goblets of the fine wine.
The Wine of Ships, as it was known. Grobus sipped at his,
watching Hawkwood with a mixture of wariness and puzzle-
ment.

"That ship has sailed beyond the knowledge of geogra-
phers," Hawkwood said at last. "She has dropped anchor in
lands hitherto unknown to man. I will not have her broken
up."

Grobus pinched wine from his upper lip. "If you will forgive me, Captain, you do not have any choice. A multitude
of heroic myths may surround the *Osprey* and yourself, but
myth does not plump out a flaccid purse—or fill a wine glass
for that matter. You already owe a fortune in harbour fees.
Even Galliardo di Ponera cannot help you with them any-
more. If you accept my offer you will clear your debts and

have a little left over for your—for your retirement. It is a fair offer I am making, and—"

"Your offer is refused," Hawkwood said abruptly, rising. "I am sorry to have wasted your time, Grobus. As of this moment, the *Osprey* is no longer for sale."

"Captain, you must see sense—"

But Hawkwood was already striding out of the inn, the bottle of Candelarian swinging from one hand.

A *multitude of heroic myths*. Is that what they were? For Hawkwood they were the stuff of shrieking nightmare, images which the passing of ten years had hardly dulled.

A slug from the neck of the bottle. He closed his eyes gratefully for the warmth of it. My, how the world had changed—some things, anyway.

His *Osprey* was moored fore and aft to anchored buoys in the Outer Roads. It was a fair pull in a skiff, but at least here he was alone, and the motion of the swell was like a lullaby. Those familiar stinks of tar and salt and wood and seawater. But his ship was a mastless hulk, her yards sold off one by one and year by year to pay for her mooring rent. A stake in a freighting venture some five years before had swallowed up what savings Hawkwood had possessed, and Murad had done the rest.

He thought of the times on that terrible journey in the west when he had stood guard over Murad in the night. How easy murder would have been back then. But now the scarred nobleman moved in a different world, one of the great of the land, and Hawkwood was nothing but dust at his feet.

Seagulls scrabbling on the deck above his head. They had covered it with guano too hard and deep to be cleared away. Hawkwood looked out of the wide windows of the stern cabin within which he sat—these at least he had not sold—and stared landwards at Abrusio rising up out of the sea, shrouded in her own smog, garlanded with the masts of ships, crowned by fortresses and palaces. He raised the bottle to her, the old whore, and drank some more, setting his feet on the heavy fixed table and clinking aside the rusted, broad-bladed hangar thereon. He kept it here for the rats—they grew fractious and impertinent sometimes—and also for the odd ship-stripper who might have the stamina to scull out this far. Not that there was much left to strip.

That scrabbling again on the deck above. Hawkwood glared at it irritably but another swallow of the good wine eased his nerves. The sun was going down, turning the swell into a saffron blaze. He watched the slow progress of a merchant caravel, square-rigged, as it sailed close-hauled into the Inner Roads with the breeze—what there was of it—hard on the starboard bow. They'd be half the night putting into port at that rate. Why hadn't the fool sent up his lateen yards?

Steps on the companionway. Hawkwood started, set down the bottle, reached clumsily for the sword, but by then the cabin door was already open, and a cloaked figure in a broad-brimmed hat was stepping over the storm sill.

"Hello, Captain."

"Who in the hell are you?"

"We met a few times, years ago now." The hat was doffed, revealing an entirely bald head, two dark, humane eyes set in an ivory-pale face. "And you came to my tower once, to help a mutual friend."

Hawkwood sank back in his chair. "Golophin, of course. I know you now. The years have been kind. You look younger than when I last saw you."

One beetling eyebrow raised fractionally. "Indeed. Ah, Candelarian. May I?"

"If you don't mind sharing the neck of a bottle with a commoner."

Golophin took a practised swig. "Excellent. I am glad to see your circumstances are not reduced in every respect, Captain."

"You sailed out here? I heard no boat hook on."

"I got here under my own power, you might say."

"Well, there's a stool by the bulkhead behind you. You'll get a crick in your neck if you stoop like that much longer."

"My thanks. The bowels of ships were never built with gangling wretches like myself in mind."

They sat passing the bottle back and forth companionably enough, staring out at the death of the day and the caravel's slow progress towards the Inner Roads. Abrusio came to twinkling life before them, until at last it was a looming shadow lit by half a million yellow lights, and the stars were shamed into insignificance.

The lees of the wine at last. Hawkwood kissed the side of the bottle and tossed it in a corner to clink with its empty fellows. Golophin had lit a pale clay pipe and was puffing it with evident enjoyment. Finally he thumbed down the bowl and broke the silence.

"You seem a remarkably incurious man, Captain, if I may say so."

Hawkwood stared out the stern windows as before. "Curiosity as a quality is overrated."

"I agree, though it can lead to the uncovering of useful knowledge, on occasion. You are bankrupt I hear, or within a stone's cast of it."

"Port gossip travels far."

"This ship is something of a maritime curiosity."

"As am I."

"Yes. I had no idea of the hatred Lord Murad bears for you, though you may not believe that. He has been busy, these last few years."

Hawkwood turned. He was a black silhouette against the brighter water shifting behind him, and the last red rays of the sun had touched the waves with blood.

"Remarkably busy."

"You should not have refused the reward the King offered. Had you taken it, Murad's malignance would have been hampered at least. But instead he has had free rein these last ten years to make sure that your every venture fails. If one must have powerful enemies, Captain, one should not spurn powerful friends."

"Golophin, you did not come here to offer me half-baked truisms or old wives' wisdom. What do you want?"

The wizard laughed and studied the blackened leaf in his pipe. "Fair enough. I want you to enter the King's service."

Taken aback, Hawkwood asked, "Why?"

"Because kings need friends too, and you are too valuable a man to let crawl into the neck of a bottle."

"How very altruistic of you," Hawkwood snarled, but his anger seemed somehow hollow.

"Not at all. Hebrion, whether you choose to admit it or no, is in your debt, as is the King. And you helped a friend of mine at one time, which sets me in your debt also."

"The world would be a better place if I had not bothered."

"Perhaps." There was a pause.

Then Hawkwood said quietly, "He was my friend too."

The light had gone, and now the cabin was in darkness save for a slight phosphorescence from the water beyond the stern windows.

"I am not the man I was, Golophin," Hawkwood whispered. "I am become afraid of the sea."

"We are none of us what we were, but you are still the master mariner who brought his ship back from the greatest voyage in recorded history. It is not the sea you fear, Richard, but the things you found dwelling on the other side of it. Those things are here, now. You are one of a select few who have encountered them and lived. Hebrion has need of you."

A strangled laugh. "I am a withered stick for Hebrion to lean on, to be sure. What service had you and the King in mind? Royal Doorkeeper, or Master of the Royal Rowboat perhaps."

"We want you to design ships for the Hebrian navy, along the lines of the *Osprey* here. Fast, weatherly ships which can carry many guns. New sail plans and new yards."

Hawkwood was speechless for a while. "Why now?" he asked at last. "What has happened?"

"Yesterday the arch-mage Aruan, whom you and I know, was proclaimed Vicar-General of the Inceptine Order here in Normannia. His first act in office was to announce the creation of a new military order. Though it is not generally known, I have been able to find out that this new body is to be composed entirely of mages and shifters. He calls them the 'Hounds of God'."

"Saint in heaven!"

"What we want you to do, Captain, is to help prepare Hebrion for war."

"What war is that?"

"One which is to be fought very soon. Not this year perhaps, but within the next few. A battle for mastery of this continent. No man will be unaffected by it—nor will any man be able to ignore it."

"Unless he drinks himself to death first."

Golophin nodded sombrely. "There is that."

"So I am to help you prepare for some great struggle with the warlocks and werewolves of the world. And in return—"

"In return you will attain a high position in the navy, and at court, I promise you."

"What of Murad? He won't like my . . . elevation."

"Murad will do as he's told."

"And his wife?"

"What of her?"

"Nothing. No matter. I will do it, Golophin. For this I'll crawl out of that bottle."

The wizard's grin shone in the gloom of the cabin. "I knew you would. How very fortunate that Grobus offered so paltry a price today. We will have need of the *Gabrian Osprey*. She is to be the prototype for a new fleet."

"You knew of that. You had a hand—"

"Damn right."

Nothing changes, Hawkwood thought. The nobility have sudden need of you, so they pluck you out of the gutter, peer at the disappointed little life they pinch twisting between their fingers, and set it down on their great gaming board where it can be put to use. Well this pawn has its own rules.

"It's dark as pitch in here. Let me light a lantern." Hawkwood fumbled for his tinderbox and after striking flint and steel a dozen times was able to coax into life a ship's lantern which still had some oil in its well. The thick glass was cracked, but that was of no moment. Its yellow kindly light

illuminated the creviced features of the wizard opposite and
blacked out the sea astern.

"So may I expect you at the gate of Admiral's Tower
tomorrow morning?" Golophin asked.

Hawkwood nodded assent.

"Excellent." The mage tossed a small doeskin bag on the
table that clinked heavily. "An advance on your wages. You
might want to outfit yourself with a new wardrobe. Quarters
will be arranged in the tower."

"Will be arranged, or have been arranged?"

Golophin rose and donned his hat. "Until tomorrow then,
Captain," and he held out a hand.

Hawkwood shook it, rising in turn. His face was a stiff
mask. Golophin turned to go, and then halted. "It is no bad
thing when personal inclination and the dictates of policy go
together, Captain. We need you, it is true, but I for one am
glad to have you besides. The court is full of well-bred
snakes. The King has need of one or two honest men around
him too."

He left, stooping as he entered the companionway. Hawkwood listened to him stride forward to the waist, and then
there was that scrabbling seagull on deck again, and then
silence.

LATER, he lay on his oars a cable's length from the *Osprey*
and watched her burn. Somehow the ship reclaimed some
of her old beauty as the flames swept up from her decks and
roared bright and blazing into the night sky. The fire reflected
wet and shining from his eyes and he sat watching until she
had burned down to the waterline and the sea began rushing
in to quench the inferno. A hissing of steam, and then a
murmuring gurgle as what was left of her hull turned over
and sank beneath the waves. Hawkwood wiped his face in
the choppy darkness.

He'd build their damn navy, and jump through whatever
hoops they put in front of him. It was a way of surviving,

after all. But his brave ship would never become a mere blueprint in some naval surveyor's office.

He picked up his oars, and began the long haul back to shore.

PART ONE

THE FALL OF HEBRION

He uncovers the deeps out of darkness,
and brings great darkness to light.
He makes nations great, and he destroys them;
He enlarges nations, and leads them away.
He takes away understanding from the chiefs
of the people of the earth,
And makes them wander in a pathless waste.

Job ch:12, v. 23–24

ONE

THE knot of riders pummelled along the sea cliffs in a billow of tawny dust. Young men on tall horses, they came to a thundering halt scant inches from the edge and sat their snorting mounts there laughing and slapping dust from their clothes. The sun, bright as a cymbal, beat down on the sky-blue sea far below and made the glitter of the horizon too bright for the eye to bear. It caused the sere mountains behind the riders to ripple and shimmer like a vision.

Cantering up to join the horsemen came another, but this was an older man, his dress sombre, and his beard gun-metal grey. His mount came to a sober halt and he wiped sweat from his temples.

"You'll break your damn fool necks if you're not careful. Don't you know the rock is rotten there at the edge?"

Most of the younger men eased their horses away from the fearsome drop sheepishly, but one remained in place, a broad-shouldered youth with pale blue eyes and hair black as a raven's feather. His mount was a handsome grey gelding which stood prick-eared and attentive between his knees.

"Bevan, where would I be without you? I suppose Mother told you to follow us."

"She did, small wonder. Now get away from the edge, Bleyn. Make an old man happy."

Bleyn smiled and backed the grey from the brink of the sea cliff one yard, two. Then he dismounted in a motion as easy as the flow of water, patted the neck of the sweating horse and slapped dust from his riding leathers. On foot he was shorter than one would have guessed, with a powerfully built torso set square on a pair of stout legs. The physique of a longshoreman topped by the incongruously fine-boned face of an aristocrat.

"We came to see if we could catch a glimpse of the fleet," he said, somewhat contrite.

"Then look to the headland there—Grios Point. They'll be coming into view any time now, with this breeze. They weighed anchor in the middle of the night."

The other riders dismounted also, hobbled their horses and unhooked wineskins from their saddles.

"What's it all about anyway, Bevan?" one of them asked. "Stuck out here in the provinces, we're always the last to know."

"It's a huge pirate fleet, I hear," another said. "Up from the Macassars looking for blood and plunder."

"I don't know about pirates," Bevan said slowly, "but I do know that your father, Bleyn, had to call up all the retainers on the estate and tear off to Abrusio with them in tow. It's a general levy, and we haven't seen one of those in . . . oh sixteen, seventeen years now."

"He's not my father," Bleyn said quickly, his fine-boned face flushing dark.

Bevan looked at him. "Now listen—"

"There they are!" one of the others shouted excitedly. "Just coming round the point."

They all stared, silent now. The cicadas clicked endlessly in the heat around them, but there was a breeze off the barren mountains at their backs.

Around the rocky headland, over a league away. Coming

into view was what resembled a flock of far-off birds perched on the waves. It was the brightness of the sails which was striking at first—the heavy swell partially hid their hulls. Tall men-of-war with the scarlet pennants of Hebrion snapping from their mainmasts. Twelve, fifteen, twenty great ships in line of battle, smashing aside the waves and forging out to sea with the wind on their starboard beam and their sails bright as a swan's wing.

"It's the entire western fleet," Bevan murmured. "What in the world . . . ?"

He turned to Bleyn, who was shading his eyes with one hand and peering intently seawards.

"They're beautiful," the young man said, awed. "They truly are."

"Ten thousand men you're looking at there, lad. The greatest navy in the world. Your—Lord Murad will be aboard, and no doubt half the Galiapeno retainers, puking their guts out I'll be bound."

"Lucky bastards," Bleyn breathed. "And here we are like a bunch of widows at a ball, watching them go."

"What is it all for? Is it a war we haven't heard of?" one of the others asked, perplexed.

"Damned if I know," Bevan rasped. "It's something big, to draw out the entire fleet like that."

"Maybe it's the Himerians and the Knights Militant, come invading at last," one of the younger ones squeaked.

"They'd come through the Hebros passes, fool. They've no ships worth speaking of."

"The Sea-Merduks then."

"We've been at peace with them these forty years or more."

"Well there's something out there. You don't send a fleet out to sea for the fun of it."

"Mother will know," Bleyn said abruptly. He turned and remounted the tall grey in one fluid movement. "I'm going home. Bevan, you stay with this lot. You'll slow me down." The gelding pranced like a sprightly ghost below him, snorting.

"You just wait a moment—" Bevan began, but he was already gone, leaving only a zephyr of dust behind.

L ADY Jemilla was a striking woman with hair still as dark as her son's. Only in bright sunlight could the grey be seen threading it through, like silver veining the face of a mine. She had been a famous beauty in her youth, and it was rumoured that the King himself had at one time honoured her with his attentions; but she was now the dutiful well-bred wife of Hebrion's High Chamberlain, Lord Murad of Galiapeno, and had been for almost fifteen years. The colourful escapades that had enlivened her youth were now all but forgotten at court, and Bleyn knew nothing of them.

Murad's fiefdom, tucked away on the Galapen Peninsula south-west of Abrusio, was something of a backwater, and the high manse which had housed his family for generations was an austere fortress-like edifice built out of cold Hebros stone. In the heat of high summer it still retained an echo of winter chill and there was a low fire burning in the cavernous hearth of Jemilla's apartments. She was running over the household accounts at her desk, whilst beside her an open window afforded a view of the sun-baked olive groves of her husband's estates like some brightly lit fragment of a sunnier world.

The clamour of her son's arrival was unmistakable. She smiled, losing ten years in an instant, and knuckled her small fists into the hollow of her back as she arched, cat-like, from the desk.

The door opened and a grinning footman appeared. "Lady—"

"Let him in, Dominan."

"Yes, lady."

Bleyn blew in like a gale, reeking of horse and sweat and warm leather. He embraced his mother, and she kissed him on the lips. "What is it this time?"

"Ships—a million ships—well a great fleet at any rate. They passed by Grios Point this morning. Bevan tells me that Murad is aboard, with the retainers he took to Abrusio last month. What's afoot, Mother? What great events are sailing us by this time?" Bleyn collapsed on to a nearby couch, shedding dust and horsehair over its antique velvet.

"He is Lord Murad to you, Bleyn," Jemilla said tartly. "Even a son must not be too familiar when his father is of the high nobility."

"He's not my father." An automatic snap of petulance.

Jemilla leaned forward wearily, lowering her voice in turn. "To the world he is. Now, these ships—"

"But we know better, Mother. Why pretend?"

"If you want to keep your head on your shoulders, then to you he must be Father also. Prate to your friends all you want—I have them watched. But in front of strangers, you will swallow this pill with a smile. Understand me now, Bleyn. I am tired explaining."

"I am tired pretending. I am seventeen, Mother—a man in my own right."

"When you cease pretending, this man you have suddenly become will no longer have a life to be tired of, I promise you. Abeleyn will not tolerate a cuckoo—not yet—for all that that Astaran whore has a womb as barren as a salted field."

"I don't understand. Surely even a bastard heir is better than no heir at all."

"It comes of the Civil War. He wants everything absolutely clear. A legitimate king's heir, with whom no one can quibble. He is not yet fifty, and she is younger. And they have that sorcerer Golophin weaving his spells, coaxing his seed into her year by year."

"And all for nothing."

"Yes. Be patient, Bleyn. He will come to his senses in the end and realise, as you say, that a bastard is better than nothing." Jemilla smiled as she said this, and her smile was not altogether pleasant. She saw how it wounded him. Well and good—it was something he would have to get used to.

She ruffled his dust-caked hair. "What is this about a fleet of ships then?"

He was sullen, slow to answer, but she could see the curiosity burning away the sulk.

"The whole battle fleet, Bevan says. What's going on, Mother? What war have we missed?"

Now it was she who paused. "I—I don't know."

"You must know. He tells you everything."

"He does not. I know little more than you do. All the households have been turned out, and there has been a Grand Alliance signed, the likes of which has not been seen since the days of the First Empire. Hebrion, Astarac—"

"—Gabrion, Torunna and the Sea-Merduks. Yes Mother, that has been old news for months now. So the Himerians are finally invading–is that it? But they have no fleet worth speaking of. And Bevan said our ships are westbound. What's out there but empty ocean?"

"What indeed? A host of rumours and legends, perhaps. A myth about to be made flesh."

"And now you talk in riddles again. Cannot you ever give me a straight answer?"

"Hold your tongue," Jemilla snapped. "You're barely seventeen summers old in the way of the world, and you think you can bandy words with me and belittle your—your father? Whelp."

He subsided, glowering.

In a softer tone she went on, "There are legends of a land out in the uttermost west, a new world that remains undiscovered and uninhabited. They are the stuff of children's bedtime stories here in Hebrion, and have been for centuries. But what if the children's tales were true—what if there was indeed a vast, unknown continent out there in the west—and what if I told you that Hebrian ships had already been there, Hebrian feet had trodden those uncharted strands?"

"I would say, bravo for Hebrian enterprise, but what has this to do with the armada I saw this morning?"

"There's been talk at court, Bleyn, and even here I have caught the gist of it. Hebrion is about to face the threat of invasion, it would seem."

"So it is the Himerians!"

"No. It is something else. Something from the west."

"The west? Why—aha—you mean there really is some

new empire out beyond the sea? Mother, this is amazing news! How can you sit there so calm? What marvellous times we live in!" Bleyn leapt up and began striding back and forth across the chamber, slapping the palms of his hands together in his excitement. His mother watched him dourly. Still a boy, with a boy's enthusiasms, and a boy's ignorance. She had thought to have done better. Perhaps if his father had truly been Abeleyn—or Murad—he would have been different, but this pup was the progeny of one Richard Hawkwood, a man Jemilla might once, ironically enough, have actually loved–the only man she might once have loved—but a commoner, and thus useless to her life and her ambitions. Still, she thought, one must work with the tools one is given. And he is my son, after all. I am his mother. And I do love him— there is no gainsaying that.

"Not an empire," she corrected him. "Or at least, not yet. Whatever it is that has arisen out there, it seems to have been connected to events here, in Normannia, for untold centuries. How, I am not sure, but the Himerians are part of it, and the Second Empire somehow within its control."

"You are very vague, Mother," said Bleyn with some circumspection.

"It is all I know. Few men anywhere know more except Lord Murad, and the King, and Golophin his wizard."

And Richard Hawkwood. The thought came unbidden to her. He too would know everything, having captained that unhappy voyage all those years ago. The greatest feat of maritime navigation in history, it was said, but the Crown had clamped down on all mention of it in subsequent years. The initial interest—nay, hysteria—had faded within a year. No log books were ever published, no survivor ever hawked his story in street-sold handbills. It was as though it had never happened.

Her husband it was who had seen to that. Murad forgot nothing, forgave nothing. The man was obsessed with ruining Richard Hawkwood—why, Jemilla could not fathom. Something had happened to them out there in the west, something horrible. It was as if Murad were trying to expunge it

from his soul. And if he could not, then he would bury every
reminder of it he could.

If he ever found out that Bleyn were actually the mariner's
son . . . Jemilla's face grew cold at the thought.

So Hawkwood had gained nothing from his great voyage,
once the initial run of banquets and audiences had run their
course. It had been a nine-day wonder, quickly forgotten.
Even the King, she thought, had been happy to have it that
way. What had happened out there, to destroy their expedition and so blight their lives?

And what was coming from that terrible place now that
warranted such preparations? Alliances, ship-building pro-
grammes, fortification projects: in the last five years Hebrion
and her allies had been preparing for a vast struggle with the
unknown. And now, it had begun. She could sense it as
surely as if it were some noisome reek brought on the back
of the wind.

Bleyn was watching her. "How can you sit here like this,
Mother—so uninterested? You're a woman, I know—but not
like any other—"

"You know so many then?"

"I know other noblewomen. You are a hawk amongst pi-
geons."

She laughed. Perhaps he was not so much of a boy as she
had thought. "I keep my place, Bleyn, as I must. Lord Murad
is not a man to cross lightly, as you know, and he prefers
that you and I stay away from court. The King prefers it that
way also. We are a skeleton long hidden in the back of a
closet. We must be patient, is all."

"I am a man now. I can sit a horse as well as any trooper,
and I'm the best fencer in all of Galiapeno. I should be out
there on those ships, or at least commanding a tercio in the
city garrison. My blood demands it. It would demand it even
were I Murad's son and not the King's."

"Yes, it would."

"What kind of education do you think I get out here in
the country? I know nothing of court or of the other nobility—"

"That's enough, Bleyn. I can only counsel patience. Your time will come."

Bleyn's voice rose. "It will come when at last I am a doddering greybeard and my youth has been poured out on the stones of this damned backwater!" He stormed out of the chamber, his shoulder thumping the door frame as he went. The dust of his passage hung in the air after him. Jemilla could smell it. Dust. All that was left of sixteen years of her life. She had aimed high once—too high—and this semi-imprisonment had been her punishment, Murad her jailer. She was lucky to be alive. But Bleyn was right. It was time to chance another cast perhaps, before sixteen more years passed in the arid dust and sunlight of this damned backwater.

TWO

THE first primroses were out, and new bracken was curling up in gothic-green shoots through the massed needles of the pinewoods. That smell in the wind—of pine resin and new grass and growing things; a clean, sharpness from which the chill was finally departing, to be replaced by something new.

The horses had caught the flavour of the air and were prancing and nipping at each other like colts. The two riders ahead of the main party let them have their heads, and were soon galloping full tilt along the flank of one of the great upland fells which formed this part of the world. When their mounts were blowing and steaming, they reined them in again, and continued at an amble.

"Hydrax is coming on well," the man said. "It seems you have a talent there, after all."

His companion, a girl or young woman, curled her lip. "I should think so. Shamarq says that if I spend any more time on horseback I'll be bow-legged. But who would notice in court dress anyway?"

The man laughed, and they rode on in companionable silence, the horses picking their way through the tough gnarls of hill heather. Once the girl pointed wordlessly skywards, to where a solitary raptor soared in the north. The man followed her finger and nodded.

Half a mile behind them a straggling band of some forty riders followed doggedly. Some were richly dressed ladies, others armoured cavalrymen. One bore a silk banner which whipped and twisted in the wind so that its device was impossible to make out. Many led heavily laden pack-mules that clanked as they walked.

The man turned in the saddle. "We'd best let them catch up. They're not all centaurs like you."

"I know. Briseis rides like a frog on a griddle. And Gebbia is not much better."

"They're ladies-in-waiting, Mirren, not horse troopers. I'll wager they sew and cook a good deal better than they ride. Well, sew at any rate."

That curl of the lip again. The man smiled. He was a broad-shouldered fellow in middle age, his once dark hair grey at the temples, giving him the look of a grizzled badger. Old scars marked his weather-beaten face and his eyes were deep-hollowed, grey as a winter sea, and there was a coldness to them that softened only when he looked upon the girl at his side. He sat his mount with the consummate ease of a born horseman, and his clothing, though well-made, was plain and unadorned. It was also black, dark as a panther's pelt with no hint of colour to relieve it.

The girl at his side, in contrast, was dressed in bright brocade heavily worked with pearls and gems, with a lace ruff at her white throat and a finely woven linen and wire headdress on her yellow hair. She sat her horse like a young queen. Her elegance was marred, however, by the battered old riding cloak she had thrown over her shoulders. It was a soldier's cloak, and had seen hard service, though it had been lovingly repaired many times. Peeping out from under its folds there appeared for a moment the wizened face of a marmoset. It sniffed the bracing air, shuddered, and withdrew once more.

"Must we go back, Father?" the girl asked her sombrely clad companion. "It's been such fun."

Her father, the King of Torunna, set his warm hand atop her fingers on the reins.

"The best things," he said quietly, "are better not savoured too long." And there came into his cold eyes a shadow that held no hope of spring. Seeing it, she took his hand and kissed it.

"I know. Duty calls once more. But I'd rather be out here like this than warm in the greatest palace of the world."

He nodded. "So would I."

The thud and snuffle and chatter of the party behind them as they caught up, and Corfe turned his horse to greet them.

"Felorin, I believe we may begin to make our way back to the city. Turn this cavalcade around, and warn the steward. We will make camp one hour before sunset. I trust you to find a suitable site. Ladies, I commend your forbearance. This last night in tents, and tomorrow you shall be in the comfort of the palace. I entrust you to the care of my Bodyguard. Felorin, the Princess and I will catch you up in a few hours. I have somewhere I wish to go."

"Alone, sire?" the rider called Felorin asked. He was a slender whip of a man whose handsome face was a swirl of scarlet tattoos. He wore a black surcoat with vermilion trimming, and a cavalry sabre bounced at his thigh.

"Alone. Don't worry, Felorin. I still know my way about this part of the world."

"But the wolves, sire—"

"We have fleet horses. Now stop clucking at me and go seek out tonight's campsite."

Felorin saluted, looking discontented and concerned, and then turned his horse about and sped off to the rear of the little column. The cavalcade, turning about, made a clanking, braying, confusing circus of soldiers, ladies and servants, restive mules, mincing palfreys. Corfe turned to his daughter.

"Come, Mirren." And he led her off into the hills at a fast canter.

THE clouds broke open above their heads, and flooding out of the blueness came bright sunlight which kindled the flanks of the fells and made them a tawny and russet pelt running with tumbled shadow. Mirren followed her father as he pounded along what appeared to be an old, overgrown track nestled in the encroaching heather. The horses' hoofs thudded on hard, moss-green gravel instead of soggy peat, and they picked up speed. The track ran straight as an arrow into the east; in summer it would be well-nigh invisible beneath the bracken.

Corfe slowed to a walk and his daughter wrestled her own mount to a similar pace beside him. Despite her youth her horse, Hydrax, was a solid bay fully as large as her father's black gelding. A martingale curbed some of his wilder headtossing, but he was still prancing mischievously under her.

"That bugger will have you off one of these days," Corfe said.

"I know. But he loves me. It's high spirits is all. Father, what's all the mystery? Where are we going? And what is this old road we're on?"

"You've not much notion of history—or geography—despite those tutors we gathered from the four corners of the world. I take it you know where we are?"

"Of course," Mirren said scornfully. "This is Barossa."

"Yes. 'The Place of Bones,' in Old Normannic. It was not always named so. This is the old Western Road, which once ran from Torunn clear to what was Aekir."

"Aurungabar," his daughter corrected him.

"Yes, by way of Ormann Dyke . . ."

"Khedi Anwar."

"The very same. This was the spine of Torunna once upon a time, this old track. The Kingsway runs to the north-west, some twelve leagues, but it's barely fifteen years old. Before Torunna even existed, before this region was known as Barossa, it was the easternmost province of the old empire. The

Fimbrians built this road we trot upon, as they built most things that have endured in the world. It's forgotten now, such are men's memories, but once it was the highway of armies, the route of fleeing peoples."

"You—you came along this way from Aurungabar when you were just a common soldier," Mirren ventured, with a timidity quite unlike her.

"Yes," Corfe said. "Yes, I did. Almost eighteen years ago." He remembered the mud, the cold rain, and the hordes of broken people, the bodies lying by the hundred at the side of the road.

"The world is different now, thank God. Up along the Kingsway they've cleared the woods and burnt off the heather and planted farms in the very face of the hills. There are towns there where before it was wilderness. And here, where the towns used to be before the war came, the land has been given back to nature, and the wolves roam unmolested. History turns things on their heads. Perhaps it is no bad thing. And there, up ahead—can you see the ruins?"

A long ridgeline rose ahead of them, a dark spatter of trees marking its crest. And at its northern end could be seen broken walls of low stone, like blackened teeth jutting up from the earth. But closer to, there rose up from the flatter land a tumulus, too symmetrical to be of nature. Atop it a stone cairn stood stark against the sky. The birdsong which had been brash and cheery about them all morning had suddenly stilled. "What is this place?" Mirren asked in a whisper.

Corfe did not answer, but rode on to the very foot of the tall mound. Here he dismounted, and gave Mirren his hand as she followed suit. The marmoset reappeared and swarmed up to her shoulder, its tail curling about her neck like a scarf.

There were stone flags set in the grass, and the pair climbed up them until they stood before the cairn on the summit. It was some five feet high, and a granite slab had been set upon its top. There were words chiselled into the dark stone.

Here lie we, Torunna's dead,
Whose lives once bought a nation liberty.

Mirren's mouth opened. "Is this—?"

"The ruins you see were once a hamlet named Armage-dir," Corfe said quietly.

"And the mound?"

"A grave barrow. We gathered all those whom we could find, and interred them here. I have many friends in this place, Mirren."

She took his hand. "Does anyone else come here any-more?"

"Formio and Aras and I, once every year. Apart from that, it is left to the wolves and the kites and the ravens. Since the mound was raised, this world of ours has moved on at a pace I would never once have believed possible. But it exists in its present form only because of the men whose bones moulder underneath our feet. That is something you, as my daughter, must never forget, even if others do."

Mirren made as if to speak, but Corfe silenced her with a gesture. "Wait."

Arrowing out of the west there came a single bird, a falcon or hawk of some kind. It circled their heads once, and then plummeted towards them. The marmoset shrieked, and Mir-ren soothed it with a caress. The bird, a large gyrfalcon, alighted on the grass mere feet away, and spent a few sec-onds rearranging its pinion feathers before opening its hooked beak and speaking in the low mellifluous voice of a grown man.

"Your majesty. We are well met."

"Golophin. What tidings from the west?"

The bird cocked its head to one side to bring one inhuman yellow eye to bear. "The combined fleet put to sea three days ago. They are cruising in the area of North Cape and have a squadron out keeping watch on the western approaches to the Brenn Isles. Nothing as yet."

"But you're sure the enemy is at sea."

"Oh yes. We've had a picket line of galliots cruising be-yond the Hebrionese for four months. In the last sennight every one of them has disappeared. And a fair portion of the northern herrin fleet has failed to make it back to port, and yet the weather has been fine and clear. There's something out there, all right."

"What of your raptor's eyes?"

A pause, as if the bird were distracted or Golophin was considering his words. "My familiar is based here, in Torunna, for the moment, your majesty, to keep whole the link between east and west."

"Charibon then. What news?"

"Ah—there I have something a little more tangible. The Himerian armies are breaking up winter quarters as I speak. They will be on the march within a fortnight I would hazard, or as soon as the Torrin Gap is free of the last drifts. The Thurian Line is awash with marching men."

"It has begun then," Corfe breathed. "After all this time, the curtain has risen."

"I believe so, sire."

"What of the Fimbrians?"

"No word as yet. They are playing a waiting game. The Pact of Neyr may have broadcast their neutrality to the world, but they will have to climb down from their fence sooner or later."

"If this yet-unseen fleet manages to make landfall it could well make up their minds for them."

"And it will also mean a two-front war."

"Yes of course."

"I trust, sire, that all your preparations are in hand?"

"The principal field army awaits only my word to march, and General Aras has the northern garrison on alert at Gaderion. You will let me know as soon as anything happens?"

"Of course, sire. May I convey to you the compliments and greetings of your Royal cousin Abeleyn of Hebrion? And now I must go."

The bird's wings exploded into a flurry of feathers and it took off like a loosed clothyard, soaring up into the spring blue. Corfe watched it go, frowning.

"So that was Golophin—or his familiar, at least," Mirren said, eyes bright. "The great Hebrian mage. I've heard so much about him."

"Yes. He's a good man, though his years are beginning to tell on him now. He took it hard, his apprentice going the way he did."

"Ah, the Presbyter of the Knights. Is it true he is a werewolf as well as a mage?"

Corfe looked at his daughter closely. "Someone has been listening at keyholes."

Mirren flushed. "It is common folklore, no more."

"Then you will know that our world is threatened by an unholy trinity. Himerius the anti-Pontiff, Aruan the sorcerer, now Vicar-General of the Inceptine Order, and Bardolin, another arch-mage, who is Presbyter of the Knights Militant. And yes, this Bardolin is rumoured to be a shifter. He was Golophin's friend, and brightest pupil. Now he is Aruan's creature, body and soul. And Aruan is the greatest of the three, for all that he has the lesser rank in the eyes of the world."

"They say that Aruan is an immortal, the last survivor of an ancient race of men who arose in the west, but who destroyed themselves in ages past with dabbling in black sorcery," Mirren whispered.

"*They* say a great deal, but for once there is a nubbin of truth under all the tall tales. This Aruan came out of nowhere scarcely six years ago now, landing at Alsten Island with a few followers in strange-looking ships. Himerius at once recognised him as some kind of messianic prodigy and admitted him to the highest circles of power. He claims to be some form of harbinger of a better age of the world. He is immensely old, that we know, but as for the lost race of conjurors—well, that's a myth, I'm sure. In any case, he has the armies of Perigraine and Almark and half a dozen other principalities to call upon, as well as the Orders of the Knights Militant and the mysterious Hounds. The Second Empire, as this unholy combine is known, is a fact of our waking world—"

"The Fimbrians," Mirren interrupted. "What will they do?"

"Ah, there's the rub. Which way will the Electorates jump? They've been hankering after a rekindling of their hegemony ever since the fall of Aekir, but this new thearchy has stymied them. I'm not sure. We will be fighting for the self-determination of all the Ramusian kingdoms, and that is not something the Fimbrians would particularly like to see. On the other hand, they do not want to watch the Himerians become invincible, either. I reckon they'll wait it out until we and Charibon have exhausted ourselves, and then step in like hyenas to pick over the bones."

"I've never known a war," Mirren said with uncharacteristic timidity. She stroked the marmoset which perched on her shoulder. "What is it like, Father?"

Corfe stared out over the barren swells of the upland moors. Sixteen years ago, this quiet emptiness had been the epicentre of a roaring holocaust. If he tried, he was sure he would hear the thunder of the cannon echoing still, as it echoed always in the dark, hungry spaces of his mind.

"War is a step over the threshold of hell," he said at last. "I pray you never experience it first hand."

"But you were a great general—you commanded armies— you were a conqueror."

Corfe looked down at her coldly. "I was fighting for survival. There's a difference."

She was undaunted. "And this next war—it also is about survival, is it not?"

"Yes. Yes, it is. We have not sought this battle; it has been thrust upon us—remember that." His voice was sombre as that of a mourner.

But the hunger and the darkness within him were crowing and cackling with glee.

THREE

"THE birds," said Abeleyn. "They follow the ships."

Over the fleet hung a cloud of raucous gulls, thousands of them. They wheeled and swooped madly and their unending shrieks hurt the air, carrying over even the creak of timber, the smash of keel striking water, the groan of rope and yard.

"Scavengers," Admiral Rovero called out from the quarterdeck below. "But it's strange, is it not, to see them so far out from land."

"I have never seen it before. The odd one, yes, but not flocks like these," Hawkwood told him.

All down the four levels of the spar deck—forecastle, waist, quarterdeck, poop—soldiers and sailors were staring upwards, past the cracking, bellied sails, the straining yards, the bewildering complexities of the rigging. The gulls circled tirelessly, screaming.

Below them the flagship shouldered aside the swell with a beautiful easy motion. The *Pontifidad* was a tall man-of-war of twelve hundred tons with seven hundred men on board, and eighty long guns which were now bowsed up tight against the closed portlids like captured beasts straining for their liberty. A floating battery of immense destructive power, she was the largest warship in the western world, the pride of the Hebrian navy.

And she may not be enough, Abeleyn thought. She and all her mighty consorts, the assembled might of four nations. What are men and ships compared to—

"Sail ho!" the lookout yelled down from the main topgallant yard. "A caravel coming out of the eye of the wind, fine on the larboard beam."

"Our reconnaissance returns," Hawkwood said. "With what news I wonder?"

The knot of men stood on the poop deck of the *Pontifidad* and awaited the approaching ship calmly. Two days before a small squadron had been sent out to the west to reconnoitre while the fleet beat up round the headland now safely astern.

Admiral Rovero called up to the lookout from the quarterdeck. "How many sail there?"

"Still just the one, sir. She's got a fore topsail carried away and I see braces on her flying loose."

Abeleyn and Hawkwood looked at one another.

"What do you think, Captain?" Abeleyn asked.

Hawkwood rubbed a hand through the peppery tangle of his beard. "I think the squadron may well have found what it was looking for."

"My thoughts also."

Admiral Rovero thumped up the companionway to the poop and saluted his monarch. "Sire, there's no one to be seen on her deck. It smells bad to me. Permission to beat to quarters."

"Granted, Rovero. Captain Hawkwood, I believe we should signal the allied contingents. Enemy to nor'-west. Clear for action."

"Aye, sir."

OVER several square miles of ocean, the fleet came to urgent, scurrying life. Fifty-three great ships and dozens of smaller carracks and caravels were travelling north-east with the breeze broad on their larboard beam. The solitary caravel, a small vessel gauging no more than a hundred tons, ran headlong before the wind towards their gaping broadsides.

The fleet was in a rough arrowhead formation. The point was formed of Hebrian ships, the largest contingent. The left barb belonged to the Gabrionese, eleven lean, well-manned vessels with crews of superb seamen. The right barb consisted of the Astarans: larger ships, but less experienced crews. And the shank of the arrowhead was made up of the Sea-Merduks. Their vessels were lighter, as were their guns, but they were crowded with arquebusiers and buckler-men.

All told, over thirty thousand men rode the waves this bright spring morning, fifty leagues off the west coast of Hebrion. It was the biggest conglomeration of naval power the world had yet seen, and its assembling had been the patient work of years. Ten days now they had been cruising westwards together, having rendezvoused off the Hebrian coast a fortnight since. All for this one day, this moment in time. This bright spring morning on the swells of the Western Ocean.

The stink of slow-match drifted up to Abeleyn from the gun deck, along with the sweat of the sailors as they hauled the huge guns outboard so that their muzzles protruded from the ship's sides like blunt spikes. Above him, in the tops, soldiers were loading the wicked little two-pounder swivels, ramming loads down the barrels of their arquebuses, hauling up buckets of seawater to fight the inevitable fires that would catch in the sails.

The caravel was less than three cables away now, and careering directly for the flagship. There was no one at her tiller, but her course was unerring.

"I don't like this. That's a dead ship with a live helm," Rovero said. "Sire, permission to blow her out of the water."

Abeleyn paused in thought, and for a moment could have sworn that the regard of all those hundreds of sailors and soldiers and marines was fastened upon him alone. At last he said: "Granted, Admiral."

The signal pennants went up, and moments later the massed ordnance of the fleet began to thunder out, awesome as the wrath of God.

The caravel disappeared in a murderous storm of spuming water. Hawkwood saw timbers flying high in the air, a mast lurch and topple enmeshed in rigging. Cannonballs fell short and overshot, but enough were on target to smash the little vessel to kindling. When it reappeared it was a dismasted hulk, low in the water and surrounded by debris. The gulls shrieked overhead as the smoke and roar of the broadsides died away.

"I hope to God we were right," Admiral Rovero murmured.

"Look at her decks!" someone yelled from the masthead.

Men crowded the ship's rail, impatient for the powder smoke to clear. The knot of officers on the poop were higher up, and thus saw it before the sailors in the waist.

Cockroaches? Hawkwood thought. My God.

As the caravel settled, black, shining things were clambering up out of her hatches and taking to the sea, for all the world like some aquatic swarm of beetles. A horrified buzz ran through the ship as the men glimpsed them.

"Back to your stations!" Hawkwood roared. "This is a king's ship, not a pleasure yacht! Bosun—start that man by the cathead."

The beetle figures tried to clasp on to the wreckage of the caravel, but it was in its death throes, circling stern-first down into a foaming grave and sucking most of them down with it. Soon there was nothing left on the surface of the sea but a few bobbing fragments of wreckage.

A yelp of pain as the bosun brought a knotted rope's end down on some unfortunate's back. The men returned to their battle-stations, but their whispering could be heard like a low surf from the poop.

"They captured our squadron, and obviously are aware of our location," Admiral Rovero said.

Whatever *they* are, Abeleyn thought. But he nodded in agreement. "That is what we wanted, after all. We cannot cruise indefinitely. The enemy must come to us." He turned to Hawkwood, and lowered his voice. "Captain, the things in that ship. Have you—?"

"No, sire. We saw nothing like that in the west."

As Hawkwood spoke there was the sudden flap and crack of wilting canvas overhead. They looked up to see the sails go limp as the wind died. For a few moments it was so silent on board that the only noise seemed to be the rasping of the sea past the cutwater. Then that faded too. The very waves became still, and in the space of half a glass the entire fleet was wallowing in a clock-calm, its formation scrambling as the ships began to box the compass. The abrupt stillness was astonishing.

"What in the world?" King Abeleyn said. "Captain, this cannot be right."

"It's not natural," Hawkwood told him. "There's sorcery at play here. Weather-working."

The ship's bell rang out, and seconds later those of the other ships in the fleet followed suit as their quartermasters collected their wits. The sound was somehow desolate in the midst of that vast, dead ocean. Seven bells. It was barely mid-afternoon. The sea was a vast blue mirror, as even and unruffled as the flawless sky above it. The fleet resembled nothing so much as a chaotic, bristling city somehow set afloat upon the ocean, and for all its teeming might, it was dwarfed into insignificance by the vastness of the element which surrounded it. The gulls had disappeared.

THE preternatural calm lasted into the evening, when a mist began to creep up on the fleet from the west. Faint as spider-silk at first, it swiftly thickened into a deep fog laden with moisture, blotting out the stars, the young moon, even the mast lanterns of all but neighbouring ships. Into the night the conches blew, arquebuses were fired at stated intervals, and lookouts posted fore and aft shouted their enquiries into the blank grey wall. The fleet drifted with flaccid sails, and crews spent anxious hours at the rail with long poles, lest they be needed to ward off a collision. All order was lost, and ships of Astarac became entangled with ships of Gabrion, and slim Merduk vessels were thumped and dunted by great Hebrian galleons.

THE Kings of Hebrion and Astarac, along with Admiral Rovero and Captain Hawkwood, met in the Great Cabin of the *Pontifidad* just after eight bells had struck the end of the last dog-watch. King Mark had set out for the flagship to confer with his Royal cousin just after the fog had descended, and had been several hours in a cutter, rowed from ship to ship until he found his goal. His face was pasty and ill-looking despite the motionless sea.

The setting was a magnificent one, the curving, gilded sweep of the stern windows glittering in the light of overhead lanterns slung in gimbals, and two eighteen-pounder culverins bowsed up snug to their ports forward. The long table that ran athwartships was covered in charts, wine glasses, and a decanter. The liquid within the latter was as level as if it sat upon dry land.

"The men are becoming tired," Hawkwood said. "We've had them at quarters for nigh on six hours. The last watch has missed its turn below decks."

"The enemy is very close—somewhere out in the fog," Rovero said harshly. "They have to be. They'll come at us ere the dawn. The men must remain at their posts."

A momentary silence. They sipped their wine and listened to the melancholy calls of the lookouts, the far-off crack of an arquebus. Hawkwood had never known a crew so quiet. Usually there was a hum of talk, a splurge of laughter, ribaldry or profanity to be heard, even as far aft as this, but the ship's company waited on deck in the dew-laden darkness with scarcely a word, their eyes wide as they watched the wall of fog swirl formlessly before them.

"And who—or what—exactly are the enemy?" King Mark asked. "Those things in the caravel were not human, or did not appear so. Nor did they seem to be shifters like those encountered by the Captain here on his expedition."

The table looked at Hawkwood. He could only shrug. "I am as much in the dark as anyone, sire. It's a fair number of years since that voyage. Who knows what they have been doing there in that time, what travesties they have been hatching?"

A knock on the cabin door, and a marine stepped in. "Lord Murad, sire. Desires an audience." The marine's face was chalky with fear.

Hawkwood and Rovero shared a swift look, but then Murad was with them, bowing prettily to his king. "I hope I see you well, sire." To their surprise his voice shook as he spoke. Water droplets beaded his face.

"You do. How was the haul to the flagship, cousin? The night is as thick as soup."

"My coxswain hailed every ship in turn until we found the *Pontifidad*. He is as hoarse as a crow and I am dew-soaked and salt-crusted. We followed in the wake of King Mark, it seems. Your majesty, forgive me"—this to Mark of Astarac who sat watching wordlessly—"Duke Frobishir of Gabrion has also been looking for the flagship, I am told. He must still be out there in the fog. A man could be rowed around all night and finish where he started, it is so thick. But I am forgetting my manners. Admiral Rovero, my compliments—and here of course is my old comrade and shipmate, Captain Hawkwood. It has been awhile, Captain, since we exchanged more than a nod at court."

Hawkwood ducked his head, face closed.

Murad had put on some flesh since returning from his ill-starred voyage to the Western Continent. He would never be plump, but there was a certain sleekness to him now which made his scarred, wedge-shaped face less sinister than it once had been. Neither would he ever be handsome in any conventional sense, but his eyes were deep-set coal gleams which missed nothing and which gazed often, it was said, on the naked forms of other men's wives. This despite his marriage to the celebrated beauty Lady Jemilla. Hawkwood met those obsidian eyes and felt the mocking challenge within them. The two men were bitter enemies, the mariner's elevation of the past few years seemingly adding an even keener edge to Murad's hatred, but they kept up a civilised enough pretence in front of the King.

Murad's initial discomfiture had fled. "I have brought you a gift, sire, something which I think we may all find intriguing, and, dare I say it, educational. With your permission." He raised his voice to a shout. "Varian! Have it brought in here!"

There was a commotion in the companionway beyond the stern cabin, men swearing and bumping. The door opened to admit four burly sailors dragging a large hessian sack which bulged heavily. They dropped it on the deck of the Great Cabin, knuckled their foreheads to the astonished company within, and then left with a strange, hunted haste.

The thing stank, of stagnant seawater and some other, nameless reek which Hawkwood could not identify, though it seemed hauntingly familiar. The men in the cabin rose to their feet to peer as Murad pulled back the mouth of the sack.

Something black and gleaming lay bundled within.

The nobleman took his poniard and ripped open the hessian with a flourish. Spilling out on to the cabin floor was what seemed at first glance to be a jumbled set of black armour. But the stink that poured out of it set them all to coughing and reaching for handkerchiefs.

"God Almighty!" Abeleyn exclaimed.

"Not God, sire," Murad said grimly. "Nothing to do with God at all."

"How did you snare it?" demanded Hawkwood.

"We trolled for it with a net one of the crew had, in the wake of the caravel's sinking. We brought up others—all dead, like this—but threw them back and kept this as the finest specimen." There was surly triumph in Murad's voice.

"At least they drown then, like normal beasts," Rovero said. "What in the Saint's name is that stuff? It's not metal."

"It's horn." Abeleyn, less ginger than the rest, had knelt beside the carcass and was examining it closely, tapping it with the pommel of his dagger. "Heavy, though. Too heavy to float. Look at the pincers there at the end of the arms! Like a giant lobster. And the spikes on the feet would pierce wood. Captain, help me here."

Together the mariner and the King grasped a segment of plate that might be said to be the helm of the creature. They tugged and grunted, and there was a sharp crack, followed by a nauseating sucking sound. The helm part came free, and the smell it released set them coughing again. Hawkwood controlled his heaves first.

"It's a man then, after all."

A contorted ebony face with snarling yellow teeth, the lips drawn back, the eyes a pale amber colour. It was a study in bone and sinew and bulging tendon, an anatomist's model.

"A man," King Mark of Astarac said, rather doubtfully.

"If they're men, then they can be beaten by other men," said Abeleyn. "Take heart, my friends. Rovero, let this news be passed on to the crew at once. It's ordinary men in strange armour we face, not soulless demons."

"Aye, sire." Rovero gave the corpse a last, dubious stare, and left the cabin.

Hawkwood, Abeleyn, Murad and Mark were left to gaze at the dripping carrion at their feet.

"It's like no kind of man I've ever seen before," Hawkwood said. "Not even in Punt are their skins so black. And see the corner teeth? Sharp as a hound's. They've been filed, I believe. Some of the Corsairs do the same to render themselves more fearsome-looking."

"Those eyes," Abeleyn muttered. "He burns in hell now, this fellow. You can see it in the eyes. He knew where he was going."

They stood in an uncomfortable silence, the agony in the dead man's face holding them all.

"He may be a man, but something dreadful has been done to him all the same," Mark said in almost a whisper. "These sorcerers . . . Will their lord, Aruan, be here in person, you think?"

Abeleyn shook his head. "Golophin tells me he is still in Charibon, marshalling his forces."

"This fleet of theirs—"

"Is very close now. It may only have been sighted once or twice in the last ten years, but it exists. Small ships it is said, lateen-rigged and bluff-bowed. Scores of them. They appear out of mists like this. They've been raiding the Brenn Isles these two years past and more, taking the children and disappearing as they came. Odd-looking ships with high castles to fore and aft."

"Like the cogs of ancient times," Hawkwood put in.

"Yes, I suppose so. But my point is that they are built for boarding. Our long guns can—can keep them at bay . . ." The King's voice fell and they all looked at one another as the same thought struck them at once. In this fog, long guns were next to useless, and an enemy ship might drift close enough to board before anyone had any notion of her.

"If our sails are empty, then theirs are also," Hawkwood said. "I've not heard tell they have any galleys, and even the most skilled of weather-workers can affect only an area of ocean—he cannot choose to propel individual ships. They're boxing the compass just like us, and these things here"—he nudged the corpse with his foot—"they can't swim it seems, which is another blessing."

Abeleyn slapped him on the shoulder. "You hearten me, Captain. It is the good sense of mariners we need now, not the paranoia of politicians. You may rejoin the admiral on deck. We shall be up presently."

Dismissed, Hawkwood left the cabin, but not before trading chill glances with Murad.

Abeleyn flicked the hessian over the snarling dead face on the deck and poured himself a long glass of wine. "I should like to keep this thing as a specimen for Golophin to examine when he next visits us, but I fear the crew would not be overly enthusiastic at the notion. And the stink!" He drained his glass.

"Mark, Murad, no formality now. I want advice as the"— he raised his empty glass ironically—"supreme commander of our little expedition. We have enough supplies for another month's cruising, and then we must put about for Abrusio. If we are not attacked tonight, then—"

"We're not going anywhere as long as this calm lasts," Murad interrupted him harshly. "Sire, while we are helpless and blind in this airless fog, it may be that the enemy is sailing past us in clear skies, and is intent on invading a kingdom stripped of its most able defenders."

"Golophin has six thousand men garrisoned in Abrusio, and another ten scattered up and down the coast," Abeleyn snapped.

"But they are not the best men, and he is no soldier, but a mage. Who's to know how his weathercock loyalties may swing if he sees this thing going against us?"

"Don't go doubting Golophin's loyalty to me, cousin. Without him this alliance would never have been possible."

"All the same, sire," Murad answered him, unabashed, "I'd as soon as seen a soldier in command back in Hebrion. General Mercado—"

"Is dead these ten years. I see where you are going with this, kinsman, and the answer is no. You remain with the fleet. I need you here."

Murad bowed. "Cousin, forgive me."

"There is nothing to forgive. And I do not believe we will be bypassed by the enemy."

"Why not, sire?"

King Mark of Astarac spoke up in the act of filling his own glass. His face had regained some of its colour. "Because there are too many ripe royal apples in this basket to let it go by unplucked. Isn't that so, Abeleyn? We're dangling out here like the worm on the end of a hook."

"Something like that, cousin."

"Hence the pomp and circumstance that attended our departure," Mark said wryly. "Bar an engraved invitation, we have done everything we could to persuade the enemy to rendezvous with us. Abeleyn, I salute your cleverness. I just hope we have not been too clever by half. When is Golophin due to drop in again?"

"In the morning."

"You can't summon him in any way?"

"No. His familiar is with Corfe, in the east."

"A pity. For all your doubts, Murad, I for one would feel a lot happier with the old boy around. If nothing else, he might blow away this accursed mist, or whistle up a wind."

"Sire, you speak sense," Murad said, with what passed for humility with him. "If the enemy has any intelligence at all of our comings and goings, then he will attack tonight, while the elements are still in his favour. I must get back to my ship."

"Don't bump into anything in the dark," Abeleyn told him, shaking his hand.

"If I do, it had best not be allergic to steel. Your majesties, excuse me, and may God go with you."

"God," said Abeleyn after he had left. "What has God to do with it any more?" He refilled the wine glasses, and emptied his own at a single draught.

THE night passed, the stars wheeled uncaring and unseen beyond the shroud of fog that held the fleet captive.

Unforgivably, Hawkwood had nodded off. He jerked upright with a start, a sense of urgent knowledge burning in his mind. As his eyes focused he took in the steady glow of the lamp motionless in its gimbals, the blur of the chart on the table before him resolving itself into the familiar coastal line of Hebrion, the shining dividers lying where they had dropped from his limp fingers. He had been dozing for a few minutes, no more, but something had happened in that time. He could feel it.

And he looked up, to see he was not alone in the cabin.

A darkness there in the corner, beyond the reach of the light. It was crouched under the low ship timbers. For an instant he thought he saw two lights wink once, and then the darkness coalesced into the silhouette of a man. Above his head eight bells rang out, announcing the end of the middle watch. It was four hours after midnight, and dawn was racing towards him over the Hebros Mountains far to the east. It would arrive in the space of half a watch. But here on the Western Ocean, night reigned still.

"Richard. It is good to see you again."

Hawkwood tilted the lamp, and saw standing in the corner of the cabin the robed figure of Bardolin. He shot to his feet, letting the lamp swing free and career back and forth to create shadowed chaos out of the cabin. He lurched forward, and in a moment had grasped Bardolin's powerful shoulders, bruising the flesh under the black robes. A wild grin split his face, and the mage answered it. They embraced, laughing—and the next instant Hawkwood drew back again as if a snake had lunged at him. The smile fled.

"What are you come here for?" His hand went to his hip, but he had unslung his baldric, and the cutlass hung on the back of his chair.

"It's been a long time, Captain," Bardolin said. As he advanced into the light, Hawkwood retreated. The mage held up a hand. "Please, Richard, grant me a moment—no calling out or foolishness. What has it been, fifteen years?"

"Something like that."

"I remember Griella and I searching the docks of old Abrusio for the *Osprey* that morning"—a spasm of pain ran across his face—"and the brandy I shared with Billerand."

"What happened to you, Bardolin? What did they do to you?"

The mage smiled.

"How the world has changed under our feet. I should never have gone into the west with you, Hawkwood. Better to have burned in Hebrion. But that's all empty regret now. We cannot unmake the past, and we cannot wish ourselves other than we are."

Hawkwood's hammering heart slowed a little. His hand edged towards the hilt of the cutlass. "You'd best do it and have done then."

"I'm not here to kill you, you damned fool. I'm here to offer you life." Suddenly he was the old Bardolin again; the dreamy menace retreated. "I owe you that at least. Of them all, you were the only one who was a friend to me."

"And Golophin."

"Yes—him too. But that's another matter entirely. Hawk-wood, grab yourself a longboat or a rowboat or whatever passes for a small insignificant craft among you mariners, and get into it. Push off from this floating argosy and her consorts, and scull out into the empty ocean if you want to see the dawn."

"What's going to happen?"

"You're all dead men, and your ships are already sunk. Believe me, for the love of God. You have to get clear of this fleet."

"Tell me, Bardolin."

But the strange detachment had returned. It did not seem to Hawkwood that it was truly Bardolin who smiled now.

"Tell you what? For the sake of old friendship I have done my best to warn you. You were always a stubborn fool, Cap-tain. I wish you luck, or if that fails, a quick and painless end."

He faded like the light of a candle when the sun brightens behind it, but Hawkwood saw the agony behind his eyes ere he disappeared. Then Hawkwood was alone in the cabin, and the sweat was running down his back in streams.

He heard the gunfire and the shrieking up on deck, and knew that whatever Bardolin had tried to warn him about had begun.

FOUR

S NOW lay bright and indomitable on the peaks of the Cim-brics, and beyond their blinding majesty the sky was blue as a kingfisher's back. But spring was in the air, even as high up as this, and the margins of the Sea of Tor were ringed with only a mash of undulating pancake ice which opened and closed silently around the bows and sterns of the fishing boats that plied its waters.

In Charibon the last yard-long icicles had fallen from the eaves of the cathedral and the lead of the roof was steaming in the sunlight. The monks could be heard singing Sext. When they were done they would troop out in sombre lines to the great refectories of the monastery-city for their midday meal, and when they had eaten they would repair to the scrip-toriums or the library or the vegetable and herb gardens or the smithies to continue the work which they offered up to God along with their songs. These rituals had remained un-changed for centuries, and were the cornerstones of monastic life. But Charibon itself, seat of the Pontiff and tabernacle of western learning, had changed utterly since the Schism of eighteen years before.

It had always been home to a large military presence, for here were the barracks and training grounds of the Knights Militant, the Church's secular arm. But now it seemed that the austere old city had exploded into an untidy welter of recent building, with vast swathes of the surrounding plain now covered with lines of wooden huts and turf-walled tents, and linking them a raw new set of gravel-bedded roads spider-webbing out in all directions. West to Almark they went, north to Finnmark, south to Perigraine, and east to the Torrin Gap, where the Cimbrics and the tall Thurians halted, leaving an empty space against the sky, a funnel through which invading armies had poured for millennia.

And on the parade grounds the armies mustered, bristling masses of armoured men. Some on horseback with tall lances and pennons crackling in the wind, others on foot with shouldered pikes, or arquebuses, and others manhandling the carriages of long-muzzled field guns, waving rammers and linstocks and sponges and leading trains of mules which drew rattling limbers and caissons. The song of the monks in their quiet cloisters was drowned out by the cadenced tramp of booted feet and the low thunder of ten thousand horses. The flags of a dozen kingdoms, duchies and principalities flapped over their ranks. Almark, Perigraine, Gardiac, Finnmark, Fulk, Candelaria, Touron, Tarber. Charibon was now the abode of armies, and the seat of Empire.

THE Fimbrian embassy had been billeted in the old Pontifical Palace which overlooked the Library of Saint Garaso and the Inceptine cloisters. Twelve men in trailworn sable, they had tramped at their fearsome pace across the Malvennor Mountains, over the Narian Hills and down on to the plains of Tor to consult with the Pontiff Himerius in Charibon. They had marched for miles amid the tented and log-hewn city which had sprung up around the monastery, noting with a professional eye the armouries and smithies and horse lines, the camp discipline of the huge host dwelling there, and the endless lines of supply wagons that came and went to the rich farmlands of the south and west, all under tribute now. Almark and Perigraine were no longer counted among the monarchies of the Five Kingdoms. Himerian presbyters ruled them, priestly autocrats answerable only to the High Pontiff himself, and King Cadamost had shaved his head and become an Inceptine novice.

It was twelve years since the Fimbrian Electors had signed the Pact of Neyr with the Second Empire, wherein they had professed complete neutrality in the doings of the continent outside their borders. They had sent an army east to aid Torunna against the Merduk, only to see half of it destroyed and the other half desert to the command of the new Torunnan king. This had brought to an abrupt halt their dreams of rekindling some form of imperial power in Normannia, and to add insult to injury they had in subsequent years seen a steady trickle of their best soldiers desert and take ship for the east, where they had joined the tercios of King Corfe and his renegade Fimbrian general, Formio. The Torunnan victories of sixteen years before had shaken the Electorates, who had long been accustomed to viewing all other western powers as inferior in military professionalism to themselves. But the heterogeneous army which Corfe had led to such savage victories against the Merduk had given them much food for thought. The Torunnans were now the most renowned soldiers in the world—at least as long as they were led by their present king. And they were now part of this Grand Alliance which encompassed Hebrion, Astarac, Gabrion, and even Ostrabar. Set against this confederation was the might of the Second Empire. At the court of the Electors it had long been decided that Fimbria would swallow her pride, bide her time and await the collision of these two titans. After the dust had cleared, then that would be the time for Fimbria to reassert her old claims on the continent, and not before—no matter how this neutrality might frustrate and even anger the common soldiers of the army, who were burning to reclaim their reputation as the conquerors of the west. But times were changing with a rapidity bewildering to those who had grown up with the twin certainties of the indivisible Holy Church and the menace of the heathen east, and Fimbria had decided to review her policies, and take stock of the new order of the world.

"I make it at least thirty thousands of infantry, and ten of cavalry," Grall said, consulting the varicoloured counters which littered the table.

Justus turned from the window and his view of Charibon's faithful streaming out of the cathedral into the square below. Almost all the clerics he saw were in black. One or two in Antillian brown here and there, but for the most part the Inceptines seemed to have virtually subsumed every other religious order in the world. In this half of the continent, at any rate.

"There are other camps," he told his companion. "Further to the east, towards the gap. They have fortresses there in the foothills of the Thurians. Their entire strength may be half as much again."

"And that's not counting their garrisons," a third raven-clad Fimbrian put in from his post by the fire. "Our intelligence indicates that they have large contingents in Vol Ephrir and Alstadt, and even as far west as Fulk."

"Hardly surprising," Grall said. "They have the resources of half the continent to draw upon, and then there are these *others* . . ." With an impatient gesture, he began scooping the counters into a leather pouch, scowling.

"It is mainly these others that we are here to find out about," Justus told him. "Armies of men, we can prepare for. But if half the rumours are true—"

"If half the rumours are true then the Second Empire has both God and the devil on its side." Grall chuckled. "I dare-say it is mostly a case of tall tales and skilful rumour-handling."

The Fimbrian at the fire was shorter, and older than the other two. His hair was a cropped silver, and his face was as hard and seamed as wood. Only his eyes gave him away. They flashed now like two cerulean gemstones. "There is more to it than that. There are strange things happening in Charibon; there have been ever since this Aruan appeared out of nowhere five, six years go and waltzed into the Vicar-

Generalship as though it had been specially set aside for him."

"Do you think the stories about him are true then, Briannon?" Grall asked. There was a mocking edge to his voice.

"The world is full of strange things. This man has opened the doors of the Himerian Church to all the sorcerers and witches of the Five Kingdoms, reversing the ecclesiastical policies of generations, and they have come flocking to him as though he were Ramusio himself. Why would he do this? Where has he come from? And what manner of man is he? That is what we are here to find out. Now, before the storm clouds break and it is too late."

A knock on the door of the chamber, and a man who might have been brother to any of those within peered inside and said, "It's time, sir. They're expecting us in a few moments."

"Very well," Briannon answered. He repaired to a side chamber for a few minutes, and when he returned some of the worst of the grime had been slapped off his uniform, and he wore a scarlet sash about his middle.

"No circlet?" Grall asked wryly. He and Justus had buckled on short swords of iron and wiped some of the mud off their boots, but aside from that they looked much as they had when they had marched into Charibon the night before.

"No. As we agreed, I am Marshal Briannon here—no relation to the Elector who happens to share my name."

THE Pontifical Reception Hall had been built to overawe. It resembled the nave of a cathedral. Every supplicant who sought an audience with the High Pontiff must needs tramp a long, intimidating path down its length towards the high dais at the end, his every move flanked by alcoves in the massive walls—every one of which held the figure of a Knight Militant in full armour, standing like a graven statue, but following everything with his eyes.

At the far end, Himerius sat on a tall throne, and on either side of him stood his Vicar-General, and the Presbyter of the Knights. Other monks were black shadows in the background, murmuring and scraping quills across parchment. Although it was a bright spring day outside, and sunlight flooded in through the tall windows that butted the vaulted roof of the building, braziers were burning around the dais, and elaborately carved wooden screens had been drawn around, so it seemed that Himerius and his advisors were cloaked in shadow and flame light, and difficult to make out after the dazzling length of the hall.

The twelve Fimbrians marched sombrely towards this darkness. Their swords had been left in the antechamber and their hands were empty but they somehow seemed more formidable than the heavily armoured Knights whom they passed by.

They came to a cadenced halt before the dais, and were enveloped in the shadow that surrounded Himerius.

Grall was listening to the opening exchanges with one part of his mind, but more of it was studying the men he saw before him. Himerius was old—in his seventies now—and his frame seemed withered and lost in the rich robes which clad it. But his eyes were bright as a raptor's, his ivory face still retaining a haggard vitality.

To his right stood a tall man in Inceptine black, with the chain of the Vicariate around his neck. He was monk-bald, but had the air about him of a great nobleman. He had a hawk nose that put even Himerius's to shame, and thick, sprawling eyebrows over deep orbits within which the eyes were mere glints. He looked somehow foreign, as though he came from the east. It was the high cruelty of the cheek-bones, perhaps. There was about him an air of command that impressed even Grall.

This was Aruan of Garmidalan, the Vicar-General of the Inceptine Order, and, some said, the true head of the Himerian Church. The power behind the throne at any rate, and an object of mystery and speculation throughout all the Normannic kingdoms.

To Himerius's left stood a different pot of fish entirely. A broad-shouldered, shaven-headed soldier in half armour with a broken nose and the scar of long helm-wearing on his forehead. In his sixties, perhaps, he looked as hale and formidable as any Fimbrian drill sergeant Grall had ever known. But there was intelligence in his eyes, and when Grall met them he felt he was being gauged and, as the eyes moved on, dismissed again. This man had seen battle, spilled blood. The violence in him could almost be smelled. Bardolin of Carreirida, Presbyter of the Knights Militant—another enigma. He had been a mage, apprentice to the great Golophin of Hebrion, but had turned against his master and now completed the triumvirate of powers here in Charibon.

"—Always a pleasure to see the representatives of the Electorates here in Charibon. We trust that your quarters agree with you, and that there will be time during your visit to discuss the many and varied subjects of importance which now concern both our fiefdoms. The Grand Alliance, as it styles itself, has been for years a warlike and threatening presence on our shared continent, and it borders both our states, yet of late its posturing has become more substantial, and we must needs consult together, I believe, as to how its ambitions may be curtailed." This was Himerius, his old voice surprisingly clear and resonant under the massive beams of the hall.

"The restraint shown by the Electorates has been admirable, considering the many hostile acts committed against it by the alliance, but we feel here at Charibon, the seat of the True Faith, that it is perhaps time that Fimbria and the Empire made common cause against these aggressors. The world is divided irrevocably. To our sorrow, our advisors tell us that war may not be long in coming, despite all our efforts to prevent it. The anti-Pontiff Albrec the Faceless and his benefactor, the murderous usurper Corfe of Torunna, not to mention the despicable despoilers of the holy city of Aekir, are all massing troops on our eastern borders. While in the west, Hebrion, Gabrion and Astarac—also in league with the Merduk—blockade our coasts and strangle trade. We pray therefore, Marshal Briannon, that your embassy is come here today to make common cause with us in this approaching struggle—one that will, with God's blessing, wipe the heresy of Albrec from our shores for ever, and bring to an end the disgusting spectacle of Merduk and Ramusian worshipping together—in the same temple, at the same altar!—as it is said they do in the iniquitous sink that is Torunn."

Grall blinked in surprise. As diplomatic statements went, this one was as subtle as an onager's kick. He wanted to glance at Briannon, to see how the Elector had received this speech—nay, this demand—but faced his front rigidly, and kept his face as blank as wood.

"Your Holiness makes many valuable points," Briannon replied, his voice hard as basalt after Himerius's music. "Too many in fact to be addressed adequately standing here. As you know, no Fimbrian embassy is ever dispatched lightly, and our presence here is evidence enough that we, also, share your concerns about the current state of affairs on our borders and yours. I will divulge to you that I stand here with the authority to make or break any treaty hitherto entered into by the Electorates. The Treaty of Neyr, guaranteeing Fimbrian neutrality in any war in which the Second Empire might become involved, has served us well over these last twelve years. But times are changing. I rejoice that you and I are of one mind in this respect, Holiness."

Himerius actually smiled. "Shall we adjourn for dinner then, my dear Marshal, and afterwards, perhaps we can meet more informally and begin to explore the new possibilities that this current state of affairs has brought to light?"

Briannon bowed slightly. "I am at your Holiness's disposal."

"I had thought Himerius to be a wily negotiator," Justus said. "He as much as stated we are either for or against him, the old buzzard."

"They were not his words," Briannon told him. "Himerius is a mere figurehead. We are dealing with this Aruan, no other, and he is confident enough of his strength that he thinks to lay down the law to the Electorates."

"What will it be then?" Grall asked impatiently. "Are we to throw in our lot with these sorcerers and priests?"

Briannon stared at him coldly. "We will do whatever is

best for our people, no matter if we have to lay down with the devil to do it." The trio of sombrely clad men tramped back to their quarters in silence after that. Grall found himself thinking of his cousin, Silus, who had deserted to Torunna not three weeks before. To serve under a soldier, he had said bitterly. The only real soldier left in the west.

WHEN the doors had boomed shut on the Fimbrians' retreating backs the three figures on the dais seemed to become animated. "We were too obvious," Himerius said discontentedly. "Master, these Fimbrians have the stiffest necks of any men alive. One has to handle them with care, courtesy, flattery."

"They tolerate these things—they do not appreciate them," Aruan said. "And they are men like any other, fearful of what the future may bring. Our friend Briannon is in fact the same Briannon who is Elector of Neyr, and should the Fimbrians ever set aside their internal differences and decide to raise up an emperor again, then he will be the man clad in imperial purple. He is not here for the exercise. I believe they will sign the new treaty. We will have Fimbrian pike within our ranks yet, I promise you. Not for a while, perhaps, but once Hebrion and Astarac fall, they will see which way the wind is blowing."

"They don't like us," Bardolin said. "They would prefer to serve under King Corfe—a fighting man."

"They would prefer to serve under no one but themselves. However, their rank and file will obey orders. It's what they're good at, after all." Aruan smiled. "My dear Bardolin, you have been very promiscuous in your comings and goings of late. I sometimes regret letting you into the mysteries of the Eighth Discipline. Do I detect a note of sympathy for this soldier-king?"

Bardolin met Aruan's hawkish gaze without flinching. "He's the greatest general of the age. The Fimbrian rank and file may obey their orders in the main, but over the past fifteen years thousands of them have flocked to his banner. 'The Orphans,' they call themselves, and they are fanatics.

I've met them in the field, and they are a fearsome thing to contend against."

"Ah, the Torrin Gap battle," Aruan mused. "But that was a small affair, and almost ten years ago. We have our own brand of fanatics now, Bardolin, and they laugh at pikes no matter who wields them. Children? *Am I not right?*"

At this the monks who stood in the shadows raised their heads, and as their cowls slipped back there were revealed the slavering muzzles of beasts. These opened their maws and howled and yammered, and then crawled forward to fawn at the feet of Aruan, their yellow eyes bright as the flickering flames of the braziers.

FIVE

THE sound came first, a noise like the massed thudding of a thousand heartbeats. The ship's company roused itself from the exhausted torpor into which it had fallen and stood on deck staring fearfully into the fog. Their officers were no wiser. King Abeleyn stood on the poop in a golden swirling soup gilded by the huge stern lanterns of the *Pontifidad*. Along the gangways of the waist marines were replenishing their slow-match, which had burned down to stubs, and all about the forecastle, waist and quarterdeck the gun crews wiped their faces, spat on their hands and exchanged wordless looks. The beating noise was all around, and growing louder as they stood. Dawn would come in an hour, but something else was coming first.

Admiral Rovero had ordered the swivel-men to remain in the tops, though up there they were on self-contained little islands adrift in an impenetrable grey sea. There was confused shouting from above now, within the fog, and the sudden, shattering bark of the wicked little swivel-guns firing in a formless barrage. Pieces of rope and shards of timber fell to the deck, shot off the yards.

"It's begun," Abeleyn said.

"Sergeant Miro!" Rovero bellowed. "Take a section up the shrouds and see what's going on there." And in a lower tone: "You, master-at-arms, go get Captain Hawkwood."

The firing intensified. Miro and his men abandoned their arquebuses and took to the shrouds, disappearing into the fog. All along the packed decks of the ship the crew looked upwards in fearful wonder as the fog began to spin in wild eddies and the shouting turned to screaming. A warm rain began to fall on their faces and a wordless cry went up from the decks as they realised it was raining blood. Then one, two, three—half a dozen bodies were falling down out of the fog, smashing off spars, bouncing from ropes, and thumping in scarlet ruin amid their shipmates below, or splashing overboard into the black sea. The volleyed gunfire sputtered out into a staccato confusion of single shots. Men on the spar decks ducked and dodged as even more dreadful debris rained down from the invisible tops: limbs, entrails, heads, warm spatters of blood. And all the while over the gunfire and the wails of the dying, that drumbeat murmur overhead.

Ashen-faced and panting, Hawkwood joined Abeleyn and Mark on the poop.

"What in hell's going on?"

No one answered him. The firing from the tops had all but died, but the shrieking went on, and now men were appearing out of the fog overhead, pouring down the rigging, sliding down backstays so swiftly as to burn the flesh from their hands. It was Abeleyn who first snapped out of the dreamlike paralysis that seemed to have seized all the men on deck.

"Marines there, fire a volley into the tops. Ensign Gerrolvo, get a grip of your men, for God's sake! All hands, all hands prepare for boarding! Sergeant-at-arms, issue cutlasses."

The spell was broken. Given orders to carry out that made sense of the nightmare, the men responded with alacrity. A ragged salvo of arquebus fire was directed towards the swirling mists into which the masts disappeared ten feet above everyone's heads, and the rest of the mariners raced to the arms barrels to seize close-combat weapons, since it was clear the great guns were useless against whatever was attacking the ship.

On the poop beside Abeleyn, Hawkwood drew his own cutlass and fought the sickening panic that was rising up his throat like a cloud. Almost he mentioned Bardolin's visitation to the Hebrian King, but then bit back his words. *You're all dead men*. It was probably too late now anyway.

Admiral Rovero was in the waist, thrusting men to their stations, kicking aside the mutilated corpses which littered the deck. He grasped one mad-eyed marine whose arm looked as though it had been chewed short at the wrist. The man stood grasping his stump and watching the arteries spurt as if they belonged to someone else.

"Miro, you got up to the maintop, didn't you? What in the name of God is happening up there?"

"Demons," Miro said wildly. "Yellow-eyed fiends. They have wings, Admiral. There's no one left alive up there."

The man was in deep shock. Rovero shook him angrily, baffled. "Get below to the sickbay. You there—Grode—help him down the hatch. Stand to your weapons, you whoresons. Remember who you are!"

All around them in the wall of mist it was possible to see the red darting flashes of small-arms fire, and seconds later to hear the muted crackle of distant volleys through a far surf of shouting. The other ships of the fleet were enduring a similar assault.

A knot of bodyguards, Hebrian and Astaran, joined Abeleyn, Mark and Hawkwood at the taffrail with drawn swords. They were in half-armour with open helms, glaring about in bewildered determination. Something swooped out of the fog above them, was lit up saffron as it wheeled into the light of the stern lanterns, and smashed full-tilt into their ranks. The men were sent sprawling like skittles. One was knocked over the ship's rail and splashed into the sea below without a sound. His armour would sink him like a stone. Hawkwood, in the midst of the tumbling, chaotic flailing of arms and legs and impotently swinging blades, glimpsed a winged shape,

featherless as a snake—wickedly swiping claws, a long bald
tail like that of a monstrous rat—and then it was gone again,
the fog spinning circles in the draughts stirred by its wing-
beats.

All the length of the ship, men were fighting off this attack
from above. Scores, hundreds of the creatures, were diving
down out of the fog, raking mariners and marines to shreds
with their wicked talons, and then disappearing again. The
masters-at-arms were manning the quarterdeck swivels and
indiscriminately blasting the air with wicked showers of
metal. Ropes and lines sliced apart by shrapnel came hissing
down on the struggling men below; falling blocks and tackle
cracking open skulls and adding to the mayhem. Hawkwood
saw what must have been the main topgallant yard—thirty
feet of stout wood frapped with iron—come searing down
like a comet trailing all its attendant rigging and tackle. It
speared through the deck and disappeared below, dragging
with it two gunners who had been caught up with its lines.
The splintered wood of the deck tore their bodies to pieces
as they were yanked through it.

"They're breaking up the ship from the masts down," he
cried. "We must get men back into the tops or they'll cripple
her."

He ran forward towards the quarterdeck ladder. Behind
him, the two Kings were helping their heavily armoured
bodyguards to their feet. Another one of the winged creatures
swept low and Hawkwood swiped at it with his iron cutlass,
hacking off one of the great talons. It crashed full into the
taffrail in a stinking flap of beating bone and leathery wings.
The six-foot stern lantern above it shuddered at the impact,
tottered, and then fell to the deck in an explosion of flame,
burning oil spraying everywhere. King Mark of Astarac was
engulfed and transformed into a blazing torch, the bodyguards beside him likewise drenched, roasting inside their
armour. Some threw themselves overboard. The King tried
to bat out the flames but they rushed hungrily up his body,
blackening his skin, withering his hair away, melting his
clothes. Dazed, and on fire himself, Hawkwood saw As-

tarac's monarch rip the flesh from his own face in his agony. Abeleyn was trying to smother the blaze with his cloak, but it caught too. One of the Hebrian bodyguards pulled his King away and lay on his body, smiting the flames which had caught in his sleeves and hair. Hawkwood rolled across the deck and beat to death the burning droplets on his own clothing. "Fire party!" he shouted. "Fire party aft!" The skin peeled off the back of his hands in perfect sheets and he stared at them, transfixed.

The stern of the ship was ablaze, the fire igniting the pitch in the deck seams and catching in the tarred rigging of the mizzen backstays. When the heat reached the second stern lantern, it exploded, spraying fiery oil as far as the quarter-deck. As the inferno took hold, it touched off the poop culverins and they detonated one after another, rearing back on their burning carriages. The spare powder charges stored beside them went up with a sound like a series of thunderous broadsides and blew huge jagged holes in the superstructure of the *Pontifidad*, the massive timbers that formed the skeleton and ribs of the ship tossed like twigs into the air along with fragments of burning men. The ship groaned like a maimed beast and there was a great tearing crack as the mizzen gave way and toppled over, tearing free the shrouds and stays and crashing into ruin down the ship's larboard side. The vessel began to list.

Hawkwood had been blasted clear of the burning poop by the powder explosions. They had rendered him deaf, and thus the scene aboard was a surreal, soundless nightmare; a dream which seemed to be happening to someone else. He picked himself up out of a tangle of broken timber and piled cordage. All around him, men were fighting the fire with pitiful chains of buckets, or slashing and shooting at the swooping shadows overhead, or dragging their wounded comrades clear of the flames. There was utter confusion, but it had not yet bled into panic. That was something.

The King. Where was he?

Rovero, one side of his face a burnt bubbled ruin, had grabbed his arm and was shouting something, but Hawk-

wood could not make it out. He ducked as another one of
the winged monstrosities dived low, and felt the wrench as
Rovero was lifted free of the deck. He seized the admiral's
hand, but toppled backwards as it came free. Rovero's decapitated torso tumbled like a rag across the deck. Hawkwood stared in horror.

Men were lifted struggling into the air and dropped with
torn throats. A sergeant of marines was grappling fifteen feet
off the deck, digging his fingers into his attacker's eyes while
the bald wings flapped furiously about him. Sailors caught
the hanging tails of their tormentors and dragged them down
whilst their comrades hacked them to pieces. But there were
hundreds of the beasts. They fastened like flies on the dead
and the living alike, wreaking carnage with no thought of
their own preservation.

Hawkwood experienced no fear, just a dazed series of decisions in his mind. He grabbed a steel marlin spike from a
fife-rail and stabbed with all his strength one of the winged
creatures that was perched on the shattered deck, feeding off
a shrieking marine. The beast reared backwards on top of
him, the wings beating in a paroxysm of agony. He crawled
out from under and knelt upon it, pinning the wings. A human face spat up at him, but the eyes were yellow as a cat's
and its fangs were as long as his fingers. Disgust and rage
overmastered him. He punched the face with his raw fists
until his knuckles cracked and broke, and the beast's glaring
eyes were burst from their sockets.

A silent explosion staggered him—he felt the blast of hot
air scorching his skin. He lurched to his feet. Some sounds
were coming back, all overlaid with a shrill hissing that filled
his head. The ship's wheel was on fire, and the binnacle. The
chain of buckets had disappeared. There was no sign of King
Abeleyn and his bodyguards—no order left now on board.
Men were fighting their own private battles for survival and
wielding anything that came to hand to beat off the enemy.
No time to reload arquebuses; the marines were swinging
them like clubs. Over the formless storm in his ears Hawk-

wood heard some shouting in despair, and saw them pointing. He turned.

Crawling over the ship's rails were hordes of the beetle-like warriors which had gone down in the caravel. Their pincers made short work of the boarding netting and their spiked feet propelled them over the side with preternatural speed. Hawkwood peered over the ship's rail and saw that a mass of smallcraft was clustered there, and grapnels were being tossed aboard by the score. The *Pontifidad* gave a lurch to starboard which sent him sliding across the packed deck. A squirming mass of humanity went with him, men sliding off their feet and rolling in the remains of their shipmates. One sailor was pitched from the main hatch square on to a baulk of broken timber that transfixed him. He writhed there in astonishment, grasping the bloody stave that now protruded from his belly, wound round with blue innards.

Crowds of the beetle-warriors swarmed across the *Pontifidad* like cockroaches crawling over some vast putrefying carcass. There was no escape for the survivors of the ship's company still on deck. They stampeded for the hatches. Hawkwood found himself in the midst of a crowd that bore him along towards the quarterdeck companionway. He fell to his knees, buffeted by the frenzied sailors, but elbowed a space and laboured upright. His numbed mind followed him down the companionway with the others, and at the foot of the companionway he paused, looking about him.

Battle lanterns still burning in the tween decks, though they hung at an angle with the list of the ship. It was suffocatingly hot, and the smoke smarted his eyes, racked coughs out of his heaving chest. He opened the door which led to the officers' quarters aft, and was met by a hungry rush of flame that tightened the skin of his face and shrivelled his eyebrows. Nothing could live there. He slammed shut the smoking door, and headed forward with no thought in his mind except to escape the flames below and the carnage above.

He passed clots of wounded men who had dragged themselves down here to die, and slipped in their blood as the

ship listed further. They must have holed her below the waterline somehow. Then the space between decks opened out
into the middle gun deck. Hawkwood found himself in a dark
nightmare lit by battle lanterns, crowded with panicked figures who were setting off the great guns in a disorderly
broadside. They had something to fire at now, but their elevation was too high; the shot was passing over the hulls of
the enemy craft grappled alongside. Hawkwood screamed at
them to depress their pieces, and when they stared at him
blankly he seized a handspike himself and wedged the nearest culverin up with a quoin so that the muzzle tilted downwards. It was loaded, and he stabbed the lighted match into
the touch-hole with a savage joy. The gun jumped back with
a roar, and beyond the port he glimpsed a spout of broken
timbers.

But up through the gunport there squeezed now a glinting
mass of the enemy, their pincers splintering wood. Hawkwood clubbed them back with the handspike, but they were
squirming in through every port on the deck. Men left the guns
and began fighting hand-to-hand, crouched under the low deck
beams. It looked like a battle fought far below the earth, in the
subterranean chamber of a steaming mine.

Part of the deck about the main hatch above their heads
collapsed in a cataclysm of burning timber. It came down on
the gun crews like a wooden avalanche. With it fell a mass
of the glinting enemy. The beetle-warriors rolled like balls,
righted themselves, and began laying about with hardly a
pause. The awful pincers lopped off men's limbs and the
black armour was impenetrable save at the joints. The gun
crews fell back. Hawkwood tried to rally them but his voice
was lost in the tumult. Stooping under the deck beams, he
struggled forward again. Another hatch leading downwards.
He followed it, borne along by a terrified mob of gunners
with the same end in mind.

The orlop. They were below the waterline now, close to
the hold.

I will die down here, Hawkwood thought. When a ship's
crew was forced below the guns, she was finished.

There was water sloshing about his ankles. Somehow the enemy had holed the ship, attacking from the sea as well as the air. The *Pontifidad* was dying, and when she gave up the struggle against the pitiless waves she would take hundreds of trapped men with her. The pride of Hebrion, she had been. Hard to grasp that such a vessel could be destroyed, and not by gunfire or storm, but by—by what?

His hands were agony to him now. Hawkwood staggered out of the way of the crowd coming down the hatch and fell to his side. The salt water scalded his burns. He crawled behind one of the great wooden knees of the ship that supported the deck beams, and there halted. The water was rising fast.

The ship shook with a dull boom and the men below wailed helplessly, realising that their doom was not far off. There was a deafening creaking roar, and then part of the very hull gave way. It burst inwards admitting an explosion of spray. Hawkwood thought he saw a massive black snout in the midst of it for a second.

The water rose at an incredible rate, thundering in through a breach some eight feet wide. Men were clawing their way back up the hatches they had so lately fought to get down. The ship lurched further to starboard with a moan of overstressed timbers. Hawkwood slid towards the breach and was enveloped in foam. He went under, sucked into a storm of swirling seawater. Fighting to see, he found broken timbers under his nose, and beyond them, darkness. He clutched them with his skinless hands and fought against the push of the water, levering himself over them. Splinters raked his belly, his thighs. Then he was spinning freely in open water, a chaotic turbulence which was sucking him down. He struck out in the opposite direction, knowing that the ship was going down and trying to bring him to the depths with it. Something struck him on the forehead and he lost ground. His lungs felt like two cinder-filled bags about to explode. His torso convulsed with the need to suck in air, water, anything, but he fought against it, kicking upwards. His sight turned red. He bared his teeth, tasted blood in his mouth, but kept struggling.

At last his head burst clear of the water for a second. He exhaled and gulped a cupful of air, then was sucked under again.

Harder this time, the fight against the undertow. His arms and legs slowed. He looked up and saw light above him, but it was too far. His limbs stopped. He drifted slowly downwards, but still would not give up, would not breathe in though his body screamed for him to do so.

Damn you. *Damn you!*

Something became entangled with his legs. It caught there and spun him around, then began to tug him upwards again. A dark blob against the light, leather straps wrapped around his ankles. He was floating towards the surface feet first. He looked down past his wriggling fingers, down into the depths, and saw there a sight he would never forget.

Scores of men, dozens of other faces turned up to the light, some calm and otherworldly, others still fighting the sea like himself. They were suspended in the clear water below, trapped and dying. And behind them, the awesome dark bulk of the *Pontifidad* sliding towards the seabed like some tired submarine titan going to her rest. Broken, mastless, but still with one or two lights twinkling. She turned over and the last lights went out. Her black hulk slid soundlessly down into the deeper blackness beyond.

Hawkwood was still rising. He broke the surface and shouted the dead poison from his lungs. He flapped his weary legs free of the thing that had saved him, and found it was a leather-strapped wineskin, half full of air. Grasping it in his arms, he sobbed in great gouts of the cold air knowing only that he was alive, he had escaped. His ship was gone, and her crew had ridden her into the depths, but her captain remained. He felt a moment of overpowering shame.

Wind on his face. The mist was clearing, and the sun was riding up the morning sky. In the east it set light to a wrack of distant cloud and turned it into a tumbled mêlée of gold and scarlet and palest aquamarine. Hawkwood raised his head. There was a slight swell, and when it lifted him on its crest he saw he was surrounded by a horrible wreckage of bodies and parts of bodies, broken spars, limp cordage. To the west a bank of fog still lay stubbornly upon the water, but it was thinning moment by moment. Through it the ships of the enemy could be seen as a forested crowd of masts, and the early sunlight sparkled off milling hosts of armoured figures on their decks. Larger hulks, low in the water and bearing only the ragged stumps of their lower yards, drifted everywhere in and out of the fog, some burning, others appearing wholly lifeless and inert. And in the brilliant blue vault of the sky above, a flock of the winged creatures was wheeling in a great spiral. Hawkwood watched as it descended, and lit upon a sinking galleon. Faint over the water came a series of shots.

Ships everywhere, looming like islands out of the mist. Hebrian galleons built to his own designs, Astaran carracks, Merduk xebecs, Gabrionese caravels. But all of them were dismasted, ablaze and sinking. The waves were thick with flotsam, the wreckage of the greatest naval armament that history had ever seen. In the space of an hour it had been annihilated.

The *Pontifidad* had been at the forefront of the fleet, the tip of the arrow; and hence it had gone down some distance from the main body of ships. Hawkwood realised that he was drifting eastwards with the breeze, away from the lingering fog banks and the terrible tangled mass of broken hulks to windward. Where they burned the water was still relatively calm; the weather-working spell was fading last at its core. But here, scarcely half a sea-mile away, the wind was picking up. Hawkwood studied the sky and watched the clouds grow and darken in the west, heralding a storm. They were leaving nothing to chance, it seemed.

Had anyone else escaped from the flagship? Again, the choking sense of shame. Seven hundred men and two kings. Lord God.

But he could not give up. He could not will himself to die. It was the same stubbornness that had kept him going all those years ago in the west. Without conscious volition he found himself scanning the pitching waves for something, anything, that might enable him to hold on to life a few hours longer.

Half a cable away a mass of wood rose and fell slowly on the swell. Deadeyes and the rags of shrouds clung to it still. Hawkwood realised it was what was left of the maintop. He struck out for it, leaving his wineskin, and for half a despairing hour fought the steeping waves with what was left of his strength. When he reached it he had not the strength to pull himself atop it, and so hung there, shivering and listless, his hands become rigid claws which no longer obeyed him. Above his head the clouds thickened, and on the wind he heard the screaming of gulls as they settled down to feast on the bounty of disaster, but he shut his eyes and hung on, no longer caring why.

A GONY in his hands. He tried to cry out as they were constricted in a merciless grip, their blisters bursting, the charred skin flaying off. He was hauled out of the water, and fell with a thump to the sodden wood of the maintop wreckage. He lay there, awash, and a scream died in his salt-crusted mouth.

"It's all right, Richard. I have you."

He opened his eyes and saw only a shadow limned black against the sky.

SIX

THE Queen's chambers were a shadowed place. Despite the spring warmth of the air outside, there were fires burning in every massive hearth, and the ornate grilles that flanked each window were shut, letting in only a pale, mangled radiance that could barely compete with the blare of the firelight.

The ladies-in-waiting all had an attractive flushed look, and their low-cut gowns afforded an intriguing glimpse of the perspiration that gleamed in the hollows of their collar bones. Corfe tugged at his own tight-fitting collar and dismissed them as they hovered around, curtseying. "Go on outside and get some air, for God's sake."

"Sire, we—"

"Go, ladies; I'll square it with your mistress."

More curtsies, and they whispered out, white hands flapping fan-like at their faces, long skirts hitched up as though they were tiptoeing through puddles. Corfe watched them go appreciatively, then collected himself.

"It's like a Macassian bath house in here!" he called. "What new fad is this, lady?"

His wife appeared from the inner bedchamber. She had a shawl wrapped about her shoulders and she leaned on an ivory cane.

"Nothing that need concern a loutish peasant up from the provinces for the day," she retorted, her voice dry and clear.

Corfe took her in his arms as carefully as though she were made of tinsel, and kissed her wrinkled forehead. It was marble-cold.

"Come now. It's Forialon these two sennights past. There are primroses out along the side of the Kingsway. What's with this skulking in front of a fire?"

Odelia turned away. "So how was your jaunt up the road of memory? I trust Mirren enjoyed it." She lowered herself into a well-stuffed chair by the fire, her blue-veined hands resting on top of her cane. As she did, a multi-legged, dark, furred ball skittered down the wall, climbed up her arm and nestled in the crook of her neck with a sound like a great cat's purr. A clutch of eyes shone like berries.

"It would do you good to take a jaunt yourself."

Odelia smiled. Her hair, once shining gold, had thinned and greyed, and her years sat heavily in the lines and folds of her face. Only her eyes seemed unchanged, green as a shallow sea in sunlight, and bright with life.

"I am old, Corfe. Let me be. You cannot fight time as though it were a contending army. I am old, and powerless. What gifts I possessed went into Mirren. I would have made her a boy if I could, but it was beyond me. The male line of Fantyr has come to an end. Mirren will make someone a grand queen one day, but Torunna must have a king to rule, always. We both know that only too well."

Corfe strode to a shuttered window and pulled back the heavy grilles, letting in the sun, and a cool breeze from off the Kardian in the east. He stared down at the sea of roofs below, the spires of the Papal Palace down by the square. The tower wherein he stood was two hundred feet high, but still he could catch the cacophony of sellers hawking their wares in the marketplace, the rattle of carts moving over cobbles, the braying of mules. "We made slow going of it for the first few days," he said lightly. "It is incredible how quickly nature buries the works of man. The old Western Road has well-nigh disappeared."

"A very good point. Our job here is to prevent nature burying *our* works after we are gone."

"We've been over this," he said wearily.

"And will go over it again. Speaking of burying things, my time on this goodly earth is running out. I have months left, not years—"

"Don't talk like that, Odelia."

"And you must start to think of marrying again. It's all very well making these pilgrimages to the past, but the future bears looking at also. You need a male heir. Lord God, Corfe, look at the way the world is turning. Another conflict ripens at long last to bloody fruition, one whose climax could make the Merduk Wars look like a skirmish. The battles may have already begun, off Hebrion, or even before Gaderion. When you take to the field, all that is needed is one stray bullet to lose this war. Without you, this kingdom would be lost. Do not let what you have achieved turn to dust on your death."

"Oh, it's my death now. A fine conversation for a spring morning."

"You have sired no bastards—I know that—but I almost wish you had. Even an illegitimate male heir would be better than none."

"Mirren could rule this kingdom as well as any man, given time," Corfe said heatedly. Again, Odelia smiled.

"Corfe, the soldier-king, the iron general. Whose sun rises and sets on his only daughter. Do not let your love blind you, my dear. Can you see Mirren leading armies?"

He had no reply for that. She was right, of course. But the simple thought of remarrying ripped open the scars of old wounds deep in his soul. Aurungzeb, Sultan of Ostrabar, had two children by—by his queen, and several more by various concubines it was said. Nasir, the only boy, was almost seventeen now, and Corfe had met him several times on state visits to Aurungabar. Black-haired, with sea-grey eyes—and the dark complexion of a Merduk. A son to be proud of. The girl was a couple of years younger, though she remained cloistered away in the manner of Merduk ladies.

Their mother, too, rarely left the confines of the harem these days. Corfe had not seen her in over sixteen years, but once upon a time, in a different world it seemed, she had been his wife, the love of his life. Yes, that old scar throbbed still. It would heal only when his heart stopped.

"You have a list, no doubt, of eligible successors."

"Yes. A short one, it must be said. There is a dearth of princesses at present."

He laughed, throwing his head back like a boy. "What does the world come to? So who is head of your list? Some pale Hebrian maiden? Or a dark-eyed matron of Astarac?"

"Her name is Aria. She is young, but of excellent lineage, and her father is someone we must needs bind to us with every tie we can at the present time."

"Abeleyn? Mark?" Corfe was puzzled.

"Aurungzeb, you fool. Aria is his only daughter by his Ramusian-born queen, sister to his heir, and hence a princess of the Royal blood. Marry her, and you bind Torunna and Ostrabar together irrevocably. Sire children on her and—"

"No."

"What? I haven't finished. You must—"

"I said no. I will not marry this girl." He turned from the window and his face was bloodless as chalk. "Find another."

"I have already put out diplomatic feelers. Her father approves the match. Your issue would join the Royal houses of Ostrabar and Torunna for all time—our alliance would be rendered unbreakable."

"You did this without my permission?"

"I am still Torunna's Queen!" she lashed out, some of the old fire flashing from her marvellous eyes. "I do not need your permission every time I piss in a pot!"

"You need it for this," he said softly, and his own eyes were winter-cold, hard as flint.

"What is your objection? The girl is young, admittedly, but then I'm not quite dead yet. She is a rare beauty by all accounts, the very image of her mother, and sweet-natured to boot."

"By God you're well-informed."

"I make it my business to be." Her voice softened. "Corfe, I'm dying. Let me do this last thing for you, for the kingdom. I know I have not been much of a wife to you these last years—"

He strode from the window and knelt on one knee beside her chair. The skin of her face was gossamer thin under his hand. He felt that she might blow away in the breeze from the windows. "You've been a wife and more than a wife. You've been a friend and counsellor, and a great queen."

"Then grant me this last wish. Keep Torunna together. Marry this girl. Have a son—a whole clutch of sons. You also are mortal."

"What about Mirren?"

"She must marry young Nasir."

He shut his eyes. The old pain burned, deep in his chest. That one he had seen coming. But marry Heria's daughter—his own wife's child? Never.

He rose, his face like stone. "We will discuss this another time, lady."

"We are discussing it *now*."

"I think not." Turning on his heel he left the darkened chamber without a backward glance.

A courtier was waiting for him outside. "Sire, I've been instructed by Colonel Heyd to tell you that the couriers are in with dispatches from Gaderion."

"Good. I'll meet them in the Bladehall. My compliments to the colonel, and he is to join me there as soon as he can. The same message to General Formio and the rest of the High Command." The courtier saluted and fled.

Corfe's personal bodyguard, Felorin, caught up with him in the corridor as he strode along with his boots clinking on the polished stone. Not a word was spoken as the pair made their way through the Queen's wing to the palace proper. There were fewer courtiers than there had been in King Lofantyr's day, and they were clad in sober burgundy. When the King passed them they each saluted as soldiers would. Only the court ladies were as finely plumaged as they had ever been, and they collapsed delicately into curtsies as Corfe blew past. He nodded to them but never slowed his stride for an instant.

They crossed the Audience Hall, their footsteps echoing in its austere emptiness, and the palace passageways and chambers grew less grand, older-looking. There was more timber and less stone. When the Fimbrians had built the Palace of Torunn it had been the seat of the Imperial Governor, who was also the general of a sizeable army. This area of the complex had originally been part of that army's barracks, but until Corfe came to the throne had been used mainly as a series of storerooms. Corfe had restored it to its original purpose, and housed within it now were living quarters for five hundred men—the Bodyguard of the King. These were volunteers from the army and elsewhere who had passed a rigorous training regimen designed by Corfe himself. Within their ranks served Fimbrians, Torunnans, Cimbric tribesmen, and even a sizeable element of Merduks. In garrison they dressed in sable and scarlet surcoats, the old "blood and bruises" that John Mogen's men had once worn. In the field they rode heavy warhorses—even the Fimbrians—and were armed with wheel-lock pistols and long sabres. Both they and their steeds were accustomed to wearing three-quarter armour, which Torunnan smiths had tempered so finely that it would turn even an arquebus ball. On the breastplate of every man's cuirass was a shallow spherical indentation where this had been put to the test.

"Where is Comillan today?" Corfe barked to Felorin.

"On the Proving Grounds, with the new batch."

"And Formio?"

"On his way in from Menin Field."

"We'll get there first then. Run ahead, Felorin, and set up the Bladehall for a conference. Maps of the Torrin Gap, a clear sand-table and some brandy—you know the drill."

Felorin gave his monarch a strange look, though his tattooing rendered his expression hard to read at the best of times. "Brandy?"

"Yes, damn it. I could do with one. Now cut along."

Felorin took off at a run, whereas Corfe's pace slowed. Finally he halted, and propped himself by a windowsill which looked out on the Proving Grounds below where a new set of recruits were being put through their paces. The glass was blurred with age but he was able to make out the man-high wooden posts sunk in the ground, and the lines of sweating men who hacked at them with the arm-killing practice swords whose blunt blades housed a core of lead. They had to strike defined spots at shoulder, waist and knee height on the right and then the left sides of the iron-hard old posts, and keep doing it until their palms blistered and the sweat ran in their eyes and their backs were raw masses of screaming muscle. Over thirty years before, Corfe had stood out there and hacked at those same posts while the drill sergeants had shouted and jeered at him. Some things, at least, did not change.

The Bladehall was new, however. A long, vaulted, church-like building, Corfe had had it constructed after the Battle of the Torian Plains ten years before, close to the old Quartermaster Stores where he had once found five hundred sets of Merduk armour mouldering and used them to arm his first command. He disliked using the old conference chambers for staff meetings because they were in the palace, and curious courtiers and maids were always in and out. Though Odelia might remind him tartly that the older venue had been good enough for Kaile Ormann himself, Corfe felt a need to break with the past. He also wanted to create somewhere for the officers of the army to come together without the inevitable delays that entering the palace complex entailed. Deep down, he also welcomed any opportunity to get out of the palace himself, even now.

Still a peasant with mud under my nails, after all this time, he thought with sour satisfaction.

Along the walls of the Bladehall were ranged suits of antique armour and weapons, tapestries and paintings depicting past battles and wars won and lost. And near the massive timber beams that supported the roof were hung the war banners and flags of generations of Torunnan armies. They had been found scattered in storerooms throughout the palace complex after Corfe had become king. Some were tattered and rotting but others, crafted of finest silk and laid aside with more care, were as whole as the day they had waved overhead on a shot-torn field.

Set into the walls were hundreds of scroll pigeonholes, each of which held a map. On the upper galleries there were shelves of books also: manuals, histories, treatises on tactics and strategy. Several sycophantic nobles had begged Corfe to write a general treatise on war years ago, but he had curtly refused. He might be a successful general, but he was no writer—and he would not dictate his clumsy sentences to a scribe so that some inky-fingered parasite might polish them up for public consumption afterwards.

Hung above the lintel of the huge fireplace at one end of the hall was John Mogen's sword, the Answerer. Corfe had carried it at the North More, at the King's Battle, and at Armagedir. A gift from the Queen, it had hung there with the firelight playing upon it for a decade now, for Torunna's King had not taken to the field in all that time.

There were large tables ringed with chairs set about the floor of the lower Bladehall, and seated at these were several young men in Torunnan military uniform, trying hard to ignore the two muddy couriers who stood wearily to one side. Corfe encouraged his officers to come in here and read when they were off duty, or to study tactical problems on the long sand-table that stood in one of the side chambers. Attendants were permanently on hand to serve food and drink in the small adjoining refectory, should that be required. In this way, among others, Corfe had tried to encourage the birth of a more truly professional officer class, one based on merit and not on birth or seniority. All officers were equal when they stepped over the threshold of the Bladehall, and even the most junior might speak freely. More importantly, perhaps, the gratuities which army commanders had traditionally accepted in return for the granting of commissions had been stamped out. All would-be commanders started as lowly ensigns attached to an infantry tercio, and they sweated it out in the Proving Grounds the same as all other new recruits. Strange to say, once Corfe had instituted this reform, the proportion of gallant young blue-bloods joining the army had plummeted. He smiled at the thought.

There was as yet no formal military academy in Torunna, as existed in Fimbir, but it was something Corfe had been mulling over in his mind for several years. Though he was an almost absolute ruler, he still had to bear in mind the views of the important families of the kingdom. They would never dare to take the field against him again, but their opposition to many of his policies had been felt in subtler ways. They would see an academy of war as a means to build up a whole new hierarchy in the kingdom, based not on blood but on military merit. And they would be right.

The young men in the Bladehall ceased their reading. They stood up as Corfe entered and he returned their salutes. The two couriers doffed their helms.

"Your names?"

"Gell and Brinian, sir. Dispatches from—"

"Yes, I know. Give them here." Corfe was handed two leather cylinders. The same dispatch would be in both. "Any problems on the road?"

"No, sir. Some wolves near Arboronn, but we outran them."

"When did you leave Gaderion?"

"Five days ago."

"Good work, lads. You look all in. Tell the cooks here to give you whatever you want, and change into some fresh clothes. I will need you back here later, but for now get some rest." The couriers saluted and, gathering up their muddy cloaks, they left for the refectory. Corfe turned to the other occupants of the hall, who had not moved.

"Brascian, Phelor, Grast." These three were standing together. At a table alone stood a dark young officer of medium height. Corfe frowned. "Ensign, forgive me, I do not recall your name."

The youngster stiffened further. "Ensign Baraz, your majesty. We have not yet met."

"Officers simply call me 'sir' in garrison. Are you part of the Ostrabarian Baraz family?"

"My mother's brother was Shahr Baraz, the Queen's bodyguard, and my grandfather was the same Shahr Baraz who took Aurungabar, your—sir. I kept the Baraz name as I was the last male of the line."

"It was called Aekir then. I do not know your uncle, but your grandfather was an able general, and a fine man by all accounts." Corfe stared closely at Baraz. "How is it that you are become an ensign in the Torunnan army?"

"I volunteered, sir. General Formio inducted me himself, not three months ago."

When Corfe said nothing Baraz spoke up again. "My family has been out of favour at the Ostrabarian court for many years. It is known all over the east that you will take loyal men of any race into your forces. I would like to try for the Bodyguard, sir."

"You will have to gain some experience then. Have you completed your Provenance?"

"Yes, sir. Last week."

"Then consider yourself attached to the General Staff for the moment. We're short of interpreters."

"Sir, I would much prefer to be attached to a tercio."

"You'll follow orders, Ensign."

The young man seemed to sag minutely. "Yes, sir."

Corfe kept his face grave. "Very good. There's to be a conference of the staff here in a few minutes. You may sit in." He nodded to the other three officers who were still ramrod straight. "As may you, gentlemen. It will do you good to see the wrangling of the staff, though you will of course say nothing of what you hear to anyone. Clear?"

A chorus of *yes sirs* and a bobbing of heads and hastily smothered grins.

●　　●　　●

Menin Field was the name given to the new parade grounds which had been flattened out to the north of Torunn. They covered hundreds of acres, and allowed vast formations to be marched and counter-marched without terrain disordering the ranks. At their northern end a tall plinth of solid stone stood dark and sombre: a monument to the war dead of the country. It towered over the drilling troops below like a watchful giant, and it was said that in times of trouble the shadows of past armies would gather about it in the night, ready to serve Torunna again.

General Formio raised his eyes from the courier-borne note to the knot of officers who sat their horses around him.

"I am wanted by the King; news from the north, it seems. Colonel Melf, you will take over the remainder of the exercise. Gribben's tercios are still a shambles. They will continue to drill until they can perform open order on the march without degenerating into a rabble. Gentlemen, carry on." He wheeled his horse away to a flurry of salutes.

Formio had years before bowed to necessity, and went mounted now like all other senior officers. He was Corfe's second-in-command in Torunn, and had been for so long now that people almost forgot he was a foreigner, a Fimbrian no less. He had changed little since the Merduk Wars. His hair had gone grey at the temples and his old wounds ached in the winter, but otherwise he was as hale as he had been before Armagedir, from whose field he had been plucked broken and dying sixteen years before. Queen Odelia had saved his life, and her ladies-in-waiting had nursed him through a series of fevered relapses. But he had survived, and Junith, one of those ladies, had become his wife. He had two sons now, one of whom would be of an age to begin his Provenance in another couple of years. He was not unique: almost all the Fimbrians who had survived Armagedir had taken Torunnan wives.

Of the circle of officers and friends which had surrounded the King in those days only he and Aras now remained, and Aras was up in the north holding Gaderion and the Torrin Gap against the Himerians. But there were fresh faces in the army now, a whole host of them. An entirely new generation of officers and soldiers had filled the ranks. They had been youngsters when Aekir had fallen, and the savage struggle to overcome the hosts of Aurungzeb was a childhood story, or something to be read in a book or celebrated in song. In the subsequent years the Merduks had become Torunna's allies. They worshipped the same God, and the same man as his messenger. Ahrimuz or Ramusio, it was all one. There were Merduk bishops in the Macrobian Church, and Torunnan clerics prayed in the temple of Pir-Sar in Aurungabar, which had once been the cathedral of Carcasson. And in the very Bodyguard of King Corfe himself, Merduks served with honour.

But the years of near-peace had bred other legacies. The Torunnan army had been a formidable force back in King Lofantyr's day; now it was widely held to be invincible. Formio was not so sure. A certain amount of complacency had crept through the ranks in recent years. And more importantly, the number of veterans left in those ranks was dwindling fast. He had no doubts about his own countrymen— war ran in their blood. And the tribesmen who made up the bulk of the Cathedrallers viewed war as a normal way of life. But the Torunnans were different. Fully three quarters of those now enrolled in the army had never experienced the reality of combat.

It had been ten years since the Himerians had sent an army into the Torrin Gap. There had been no effort at diplomacy, no warning. It was obvious to the world that the regime which was headed by one pontiff could never recognise or treat with the regime which protected another.

The enemy had advanced tentatively, feeling their way eastwards. Corfe had moved with breakneck speed, a forced march out of Torunn that left a tenth of the army by the side of the road, exhausted. He had not paused, but had launched into the enemy with the Cathedrallers and the Orphans alone, and had thrown them back over the Torian Plains with huge loss. Formio remembered the wreckage of the Knights Militant as they counter-charged his lines of pikes with suicidal courage but little tactical insight. The big horses, disembowelled and screaming. Their riders pinned by the weight of their armour, trampled to a bloody mire as the Cathedrallers rode over them to finish the job. The Battle of the Torian Plains seemed to have given the Himerian leadership pause for thought. It was said that the mage Bardolin had been present in person, though it had never been confirmed.

Not once since then had there been a general engagement. The enemy had built outposts of stone and timber and turf and had advanced them as far into the foothills as he dared, but he had not cared to risk another full-scale battle. The Thurian Line, as this system of fortifications had come to be known, now marked the border between Torunna and the Second Empire.

Ten years, and another turnover of faces. The men of the Torunnan army were as well trained as a professional like King Corfe could make them, but they were essentially unblooded.

This was about to change.

In the Bladehall the fires had been lit and the map-table was dominated by a representation of Barossa, the land bounded by the Searil and Torrin rivers to east and west, and by the Thurians in the north. Blue and red counters were dotted about the map like gambling tokens. In some respects, Formio thought grimly, that is what they were.

"How are they shaping up, General?" Corfe asked the Fimbrian. He held an empty brandy glass in one fist and a crumpled dispatch in the other. Surrounding him were a cluster of other officers, several of whom looked as though they had yet to start shaving.

"They're good, but only on a parade ground. Take them out in the rough and their formations go all to pieces. They need more field manoeuvres."

Corfe nodded. They will get them soon enough. Gentlemen, we have dispatches just in from Aras in the north. The Sea of Tor is now largely clear of ice, and Himerian transports are as thick upon it as flies on jam. The enemy is massively reinforcing his outposts in the gap. At least two other armies are marching down from Tarber and Finnmark. They began crossing the Tourbering river on the fifteenth."

"Any idea about numbers, sir?" a squat, brutal-looking officer asked.

"The Finnmarkan and Tarberan forces total at least forty thousand men. Added to the troops already in position, and I believe we could well be talking in the region of seventy thousand."

There was a murmur of dismay. Aras had less than half that in Gaderion.

"It will take them at least four or five days to cross the river. Aras sent out a flying column last month which burned the bridges, and the Tourbering is in full spate with the meltwater from the mountains."

"But once they're across," the squat officer pointed out, "they'll make good time across the plains south of there. Any word on composition, sir?"

"Very little, Comillan. Local intelligence is poor. We do know that King Skarp-Hedin is present in person, as is Prince Adalbard of Tarber. The northern principalities have historically been weak in cavalry. Their backbone is heavy infantry."

"Gallowglasses," someone said, and Corfe nodded.

"Old-fashioned, but still effective, even against horse. And their skirmishers continue to use javelins. Good troops for rough ground, but not of much account in the open. My guess is that the Himerians will send out a screen of the light northern troops before probing with their heavies."

They all stared at the map and its counters. Now the red blocks laid square across the inked line of the Tourbering river had a distinctively menacing air. Similar blocks were set in a line north-east of the Sea of Tor. Opposing them all was the single blue square of Aras's command.

"If that's their plan, then it buys us some time," Formio said, breaking the silence. "The northerners will be almost two weeks marching across the Torian Plains."

"Yes," Corfe agreed. "Enough time for us to reinforce

Aras. I plan to transport many of our own troops upon the Torrin, which will save time, and wear and tear on the horses."

"This is it then, Corfe?" Formio asked. "The general mobilisation?"

Corfe met his friend's eye. "This is it, Formio. All roads, it seems, lead to the gap. They may try and sneak a few columns through the southern foothills, but the Cimbriani will help take care of those. And Admiral Berza is liaising with the Nalbeni in the Kardian to protect that southern flank."

"Bad terrain," Comillan said. His black eyes were hooded and he tugged at the ends of his heavy moustache reflectively. "Those foothills up around Gaderion are pretty broken. The cavalry will be next to useless, unless we remount them on goats."

"I know," Corfe told him. "They've pushed their outposts right up to the mountains, so we've little room to manoeuvre unless we abandon Gaderion and fall back to the plains below. And that, gentlemen, will not happen."

"So we're on the defensive, then?" a voice asked. The senior officers turned. It was Ensign Baraz. His fellow subalterns stared at him in shock for a second and then stood wooden and insensible. One moved slightly on the balls of his feet, as though he would like to be physically disassociated from his colleague's temerity.

"Who in hell—?" Comillan began angrily, but Corfe held up a hand.

"Is that your conclusion, Ensign?"

The young man flushed. "Our forces have been brought up thinking of the offensive, sir. It's how they are trained and equipped."

"And yet their greatest victories have been defensive ones."

"The strategic defensive, sir, but always the tactical offensive."

Corfe smiled. "Excellent. Gentlemen, our young friend has hit the nail on the head. We are fighting to defend Torunna,

as we once fought to defend it from his forefathers—but we
did not win that war by sitting tight behind stone walls. We
must keep the enemy off-balance at all times, so that he can
never muster his strength sufficiently to land a killer blow.
To do that, we must attack."

"Where, sir?" Comillan asked. "His outposts are well
sited. The Thurian Line could soak up an assault of many
thousands."

"His outposts should be assaulted if possible, and in some
force. But that is not where I intend the heaviest blow to
fall." Corfe bent his head. "Where could we do the most
damage, eh? Think."

The assembled officers were silent. Corfe met Formio's
eyes. The two of them had already discussed this in private,
and had violently disagreed, but the Fimbrian was not going
to say a word.

"Charibon," Ensign Baraz said at last. "You're going to
make for Charibon."

A collective hiss of indrawn breath. "Don't be absurd,
boy," Comillan snapped, his black eyes flashing. "Sir—"

"The boy is right, Comillan."

The commander of the Bodyguard was shocked speechless.

"It can't be done," someone said.

"Why not?" Corfe asked softly. "Don't be shy now, gentlemen. List me the reasons."

"First of all," Comillan said, "the Thurian Line is too
strong to be quickly overrun. We would take immense casualties in a general assault, and a battering by artillery
would give the enemy enough time to bring up masses of
reinforcements, or even build a second line behind the first.
And the terrain. As was said earlier, our shock troops need
mobility to be most effective. You cannot throw cavalry, or
even pikemen, at solid walls, or over broken ground."

"Correct. But forget about the Thurian Line for a moment.
Let us talk about Charibon itself. What problems does it
pose?"

"A large garrison, sir?" one of the ensigns ventured.

"Yes. But don't forget that most of the troops about the monastery-city will be drawn eastwards to assault Gaderion. Charibon is largely unwalled. What defences it has were built in the second century, before gunpowder. As fortresses go, it is very weak, and could be taken without a large siege train."

"But to get to it you would have to force the passage of the Thurian Line anyway," Colonel Heyd of the cuirassiers pointed out. "And to do that, Charibon's field armies would have to be destroyed. We have not the men for it."

"I had not finished, Heyd. Charibon's man-made defences may be weak, but her natural ones are formidable. Look here." Corfe bent over the map on the table. "To the east and north she is shielded by the Sea of Tor. To the southeast, the Cimbrics. Only to the west and north are there easy approaches for an attacking army, and even then the northern approach is crossed by the line of the Saeroth river, Charibon does not need walls. It is guarded by geography. On the other hand, if the city were suddenly attacked, with its forces heavily engaged to the east in the Torrin Gap, then the enemy would have an almost impossible time recalling them to her defence. The problems bedevilling an attacker would suddenly be working against the defender. The only swift way to recall them would be to transport them back across the Sea of Tor in ships. And ships can be burnt."

"All well and good, sir," Comillan said, clearly exasperated, "if our troops could fly. But they can't. There are no passes in the Cimbrics that I know of. How else do you suggest we transport them?"

"What if there were another way to get to Charibon, bypassing the Thurian Line?"

Dawning wonder on all their faces save Formio's.

"Is there such a way, sir?" Comillan asked harshly.

"There may be. There may be. The point is, gentlemen, that we cannot afford a war of attrition. We are outnumbered, and as Ensign Baraz pointed out, on the defensive. I do not want to go hacking at the tail of the snake—I intend to cut off its head. If we destroy the Himerian Triumvirate, this continent-wide empire of theirs will fall apart."

He straightened up from the map and stared at them all intently. "I intend to lead an army across the Cimbrics, to assault Charibon from the rear."

No one spoke. Formio stared at the map, at the line of the Cimbrics drawn in heavy black ink. They were the highest peaks in the world, it was said, and even in spring the snow on them lay yards deep.

"At the same time," Corfe went on calmly, "Aras will assault the Thurian Line. He will press the assault with enough vigour to persuade the enemy that it is a genuine attempt to break through to the plains beyond, but what he will actually be doing is drawing off troops from the defence of the monastery-city. A third operation will be a raid on the docks at the eastern end of the Sea of Tor. The enemy transport fleet must be destroyed. That done, and we have him like a bull straddling a gate."

"But first the Cimbrics must be crossed," Formio said.

"Yes. And of that I shall say no more at present. But make no mistake, gentlemen, we must win this war quickly. The first battles have already begun. I have communications from the west to the effect that the fleet of the Grand Alliance is about to go into action. A Fimbrian embassy has been reported at Charibon. It is likely that Himerian troops have been granted passage through Fimbria to attack Hebrion, and we know they are massing on the borders of eastern Astarac. We are not alone in this war, but we are the only kingdom with the necessary forces to win it."

Formio continued to stare at his king and friend. He drew close. "No retreat, Corfe," he said in a pleading murmur. "If you fail in front of Charibon, there is *no retreat*."

"What of the Fimbrians?" Heyd, the square, straight-lipped officer who was commander of the Torunnan cuirassiers asked.

"They are the great unknown quantity in this equation. Clearly, they favour the Empire for the moment, but only because they consider our armies to be the greater threat. I believe they think they can manage Aruan—consider how easy it would be for them to send a host eastwards to sack Charibon. If we are considering it, you may be sure they have. No, they want the Empire to break us down, along with the other members of the Alliance, and then they will strike, thinking to rebuild their ancient hegemony out of the ruins of a war-torn continent. They are mistaken. Once the true scale of this war becomes apparent, I am hoping they will think again."

"And if they don't?" Formio asked, looking his king in the eye.

"Then we'll have to beat them as well."

SEVEN

THERE was a storm, out in the west. For two days now the people of Abrusio had watched it rise up on the horizon until the boiling clouds blotted out fully half the sky. Each evening the sun sank into it like a molten ball of iron sinking into a bed of ash, its descent lit up by the flicker of distant lightning. The clouds seemed unaffected by the west wind that was blowing steadily landwards. They towered like ramparts of tormented stone on the brim of the world, the harbingers of monstrous tidings.

Abrusio was a silent city. For days the wharves had been crowded with people—not dockworkers or mariners or longshoremen, but the common citizenry of the port. They stood in sombre crowds upon the jetties and all along the waterfront, talking in murmurs and staring out past the harbour moles to the troubled horizon beyond. Even at night they remained, lighting fires and standing around them like men hypnotised, watching the lightning. There was little ribaldry or revelry. Wine was passed round and drunk without enjoyment. All eyes were raised again and again to the mole beacons at the end of the Outer Roads. They would be lit to signal the return of the fleet. To signal victory perhaps, in a war none of the people standing there truly understood.

They could be seen from the palace balconies, these waterfront fires. It was as though the docks were silently ablaze. Golophin had reckoned there were a hundred thousand people—a quarter of the city's population—standing down there with their eyes fixed on the sea.

Isolla, Queen of Hebrion, stood with the old wizard and looked out at the storm-racked western ocean from one of those palace balconies. She was a tall, spare woman in her forties with a strong face and freckled skin. Her wonderful red-glinting hair had been scraped back from that face and was covered by a simple lace hood.

"What's happening out there, Golophin? It's been too long."

The wizard set a hand lightly on her shoulder. His glabrous face was dark and set and he opened his mouth to speak, then paused. The hand left her shoulder and bunched into a bony fist. Faint around it grew an angry white glimmer. Then it faded again.

"They're stopping me from going to him, Isolla. It's not Aruan, it's someone or something else. There is a powerful mage out there in that storm, and he has thrown up a barrier that nothing, not ships or wizards or even the elements of the sea and earth itself, can penetrate. I have tried, God knows."

"What can cannon and cutlasses do against such magic?"

The wizard's jaw clenched. "I should have been there, it's true. I should have been there."

"Don't torture yourself. We've been over this."

"I—I know. He picked his moment well, Isolla. My only hope is that this mage, whoever he is, will have expended himself maintaining this monstrous weather-working spell, and so will not be able to aid in any attack on the ships. They will have to be assaulted using more conventional means, and thus valour, cold steel and gunpowder may yet count for something for those who are trapped out there."

She did not look at him. "And if they do not count for enough? What do we do then?"

"We make ready to repel an invasion."

"An invasion of *what*, Golophin? The country is near panic, not knowing who we war with. The Second Empire, some say. The Fimbrians say others. In the name of God, what exactly is out there?"

The old wizard did not reply, but traced a glowing shape in the air with one long finger. The shape of a glyph flashed for a second and was gone. Nothing. It was like staring at a stone wall.

"We fight Aruan, and whatever he has brought out of the Uttermost West with him. We know not exactly what we fight Isolla, but we know that it is dedicated to the overthrow of every kingdom in the west. They are out there, in that storm, our enemies, but I cannot tell you what manner of men they are, or if they are men at all. You have heard the stories which have come down through the years, the tales about Hawkwood's voyage. Some are fanciful, some are not. We know there are ships, but we do not know what is in them. There is a power, but we are not sure who wields it. But it is coming. And I fear that our last attempt to rebuff it has failed." His voice was thick with grief and a strangled fury.

"It has failed."

ONE half of the night sky had been obliterated, but the other was ablaze with stars. It was by these that Richard Hawkwood navigated his little craft. He had found a scrap of canvas that afternoon, barely big enough to cover a nobleman's table, and he had rigged up a rude mast and yard from broken ships' timbers. Now the steady west wind was blowing him back towards Hebrion, though the maintop wreckage that formed his raft was awash in a two-foot swell, and he had to keep one end of the knotted stay that kept his little mast erect tied round his pus-oozing and skinless fist.

His companion, hooded and anonymous, squatted unconcernedly on the sodden wood as the swell broke over them both and caked them with salt. Hawkwood wedged himself in place, shivering, and regarded the hooded figure with the burning eyes of a fever victim.

"So you came back. What is it this time, Bardolin? Another warning of imminent catastrophe? I fear you are talking to the wrong man. I am fish bait now."

"And yet, Richard, you strive to survive at every turn. Your actions contradict the brave despair of your words. I have never seen one so determined to live."

"It is a weakness of mine, I must confess."

The hood shook with what might have been a silent chuckle. "I have news for you. You will survive. This wind will waft you back into the very port you sailed from."

"It's been arranged, then."

"Everything has been arranged, Captain. Nothing is left to chance in this world, not anymore."

Hawkwood frowned. Something about the dark figure seated opposite him made him hesitate. Then he said: "Bardolin?"

The hood was thrown back, to reveal a hawk-nosed, autocratic face and a hairless pate. The eyes were black hollows in the night, like the sockets in a skull.

"Not Bardolin."

"Then who in the hell are you?"

"I have many names, Richard—I may call you Richard? But in the beginning I was Aruan of Garmidalan." He bowed his head with mocking courtesy.

Hawkwood tried to move, but the murderous lunge he had attempted turned into a feeble lurch. The rope which belayed his little mast had sunk into the burnt flesh of his palm and could not be released. The pain made him retch emptily. Aruan straightened and levered the mast back into place. The canvas flapped, then drew taut again. The two men sat looking at one another as the raft rose and fell on the waves, their crests glittering in the starlight.

"Come to finish the job?" Hawkwood croaked.

"Yes, but not in the way you think. Compose yourself, Captain. If I wished you dead I would not have permitted

Bardolin to visit you, and I would not be here now. Look at you! This suffering could have been avoided had you but followed your friend's advice of last night. Your sense of honour is admirable, but misguided."

Hawkwood could not speak. The pain of his salt-soaked burns was a ceaseless shuddering agony, and his tongue rasped like sand against his teeth.

"You are to be my messenger, Richard. You will return to Abrusio and relay my terms."

"Terms?" The word felt like crushed glass in his mouth.

"Hebrion and Astarac are defeated, their kings dead, their nobility decimated. Their eggs, shall we say, were all in the one basket. Yes, you will tell me that their land armies are intact, but you have seen the forces at my disposal. There is no army in the world which can stand against my children, even if it is commanded by a Mogen, or a Corfe. I was of Astarac myself once upon a time. I have no wish to see these kingdoms laid waste. I am not a barbarian."

"You are a monster."

Aruan laughed softly. "Perhaps, perhaps. But a monster with a conscience. You will survive, as I have always allowed you to survive, and you will go to your friend Golophin. Hebrion and Astarac must surrender to me, unless you wish to see them suffer the same fate as the fleet they sent against me. It may be better this way, now I think of it. You are a very convincing survivor of disaster, Captain, and you are a good witness."

"You go to hell."

"We are all in hell already. Imagine my hosts running amok through all the kingdoms of the west. Imagine the blood, the terror, the mountains of corpses. You want that no more than I. And Golophin, especially, will know that I make no idle boasts. I mean what I say. Hebrion and Astarac must surrender to the Second Empire, hand over all that remains of their nobility, and accept my suzerainty. If they do not, I will make of them a desert, and their peoples I will render into carrion."

Aruan's eyes lit up as he spoke with a hungry yellow light

that had nothing human about it. His voice thickened and deepened. A powerful animal stink lingered a moment, and then was swept away by the wind.

Hawkwood stared at the lightning-shot clouds in their wake. His eyes stung and smarted. "What manner of thing are you?"

"The new breed, you might say. The future. For centuries men have been pouring their energies into the fighting of their endless, worthless wars, many started in defence of a God they have never seen. Or else they cudgel their brains to think up more efficient ways of winning them—this they call science, the advance of civilisation. They turn their backs on the powers within them, because these are deemed evil. But what is more evil, the magic that heals a wound or the gunpowder that inflicts it? It is baffling to me, Hawkwood. I do not understand why so many clever men think that I and my kind are such an abomination."

"I never thought so. I've hired weather-workers before now and been damned glad of them. Torunna's Queen is a witch, it is said, and is respected across the continent. The mage Golophin has been Abeleyn's right hand for twenty years. And Bardolin—"

"Yes—and Bardolin?"

"He was my friend."

"He is yet."

"I doubt that somehow."

"You see? Suspicion. Fear. These names you drop are isolated instances, the exceptions that prove the rule. Four hundred years ago every royal court had a mage, every army had a cadre of wizards, and every city a thriving Thaumaturgists' Guild. Hedge-witches and oldwives were a part of ordinary life. That cursed Ramusio changed everything, he and his ravings. This God you people worship has hounded my people to the brink of extinction. How can you blame us for fighting back?"

"It was your creature, Himerius, who instigated the worst of the purges eighteen years ago. How was that fighting back?"

Aruan paused. The yellow light flickered again. "That was a means to an end, painful but necessary. I had to separate my folk from yours; make clear to all men the division between the two."

"Otherwise, you might have found wizards ranged against you when you attacked the western kingdoms, fighting for their own kings. Your cause would not be so clear-cut. You want power. Don't try to dress it up as a crusade."

Aruan laughed. "You are a perceptive man, Richard. Yes, I want power. Why shouldn't I? But in this world, unless you are somebody's son you are nothing. You know that as well as anyone. Why should mankind be ruled by a flock of fools just because they were dropped in a royal bed? I want power. I have the means to take it. I will take it."

Again, Hawkwood stared past his companion, into the storm-shot western sky where the lightnings shivered and the black clouds blotted out the stars. Those fine ships, those kings of men and that huge armament with its guns and its banners and its tall beauty.

"All gone. All of them."

"Very nearly all. It is a shock, I know. Men place such confidence in an array of power that it blinds them to its weaknesses. Ships must float, and must have wind to propel them."

"We should have had weather-workers of our own."

"There are none left, not in all the Five Kingdoms. Whatever you say, they are mine now, the Dweomer-folk. They have suffered for centuries under the rule of blind, bigoted fools. No longer. Their hour is come at last. This narrow land, Captain, is about to be fashioned anew."

"Golophin did not turn traitor. Not all the Dweomer-folk think of you as their saviour."

"Ah yes. My friend Golophin. I have not given up on him yet. You and he are very similar—stubborn to the core. Men who cannot be browbeaten or threatened or bought. That is why he is such a prize. I want him to see sense in his own time, and I am willing to wait."

"Corfe of Torunna will never bow the knee to you either."

"No. Another noble and misguided fool. He will be destroyed, along with that much-vaunted army of his. My storm will fell the oaks and leave the willows standing, and this little continent of yours will be a better place for it."

"Save your breath. I caught a glimpse of that better place of yours in the fog. I want no part of it."

"That is a pity, but I am not surprised. These are the labour pangs of the world. There will be pain, and blood, but a new beginning when it is over. The night is darkest just before the dawn."

"Spare me the rhetoric. You sound to me the same as any other grasping noble. You're not making a new world, you're just grabbing at the old and destroying anything that stands in your way. Those who fish the seas or till the land will have a change of masters, but their lives will not change. They'll pay their taxes to a different face, is all."

Aruan bent towards Hawkwood with a smile that was a snarled baring of teeth. "You are wrong there, Captain. You have no idea what I have in store for the world." He stood up, seemingly unaffected by the pitching of the raft. "Deliver my terms to Golophin. He may take them or leave them; I do not negotiate. This wind will bear you home in another day or two. Stay alive, Hawkwood. Deliver your message, and then find a hole to crawl into somewhere. My forbearance is at an end."

And he was gone. Hawkwood was alone on the raft, the waves black and cold in the night. His hands were cramped in salt-racked torture and the fever in him beat up a blaze within his blood. He shouted wordless defiance at the empty sea, the blank glitter of the uncaring stars.

DAWN saw the Hebros Mountains rise blue and tranquil out of the horizon—but they were to the north. Hawkwood was baffled for a few minutes until he realised that some time in the night he must have passed Grios Point. He had travelled some thirty leagues.

The wind had backed several points in the last few hours and was still right aft, but now it was blowing west-south-

west. He was being propelled up the Gulf of Hebrion, and
the spindrift was flying off the crests of the waves in stream-
ers around him, while the rope which supported his little
mast had disappeared into a mound of tight, puffed flesh that
had once been his hand.

The sunlight hurt his eyes and he clenched them shut,
drifting in and out of delirium. It was the sound of gulls that
woke him, a great derisive cloud of them. They were hovering and fighting over a small cluster of herrin-yawls which
were hove-to half a league away. The crews were hauling in
the catch of the night hand over fist, and even from where
he was Hawkwood could see the silver glint of fish flanks
as they squirmed in the bulging nets. He tried to rise, to
shout, but his throat had closed and he was too weak to raise
so much as an arm. No matter. The breeze was at his back,
and sending his unwieldy craft right into their midst. Half a
glass maybe, and he would be hauled in along with their
glinting catch, bearing his fearsome message for the kingdom. And after that was done, if he still lived, he would
follow Aruan's advice, and find a hole to climb into. Or
maybe the neck of a bottle.

"WHERE is he?" Isolla asked urgently.
        "Peace, Isolla. He is being carried here as we speak
by a file of marines."

"A file may not be enough. Do you hear the crowds down
there? I have ordered out the garrison. The city is ablaze
with torches."

Golophin listened. It was a sound like the surf of a distant,
raging sea. Tens of thousands of people in a panicked fever
of speculation, clogging the streets, choking the city gates.
A mob maddened by fear of the unknown. All this in the
space of a few hours. Rumour sped faster than a galloping
horse, and all over the city men were wailing that the fleet
was destroyed, and that they were now about to face an invasion of—what? That was the core of the panic. The ignorance. The yawl which bore the survivor had put in to the
Inner Roads late in the afternoon, and the marines sent to

fetch him to the palace were moving more slowly than the speculation.

"Have you summoned the nobles?"

"What is left of them. They're waiting in the abbey. My God, Golophin, what does it mean?" There were tears in her eyes, the first time he had seen her weep in many years. She truly loved Abeleyn, and now she was jumping to conclusions about his fate like everyone else. Golophin felt a pang of pure despair. He knew in his heart what this castaway they had found would tell him. But he had to hear it aloud, from someone who had been there.

A thump on the door. They had repaired to the Queen's chambers, as the rest of the palace was in an uproar.

All the best officers of the kingdom had been on board those proud ships. All that were left were time-servers and passed-over incompetents. Hebrion had been decapitated.

If the fleet is lost, Golophin reminded himself. The door was thumped again.

"Enter," Isolla called, composing herself. A burly marine with a livid scratch on his face put his head round the door. All the maids had been sent away.

"Your majesty, we have him here. We brought him on a handcart, but that got snarled up, so we—"

"Bring him in," Golophin snapped.

It was Hawkwood. They had not known that. Isolla's hand went to her mouth as the marines carried him in. They set him on the Queen's own four-poster and then stood like men who have had the wind knocked out of them. They were all looking at Golophin, then at the wrecked shape on the bed as though waiting for some explanation. In a kindlier voice, Golophin said; "There's wine in the antechamber, Sergeant. You and your men help yourselves, and remain there. I shall want to question you later."

The marines saluted and clanked out. As the door banged shut behind them Golophin leaned over the body on the bed. "Richard. Richard, wake up. Isolla, bring over that ewer, and the things on the tray. Water, lots of it. Hunt up one of those bloody maids."

Hawkwood had been terribly injured. Half his beard had been burnt off and his face was a raw, glistening wound which was bubbled with blisters and oozing fluid. His arms and chest had also suffered, and his right fist was a mass of scorched tissue from which a sliced rope's end protruded. He was caked with salt and what looked like old blood.

Golophin trickled water over the split lips and sprinkled drops over the eyelids. "Richard." His fingers wriggled and conjured a tiny white ball of flame in the air. He flicked it as one might bat at an annoying fly, and it smote the unconscious mariner on the forehead, sinking into his flesh in the glimmer of a second.

Isolla returned, a maid behind her bearing all manner of cloths and bottles and a steaming bowl. The maid was wide-eyed as an owl, but fled instantly at one look from her mistress.

Hawkwood opened his eyes. The white of one was flooded scarlet.

"Golophin." A cracked whisper. The wizard trickled more water over his lips and Hawkwood burst into a racking cough.

"Cradle his head, Isolla; raise it up."

The Queen rested the mariner's battered head on her breast, tears sliding silently down her face.

"Richard, can you talk?" Golophin asked gently.

The eyes, one garish red, glared wildly for a second, terror convulsing his body. Then Hawkwood relaxed like a puppet whose strings have been snipped.

"It's gone. The whole fleet. They destroyed it, Golophin. Every ship."

Isolla shut her eyes.

"Tell me, Captain."

"Weather-working—a calm and fog. Monsters out of the air, the sea. Thousands. We had no chance."

"They're all—"

"Dead. Drowned. Oh God!" Hawkwood's lips drew back from his black gums and a hoarse cry ripped out of him. "Pain. Ah, stop, stop." Then it passed.

"I will heal you," Golophin said. "And then you will sleep for a long time, Richard."

"No! Listen to me!" Hawkwood's eyes blazed with fever and anguish. "I saw him, Golophin. I spoke to him."

"Who?"

"Aruan. He let me go. He sent me back." Hawkwood sobbed dryly. *"I bear his terms."*

A hand of pure ice closed about Golophin's heart. "Go on."

"Surrender. Hand over the nobles. Hebrion and Astarac both. Or he'll destroy them. He can do it. He will. They're coming here on the west wind Golophin, in the storm."

It poured out of him in a stream of tumbled words. The raft. Aruan's appearance. His words—his implacable reasoning. At last Hawkwood's voice sank into a barely audible croak. "I'm sorry. My ship. I should have died."

Isolla caressed his unburnt cheek. "Hush, Captain. You have done well. You can sleep now." She looked at Golophin and the old wizard nodded, his face grey.

"Sleep now. Rest."

Hawkwood stared up at her, and the ghost of a smile flitted across his face. "I remember you." Then coughing took him, a fit that made him jump in Isolla's arms. He fought for breath. Then his eyes rolled back, and the air came out of him in a long, tired exhalation. He was still.

"He has suffered too much," Golophin said. "I was impatient. I am a fool."

Isolla bent her head and her shoulders trembled, but she made not a sound.

"He is dead then," she said at last, calmly.

Golophin set a hand on Hawkwood's chest, and shut his eyes. The mariner's body gave a sudden jolt, and his limbs quivered.

"I will not permit him to die," Golophin said fiercely, and as he spoke the Dweomer blazed up in him and spilled out of his eyes, his fingertips. It coiled out of his mouth like a white smoke. "Get away from him, Isolla."

The Queen did as she was told, shielding her eyes against

the brilliance of Golophin's light. The wizard had been transformed into a form of pure, pulsing argent. The light waxed until it was unbearable to look at, becoming a shining swirl, a sunburst, and then with a shout it left him and hurled into the inert form on the bed. There was a noiseless concussion that blew out the lamps and sent the bedclothes spiralling into the air even as they crackled and shrivelled away to nothing, and Hawkwood's body thrashed and twitched like the plaything of a mad puppeteer.

The room plunged into darkness save for where Golophin crouched by the bed, breathing hard. The werelight still shone out of his eyes dementedly. Isolla was standing at the far wall as if fixed to it. Something powdery and light was snowing down upon her head, and there was an inexplicable tautness to one side of her face.

"Light a candle," the wizard's voice said. The lambency of his stare faded and the room was pitch-dark. On the bed, something was groaning.

"I—I can't see, Golophin," Isolla whispered.

"Forgive me." A fluttering wick of werelight appeared near the ceiling. Isolla reached for the tinderbox, and retrieved a candle from the floor. The backs of her hands, her clothing, were covered in a delicate layer of white ash. She struck flint and steel, caught the spark in the ball of tinder, and fed it to the candle wick. A more human radiance replaced the werelight.

Golophin laboured to his feet, beating the ash from his robes. When he turned to her Isolla caught her breath in shock. "My God, Golophin, your face!"

One side of the old wizard's countenance had been transformed into a tormented mass of scar tissue, like that of a burn long healed. He nodded. "The Dweomer always exacts a payment, especially when one is in a hurry. Ah, child, I am so sorry. You should not have been here for this. I thought that I alone would suffice."

"What do you mean?"

He came forward and stroked her cheek gently, the strange tautness there. "It took you too," he said simply.

She felt her skin. It was ridged and almost numb in a line running from the corner of her eye to her jaw. Something in her stomach pitched headlong, but she spoke without a quaver. "It's no matter. How is he?"

They turned to the bed, holding the candle over the blasted coverlet, the ash-strewn and smoking mattress. Hawkwood's ragged, scorched clothes had disappeared. He lay naked on the bed breathing deeply. His beard had gone, and the hair on his scalp was no more than a dark stubble, but there was not a mark on his body. Golophin felt his forehead. "He'll sleep for a few hours, and when he wakes, he'll be as hale as ever he was. Hebrion has need of him yet.

"Stay here with him, my dear. I must go and take the temperature of the city, and there are one or two errands to be run also." He looked closely at Isolla, as though deliberating whether to tell her something, then turned away with a passable pretence at briskness. "I may be gone some time. Watch over our patient."

"As I once watched over Abeleyn?" The grief was raw in her voice. She remembered another evening, a different man restored by Golophin's power. But there had been hope back then.

Golophin left without replying.

EIGHT

A procession of dreams, all brightly lit and perfectly co-
herent, travelled along the trackways of Hawkwood's
mind. Like paper lanterns set free to soar, they finally burned
themselves up and came drifting sadly back down in ash and
smoke.

He saw the old *Osprey* blazing in the night, sails of flame
twisting and billowing from her decks. At her rail stood King
Abeleyn, and beside him, Murad. Murad was laughing.

He watched as, like a succession of brilliantly wrought
jewels, a hundred ports and cities of the world winked past.
And with them were faces. Billerand, Julius Albak, Haukal,
his long-forgotten wife Estrella. Murad. Bardolin. These last
two were linked, somehow, in his mind. There was something they shared which he could not fathom. Murad was
dead now—even in the dream Hawkwood knew this, and
was glad.

At the last there came a red-haired woman with a scar on
her cheek who pillowed him on her breast. He knew her. As
he studied her face the dreams faded, and the fear. He felt

as though he had made landfall after the longest of voyages, and he smiled.

"You're awake!"

"And alive. How in the world—" and he saw her face clearly now, the line of ridged tissue down one side, like the trail of a sculptor's fingers in damp clay.

Her own fingers flew to it at once, covering it. Then she dropped her hand deliberately, stern as the Queen she was. She had been weeping.

The room was gloomy and cold in the pre-dawn greyness. A fire in the hearth had sunk to smoking embers. How long had he been here? What had been happening? There was no pain. His life's slate had been wiped clean.

"Golophin saved you, with the Dweomer. But there was a price. He is far worse than I. It is not important. You are alive. He will be here soon."

Isolla rose from the bedside, his eyes following her every move with a baffled, helpless pain. He ran a hand over his own features and was astounded.

"My beard!"

"It'll grow back. You look younger without it. There are clothes by the side of the bed. They should fit. Come into the antechamber when you are ready. Golophin wants to talk to us." She left, walking stiffly in a simple and unadorned court gown.

Hawkwood threw aside the covers and studied his body. Not a mark. Even his old scars of twenty years had disappeared. He was as hairless as a babe.

Feeling absurdly embarrassed, he pulled on the clothing which had been left out for him. He was parched, and drained at a gulp the silver jug of springwater sitting beside them. He felt as though he must crack every joint in his body to bend it back into shape, and spent minutes stretching and bending, getting the blood flowing again. He was alive. He was whole. It was not a miracle, but it seemed more than miraculous to him. Despite all that he had seen of the workings of magic through the years, certain aspects of it never failed to stun him. It was one thing to call up a storm—it was the kind of thing he expected a wizard to do. But to mould his own flesh like this, to smooth out the burns and heal his cracked, smoke-choked lungs—that was truly awe-inspiring.

What price had been paid for the gift of this life? That lady on the other side of the door. She had paid for his scars with her own. She, Hebrion's Queen.

When he stepped through the doorway his face was as sombre as that of a mourner. In his life he had not made a habit of frequenting the bedchambers of royalty and he was at a loss as to whether he should bow, sit down or remain standing. Isolla was watching him, drinking a glass of wine. The antechamber was small, octagonal, but high-ceilinged. A fire of blue-spitting sea coal burned in the hearth and there was a pretty tumble of women's things here and there on the chairs, a full decanter on the table, ruby and shining in the firelight, beeswax candles burning in sconces in the walls, their fine scent mingling with Isolla's perfume. Heavy curtains were drawn across the single window, so that it might have been the middle of the night, but Hawkwood's internal clock knew that dawn had come and gone, and the sun was rising up the sky now.

"There is no formality here, Captain. Help yourself to some wine. You look as though you had seen a—a ghost."

He did as he was bidden, unable to relax. He wanted to twitch aside the curtains and peer out to see what was in the morning sky.

"I have met you before, have I not?" she said stiffly.

"I have been at a levee or two over the years, lady. But a long time ago I met you on the North Road. Your horse had thrown a shoe."

She coloured. "I remember. I served you wine in Golophin's tower. Forgive me Captain, my wits are astray."

Hawkwood bowed slightly. There was nothing more to be said. But Isolla was trying to say something. She stared into her wine and asked at last: "How did he die? The King."

Hawkwood swore silently. What could he possibly tell this woman that would make her sleep any easier at night? That her husband had been burned, ripped apart, drowned? She raised her head and saw what he would not say in his eyes.

"So it was bad, then."

"It was bad," he said heavily. "But truly, lady, it did not last long, for any of them."

"And my brother?"

Of course, she was Mark's sister. This woman was now one of the last survivors of two Royal lines—perhaps the last indeed.

"For him also it was quick," he lied, staring her down, willing her to believe him. "He died scant feet away from Abeleyn, the two on the same quarterdeck." On my ship, he thought. Two kings and an admiral died there, but not I. And the shame seared his soul.

"I'm glad they died together," she said thickly. "They were like brothers in life, save that Mark always hated the sea. How was it that he was not on his own flagship?"

Hawkwood smiled, remembering the green-faced and puking Astaran King being hauled over the side of the *Pontifidad* in a bosun's chair. "He came for a conference and—and kept putting off the return journey."

That made her smile also. The room warmed a little.

A discreet knock at the door, and Golophin came in without further ado. Hawkwood had to collect himself for a moment at the sight of the old man's face. God in heaven, why had they done it?

The wizard was a gaunt manikin with white parchment skin that rendered his purple and pink scars all the more startling. But he grinned at Hawkwood as the mariner stood with his untasted wine in his fist.

"Good, good. A perfect job. You had us worried there for a while, Captain." Isolla took his heavy outer robe like a girl helping her father, and gave him her own glass. He drained it in one swallow, then stepped across to the window and swept back the curtains.

The window faced west, and looked out into a vast, boiling darkness. Hawkwood joined the wizard to stare at it. "Blood of God," he murmured.

"Your storm is almost upon us, Captain. It made good time during the night."

The cloud was twisted and stretched into a great bastion of shadow which filled the entire western horizon. It was shot through with the flicker of lightning at its base and writhed in tormented billows with a motion that seemed almost sentient.

"The city has been swarming like a wasps' nest all night, and the sight of that this morning has been enough to tip things over the edge. Already there is a throng of soldiers, sailors and minor nobles in the abbey, all talking without listening. The garrison, such as it is, is out on the streets, but the panic has already begun. They're streaming out of North Gate in their thousands, and ships in the harbour have dumped their cargoes and are offering passage out of Hebrion instead, to anyone who has a king's ransom in his purse."

"No one said a word," Isolla said wonderingly. "One castaway is brought ashore, and the whole country expects the worst. Storm or no storm, have they no faith? It's madness."

"The fishermen found me floating on the broken maintop of a Great Ship. Some of them recognised me as the captain of the flagship. And I would answer none of their questions," Hawkwood told her gently. "Victory is not so close-mouthed. They know that the fleet has met with some disaster."

"Plus, I believe that a few of the palace maids have been more ingenious in their curiosity than I gave them credit for," Golophin went on. "At any rate, the secret is out. The fleet, and our King are no more—this much is now common knowledge. Aruan's terms have not yet been bruited abroad though, which is a blessing. We must have no more maids or valets in this wing of the palace, if it is to stay that way. I have posted sentries further down the passage."

"What do we do now?" Isolla asked slowly, her eyes fixed on the preternatural tempest which was rolling towards them on the west wind. She was no ingénue, but nothing in her life had prepared her for this sudden, crushing weight of responsibility. She did not even know the name of the officer who now commanded the army.

Golophin looked at Hawkwood, and found that the mariner was watching the Queen with a strange intentness. He nodded to himself. He had been right there, all those years ago, and he was still right. That could be for the good.

He pursed his lips. "Abrusio has a garrison of some six thousand men left to her. The marines went with the fleet, as did all the Great Ships. All we have left are dispatch-runners and a few gunboats. There are small garrisons in Imerdon and up on the border with Fulk, but they are weeks away."

"There are the mole forts," Isolla said. "In the Civil War they held up Abeleyn's fleet for days."

"These things," Hawkwood said slowly, "can fly."

"What were they, Captain?" Golophin asked. Even at a time like this, he seemed more curious than appalled.

"I saw one once before, in the jungle of the Western Continent. I believe they were men at one time, but they have been warped beyond humanity. They are like great bats with tails, and the talons of a raptor. And they number many thousands. There is a fleet out there also, mostly composed of lesser ships, and on board it are black-armoured warriors with pincers for hands and a carapace like that of a beetle. They swarm like veritable cockroaches in any case. Abrusio cannot stand against that. Her best men died off North Cape and her citizens, from what you tell me, are in no mood to stand and fight."

"She is doomed then," Isolla murmured.

Golophin's face was a demonic mask. "I believe so. Hebrion, at least, must accept Aruan's terms, or see bloodshed that will make the Civil War pale into insignificance."

"He wants the nobles handed over too," Hawkwood reminded him. "He intends to extinguish the aristocracy of the whole kingdom."

Both men looked at Isolla. She smiled bitterly. "I care not. My husband and my brother are both dead. I may as well join them."

Golophin took her hand. "My Queen, you have been like a daughter to me, one of the few folk I have trusted in this long, absurd life of mine. This man here is another such, though he has not always known it. Abeleyn your husband was the third, and Bardolin of Carreirida was the fourth. Now only you and Hawkwood remain." As she hung her head he gripped her fingers more tightly. "I speak to you now as a Royal advisor, but also as a friend. You must leave Hebrion. You must take ship with a few of the household whom you in your turn can trust, and sail from these shores. And you must go soon, within the day."

Isolla looked shaken. "Where shall I go?"

It was Hawkwood who answered. "King Corfe still rules in Torunna, and his army is the greatest in the world. You should go to Torunn, lady. You will be safe there."

"No. My place is here."

"Hawkwood is right," Golophin said fiercely. "If Aruan captures you then all hope for the future is lost. The people must have some continuity in the times to come. And you must go by sea; the land route to the east is closed." He raised a hand. "Let us hear no more on this matter. I have already spoken to the Master of Ships down in Admiral's Tower. A state xebec awaits you as we speak. Hawkwood here will captain it. You ought to leave, I am told, with a certain combination of tides, the—the—"

"The ebb tide," Hawkwood told him. "It happens at the sixth hour after noon. The xebec is a good choice. She's lateen-rigged, and with this westerly she'll have a beam wind to work with to get out of the harbour—precious little leeway, mind. But you'll find some other skipper. I'm staying here."

Isolla and Golophin both glared at him.

"I survived my King, my admiral and my ship—despite being her captain," Hawkwood said simply. "I'm not running away again."

"Bloody fool," Golophin said. "And what service will you render here in Hebrion, apart from having that stiff neck of yours chopped through?"

"I might make the same point to you. You're staying, it seems—and for what?"

"I can be in Torunn in the blink of an eye if I so choose."

"You look as though a child could knock you over with a willow wand."

"He's right, Golophin," Isolla said quickly. "Are your powers in need of recuperation? You do not look well." She appeared momentarily exasperated by her own timidity. Hawkwood saw her jaw harden. But then Golophin, ignoring her, was poking him in the chest with a bony forefinger.

"Aruan told you his forbearance is at an end. Twice now he's let you live, to suit his own ends. He will not do so again. Plus, this ship needs an experienced navigator. You will be travelling the entire length of three seas to reach Torunn. You are going, Captain. And you, lady—even if I were not your friend, I would insist that, as Hebrion's reigning Queen, you must go. And you will, if I have to have you bundled up in a sack. Hawkwood, I charge you with her protection. Now let us hear no more about it. As it happens, I have a reason for staying, and you have given me reason to believe Aruan will not have me slain out of hand. Nor am I defenceless, so rest your minds from that selfless worry and start preparing for your voyage. There are tunnels under the palace that lead almost to the waterfront; Abeleyn had them dug ten years ago, so you will be able to leave without creating even more of a panic than already exists. Isolla knows where they are. You will leave by them as soon as you possibly can."

"I can't do that. I must speak to the nobility before I go. I can't just sneak away," Isolla protested.

Golophin finally let slip the leash on his temper. *"You can and you will!"* A cold light blazed in his eyes. They burned like white flames and the fury in them made Isolla retreat a step. "By Ramusio's beard, I thought you had better sense. Do you think you can give a cheery little speech to the nobles and then expect to trip lightly away? This kingdom is about to enter a dark age that none of us can imagine, and the storm of its wings is almost upon us. I have no more time to sit here and wrangle with stiff-necked fools and silly little girls. *You will both do as I say.*"

The light in his eyes faded. In a more human voice he said, "Hawkwood, a word with you outside."

The mage and the mariner left the shocked Queen behind and stood outside her door. Hawkwood watched Golophin warily, and the old wizard grinned.

"What do you think? Did I put the fear of God into her?"

"You old bastard! And into me too."

"Good. The eyes were a nice touch, I think. Listen Richard, you must get her down to that damned ship by mid-afternoon at the latest. Your vessel is called the *Seahare*, and is berthed in the Royal yards at the very foot of Admiral's Tower. Do not ask how I purloined her; I would blush to tell you. But she is yours, and all the paperwork is . . ." He grinned again. "Irrelevant. Everything is ready or almost so. They're lading her with extra stores but she's a flyer, not a fighter—so they tell me—and if I start sending marines aboard it'll arouse suspicion. The current captain is on shore leave, no doubt dipping his wick in some bawdy house. I have spoken to the harbour master, and you are expected, but your passengers are anonymous nobles, no more."

"Nobles? So who are the others?" Hawkwood asked.

"I'm not yet sure there will be others. That is what I am going to find out now. Just get Isolla down to that ship. And—and look after her, Richard. Quite apart from being Queen, she's a fine woman."

"I know. Listen Golophin, I haven't thanked you—"

"Don't bother. I need you as much as you needed me. Now I must be gone." Golophin gripped his arm. "I will see you again, Captain, of that you may be sure."

Then he was off, striding down the passageway like a much younger man, albeit one who looked as though he had not eaten in a month.

A flurry of packing—and Hawkwood conscripted into the process by dark little Brienne, Isolla's Astaran maid, who had been with her since childhood. Isolla white-faced and silent, still believing Golophin's rage to be genuine. And then a subterranean journey, the little trio hurrying and stumbling by torchlight, weighed down with bags and even a small trunk. From the palace to Admiral's Tower was the better part of half a league, and the first third of the way was a steep-stepped descent of dripping stone, the Queen leading the way with a guttering torch, Hawkwood and Brienne following, unable to see their own feet for the burdens they carried. Hawkwood stepped once on the wriggling softness of a rat, and stumbled. At once, Isolla's strong hand was at his elbow, helping him to his feet. The Queen's face was invisible under a hooded cloak but she was as tall as a man, and up to the burden. Hawkwood found himself admiring her quick, sure gait, and the slender fingers which held aloft the torch. Her perfume drifted back to him as they laboured along, an essence of lavender, like the scent of the Hebros foothills in summer.

At last they came to a door which Isolla unlocked and left open behind them, and stepped out into the lower yards of the tower. All about them was the tumult of the wharves, the screaming gulls. Sea smells of rotting fish and tar and wood and salt. A forest of masts rose up into a clear sky before them, and the sunlight was dazzling, blinding after their underground journey. They stood blinking, momentarily bewildered by the spectacle. It was Hawkwood who collected his wits first, and led them to their vessel where it floated at its moorings in the midst of a crowd of others.

THE *Seahare* was a lateen-rigged xebec of some three hundred tons, a fast dispatch-runner of the Hebrian navy with a crew of sixty. Three-masted, she could run up both lateen and square-rigged yards depending on the wind. She was a sharp-beaked ship with an overhanging counter and a narrow keel, but she was nonetheless wide in the beam to enhance her stability as a sail platform. Her decks were turtle-built so that any seas which came aboard might run off into the scuppers at once, and above the decks were gratings which ran from the centre line to the ship's rail so that

her crew might work dry-shod whilst the water ran off below
them. As Golophin had said, she was built for speed, not
warfare, and though she had a pair of twelve-pound bow-
chasers her broadside amounted to half a dozen light sakers,
more to counter a last-minute boarding than to facilitate any
real sea battle. Hawkwood's arrival was greeted with un-
friendly stares, but as soon as the ladies were below he began
shouting out a series of orders which showed that he knew
his business. The first mate, a Merduk named Arhuz, was a
small, compact man, dark as a seal. He had sailed with Julius
Albak thirty years before, and like all of the other sailors he
knew of Richard Hawkwood and his great voyage, as a man
remembers the nursery rhymes learned as a child. Once the
knowledge of the new captain's identity had spread about the
ship the men set to work with a will. It was not every day
they were to be skippered by a legend.

A great deal of stores had still to be taken on board, and
the main hatch was gaping dark and wide as the men hauled
on tackles from the yardarms to lower casks and sacks into
the hold. Others were trundling more casks from the vast
storerooms under the tower, whilst yet more were coiling
away spare cables and hauling aboard reluctant goats and
cages of chickens. It looked like chaos, but it was a controlled chaos, and Hawkwood was satisfied that they would
complete their victualling in time for the evening tide.

The Royal yards had not yet been engulfed by the panicked disorder that was enveloping the rest of the waterfront,
but that disorder was audible beyond the massive walls
which separated them from the Inner Roads. Fear was rank
in the air, and all the while men looked over their shoulder
at the approaching storm which was towering in the west,
and swallowing up ever more of the sky as it thundered eastwards. Hawkwood needed no charts in this part of the world;
he knew all the coasts around Abrusio as well as the features
of his own face, and that face grew grave as he considered
what it would be like to beat out of the Inner Roads under
a strong westerly. Handy as the xebec might be at dealing
with a beam wind, she would have to win some leeway once

they made it into the gulf, or that wind might just push them headlong on to the unforgiving coast of Hebrion. But they would have the ebbing flow of the tide beneath the keel, to draw them out of the bay and into the wider gulf beyond. He hoped that would be enough.

Through the years, Hawkwood had taken ships uncounted out of this port into the green waters of the gulf, and then beyond, to Macassar of the Corsairs, to Gabrion which had spawned him and of which he remembered almost nothing now. To the coasts of hot Calmar and the jungles of savage Punt. But all those memories faded into a merry silence beside the one voyage which had made his name. The one that had broken him. No good had come of it that he could see, least of all to himself. But he knew that it would always be irrevocably linked to him—among mariners at least. He had earned a place in history; more importantly, perhaps, he had won a hard-bought right to stand tall in the ranks of the mariners of yore. But he took no pride in it. He knew that it counted for nothing. Men did things because they had to do them, or because they seemed the only thing to do at the time. And afterwards they were lauded as heroes. It was the way the world worked. He knew that now.

But this woman below, she mattered. She mattered to the world, of course—it was important that she survive. But most of all she mattered to him. And he dared not delve deeper into that knowledge, for fear his middle age might come laughing back at him. It was enough that she was here.

For a while Richard Hawkwood, standing there on the quarterdeck of another man's ship with doom approaching out of the west, watched the sailors ready his vessel for sea, and knew that she was below, and was inexplicably happy.

A commotion down on the wharves. Two riders had galloped through the gate and come to a rearing halt before the xebec, scattering mariners and panicking the gulls. A man and a woman dismounted, tawny with dust, and without ceremony or introduction they ran up the gangplank hand in hand, leaving their foam-streaked and blowing mounts standing. Hawkwood, jolted out of his reverie, shouted for the master-at-arms and met them at the rail.

"What the hell is this? This is a king's ship. You can't—"

The woman threw back her richly embroidered hood and smiled at him. "Hello, Richard. It has been a long time."

It was Jemilla.

PART TWO

THE SOLDIER-KING

But I've said goodbye to Galahad,
And am no more the Knight of dreams and show:
For lust and senseless hatred make me glad,
And my killed friends are with me where I go . . .

Siegfried Sassoon

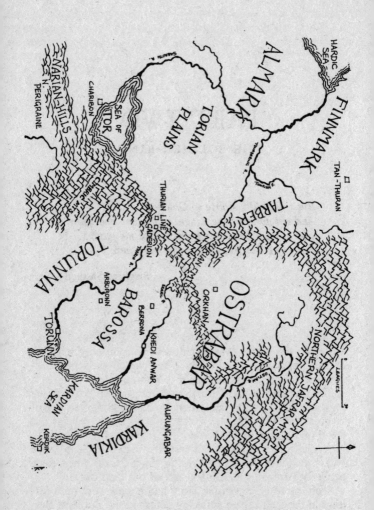

NINE

GADERION had begun life as a timber-built blockhouse
on a stream-girt spur of the Thurian mountains. The
Fimbrians had stationed troops there to police the passage of
the Torrin Gap and levy tolls on the caravans that passed
through from west to east, or east to west. When their empire
fell apart the station was abandoned, and the only relic left
of their presence was the fine road which they had constructed to speed the passage of their armies.

The Torunnans had built a series of staging posts in the
gap, and around these had grown up a straggling network of
taverns and livery stables which catered for travellers. But
these had withered away over the years, first of all in the
retrenchment which had followed the crisis of the Merduk
Wars, and then in the years after the Schism, when trade
between Torunna and Almark had all but died out.

More recently, a Merduk army had begun work on a fortress in the gap, before suffering defeat in the Battle of Berrona. King Corfe, in the years following Armagedir, had had
the entire region surveyed, and at the point where the road

was pinched in a narrow valley between the buttresses of the two mountain chains, he had had a hilltop spur levelled, and on its summit had constructed a large fortress complex which in size at least would come to rival long-lost Ormann Dyke. In the subsequent years the defences had been extended for almost half a league, to command the entire pass, and Gaderion now consisted of three separate fortifications, all connected by massive curtain walls.

To the south-east was the donjon on its steep spur of black rock. This was a squat citadel with walls fully fifty feet thick to withstand siege guns. There was a spring within its perimeter, and below it bomb proofs had been hewn out of the living gutrock to house a fair-sized army, and enough supplies to sustain them for at least a year. Here also were the administrative offices of the garrison, and the living quarters of the commanding officer. In the midst of these was a taller feature, a blunt spike of rock which at one time in the youth of the world had been a plug of molten lava within the walls of a volcano. The walls had worn away, leaving this ominous fist of basalt standing alone. There had been a pagan altar on its summit when Corfe's engineers had first surveyed it. Now it had been partially hollowed out with immense, costly, dangerous labour, and provided a last-ditch refuge within the donjon itself, and a lofty look-out which gave a bird's-eye view of the entire Torrin river valley and the mountains on either side. Light guns had been sited in embrasures in its impregnable sides, and they commanded every approach. Men called this ominous-looking tower of stone the Spike.

The donjon and the Spike loomed over this flat-floored valley, which was perhaps three quarters of a mile wide. The soil here was fertile and dark, watered by the chill stream which hundreds of miles to the south and east grew into the Torrin river, and the soldiers of the garrison tended plots of land in the shadow of the fortress despite the mountain-swift growing season and the killer frosts of the winter. There were currently twenty-eight thousand men stationed at Gaderion. Many of them had wives who lived nearby, and a scattering of stone and log houses dotted the valley east of the walls.

Officially, this was frowned upon, but in fact it was discreetly tolerated, else the separation between the men and their families would have been well-nigh unsupportable.

Square in the middle of the valley was a low, circular knoll some fifty feet high, and on this had been built the second of Gaderion's fortresses. The redoubt was a simple square structure with triangular casemates at each corner to catch any foes who reached the walls in a deadly crossfire. The North Road ran through it under the arches of two heavily defended gates, and before these gates were two redans which each mounted a battery of guns. Within the walls were housed the stables of the Royal couriers who kept Gaderion in touch with the larger world, and it was here also that the main sortie force of the fortress was billeted: some eight thousand men, half of them cavalry.

The last of Gaderion's fortresses was the Eyrie. This had been tacked on like a swallow's nest to the steep cliffs of the Candorwir, the mountain whose peak overlooked the valley on its western side. The stone of Candorwir had been hollowed out to accommodate three thousand men and fifty great guns, and the only way they could be reached was by a dizzy single-track mule path which had been blasted out of the very flank of the mountain. The guns of the Eyrie and the donjon formed a perfect crossfire which transformed the floor of the Torrin valley into a veritable killing ground in which each feature had been mapped and ranged. The gunners of Gaderion could, if they wished, shoot accurately at these features in the dark, for each gun had a log board noting the traverse and elevation of specified points on the approach to the walls.

The three fortresses, formidable in themselves, had a weak link which was common to all. This was the curtain wall. Forty feet high and almost as thick, it ranged in strange tortuous zig-zags across the valley floor connecting the donjon to the redoubt and the redoubt to the cliffs at the foot of the Eyrie. Sharp-angled bartizans pocked its length every three hundred yards, and four thousand men were stationed along it, but strong though it seemed, it was the weakest element

of the defences. Only a few guns were sited in its casemates,
as Corfe had long ago decided that it was the artillery of the
three fortresses which would protect the wall, not the wall
itself. If it were overrun, then those three would still dominate the valley too thoroughly to allow the passage of troops.
To force the passage of the Torrin Gap, an attacker would
have to take all of them: the donjon, the redoubt, and the
Eyrie. All told, twelve thousand men manned their defences,
which left a field army of sixteen thousand to conduct offensive operations and patrols. Once this had seemed more
than ample, but General Aras, officer commanding Gaderion,
was no longer so sure.

SOME six leagues to the north and west of Gaderion the
narrow, mountain-girt gap opened out into the wider land
of the Torian Plains beyond, and in the tumbled foothills
which marked the last heights of the mountains a line of turf
and timber structures signalled the beginning of the Thurian
Line, the easternmost redoubt of the Second Empire. Here,
with the conscripted labour of thousands, the forces of Himerius had reared up a great clay and wood barrier, part defensive wall, part staging post. It meandered over the grassy
hills like a monstrous serpent, bristling with stockades and
gabions and revetments. There were few heavy guns stationed along it, but huge numbers of men patrolled its unending length, and to the rear they had constructed sod-walled
towns and roads of crushed stone. The smoke of their fires
could be seen for miles, an oily smudge on the hem of the
sky, and their shanty towns were surrounded by muddy quag-
mires through which columns of troops trudged ceaselessly,
and files of cavalry plunged fetlock-deep. Here were garrisoned men of a dozen different countries and kingdoms
reaching from Fulk in the far west to Gardiac in the heights
of the Jafrar. Knights of Perigraine, looking like chivalric
relics on their magnificently caparisoned chargers. Clanking
gallowglasses from Finnmark with their greatswords and
broadaxes. Almarkan cuirassiers with pistols strapped to their
saddles. Knights Militant, as heavily armoured as the Peri-

grainians, but infinitely more businesslike. And Inceptines, no longer monks in habits, but now tonsured warriors on destriers wielding maces and clad in black-lacquered steel. They led ragged columns of men who wore no armour, wielded no weapons, but who were the most feared of all Himerius's soldiers: the Hounds of God. When a troop of these trotted down one of the muddy garrison streets, everyone, even the hulking gallowglasses, made room for them. The Torunnans had yet to meet these things in battle, but they were the secret weapon upon which the Empire based many hopes.

A savage, low-intensity warfare had flickered over this disputed ground between the two defence lines now for several months. Each side sent out patrols to gather intelligence on the other, and when these met no quarter was asked or given. Scarcely two sennights previously, a Torunnan flying column of a thousand cuirassiers had slipped through the foothills to the north-east of the Thurian Line undetected, and had burned the bridges over the Tourbering river a hundred miles to the north. However, on their way back the Himerians had been ready for them, and barely two hundred of the heavy horsemen had survived to see the walls of Gaderion again.

A small group of lightly armed Torunnan cavalry reined in as evening drew on and prepared to bed down for the night on a low bluff within sight of the endless skein of lights that was the Thurian Line. They had been out of Gaderion three days on a reconnaissance, riding the entire length of the enemy fortifications, and were to return to barracks in the morning. Half their number stood guard while the rest unsaddled, rubbed down and fed their mounts, and then unrolled their damp bedrolls. When this had been done, the dismounted troopers remained standing and watchful as their comrades did the same. Five dozen tired, grimy men who wanted nothing more than to get through the night and back to their bunks, a wash, and a hot meal. The Torunnans were forbidden to light fires when between the lines, and thus their camps had been chill and cheerless, their food ration scarcely less so. By the time the horse lines were pegged out in the wooded ground at the foot of the bluff and the animals hobbled and deep in nosebags, it had become almost fully dark, the last light edging down behind the jagged sentinel bulk of Candorwir behind them, and the seven stars of the Scythe bright and stark in a cloudless night sky.

The troopers' young officer, a lanky youth with straw-coloured hair, stood watching the line of lights glittering on the world perhaps ten miles away to the north and west. They arced across the land like a filigree necklace, too delicate to seem threatening. But he had seen them up close, and knew that the Himerians decorated those ramparts with Torunnan heads mounted on cruel spikes. The bodies they left out as carrion within gunshot of the walls.

"All quiet, sir," the troop sergeant told his officer, a shadow among other, faceless shadows.

"All right, Dieter. Turn yourself in as well. I reckon I'll watch for a while."

But the sergeant did not move. He was staring down at the Thurian Line like his officer. "Funny, behind the walls it's lively as an ant's nest someone has poked with a stick,' but there's not hide nor hair of the bastards out here. Not one patrol! I haven't seen the like, and I've been stationed up here these past four years."

"Yes, there's a bad smell in the air all right. Maybe the rumours are true, and it's the start of the war at last."

"Saint's blood, I hope not."

The young ensign turned to his sergeant, his senior by twenty years, and grinned. "What's that? Aren't you keen to have a go at them, Dieter? They've been skulking behind those ramparts for ten years now. It's about time they came out and let us get at them."

Dieter's face was expressionless. "I was at Armagedir, lad, and in the King's Battle before that. I was no older than you are now and thought much the same. All young men's minds work the same way. They want to see war, and when they have seen it, they never want to see it again, providing they live through it."

"No glory, eh?"

"Roche, you've been up here a year now. How much glory have you seen?"

"Ah, but it's just been this damn skirmishing. I want to see what a real fight is like, where the battle lines are a mile long and the thunder of it shakes the earth."

"Me, I just want to get back to my bed, and the wife in it."

"What about young Pier? He'll soon be of an age to sit a saddle or shoulder a pike. Is he to follow you into the tercios?"

"Not if I can help it."

"Ah, Dieter, you're tired is all."

"No, it's not that. It's the waiting, I think. These bastards have been building things up for a decade now, since the Torian Plains battle. They own everything between the Malvennors and the Cimbrics, right up to the sultanates in the Jafrar, and still they want more. They won't stop till we break 'em. I just want to get on with it, I suppose. Get it over with."

He stopped, listening. In the horse lines among the trees the animals were restless and quarrelsome, despite being as tired as their riders. They were tugging at the picket ropes, trying to rear though their forelegs were securely hobbled.

"Something in the wind tonight," the young ensign said lightly, but his face was set and hard.

The night was silent save for the struggling horses. The sentries down at the lines were trying to calm them, cursing and grabbing at their skewed nosebags.

"Something," Dieter agreed. "Sir, do you smell that?"

The ensign sniffed the air doubtfully. "There must be an old fox's den nearby. That's what is spooking the horses."

"No, it's different than that. Stronger."

One of the sentries came running up to the two men with his sabre drawn. The metal glinted coldly in the starlight.

"There's something out there in the dark sir, something moving. It was circling the camp, and then I lost it in that gully down on the left. It's in the trees."

The young officer looked at his sergeant. "Stand to."

But the nickering of the horses exploded into a chorus of terrified, agonising shrieks that froze them all where they stood. The sentries came running pell-mell from the horse lines, terrified. "There's something down in there, Sergeant!"

"Stand to!" Dieter yelled at the top of his voice, though all through the bivouac men were already struggling out of their bedrolls and reaching for their weapons.

"What the hell's going on down there?"

"We couldn't see. They came out of the gully. Some kind of animals, black as a wolf's throat and moving on their hindquarters like men. But they aren't men, sir."

Horses were trying pitifully to drag themselves up the rocky slope to the bivouac where their riders stood, trailing their picket ropes. But their forelegs were securely hobbled and they reared and screamed and tumbled to their sides and kicked out maniacally to their rear. The men could see the black berry-shine of blood on them now. One had been disembowelled and was slipping in its own entrails.

"Sergeant Dieter," the ensign said in a voice that shook, "take a demi-platoon down to the horse lines and see what is happening there."

Dieter looked at him a moment and then nodded. He bawled out at the nearest men and a dozen followed him reluctantly down into the wooded hollow from which the hellish cacophony of dying beasts resounded.

The rest of the men formed up on the bluff and watched them as they struck a path through the mêlée of terrified and dying beasts still struggling out of the trees. Two men were knocked from their feet. Dieter left them there, telling them to unhobble every horse they could. The terror-stricken animals mobbed the men, looking to their riders for protection. Then Dieter's group disappeared into the bottomless shadow of the wood that straggled along the foot of the bluff.

A stream of horses was galloping up the slope now as they were loosed of their restraints. The men tried to catch and soothe them but most went tearing off into the night. The men gathered around the ensign were as much baffled as afraid, and angry at the savagery of the attack on their horses. Many of the mounts that had escaped were bleeding from deep-slashed claw marks.

A single shout, cut short, as though the wind had been knocked out of the shouter.

"That was Dieter," one of the men on the bluff said.

There were alder and birch down in the hollow below the bivouac, and these began thrashing as though men were shaking their branches. Cursing the darkness, those on the hill peered down the slope, past the keening, crippled horses that littered the ground, and saw a line of black figures loom out of the trees like a cloud of shadow. The smell in the air again, but stronger now—the musk-like stink of a great beast. Something sailed across the night sky and thudded to the ground just short of their feet. They heard a noise that afterwards many would swear had resembled human laughter, and then one of their number was pointing at the thrown object lying battered and glistening on the earth before them. Their sergeant's head.

The things in the trees seemed to melt away into the darkness, branches springing back to mark their passing. The men on the hill stood as though turned to stone, and in the sudden quiet even the screaming of the horses died away.

THE lady Mirren's daily rides were a trial to both her assigned bodyguards, and her ladies-in-waiting. Each morning just after sunrise, she would appear at the Royal stables where Shamarq, the ageing Merduk who was head groom, had her horse Hydrax saddled and waiting for her. With her would be the one among her ladies-in-waiting who had chosen the short straw that morning, and a suitable young officer as escort. This morning it was Ensign Baraz, who had been kicking his heels about the Bladehall for several days until he had caught the eye of General Comillan. He had accepted his new role with as much good grace as he could muster, and now his tall grey stood fretting and prancing beside Hydrax, a pair of pistols and a sabre strapped to its saddle. Gebbia, the lady who was to accompany them,

had been assigned a quiet chestnut palfrey which she nonetheless eyed with something approaching despair.

The trio set off out of the north-west postern in the city
walls and kicked into a swift canter, Gebbia's palfrey bobbing like a toy in the wake of the two larger horses ahead.
Mirren's marmoset clung to her neck and bared its tiny teeth
at the fresh wind, trying to lick the air with its tongue. The
riders avoided the wagon-clogged Kingsway, and struck off
towards the hills to the north of the city. Not until the horses
were snorting and blowing in a cloud of their own steam did
Mirren rein in. Baraz had kept pace with her but poor Gebbia
was half a mile behind, the palfrey still bobbing simple-
mindedly along.

"Why a court lady cannot be made to ride a decent horse
I do not know," Torunna's Princess complained.

Baraz patted his sweating mount's neck and said nothing.
He was regretting the King's momentary interest in him, and
was wondering if he would ever be sent to a tercio to do
some real soldiering. Mirren turned to regard his closed face.

"You sir, what's your name?"

"Ensign Baraz, my lady—yes, that Baraz." He was getting
tired of the reaction his name produced, too.

"You ride well, but you seem more put out even than
Gebbia. Have I offended you?"

"Of course not, lady." And as she continued to stare at
him, "It's just that I was hoping for a more—more military
assignment. His majesty has attached me to the High Command as a staff officer—"

"And you wanted to get your hands dirty instead of es-
corting galloping princesses about the countryside."

Baraz smiled. "Something like that."

"Most of the young bloods are very keen to escort the
galloping Princess."

Baraz bowed in the saddle. "I am uncouth. I must apologise, lady. It is of course an honour—"

"Oh, stow it, Baraz. It's not as though I blame you. Were
I a man, I would feel the same way. Here comes Gebbia.
You would think she had just ridden clear across Normannia.

Gebbia! Clench your knees together and kick that lazy screw a little harder or you'll lose us altogether."

Gebbia, a pretty dark-haired little thing whose face was flushed with exertion, could only nod wordlessly, and then look appealingly at Baraz.

"We should perhaps walk them a while to let them cool down," he ventured.

"Very well. Ride beside me, Ensign. We shall head up to the hilltop yonder, and then maybe I'll allow you to race me."

The three horses and their riders proceeded more sedately up the long heather and boulder-strewn slope, whilst before them the sun rose up out of a roseate wrack of tumbled cloud on the undulating horizon. A falcon wheeled screaming out of the sun towards Torunn and shrank to a winged speck within seconds, though Mirren followed its course keenly with palm-shaded eyes. The marmoset gibbered unhappily and she shushed it. "No Mij, it was just a bird is all."

"You understand him?" Baraz asked, curious.

"In a way. He's my familiar," and she laughed as his eyes widened. "Didn't you know that Dweomer runs in the blood of the Fantyrs? The female line, at any rate. From my mother I gained witchery and from my father the ability to ride anything on four legs."

"You can cast spells then?"

"Would you like me to try?" She wagged the fingers of one hand at him and he recoiled despite himself. Mirren laughed again. "I have little talent, and there is no one to tutor me save Mother. There are no great mages left in Torunna. They have all fled to join Himerius and the Empire, it is said."

"I have never seen magic worked."

Mirren waved an arm, frowning, and Baraz saw a haze of green-blue light follow in its wake, as though trailed by her sleeve. It gathered on her open palm and coalesced into a ball of bright werelight. She sent it circling in a blazing blur round Baraz's astonished face, and then it winked out like a snuffed candle.

"You see? Mountebank tricks, little more." She shrugged with a rare sadness, and he saw at once her father's face in hers. Her eyes were warmer, but the same strength was in the line of the jaw and the long nose. Baraz began to regret his assignment a little less.

Mirren stared at him with the sadness still on her face, then turned to her lady-in-waiting.

"Don't try to keep up with us, Gebbia; you'll only fall off." And to Baraz: "Ready for that race?"

Without another word she let out a yell and kicked Hydrax on. The big bay sprang into an instant canter, then quickened into a full-blooded gallop, his black mane flying like a flag. Baraz watched her go, startled, but noting how well she sat, sidesaddle or no, and then dug both heels into his own horse's flanks.

He had thought to go easy on her, and let her stay a little ahead, but he found instead that she was leaving him quickly behind, and had to ride in earnest, his grey dipping and rising under him on the rough ground. Once he had to pull up hard on the reins as the gelding tripped and almost went headlong and it took every ounce of his skill to draw level with her as they reached the broad plateau at the summit of the ridge-line, and she slowed to a canter again, then a trot, and finally a slow walk.

"Not bad," Mirren told him. The marmoset had wrapped itself around her neck and was as bright-eyed as she. "Now Mij, ease off a little there; you'll have me strangled."

There was a rough upland track here on the ridge, and as they walked their horses along it they could look down on the sprawl of the capital behind them. They were some five or six miles out of the gates, now, and poor Gebbia was a mere dot on the land below, still trotting gamely upwards.

They passed the ruins of a house, or hill croft, its roof beams long since fallen in like charred ribs in the crumbling shadow of its walls.

"My father tells me there were many farms here in the hills outside the city before the war. Then the Merduks came and—" Mirren coloured. "Ensign Baraz, I am so sorry."

Baraz shrugged. "What you say is true lady. My people raped this part of the world before your father threw them back at Armagedir. It was an ugly time."

"And now a descendant of the great Shahr Baraz of Aekir wears a Torunnan uniform and takes orders from a Torunnan king. Does that not seem odd to you?"

"When the Wars ended I was a toddler. I grew up knowing that Ramusio and Ahrimuz were the same man. I have worshipped alongside Ramusians all my life. The older men remember things the way they were, but the younger know only the world the way it is now. And it is better this way."

"I certainly think so."

They smiled at each other in the same moment, and Baraz felt a warmth creep about his heart. But the moment was broken by the urgent squeaks of Mirren's familiar.

"Mij! What in the world is wrong?"

The little animal was clambering distractedly about her shoulders, hissing and crying. She halted her horse to calm it and Baraz took her reins as she bodily seized the tiny creature and stared into its face. It grew quiet, and whimperingly climbed into the hollow of her hood where it lay chittering to itself.

"He's terrified, but all he can show me is the face of a great black wolf." Mirren took back her reins, troubled.

"There's someone on the track ahead of us," Baraz told her. He loosened his sabre in its scabbard. A tall figure was standing some way in the distance, seemingly oblivious of their presence. He was motionless as a piece of statuary, and was staring down at the walls of the capital, mustard-coloured in the morning light, and the blue shine of the estuary beyond where the Torrin widened on its way to the sea.

"He doesn't look dangerous," Mirren said. "Oh, Baraz, stop topping it the bodyguard. It's just a beggar or vagabond. Look—there's another one, off to one side. They seem lost, and old, too."

They rode up to the men, who appeared to be absorbed in the contemplation of the city in the distance. One was sitting with his back to a stone and a hood which seemed like a monk's cowl was pulled over his head. He might have been asleep. The other was dressed in a travel-stained robe, buff-coloured with dust, and a wide-brimmed hat which hid his face in shadow. A bulging haversack hung from one bony shoulder.

"Good morning, fathers," Baraz greeted them as they approached. "Are you heading for the city?"

The man on the ground did not stir, but the other answered. "Yes, that is my goal." His voice was deep as a well.

"You've a fair step to go then."

The man did not reply at once. He seemed weary, if the sag of his shoulders was anything to go by. He looked up at the two riders and for the first time they saw his face and gasped involuntarily.

"Who might you two be then?"

"I am Ensign Baraz of the Torunnan army, and this is—"

"The Princess Mirren, daughter of King Corfe himself. Well, this is a happy chance." The man smiled, and they saw that despite the ruin which constituted one side of his face, his eyes were kindly.

"How do you know who I am?" Mirren demanded.

And now the man sitting on the ground raised his head and spoke for the first time. "Your familiar told us."

Baraz drew his sabre and nudged the grey forward until he was between Mirren and the strange pair. "State your names and your business in Torunna," he rasped, dark eyes flashing.

The man on the ground rose to his feet. He also seemed tired. The two might have been nothing more than a pair of road-weary vagabonds, but for that last statement, and the aura of unquiet power which hung about them.

"They're wizards," Mirren said.

The disfigured older man doffed his wide-brimmed hat. "Indeed we are, my dear. Young man, our business is our own, but as for our names, well I am Golophin of Hebrion, and my companion—"

"Will remain nameless, for now," the other interrupted. Baraz could see a square jaw and broken nose under the cowl, but little else.

"Golophin!" Mirren cried. "My father speaks often of you. The greatest mage in the world, it is said."

Golophin chuckled, replacing his hat. "Perhaps not the greatest. My companion here might bridle at such an assumption."

"What are you doing here in Torunna? I thought you were still in Abrusio."

"I have come to see King Corfe, your father. I have some news for him."

"What of your taciturn comrade?" Baraz asked, pointing at him with his sword.

As he gestured with the blade the weapon seemed to flick out of his grip. It spun coruscating in the air for a second and then flicked away into the heather, stabbing into the ground so that the hilt stood quivering. Baraz shook his hand as though it had been burned, mouth gaping.

"I do not like blades pointed in my face," Golophin's companion said mildly.

"You had best leave us be," Golophin told Baraz. "My friend and I were in the middle of a little altercation when you arrived, hence his testiness."

"Golophin, there is so much I must ask you," Mirren said.

"Indeed? Well child, you may ask me anything you like, but not right now. I am somewhat preoccupied. It might be best if you said nothing of this meeting. The fewer folk who know I am here the better." Then he looked at his companion, and laughed. The other's mouth crooked under the cowl in answer.

"You may tell your father, though. I will see him tonight, or possibly tomorrow morning."

"What is this news you have come to deliver? I will take it to him."

Golophin's ravaged face hardened into a mask. "No, one so young should not have to bear such tidings." He turned to Baraz. "See the lady safe home, soldier."

Baraz glared at him. "You may be sure I will."

• • •

SPRING might be in the air, but up here in the hills there was still an algid bite to the air when the wind got up, and as the day drew on Golophin and his companion kindled a fire with a blast of rubescent theurgy and sat on pads of gathered heather warming themselves at the transparent flames. As the afternoon waned and the sun began to slide behind the white peaks of the Cimbrics in the west, Golophin was aware that a third person had joined them, a small, silent figure which sat cross-legged just outside the firelight.

"That is an abomination," the old mage told his companion.

"Perhaps. I am no longer sure I care greatly. One can become accustomed to all sorts of things, Golophin." The speaker had thrown back his cowl at last and now was revealed as a middle-aged man with close-cropped grey hair and a prize-fighter's face. He reached into the breast of his habit and brought forth a steel flask. Unscrewing the top, he took a sip and then tossed it across the fire. Golophin caught it deftly and drank in his turn. "Hebrionese akvavit. I applaud your taste, Bard."

"Call it a perk of the job."

"Call it what it is: spoils of war."

"Hebrion was my home also, Golophin."

"I have not forgotten that, you may be sure."

A tension fizzled across the flames between them, and then slackened as Bardolin chuckled. "Why Golophin, your hauteur is almost impressive."

"I'm working on it."

"It is pleasant, this, sitting here as though the world were not on fire around us, listening to the hunting bats and the sough of the wind in the heather. I like this country. There is an austerity to it. I do not wonder that it breeds such soldiers."

"You met these soldiers in the field I hear, a decade ago. So are you become a general now?"

Bardolin bowed. "Not much of a one, it must be said. Give

me a tercio and I know what to do. Give me an army and I will admit to being somewhat ill at ease."

"That doesn't bode well for your master's efforts in this part of the world, Presbyter."

"We have generals, Golophin, ones who may surprise you. And we have numbers. And the Dweomer."

"The Dweomer as a weapon of war. In the days before the Empire—the First Empire—it is said that certain kings fielded regiments of mages. But it has never been recorded that they tolerated the presence of shifters in their armies. Not even the ancients were barbarian enough for that."

"You speak whereof you know nothing."

"I know enough. I know that the thing seated across the fire from me is not Bardolin of Carreirida, and the succubus which hides silent in the shadows behind you was not conjured up for his comfort."

"And yet she is a comfort, nonetheless."

"Then why are you here? To sit and wax nostalgic about the old days?"

"Is that so inexplicable, so hard to believe?"

Golophin dropped his eyes. "I don't know. Ten, twelve years ago I thought there was a part of my apprentice which could still be saved. I am no longer so sure. I am consorting with the enemy now."

"It does not have to be that way. I am still the Bardolin you knew. Because of me, Hawkwood is alive."

"That was your master's whim."

"Partly. The survival of the other had nothing to do with me though, you may be sure."

"What other?"

"The Presbyter of Hebrion's right hand."

"I don't understand, Bard."

"I can tell you no more. I, also, am consorting with the enemy do not forget."

The two wizards stared at each other without animosity, only a gentle kind of sadness.

"It is not as though Hebrion has been destroyed, Golophin," Bardolin said softly. "It has merely suffered a change in ownership."

"That sounds like the self-justification of the thief."

"You are so damned wilfull—and wilfully blind." Here Bardolin leaned forward so that the firelight carved a crannied mask out of his bluff features.

The fleet did not make landfall in Hebrion out of a mere whim, Golophin. Your—our—homeland is vital to Aruan's plans. It so happens that Hebrion, and the Hebros Mountains, were once part of the Western Continent."

"How can you—"

"Let me finish. At some time in the unimaginable past Normannia and the west were one great land mass, but they split apart aons ago, drifting like great lilypads and letting the ocean flood in between them. Aruan and his chief mages have been conducting research into the matter for many years."

"So?"

"So, there is something, some element or mineral in the very bowels of the Western Continent which is in effect the essence of the energy we know as *magic*. Pure theurgy, running like a vein of precious ore through the very bedrock of the earth. It is that which has made Aruan what he is."

"And you what you have become, I take it."

"This energy runs through the Hebros also, for the Hebros and the mountains of the Western Continent were once part of the same chain. That is why Hebrion has always been home to more of the Dweomer-folk than any other of the Five Kingdoms. That is why Hebrion had to fall. Golophin, you have no conception of the great researches that are underway, in the west, at Charibon, even in Perigraine. Aruan is close to solving an ancient and paramount riddle. What are the Dweomer-folk, and how were they created? Is it in fact possible to imbue an ordinary man with the Dweomer, and make of him a mage?"

Golophin found his bitter reply dying in his mouth. Despite himself, he was fascinated. Bardolin smiled.

"Think of the progress this army of mages can make in

the pursuit of pure knowledge, given all the materials they need, allowed to proceed in peace with their studies. Golophin, for the first time in history, the bowels of the Library of St. Garaso in Charibon have been opened up and laid bare. There are treatises and grimoires down there that predate the First Empire. They have been sealed away by the Church for centuries, and now they are finally being studied by those who can understand them. I have seen a first edition of *Ardinac's Bestiary*—"

"No! They were all destroyed by Willardius."

Bardolin laughed, and threw his hands up in the air. "I've seen it, I tell you! Golophin, listen to me, think about this. Imagine what a mind like yours, allied to that of Aruan, could mean for the progress of learning, both theurgical and otherwise. An eighth Discipline is only the beginning. This is a precious opportunity, a crux of history right here and now, with the bats squeaking round our ears in the hills north of Torunn. It may be there are things about our regime that you find distasteful—no man is perfect, not even Aruan. But damn it all, our motives are pure enough. To lead mankind down a different path.

"At this time, there is a fork in the road. Man can either follow what he terms as science, and develop ever more efficient means of killing, and build a world where there is no place for the Dweomer, and which will eventually see its death. Or he can embrace his true heritage, and become something entirely different. A society can be created in which theurgy is part of daily commerce, and learning is treasured above the soot-stained tinkering of the artisan. At this point in history, mankind must choose between these two destinies, and that choice will be made in a tide of blood, because that is the way of revolutions. But that, regrettable though it may be, does not make the choice invalid.

"Join us, Golophin, in the name of God. Perhaps we can spare the world some of that bloodletting."

The two men stared intently across the fire at one another. Golophin could not speak. For the first time in his long life he did not know what to say.

"I'm not asking you to decide now. But at least think about it." Bardolin rose. "Aruan has been away from Normannia a long time. It is a foreign country to him. But that is not true for us. Learned though he is, we possess a familiarity with this world of today that he lacks. He respects you, Golophin. And if your conscience still niggles, think on this: I am convinced you would have more influence over his deeds as a counsellor and friend rather than as an antagonist.

"As for me, my friend you have always been, and yet remain—whatever you might choose to believe."

Bardolin rose to his feet with the smooth alacrity of a much younger man. "Think about it, Golophin. At least do that. Farewell."

And he was gone, only a slight stirring in the air, a faint whiff of ozone to mark his passing. Golophin did not move, but stared into the firelight like a blind man.

TEN

THE Bladehall was crowded, bubbling with talk that rose to the tall roof beams in a babble of surmise. Virtually every senior officer in the country was present with the exception of Aras of Gaderion, but he had sent a staff officer-cum-courier to represent him and to inform the High Command of recent events at the gap.

The King entered without ceremony, limping a little as he always did when he was tired. It was common knowledge about the palace that most nights lately he slept in a chair by the Queen's bed. She was very low now, and would not last more than a few more days. Only the day before, a formal embassy had been sent out to Aurungabar on her express orders, and the court was still in a feverish frenzy of speculation as to what it might signify. It was as well to steer clear of the King, though. His temper, never particularly equable, had become truly savage of late.

The hall hushed as he entered, flanked by General Formio and a tall, horribly scarred old man in travel-stained robes who bore a haversack on one shoulder. Corfe's personal bodyguard, Felorin, brought up the rear, watching the stranger's back warily. The little group came to a halt in front of the map-table and Corfe scanned the faces of the assembled officers. They were staring at his aged companion with avid curiosity.

"Gentlemen, I would like to introduce you to the mage Golophin of Hebrion, one-time chief advisor to King Abeleyn. He is here with tidings from the west which take precedence over all other matters for the moment. Golophin, if you please."

The old wizard thanked Corfe and then stared at the hungry faces which surrounded him much as the King had done. His mellifluous voice was without its customary music as he spoke.

"King Abeleyn of Hebrion is dead, as is King Mark of Astarac, and Duke Frobishir of Gabrion. The great naval armament which they commanded is destroyed. The fleet of the westerners has made landfall in Hebrion, and that kingdom has surrendered to the foe."

A second of stunned silence, and then everyone began talking at once, a tumult of horrified exclamations, questions lost in the clamour. Corfe held up a hand and the noise tailed away. The Torunnan King's face was grey as marble.

"Let him continue."

Golophin, unbidden, had filled a glass from the decanter on the table, and drained it at a draught. He smelled of woodsmoke, sweat, and another evocative stink much like the charged air of a thunderstorm. A vein throbbed like a blue worm in the hollow of one temple.

"Himerian troops are on the march. They are riding out from Fulk, down both sides of the Hebros towards Imerdon and the northern Hebrionese coast. An army has crossed from Candelaria into East Astarac and has defeated the Astarans in the foothills. Garmidalan is about to stand siege, if it is not besieged already. And if my information is correct, another Himerian army is making for the passes of the Malvennors as we speak, to take Cartigella from the rear."

"How do you know all this?" General Comillan asked, his thick moustache bristling like a besom.

"I have a—a reliable source in the Himerian camp."

"Won't they at least put up some resistance?" one Torunnan asked incredulously.

"Not in Hebrion. It has been agreed that there will be no pillage, no sacking of Abrusio, in exchange for a bloodless occupation. In Astarac the military has been caught off-guard, as have we all. They are in full retreat westwards. The garrison of Cartigella is capable enough, though, and will probably stand siege under Cristian, the Crown Prince." Golophin filled his glass again, peered into it as though it were hemlock, and tossed it off.

"But Cartigella's fall is only a matter of time."

"Gentlemen," Corfe said softly, "we are at war. The general mobilisation is under way. I signed the Conscription Decree not half an hour ago. As of now, this kingdom is under martial law, and every able-bodied man in the country is being called to the colours. No exceptions. Comillan, Formio, in the morning you will begin processing the first batch of conscripts. I want them knocked into shape as quickly as possible. Comillan, the Bodyguard will act as the kernel of the new training cadre—"

"Sir, I protest."

"Your protest is noted. Colonel Heyd, I am drawing up a command for you which you will take north to reinforce Aras within two days. Colonel Melf."

"Sir?"

"You also are to have an independent command. Once the Merduk contingents arrive from Aurungabar you will set off, and take it south, to the port of Rone. Your area of operations will be the southernmost foothills of the Cimbrics, where the mountains come down to the Levangore itself. The enemy may well try to sneak a column round our southern flank that way. You will be liaising with Admiral Berza."

"Sir!" Melf, a tall, lean man who looked like a peasant farmer, beamed.

"What of the main body of the army, sir?" Formio asked.

"It will remain here in Torunn for the time being, under my command. That means the Cathedrallers, your Orphans Formio, and the Bodyguard, of course. Ensign Roche, my apologies for keeping you waiting. What news from Aras?"

The young officer seemed to gulp for a second, then jerkily proffered a dispatch case. "Sir—"

"Read it out, if you please. All present needs must hear it."

Ensign Roche flipped off the lid of the leather tube and unrolled the paper within. He cleared his throat. "It is dated six days ago, sir.

" 'Corfe, I write in haste and without ceremony. The bearer of this dispatch will give you a fuller picture of conditions up here than my penmanship ever can. He has experienced them first-hand. But you must know this—we have been swept out of the plains entirely by a large-scale advance of the enemy. Not one patrol can be sent out without encountering huge numbers of the foe, and in the past week we have lost heavily in men and horses. I have been tempted to essay a large-scale sally myself, but prefer to wait for your approval before attempting so major an operation. The Finnmarkans and Tarberans are still not yet up, thanks to our bridge-burning, but the Himerians have numbers enough without them it seems. I would hazard that they have already stripped Charibon of much of its garrison. They mean to take Gaderion, that much is plain.*

" 'There is more. We are encountering something new, something which the bearer will be able to inform you of more fully. These Hounds, as they are called— they are beasts of some kind, or men that can become beasts at will. The rumours have been flying about the continent for years, as we all know, but I have had patrols, demi-tercios of good men, slaughtered like rabbits by these things, always in the night, half-glimpsed. Our intelligence-gathering is non-existent* *now. I believe that soon we will be under siege.*

" 'Man for man, we are better soldiers than the foe, but this new thing we do not know how to fight, and there are no Dweomer-folk about to advise us. I need reinforcements, but also I need a way to fight back. I need to know how to kill these things.

" 'Officer Commanding Gaderion, Nade Aras.' "

There was a concussive silence, as though the wind had been taken out of all their mouths. Corfe spoke first. "Ensign Roche, you have encountered these things General Aras speaks of?"

"I have, sir."

Corfe flapped a hand impatiently. "Tell us."

Briefly, tonelessly, Roche recounted the fate which had befallen his patrol two sennights before. The attack of the fearsome, half-seen beasts, the death of his sergeant.

"We found the bodies in the wood after it had gone, sir. They had been torn into pieces, twelve men. We had only heard that one shout. We saddled what horses remained, doubled up in the saddles and made our way back into Gaderion that same night."

"You left the bodies unburied?" Comillan snapped.

Roche ducked his head. "I am afraid so, sir. The men were panicked, and I—"

"It's all right, Ensign," Corfe said. He turned to the old mage who stood at his side listening intently. "Golophin, can you enlighten us?"

The wizard sighed heavily and stared into his empty glass. "Aruan and his cohorts have been experimenting for years, perhaps centuries. They have taken normal men and made them into shifters. They have taken shifters and twisted them into new forms. They have bred unnatural beasts for the sole purpose of waging war, and these are now being unleashed upon the world. They destroyed the allied fleet, and now they will take part in the assault upon Torunna."

"I ask you Aras's question: how do we kill these things?"

"It's quite simple. Iron or silver. One nick from a point or a blade made of either and the Dweomer which flows through the veins of these creatures has its current disrupted, and they die instantly."

Corfe seemed slightly incredulous. "That's it?"

"That's it, sire."

"Then they are not so fearsome after all. You hearten me, Golophin."

"The swords and pike-points of the army are made of tempered steel," Formio said wryly. "They will not bite, it seems. Nor will the lead of our bullets." He looked quizzically at the old wizard.

"Correct, General."

"We must get the smithies busy, then," Corfe broke in. "Iron blades and pike-points. And I'm thinking maybe some kind of iron barbs which can be fitted on to armour. We'll make of every man a deadly pincushion, so that if these things so much as lay a paw on him, they'll send themselves off to hell."

The mood in the Bladehall lightened somewhat, and there were even some chuckles. The news from the west was bad, yes, but Hebrion and Astarac were not Torunna, and Abeleyn was no Corfe. The very sea itself might be subjugated to the will of Aruan and his cohorts, but there was no force on earth that would stop the Torunnan army once it had begun to march.

"Gentlemen," Corfe said then, "I believe you all know your duties for now, and Lord knows there's enough to be getting on with. You are dismissed. Ensign Baraz—you will stay behind."

"Corfe," Formio said in a low voice, "have you thought any more on our discussion?"

"I have, Formio," the King replied evenly, "and while you make very valid points, I believe that the possible gains outweigh the risks."

"If you are wrong—"

"There is always that chance." Corfe smiled, and gripped Formio by the shoulder. "We are soldiers, not seers."

"You are a king, not some junior commander who can be spared to hare off on a whim."

"It's no whim, believe me. If it succeeds, it will bring down the Second Empire. That makes the gamble worthwhile."

"Then at least let me come with you."

"No. I need to leave behind someone I trust—someone who could be regent if the worst occurs."

"A Fimbrian?"

"A Fimbrian who is my closest friend, and most trusted commander. It must be you, Formio."

"The nobility will never wear it."

"The Torunnan nobility is not the fractious beast it once was. I have seen to that. No, you would have the backing of the army, and that is all that matters. Now let us hear no more of this. Continue the preparations, but discreetly."

"Will you let him into our little secret?" Formio asked, nodding at Golophin, who was conversing with Ensign Baraz on the other side of the hall. Nearly all the other officers had left by now and the fire cracked and spat loudly in the sudden quiet. Felorin stood watchful as always in the shadows.

"I believe I will. He may be able to make some suggestion. There is always that bird of his anyway, a hell of a useful thing to have around."

Formio nodded. "There is something though, Corfe— something about Golophin which does not feel right."

"Explain."

"Nothing, perhaps. It is just that sometimes I feel he should hate more. He has seen his king slain, his country enslaved, and yet I sense no hatred, hardly any anger in him."

"What are you now, some kind of mind-reader?" Corfe grinned.

"I find myself not wholly trusting him, is all."

Corfe clapped him on the back. "Formio, you are getting old and cantankerous. I'll see you later down at Menin Field. We'll go over those new formations again. But talk to the Quartermaster-General for me. Let's see how much scrap iron we can come up with."

Formio saluted, spun on his heel, and left as crisply as a young officer fresh off the drill square.

"A good man, I think," Golophin said, walking over from the fire. "You are lucky in your friends, sire."

"I have been lucky, yes," Corfe said. Formio's words had unsettled him. He stared at the old wizard closely. "Golophin, you said you had a reliable source in the Himerian camp. Would it be out of place for me to ask who it might be?"

"I would rather that his identity remained secret for now. He is an ambivalent sort, sire, a man unsure as to where his loyalties lie. They are sorry creatures, these fellows who cannot make up their minds what is black and what is white. Do you not think?" The mage's smile was disconcertingly shrewd.

"Indeed." There was a brief moment where their eyes locked, and something akin to a struggle of wills took place. Golophin dropped his gaze first. "Was there anything else, sire?"

"Yes, yes, there was. I was wondering if—that is to say—" Now it was Corfe who looked down. Quietly, he said, "I thought you might call in on the Queen. She is very low, and the physicians can do nothing. Old age, they say, but I believe there is more to it than that, something to do with your . . . realm of expertise."

"I should be glad to, sire." And here the wizard's eyes met Corfe's unflinchingly. "I am flattered that you should trust me in such a grave matter." He bowed deeply. "I shall call on her at once, if that is convenient. Now, if you will excuse me sire, I have things to attend to."

"Your suite is adequate?"

"More than adequate, thank you, sire." The wizard bowed again, and left, his robes whispering about him.

The man had served kings faithfully and unstintingly for longer than Corfe's lifetime. Formio was merely being a cautious Fimbrian, that was all. The King of Torunna rubbed his temples wearily. God, to get clear of the palace, the city, to get back on a horse and sleep under the stars for a while.

Sometimes he thought that there were so many things contained in his head that one day it would bulge and burst like an overripe melon. And yet when he was in the field it was as though his mind were as clear as the tip of an icicle.

I never should have been King, he thought, as he had thought so often down the years. But I am here now and there is no other.

He collected himself, strode across to the fire where Ensign Baraz stood stiff and forgotten.

"You've met the great Golophin, I see. What do you make of him?"

Baraz seemed startled by the question. "He asked me about my grandfather," he blurted out. "But there was not much I could tell him that is not in the history books. He wrote poetry."

"Golophin?"

"Shahr Ibim Baraz sire. 'The Terrible Old Man' he was called by his men."

"Yes. Sometimes we called him that too, and other things besides," Corfe said wryly. "Whatever happened to him?"

"No one knows. He left camp and some say he set out for the steppes of his youth, at the very height of his victories."

"As well for Torunna he did. Baraz, Princess Mirren speaks very highly of you. She seems to think that you are a very gallant young officer and has asked that you accompany her on her daily rides from now on. What would you say to such a proposal?"

Baraz's face was a picture of pleasure and chagrin.

"I am honoured by the lady's confidence, sir, and I would esteem it a great privilege to be her morning escort."

"But."

"But I had hoped to be attached to the field army. I have not yet commanded anything more than a ceremonial guard, and I was hoping to be assigned to a tercio."

"You think your time spent with the General Staff is wasted then?"

Baraz's dark face flushed darker. "Not at all sir, but if an officer has never commanded men in the field, what kind of officer is he?"

Corfe nodded approvingly. "Quite right. I'll make a bargain with you, Baraz, one that you had best not give me cause to regret."

"Sir?"

"You will remain Princess Mirren's escort for the time being, and will remain attached to the staff as interpreter. In fact I will have need of you in that capacity this very evening. But when the time comes I promise that you will have a combat command. Satisfied?"

Baraz smiled uncertainly. "I am at your command, of course, sir—I merely follow orders. But thank you, sir."

"Good. Dismissed."

Baraz saluted and left. There was a jauntiness to his stride that made Corfe pause. Before Aekir, there had been something of the young officer's eagerness in himself. That urge to make a name for himself, the desire to do the right thing. But in Aekir his soul had been re-tempered in a white-hot crucible, and had made of him someone else.

T HE face was like that of a bloodless doll, lost in the wasteland of blinding linen that surrounded it. So slight was the wizened form under the coverlet that it might not have been there at all, a mere trick of the lamplight perhaps, a shadow conjured up by the warm flames leaping in the hearth. But then the eyes opened, and life glistened out of them. Bloodshot with pain and exhaustion, they yet retained some of their old fire, and Golophin could well picture the beauty that had once filled the wasted face.

"You are the Hebrian mage, Golophin." The voice was slight but clear.

"Yes, lady."

"Karina, Prio, leave us." This to the two ladies-in-waiting who sat silent as mice in the shadows. They curtseyed, their skirts scraping on the stone floor, and snicked shut the door behind them.

"Come closer, Golophin. I have heard a lot about you."

The wizard approached the bed and as the firelight fell on his ravaged face the Queen's eyes widened slightly.

"Hebrion's fall left its mark on you, I see."

"It is a light enough burden, compared to some."

"My husband asked you to come here?"

"Yes, lady."

"That was thoughtful of him, but useless, as we both know. I would have sent for you in any case. There are so few folk of intelligence I can converse with these days. They all troop in here and look dutifully mournful—even Corfe—and I can get little sense out of them. I am near the end and that is that." She hesitated, and said in a more ragged tone, "My familiar is dead. He went before me. I had not imagined there could be such pain, such a loss."

"They are part of us," Golophin agreed, "and with their passing goes something of our own souls."

"You wizards, you can create them I am told, whereas we Dweomer-poor witches must wait for another to come along. Myself, I shall have no need of another. But I do miss poor Arach." Then she seemed to collect herself. "Where are my manners? You may sit and have some wine, if you do not mind drinking from a glass a queen has used before you. I would call a maid, but then there would be an interminable fuss, and I grow impatient with advancing years."

"As do we all." Golophin smiled, filling the glass. "The old have less time to waste than the young."

She stared at him in silence for a minute and seemed to be testing words in her mouth. Her eyes were bright as fevered jewels.

"What of you now, Master-Mage? Where do you call home?"

"I have none, lady. I am a vagabond."

"Will Hebrion see you again?"

"I hope so."

"You would be very welcome here as an advisor at court."

"A Hebrionese wizard? I think you may exaggerate."

"We have all manner of foreigners in Torunna these days. Formio is Fimbrian, Comillan a Felimbric tribesman, Admiral Berza a Gabrionese. Our Pontiff, Albrec, is an Almarkan. The flotsam and jetsam of the world end up in Torunna. You know why?"

"Tell me."

"The King. They are moths to his candle. Even those haughty Fimbrians come trickling over the mountains to join him, year by year. And in his heart he hates it. He would rather be the simple nobody he was before Aekir's fall. I have watched him these seventeen years and seen the joy leech out of him day by day. Only Mirren lifts his heart. Mirren, and the prospect of leading an army into battle."

Golophin stared at Odelia wonderingly. "Lady, your candour is disarming."

"Candour be damned. I will be dead within the week. I want you to do something for me."

"Anything."

"Stay here with him. Help him. When I go there will be only Formio left for him to confide in. You have spent your life in the service of kings. End it in the service of this one. He is a soldier of genius, Golophin, but he needs someone to guide him through the silken quagmire that is the court. He, also, is less patient than he was, and will brook no opposition to what he sees as right. I would not have such a man end his days a tyrant, hated by all."

"Surely that is not possible."

"There is a black hole in his soul, and once he sets his mind to something he will shift earth and heaven to accomplish it, recking nothing of the consequences. In the years he has been King I have tried to make him see the value of compromise, but it is like trying to reason with a stone. He must have someone of experience in the darker wiles of the world beside him, to help him see that a sword is not the answer to everything."

"You flatter me, lady. But the confidence of a king is not an easily won thing."

"He admires competence and plain speaking. From what I have heard you possess both. But there is another thing. When I am gone there will not be a single practitioner of the

Dweomer at court, save only my daughter. She also needs guidance. There is a wellspring of power in her that quite eclipses anything in my experience. I would not have her explore the Dweomer alone." Odelia looked away. Her withered hands picked restlessly at the heavy weave of the coverlet. "I would she had been born without it. It would make her life easier.

"Your people and mine have chosen a different side in this war, Golophin. The wrong side. They had little choice in the matter, it is true, but they will suffer for it. They may even be destroyed by it."

Something astonishing dawned on Golophin.

"You are against this war."

Odelia managed a tight smile. "Not against it, but I have my doubts about fighting it to the bitter end. The Dweomer runs in my blood as it does in yours, and in my daughter's. I believe this Aruan to be evil, but many of the aims he espouses are not. We will not be fighting Merduks in the time to come, but fellow Ramusians—not that there is much to tell between us all now, I suppose. And I do not want a pogrom of the Dweomer-folk to stain Corfe's victory, if he should gain one. There must come an end to this senseless persecution of those who practise magic."

Golophin felt a wave of relief. He was not a traitor then. His doubts were not his alone. And Bardolin might not be the evil puppet he had feared, but a man trying to do the right thing in difficult circumstances. The thing he had so wanted to be true might well be so.

"Lady," he said, "you have my word that when the time comes I will be by your husband's side. If needs be I will make myself his conscience."

Odelia closed her eyes. "I ask no more. Thank you, Brother Mage. You have eased an old woman's mind."

Golophin bowed, and as he did he found himself thinking that here in Torunna he had found a king and queen who were somehow larger than the monarchs he had known hitherto. Abeleyn, who had become a good ruler before the end, even a great one, seemed now but a boy beside Corfe of

Torunna, the soldier-king. And this frail woman breathing her last before him: she was a worthy consort. There was a greatness here in this country that would remain the stuff of legend, no matter how many centuries passed it by.

He laid a hand on the Queen's forehead and her eyes fluttered open, the lashes feathering against his palm.

"Hush now."

The Dweomer in Odelia had sunk down to a smoking ember. It would never kindle into light again, but it was all that was keeping her alive. That, and this woman's indomitable will. She might have been a mage—the promise was there—but she had never undergone the training necessary to make her powers bloom. Anger stirred in Golophin. How many others, humble and great across this blinkered world, had wasted their gifts similarly? Bardolin was right. The world could have been different, could still be different. There might still be time.

He gave Odelia sleep, a heavy healing sleep, and with his own powers he stoked up that last ember glowing within her, coaxed it into a last flicker of life. Then he sat back, poured himself some more of the fragrant wine, and mused upon the crooked course of this darkening earth.

ELEVEN

AURUNGZEB stirred lazily with a kiss of silk hissing about his hams. "I like that woman. I have always liked her. As direct as a man, but with a mind as subtle as an assassin's."

He rolled over in the bed and the sturdy hardwood frame creaked under him. The white-limbed girl who shared it with him scurried nimbly out of the way as his vast bulk settled and he sighed comfortably.

Ancient Akran, the vizier, leant on a staff that had once been ceremonial but now was genuinely necessary. He stood on the other side of a curtain of gauzy silk which hung like fog around the Sultan's monumental four-poster.

"She is . . . remarkable, my Sultan, it must be said. Making arrangements for her husband's wedding while she, his wife, is yet living. That argues a formidable degree of will."

"He will accept, of course. But I find myself worrying all the same. Perhaps we sent out the embassy too soon. I am not convinced that he will see past the unseemly haste of the thing. Corfe is as cold and murderous as a winter wolf, but there is a stiff propriety about him. These Ramusians—well, they are not Ramusian any longer, I suppose, but our brothers-in-faith after all—they see marriage in a different light to the rest of us. The Prophet, may God be good to him, never said that a man should have one spouse only, and for a monarch, well . . . How can a man maintain his dignity with just the one wife? How can he be wholly sure of a son to follow him? Torunna's Queen may be a marvellous woman in many respects, but that did not stop her womb from proving as barren as a salted field. Or near as damn it. One child in sixteen years, and a girl at that. And the bearing of it rendered her a virtual invalid by all accounts. If he has any red blood in his veins at all, Corfe ought to jump at this chance. A beautiful young woman to share his bed and bear him sons? And she *is* beautiful, Akran. As fair as her mother once was.

"No, unseemly haste or not, Torunna's Queen and myself are of the one mind on this matter. And the fruit of this new union will be my grandchild. Think of that, Akran! My grandson on the throne of Torunna!"

Akran bowed, straightening with the aid of his staff and stifling a groan. "And what of this other union, sire? The Prince Nasir is impatient to know more of his intended bride."

Aurungzeb's grin faded into the bristling darkness of his beard. He levered himself into a sitting position, helped by the nude girl beside him, and while she leant against his back to keep him upright, he stroked his bearded chin with one plump, hairy hand, the rings upon it sparkling like a brilliant, tiny constellation.

"Ah, yes. The girl. A good match, a balancing of the scales." He lowered his voice and peered into the grey mist of the surrounding gauze. "They say she is a witch, you know. Like her mother."

"It may be court gossip sire, no more."

"It matters not; that shall be Nasir's problem, not mine." He boomed with sudden laughter, shaking the slim, straining shoulders of the girl who was supporting him.

"The Prince has expressed a wish to see this girl before he marries her. He is in fact relaying through me a request to go to Torunn to meet this Princess Mirren face to face." Akran licked his thin lips nervously.

Aurungzeb frowned. "He will hold his tongue and do as he is told. What does it matter to him how this girl looks? He will plough her furrow and plant in her a son, and then for recreation he shall have a garden of concubines. The young! They hatch such absurd ideas."

"He also would like to visit Torunn in order to—"

"What? Spit it forth."

"He wants to see something of his mother's homeland."

Aurungzeb's eyebrows shot up his face like two caterpillars on strings. "Does something ail the boy?"

Akran coughed delicately. "I believe the Queen has been telling him stories about the history of her people. I beg your pardon, my Sultan. I mean the people she once belonged to."

"I know what you mean," Aurungzeb growled. "And I was aware of it. She has been filling his head with tall tales of John Mogen and Kaile Ormann. She would do better to prate to him of Indun Meruk or Shahr Baraz."

With a titanic heave, the Sultan hauled himself off the bed. He struggled through the flimsy veil that surrounded it, and sashed close his silk dressing gown. Barefoot, he padded over to a small gilt table that glittered in the light of the overhead lamps. His soles slapped loudly on the marble floor, for he was an immense man with a pendulous paunch. He gently lifted the brindled length of his beard out of the bosom of his robe and poured himself a goblet of sharp-smelling amber liquid from a silver jug.

He sipped at it, his face changing. There was no trace of joviality left in it now. His eyes were two black stones.

"What do we know of the current situation at Gaderion?" he snapped.

"There has been fighting in the open country between the two defensive lines, sire, and the Torunnans may have had the worst of it. In any case, our spies tell us that conscription has begun in earnest, and martial law declared."

Aurungzeb grunted. "He will be wanting troops, under the terms of the treaty. I suppose I shall have to give him some. We are allies, after all, and with these marriages . . ." He broke off, chin sunk in his chest.

"There are times, Akran, when I wonder if it is all but a dream. Everything that has happened since Armagedir. Here are we, two countries whose faith is the same in all but name, who are about to be joined by the closest of dynastic ties—so close that, if they take, then these two Royal lines will become virtually one. And yet twenty years ago we were each striving for the annihilation of the other in the most savage war that history has yet seen. Old habits have not died hard; they have withered away like morning mist as the sun climbs. I try to tell myself that all this is for the best, for all our peoples, but still something within me is astonished by it, and is still waiting for the war to begin again. And then this Second Empire, arising out of thin air and empty theology to dominate the world—" He shook his head like a baffled old bear. "Strange times indeed."

He mused some more.

"I tell you what: Nasir shall indeed go to Torunn. He shall lead the contingent of reinforcements that the treaty obliges us to render, and he shall see the face of his bride-to-be. But he shall also make a first-hand report on the state of the Torunnan military, and the current situation up at the gap. His wide-eyed enthusiasm may well get us farther than the shadowed creeping of our spies."

"He is young, sire . . ."

"Bah, at his age I had already fought in half a dozen battles. The younger generation has no idea—" Here Aurungzeb halted, interrupted by the boom of the chamber doors as they were rolled back by a pair of bald-pated eunuchs.

Through the ornate doorway strode a tall woman in cobalt blue silk. A veil covered her face, but above it two grey eyes flashed from under stibium-darkened brows. Her sandal-clad feet clapped on the marble. Behind her a gaggle of veiled women huddled nervously, and dropped to their knees as the

Sultan's baleful glare swept over them. In the four-poster, the slim girl pulled the sheets over her head.

"My Queen—" Aurungzeb began with a voice like thunder, but the woman cut him short.

"What is this I hear about a marriage between Aria and the Torunnan King? Is it true?"

The vizier backed away discreetly and signalled for the eunuchs to close the doors again. They did so, the sonorous boom passing unnoticed as Aurungzeb and his Queen stood glaring at one another.

"Your presence in the harem is both awkward and insulting," Aurungzeb bellowed. "A Merduk queen—"

"It is true?"

Something went out of Aurungzeb, some kind of self-righteous outrage. He turned away and studied his forgotten wine goblet as if reluctant to meet the fire of her eyes. "Yes, it is true. There have been negotiations, and both parties are in favour of the match. I take it you have some objection."

To his surprise she did not speak. He turned back to her enquiringly and found that she was standing rigid as wood, her hands clasped together, and the beautiful eyes alight above the veil with tears that would not fall.

"Ahara?" he asked, startled.

She lowered her head. "Who thought up this match? The man's wife is not yet dead."

"Actually it was she who suggested it, through our regular diplomatic couriers. She is dying, it seems, and wishes her husband's line to be secured. Torunna needs a male heir. And what better way to cement the bond between our two countries? Nasir shall marry Corfe's daughter at the same time. It will be quite touching I am sure." Here Aurungzeb stopped. "Ahara, what is wrong?"

The tears had slipped down inside the veil. "Please do not do this. Do not make Aria do this thing." Her voice was low and there was a throb in it.

"Why ever not?" Aurungzeb was a picture of exasperation and perplexity.

"She is . . . she is so young."

Aurungzeb smiled indulgently and took Ahara in his arms. "It is hard for a mother, I know. But these things are necessary in affairs of state. You will become used to the idea in time, as will she. This Corfe is not a bad fellow. A little austere, perhaps, but he will be good to her. He had better be; she is my daughter, after all. With this our two houses will be joined for all time. Our peoples will become even closer." Aurungzeb tried to hug her more tightly. It was like embracing a pillar of stone. Over her shoulder, he nodded meaningfully at Akran. The vizier rapped on the chamber doors. "The Queen is leaving. Make way."

Aurungzeb released her. He tilted up her chin and kissed her through the veil. Her eyes were empty, expressionless, their tears dried.

"That is more like it. That is the bearing of a Merduk queen. Now I feel you may need a rest, my sweetness. Akran, see the Queen back to her apartments. And Akran, see that Serrim gives her something to calm her nerves." Another meaningful look.

Ahara, or Heria as she had once been, left without another word. Aurungzeb stood with his hands on his broad hips, frowning. She was Nasir's mother, hence the dam of a future sultan. And he had made her his queen—almost seventeen years now she had been his wife. But there was some part of her she kept always hidden, even now. Women! So many times more difficult to deal with than men. He thought she confided in old Shahr Baraz, but that was all. And he—you would think he was her father the way he watched over her.

A purr from the bed. "My Sultan? It grows cold here. I need to be warmed."

He rubbed his chin. Since Nasir was going to get a look at his new wife, why not do Corfe the same courtesy? Yes, Aria would also go, with a suitable chaperone from the harem. Her beauty would melt that stiff-necked propriety of his, and he would see sense. Excellent. Now where might this glorious double wedding be held? Aurungabar for choice—Pir Sar would be such a magnificent setting. No, Corfe would insist on it being in Torunn. He was King of

Torunna after all. But it must be soon. This war was erupting around their ears, and once it had blossomed into full flower Corfe would no doubt take the field, perhaps not to return to the capital for months. Yes, let it happen in Torunn, and straight away. In fact, let Aria take the road at once.

Then Aurungzeb remembered that Odelia had not yet breathed her last. He said a quick, furtive prayer of apology to the Prophet for being so presumptuous. He liked and respected Torunna's present Queen; their letter correspondence had been a stimulating challenge. But he needed her dead, soon.

THE Queen of Ostrabar sat in her chambers like a porcelain vase set aside in a velvet-padded box. She sat straight-backed on a divan and stared through the fretwork of an ornately carved shutter at the teeming sprawl of the city below. This place had been her home throughout her life, though in different guises. Once it had been Aekir, and she had been Heria. Now it was Aurungabar, and she was Ahara. She was a queen, and the man who had been her husband was a king. But of different kingdoms.

When she thought about it like that she had to marvel at the joke fate had played upon Corfe and herself. It had been a long time. She was past youth now, sliding into middle age with grown-up children by a man for whom she felt nothing but distaste.

And her daughter was destined, it seemed, to marry the man who had once been her husband.

How could Corfe do this to her, or to himself? Had he changed that much? Perhaps the passing years had healed or hardened him. Perhaps he was entirely a king now, with a politician's pragmatism. A matter of state, was that it?

"You sent for me, Mother?" It was Aria by the door, in the Queen's Wing and thus unveiled, a willowy version of herself as a young woman. Perhaps that was it. The resemblance to the ghost of a woman he once had loved.

"Mother?"

"Come sit with me, Aria."

The girl joined her. Heria smoothed back the raven hair from her cheek with a smile. There was a dreamy sense of unreality that fogged her mind, but it was not unpleasant. Serrim, the ageing eunuch, had a small chest full of every potion and herb and drug that the east produced, and he had made her eat a tiny cube of pure *kobhang* an hour before. He and that wizened crow Akran had watched her swallow it down with ill-concealed relief. It was not that they were afraid of her, but they were the butts of Aurungzeb's anger when she committed some transgression, such as walking unaccompanied in the market, or receiving a male visitor without a eunuch present. The rules seemed to have become more stifling over the years, partly because she was the mother of the Sultan's heir, and partly because as a noble matron she was supposed to set an example, to lead a veiled life of discretion and inoffensiveness. She was no longer even allowed to ride a horse, but must be borne in a palanquin like some kind of aged libertine.

"Have you heard the rumours too, Aria?"

"About my wedding? Yes, Mother." The girl's eyes fell. "I am to be married to the King of Torunna, and Nasir is to marry his daughter."

"You know then. I am sorry. You should have heard it from me."

"It's all right. I know what is expected of me. I suppose it will be quite soon now. In the kitchens they are talking about a caravan being prepared for Torunn, and Nasir is to lead an army to help King Corfe. Imagine Mother, Nasir leading an army!" She smiled. She was a quiet, grave girl, but the smile lit up her face.

Heria looked away. "He will be fine, as will you."

"Will you be coming with us?"

The question rocked her. "I—I don't know." A maniac notion filled her head, a vision of herself at her daughter's wedding, flinging herself at the groom, begging him to remember her. She blinked her stinging eyes clear. "Perhaps."

Aria took her hand. "What is he like, Mother? Is he very old?"

She cleared her throat. "Corfe? He is—he is not so old."

"Older than you?"

She gripped her daughter's fingers tightly. "A little older. Some years older."

Aria looked thoughtful. "An old man. They say he is lame, and bad-tempered."

"Who says?"

"Everyone. Mother, my hand . . ." Heria released it. "Are you all right, Mother?"

"I'm fine, my dear. Tired. Ask the maids to bring in a blanket. I believe I may well lie here and doze a while."

Aria did not move. "They've been giving you more of their drugs, haven't they?"

"It calms me, Aria. Don't be worried."

Don't be worried, she thought. You are to marry a good man. The best of men. She closed her eyes. Aria eased her back on to the divan and stroked her hair. "It will be all right, Mother. You'll see," she whispered, her lovely face grave again.

Heria slept, and from below her closed eyelids the tears trickled down soundlessly.

THERE was an hour before the dawn, in the black throat of the night, when even a city as large as Torunn slept. Corfe's horse picked its way through the streets unhindered and he rode it with the reins loose on its neck as though the tall gelding knew the way better than he. And perhaps it did, for the bay destrier brought Corfe unbidden to the North Gate, where he saluted the sleepy gate guards and they, grumbling and unaware of his identity, opened the tall postern for him to lead his mount through. Once beyond the city walls he let the gelding have its head, and it burst into a fast canter. The moon was riding high and gibbous in a star-brilliant sky, but it was just possible to make out the glimmerings of the dawn speeding its way up over the distant ramparts of the Jafrar in the east. Corfe left the pale ribbon of the Kingsway and headed north, his steed dipping and rising under him with the undulating ground. But he kept his knees clamped to the gelding's sides and a loose bite on the reins, and almost it seemed that he might be afloat in a grey moonlit sea upon some bobbing ship, save for the eager grunts of the horse and the creak of the saddle under him.

He reined in at last, and the steam of his mount's sweat rose around him, clean and acrid at the same time. Dismounting, he hobbled the gelding with the ease of long practice, and after he had slipped off bridle and saddle, he rubbed it down with a wisp of coarse upland grass. The gelding clumped away, happy to nose at the yellow grass and sniff for better fare. And Corfe sat on the swell of the hill, grey in the moonlight, and stared not east at the gathering dawn, but west to where the Cimbrics loomed up dark and forbidding in the dregs of the night.

Tribesmen's tales told of a hidden pass in those mountain fastnesses, a narrow way where determined men had once forged a passage of the terrible mountains. The journey was semi-legendary—the reputation of the Cimbrics as the harshest peaks in the world had been well-earned—but it had happened. And Corfe had a map of the route.

Almost four centuries before, when the Fimbrians had been lords of the world, they had sent out exploratory expeditions to all corners of the continent. One of those expeditions had had as its mission the discovery of a pass through the Cimbrics. They had succeeded, but the cost had been horrendous. Albrec, High Pontiff of Torunna and all the Macrobian Kingdoms, had discovered the text of the expedition's log in the Inceptine archives of Torunn cathedral. He seemed to consider the discovery of unique and ancient documents to be part of his calling. Or perhaps it was a hobby of his. Corfe smiled at the moonlit night. Even now that Albrec was a middle-aged man at the head of a large and influential organisation, there was something of the enthusiastic boy about him when it came to a dusty manuscript or mildewed grimoire. This ancient record, an untidy bundle of dog-eared and mouldering papers, he had shown to Corfe on a whim, never guessing how important it might prove.

For Corfe intended to use the log to take an army across the Cimbrics and win the war at a stroke.

It was a huge gamble, of course; the log might be a fiction, or at the least hopelessly out of date. But the alternative to such a bold stroke would be either a full frontal assault on the Thurian Line, or a fall back to the purely defensive business of holding Gaderion and hoping for the best. To try and break through the Thurian Line would be foolhardy to the point of lunacy. It was too heavily fortified, and the defenders would outnumber the attackers many times over. As for the magnificent works at Gaderion, formidable though they were, Corfe placed little faith in the merits of a static defence, and had done since Aekir, all those years ago. He had seen supposedly impregnable cities and fortresses fall too often to be sanguine about the chances of containing the Himerians up at the gap.

There was snow still clinging to the flanks of the Cimbrics. It glowed in the bright moonlight, and the mountains seemed to be disembodied, luminous shapes that hung suspended over the shadowed expanse of the darkened land at their feet. Deep in the midst of the range, the snow remained inviolate all year round, and even among the lesser peaks the drifts would still be deep and cold. Spring took its time in the high places.

The Fimbrian expedition, three hundred strong, had started out in the Year of the Saint 117, with the melting of the first snows, and once they had fought their way into the centre of the range they had travelled along the backs of huge glaciers as though they were a network of roads amid the tall peaks which spawned them. Crevasses and avalanches had killed them by the score, but in the end they had won through thirty leagues of the most forbidding terrain in the world, and had come finally to the shores of the Sea of Tor, and the trading post of Fort Cariabon as it then was. Even with the renowned stamina and endurance of the Fimbrians, they had been two weeks on the mountainous section of the journey, and half of them had been left frozen corpses upon the flanks of those mountains.

Corfe had been mulling over the log for months, and had
interviewed a succession of Cimbric tribesmen to test its ve-
racity. Nothing they had told him about the region contra-
dicted the account, and he was convinced that the route was
still feasible, if difficult. He could see no other way of winning this war.

His horse, bored with the winter-dry grass, nosed his neck
and its warm breath blew down his nape. He rubbed the
velvet-soft nostrils absently, and turned his head to peer eastwards.

The rising sun had still to clear the Jafrar, but its promise
was clear in the lightening sky. A skein of cloud had caught
in the summits of the eastern mountains and looked as
though it had been set afire from below. Behind it the sky
was palest aquamarine, a pink glow riding up it moment by
moment.

He turned his gaze north-east, to where the Thurians stood,
the first flush of the dawn beginning to pale their eastern
sides. The world he knew was defined by the brutal majesty
of mountains. The Cimbrics, the Thurians, the Jafrar. They
gave birth to the rivers which watered the world. The Ostian,
the Searil, the Torrin. Somewhere out there in the low country leading down to the Kardian Sea there stood Aurungabar,
capital of Ostrabar. He had been there as King and had seen
the huge labour of rebuilding which the Merduks had un-
dertaken. Mynius Kuln's vast Square of Victories still remained, opening out from the foot of what had been the
cathedral of Carcasson; but it was called *Hor el Kadhar* now,
Glory of God. The old Pontifical Palace was now the pleasure garden of the Sultan wherein his harem had been installed. And somewhere among those buildings there slept
right at this moment the woman who had been Corfe's wife.

Why he should find himself thinking about her at this moment he did not know, except that it was usually on waking
and on going to sleep that he saw her most clearly. Those
ill-defined periods of the day between darkness and light. Or
perhaps she was lying awake herself in the pre-dawn murk,
and thinking of him. The thought made his heart beat faster.

But the woman he pictured in his mind was young, not much more than a girl. She would be almost out of her thirties now, a mature woman. And he, he was a greying martinet with a halt leg. They were strangers, complete and utter. And yet the pain remained.

Was she thinking of him at this moment? There was the oddest pain in his breast, a wrench as though something there had suddenly constricted. He pushed the balls of his palms into his eyes until the lights flared, and the pain faded. He was too old to be entertaining such fancies.

He knew he would marry this girl who was his wife's daughter. It was necessary for the good of the kingdom, and he had sacrificed so much to that end that he could not imagine doing otherwise.

BUT there was a deeper, darker reason for doing so that he would not even contemplate admitting to himself. In marrying Aria, he would possess something of Heria again, and perhaps that would help calm his snarling soul. Perhaps.

TWELVE

IN squares and at street corners the people gathered in sub-dued crowds while those who could read relayed the content of the daily bulletins to their fellow citizens.

> *This day were executed Hilario, Duke of Imerdon, Lord Queris of Hebriera, and Lady Marian of Fulk, they having been found guilty of conspiring against the Presbyter of Hebrion, Lord Orkh. May Almighty God have mercy on their souls.*
>
> *A reward of five hundred silver crowns is offered for information leading to the arrest and apprehension of the following . . .*

And here a long list of names followed, which those reading the bulletin intoned in stentorian voices, watching always to see if any of the Knights Militant, or worse an Inceptine, were near.

No one knew how or where the executions took place, and the names of the dead all belonged to the nobility of Hebrion.

Thus while the common folk might feel anger, even outrage, at this unseen slaughter of their betters, they were largely unaffected by it. And besides, there was a new nobilty to get used to.

Thus the life of Abrusio, which had shuddered to a trembling halt for days after the first landings, slowly began to return to something approaching normality. Market stalls were cautiously opening again, and taverns began to fill up in the evenings as folk became less afraid to walk the streets at night. There was no curfew, no martial law, just the daily bulletins, their wording unchanged but for the names they listed. Even the soldiers of the garrison had been merely told to stack arms and return to barracks. There was talk of a treaty having been signed, a peaceful annexation, and certainly the new rulers of Hebrion were busy men. They had taken up residence not in the palace but in the old Inceptine abbey, as befitted a group of churchmen, and from the abbey the couriers rode in unending streams, while in the harbour every Royal vessel remaining had received a boarding party of Himerians and was frantically readying to put to sea.

It was not so bad, on the whole, and people looked back to the hysteria which had followed the rumours of the fleet's destruction with a kind of abashed wonder. They forget, or chose not to remember, the storm which had smote the city, the thunderheads which had hidden the sun and darkened the face of the waters at noon, and the sea lightnings which had capered madly, striking people in the streets, setting light to houses. Only the deluge which had followed had stopped the city from burning a second time. The black clouds had burst overhead and people had scurried for cover as the rain came down in rods, flattening the waves which the west wind had reared up, turning the steep streets in the Upper City into tawny rivers.

There were those who said that in the heart of the lightnings and the hammering rain the sky had not been empty. Things had been circling below the lowering clouds. Monstrous things which were not birds. But people chose not to dwell on that now, and those who insisted were ignored and even ridiculed.

As the storm had lifted, and the daylight returned, the horizon had become dark with ships. There were a few fools who wiped the rain out of their eyes and cheered the return of King Abeleyn, but they were soon hushed. Out of the west, the enemy had come to claim his prize.

The soldiers of the garrison, many little more than frightened boys, ran out the great guns of the mole forts and barricaded the wharves of the waterfront. A few public-spirited citizens helped them, but most locked themselves indoors, as if they could somehow will the invaders away, while many others choked the city gates with wagons and carts and laden mules, and set off for the dubious sanctuary of the Hebros Mountains. Perhaps a hundred thousand of Abrusio's population departed in this manner, churning up the North Road in a frenzied exodus. In their midst rode many noblemen with fortunes stuffed into bulging saddlebags, and a canny teamster might line his pockets handsomely if he were willing to sell his cart to some desperate aristocratic family.

The enemy fleet had backed their topsails within a half league of the moles and there they had ridden out the breeze, which had backed round to south-south-east. Only a few Himerian vessels had put in towards the Inner Roads, flying flags of truce. Archaic, cog-like ships, they had sailed smoothly past the staring gun crews of the moles and moored at the foot of Admiral's Tower and disgorged not the beasts of nightmare that the populace had feared, but a dignified group of black-clad clerics under a flapping white flag. The gunners of the mole forts had held their fire in fear as much as anything else, for the fleet which had hove-to beyond Abrusio's massive breakwaters was larger than anything they had ever seen. And what was more, on the decks of those innumerable ships there were massed tens of thousands of armoured figures. They might take a heavy toll of such a host, should the Himerians try to force the passage of the moles, but they would be overwhelmed in the end. Their senior officers, all well-bred second-raters, had fled the city days earlier and so the common soldiery of Abrusio, in the absence of definite orders, waited to see what might happen. They trusted to the white flags of the invaders and the rumours of the mysterious treaty which had been doing the rounds of the city ever since the flight of the Queen.

A few of the more prosperous citizens who possessed some backbone met the Himerian delegation on the waterfront and were told with firm affability that they were now subjects of the Second Empire, members of the Church of Himerius and, as such, guaranteed protection from any form of rapine or pillage. This cheered them considerably, and they went down on their knees to kiss the ring of the dark-skinned leader of the invaders whose eyes were an unsettling shade of amber. He introduced himself as Orkh, now Presbyter of Hebrion, and his accent was strange, with something of the east about it. When he stumbled in his understanding of the Abrusians' babbling, a hooded figure at his side clarified their words in a low voice and an accent that was unmistakably Hebrian.

Since then a few more ships had put in, but to the astonishment of the citizenry the vast Himerian fleet had disappeared. Old sailors mending nets down on the waterfront sniffed the wind, now veering to the west again, and looked at each other mystified. Square-rigged vessels such as the Himerian cogs ought to have been embayed in the Gulf of Hebrion by such a breeze, or even run aground. But they had sailed away in the space of a night, seemingly against the wind, and against all that was natural to seafaring experience.

Those ships which had put ashore had disembarked perhaps a thousand troops, and these were all the occupation force that it would seem the Second Empire deemed necessary to hold Abrusio, though rumours had come to the city of more armies on the march in the north and the east. There had been a battle on the borders with Fulk, and the Hebrian forces there were in panicked retreat, it was said. Pontifidad, capital of the Duchy of Imerdon, had capitulated to the invaders after defeat in a battle before her very walls. The Duke of Imerdon had fled for his life with Knights Militant in hot pursuit. And there were even hazier rumours, which no one could verify or account for, that the Himerians had landed in Astarac, and were preparing to besiege Cartigella.

The occupiers of Abrusio were a strange and disparate body. Many wore the robes of Inceptines, but over those robes they had donned black half-armour and they went gauntleted and armed with steel maces. They rode shining ebony horses which were tall and gangling as the camels of the east, and gaunt as greyhounds. Very many of these fearsome clerics were black men, who looked as though they might hail from Punt or Ridawan, but they spoke together in a language that even the most well-travelled mariner had never heard before, and many of them rode with an homunculous perched on their shoulders, or flapping about their shaven heads.

There were Knights Militant who rode the same weird breed of horses as their Inceptine brothers, but who kept their faces hidden, their eyes glinting behind the T-shaped slot in their closed helms. But the most mysterious of the invaders were those whom the foreign clerics referred to simply as the "Hounds." These were a type of men who went about in straggling troops, always accompanied by a mounted Inceptine, and they looked as though they came from every nation under heaven. They went barefoot, dressed always in rags, and there was something vulpine and horribly eager about their eyes. They spoke seldom, and had little dealings with the populace, the Inceptines leading them like a shepherd his sheep—or an overseer his slaves—but unarmoured and ill-kempt though they might be, they frightened the folk of Abrusio more than any of the other Himerians.

"THEY have eschewed the coastal route, the shorter voyage, and have struck out for the open sea," Lord Orkh, Presbyter of Hebrion, said in his sibilant, heavily accented Normannic.

"And they are already out of the range of our airborne contingents I take it, or else this conversation would be entirely different."

Orkh licked his lipless mouth. In the darkened room his fulvous eyes glowed with a light of their own and his skin had a reptilian sheen about it.

"Yes, lord. We expected them to make for the Hebrian Gulf, and the direct route to the Astaran coast, but they—"

"They outsmarted you."

"Indeed. This man who captains the *Seahare* is a mariner of some repute and is known to you, I believe. Richard Hawkwood, a native of Gabrion."

The simulacrum to which Orkh was speaking went silent. It was a shimmering, luminous likeness of Aruan, and now it frowned. Orkh bent his head before its pitiless gaze.

"*Hawkwood.*" Aruan spat the word. Then, abruptly, he laughed. "Fear not, Orkh. I am a victim of my own whim it would seem. Hawkwood! He has more bottom than I gave him credit for." His voice lowered into something resembling the purr of a giant feline. "You have, of course, set in place an alternative plan for the interception of the Hebrian Queen."

"Yes, lord. As we speak, a swift vessel is putting out from the Royal yards."

"Who commands?"

"My lieutenant."

"The renegade? Ah yes, of course. A good choice. His mind is so consumed by irrational hatred that he will fulfil his mission to the letter. How many days start does Hawkwood have?"

"A week."

"A week! There are weather-workers among the pursuers, I take it."

Orkh hesitated a moment and then nodded firmly.

"Good. Then we shall consider that loose end taken care of. What of the Hebrian treasury?"

Here Orkh relaxed a little. "We captured it almost entirely intact, my lord."

"Excellent. And the nobility?"

"Hilario, Duke of Imerdon we executed today. That more or less wipes out the top tier of the aristocracy."

"Aside from your turncoat lieutenant, of course."

"He is entirely ours, my lord, I can vouch for it personally. And his status will be useful once things have settled down somewhat."

"Yes, I suppose it will. He is a tool apt for many uses. I do not regret sparing him as I do Hawkwood. But had I allowed Hawkwood, as well as Abeleyn, to die at that time I could well have lost Golophin." Aruan's shade settled its chin on its chest pensively. "I would I had more like you, Orkh. Men I can truly trust."

Orkh bowed.

"But Golophin will see sense yet, I guarantee it. Good! Get that money in the pockets of those who will appreciate it. Buy every venal soul you can and handle Hebrion with a velvet glove. It is silver filigree to Torunna's iron. Corfe's kingdom we must crush, but Hebrion, ah, she must be wooed . . . How soon before we can expect the fleet off Cartigella?"

"My captains tell me that with the aid of their weather-workers they will drop anchor before the city in eight days."

"That will do. I believe that will do. Cartigella will be invested by land and sea, and will be made to see sense as Hebrion has."

"You don't think that the Hebrion Queen is making for her homeland?"

"If she is, the fleet will snap her up, but I doubt it. No, I sense Golophin's hand at work here. He must have healed Hawkwood and spirited the Queen away. He is in Torunn now, and that is where I believe she is going. They are touch-ingly fond of one another, I am told. All these splendid people we must kill! It is a shame. But then if they were not so worthy, they would not be worth killing." He smiled, though his face remained without humour.

"Make sure our noble renegade catches this Isolla, Orkh. With her gone, Hebrion will acquiesce to our rule that much more easily. And I will give the kingdom to this man when he kills her. It will doubtless lend even more of an edge to his eagerness when I inform him of his reward. You, I will

install in Astarac, for it will prove more troublesome than
Hebrion I believe, and you will have to keep an eye on Gabrion. Does that satisfy you?"

For an instant what might have been a thin black tongue
flickered between Orkh's lips. "You honour me, lord."

"But now the war in the east gathers pace. The assault on
Gaderion will begin soon, and the Perigrainian army is preparing to move on Rone from its bases in Candelaria. We
will enter Torunna through the back door while knocking at
the front. Let their much-vaunted soldier-king try being in
two places at once." Again, the perilous, triumphant smile.
The simulacrum began to fade.

"Do not fail me, Orkh," it said casually, and then winked
out.

THE *Hibrusian* was a sleek barquentine which displaced
some six hundred tonnes and had a crew of fifty. Square-
rigged on the foremast, she carried fore-and-aft sails on main
and mizzen, and was designed to be handled by a small
ship's company. The Hebrian navy had built her to Richard
Hawkwood's experimental designs and her keel had been
laid down barely a year before. She had been conceived as
a formidable kind of Royal yacht to transport the King and
his entourage on visits abroad, and was luxuriously appointed
in every respect. The Himerians had found her laid up in dry
dock and had at once launched her down the slipway on
Orkh's orders. Renamed the *Revenant* by someone with a
black sense of humour, she floated at her moorings now some
way from shore in the Outer Roads. Her crew had been treb-
led by the addition of Himerian troops of all kinds, and she
awaited a signal from Admiral's Tower to cast off and go
hunting.

The signal came. Three guns fired at short intervals, three
bubbles of grey smoke from the battlements preceding the
distant boom of their detonation. The *Revenant* slipped her
moorings, set jibs and fore-and-aft courses on main and mizzen, and began to carve a bright wake through the choppy

sea with the wind square on her starboard beam. On her
quarterdeck, the thing which had once been Lord Murad of
Galiapeno grinned viciously at the southern horizon, an homunculous perched on its shoulder and chuckling into its ear.

THIRTEEN

"KEEP her thus until four bells," Hawkwood told the helmsman. "Then bring her one point to larboard. Arhuz!"

"Skipper?"

"Be prepared to send up the mizzen topsail when we alter course. If the wind backs call me at once. I am going below."

"Aye, sir," Arhuz answered smartly. He checked the xebec's course on the compass board and then swept the decks with his gaze, noting the angle of the yards, the fill of the sails, the condition of the running rigging. Then he watched the sea and sky, noting the direction of the swell, the position of clouds near and far, all those almost indefinable details which a master-mariner took in and filed away without conscious volition. Hawkwood clapped him on the shoulder, knowing the *Seahare* was in good hands, and went below.

He was exhausted. For days he had been on deck continually, snatching occasional dozes in a sling of canvas spliced to the mizzen shrouds, and eating upright on the xebec's narrow quarterdeck with one eye to the wind and another to the sails. He had pushed the crew and the *Seahare* very hard, straining to extract every knot of speed out of the sleek craft and keeping the helmsmen on tenterhooks with minute variations of course to catch errant breezes. The log had been going continually in the forechains and a dozen times a day (and night) the logsman would cast his board into the sea while his mate watched the sands trickling through the thirty-second glass and cry *nip* when the time ran out. And the line would be reeled back in and the knots which had been run out by the ship's passage counted. So far, with a beam wind like this to starboard, the fore-and-aft rig of the xebec was drawing well, and they were averaging seven knots. Seven long sea miles an hour. In the space of six days, running due south, they had put almost a hundred and ninety leagues between themselves and poor old Abrusio, and by Hawkwood's calculations had long since passed the latitude of northern Gabrion, though that island lay still three hundred miles eastwards. Hawkwood had decided to avoid the narrow waters of the Malacar Straits, and sail instead south of Gabrion itself, entering the Levangore to the west of Azbakir. The straits were too close to Astarac, and too easily patrolled. But a lot depended on the wind. While veering and backing a point or two in the last few days, it had remained steady and true. Once he changed course for the east, as he would very soon, he would have to think about sending up the square-rigged yards, on the fore and mainmasts at least. Lateen yards were less suited to a stern wind than square-rigged ones. The men would be happier too. The massive lateen yards, which gave the *Seahare* the look of some marvellous butterfly, were heavy to handle and awkward to brace round and reef.

He rubbed his eyes. A packet of spray, knocked aboard by the swift passage of the ship's beakhead, drenched the forecastle. The xebec was riding the swell beautifully, shouldering aside the waves with a lovely, graceful motion and almost no roll. Despite this, seasickness had afflicted his supercargo almost from the moment they had left the shelter of Grios Point, and they had remained in their cabins. A fact for which he was inordinately grateful. He had too much to think about to worry about a sparring match between Isolla and Jemilla. And the boy, whose whelp was he? Murad's in the eyes of the world, but Hawkwood had heard court rumours about his parentage. And why else would Golophin have inveigled a passage out of Hebrion for him and his mother if there was not some Royal connection? Here he came now, hauling himself up the companionway and looking as eager as a young hound which has sighted a fox. Alone of the passengers he was unaffected by seasickness, and seemed in fact to revel in their swift southward passage, the valiant efforts of the ship. Hawkwood had had several conversations with him on the quarterdeck. He was pompous for one so young, and full of himself of course, but he knew when to keep his mouth shut, which was a blessing.

"Captain! How goes our progress?" Bleyn asked. The other occupants of the quarterdeck frowned and looked away. They had taken to Richard Hawkwood very quickly once he had proved that he was who he had claimed to be, and they thought that this boy did not address him with sufficient respect.

Hawkwood did not answer him for a second, but studied the traverse board, looked at the sails, and seeing one on the edge of shivering barked to the helmsman, "Mind your luff." Then he looked humourlessly at Bleyn. He had been about to go below and snatch some sleep for the first time in days and he was damned if some chattering popinjay was going to rob him of it. But something in Bleyn's eyes, some element of unabashed exuberance, stopped him. "Come below. I'll show you on the chart."

They went back down the companionway and entered Hawkwood's cabin, which by rights should have been the finest on the ship. But Hawkwood had given that one to Isolla, and retained for himself that of the first mate. He had a pair of scuttles for light instead of windows and both he and Bleyn had to stoop as they entered. There was a broad table running athwartships which was fastened to the deck with brass runners, and pinned open upon it a chart of the

Western Levangore and the Hebrian Gulf. Hawkwood picked up the dividers and consulted his log, ignoring Bleyn. The boy was staring about himself, at the cutlasses on the bulkhead, the battered sea-chest, the quadrant hung in a corner. At last Hawkwood pricked the bottom left corner of the chart. "There we are, more or less."

Bleyn peered at the chart. "But we are out in the middle of nowhere! And headed south. We'll soon drop off the edge of the map."

Hawkwood smiled and rubbed at the bristles of his returning beard. "If you are being pursued, then nowhere is a good place to be. The open ocean is a grand place to hide."

"But you have to turn eastwards soon, surely?"

"We'll change course today or the next, depending on the wind. Thus far it has been steady, but I've never yet known a steady westerly persist this long in the gulf. In spring the land is warming up and pushing the clouds out to sea. Southerlies are more usual in this part of the world, and heading east we should have a beam wind to work with again. Thus I hesitate to lower the lateen yards."

"They're better when the wind is hitting the ship from the side, are they not?"

"The wind is *on the beam*, master Bleyn. If you're to sound like a sailor you must make an effort to learn our language."

"Larboard is left and starboard is right, yes?"

"Bravo. We'll have you laying aloft before we're done."

"How long before we reach Torunn?"

Hawkwood shook his head. "This is not a four-horse coach we are in. We do not run to exact timetables, at sea. But if the winds are kind, then I would hazard that we should meet with the mouth of the Torrin Estuary in between three and four weeks."

"A month! The war could be over in that time."

"From what I hear, I doubt it."

There was a muffled thump on the partition to one side, someone moving about. The partitions were thin wood, and Bleyn and Hawkwood looked at one another. It was Jemilla's cabin, though the word "cabin" was a somewhat ambitious term for her kennel-like berth.

"Do you know much about this King Corfe?" Bleyn asked.

"Only what Golophin has told me, and popular rumour. He is a hard man by all accounts, but just, and a consummate general."

"I wonder if he'll let me serve in his army," Bleyn mused.

Hawkwood looked at him sharply, but before he could say anything there was a knock at his door. It was opened straight after to reveal Jemilla standing there, wrapped in a shawl. Her hair was in tails around her shoulders and she looked pale and drawn, with bruised rings about her eyes.

"Captain, you have come downstairs at last. I have been meaning to have a word with you for days in private. I could almost believe you have been avoiding me. Bleyn, leave us."

"Mother—"

She stared at him, and he closed his mouth at once and left the cabin without another word. Jemilla shut the door carefully behind him.

"My dear Richard," she said quietly. "It has been a long time since you and I were alone in the same room together."

Hawkwood tossed the dividers on the chart before him. "He's a good lad, that son of yours. You should stop treating him like a child."

"He needs a father's hand on his shoulder."

"Murad was not the paternal type, I take it."

Her smile was not pleasant. "You could say that. I've missed you, Richard."

Hawkwood snorted derisively. "It's been eighteen years, Jemilla, near as damn it. You've done a hell of a job of pretending otherwise." He was surprised by the rancour in his voice. He had thought that Jemilla no longer mattered to him. The fact that both she and Isolla were on board confused him mightily, and though the ship had needed careful handling to enable the fastest possible passage since Abrusio, he had been using that as an excuse to stay up on deck, in his own world as it were, leaving the complications below.

"I'm rather busy, and very tired. If you have anything to discuss it will have to wait."

She moved closer. The shawl slipped to reveal one creamy shoulder. He gazed at her, fascinated despite himself. There was a lush ripeness about Jemilla. She was an exotic fruit on the very cusp of turning rotten, and wantonness in her seemed not a vice but the expression of a normal appetite.

She kissed him lightly on the lips. The shawl slipped further. Below it she wore only a thin shift, and her heavy round breasts swelled through it, the dark stain of the nipples visible beneath the fabric. Hawkwood cupped one breast in his callused palm and she closed her eyes. A smile he had forgotten played across her lips. Half triumph, half hunger. He placed his mouth on hers and she gently closed her teeth on his darting tongue.

A knock on the door. He straightened at once and drew back from Jemilla. She wrapped her shawl about her again, her eyes not leaving his.

"Come in."

It was Isolla. She started upon seeing them standing there together, and something in her face fell. "I will come back at a better time."

Jemilla curtseyed to her gracefully. "Do not depart on my account, your majesty. I was just leaving." As she passed the Queen in the doorway, the shawl unaccountably slipped again. "Later, Richard," she called back over her naked shoulder, and was gone.

Hawkwood felt his face burning and could not meet Isolla's eyes. He scourged himself for he knew not what. "Lady, what can I do for you?"

She seemed more disconcerted than he. "I did not know that the lady Jemilla and you were . . . familiar to each other, Captain."

Hawkwood raised his head and met her eyes frankly. "We were lovers many years ago. There is nothing between us now." Even as he said it he wondered if it were true.

Isolla coloured. "It is not my business."

"Best to have it in the open. We'll be living cheek-by-jowl

for the next few weeks. I will not dance minuets around the truth on my own ship." His voice sounded harsher than he had intended. In a softer tone he asked: "You are feeling better?"

"Yes. I—I think perhaps I am gaining my sea legs."

"Better to go up on deck and get some fresh air. It is fetid down here. Just do not look at the sea moving beyond the rail."

"I will be sure not to."

"What was it you wished to speak of, lady?"

"It was nothing important. Good day, Captain. Thank you for your advice." And she was gone. She banged her knee on the jamb of the door as she left.

Hawkwood sat down before the chart and stared blindly at the parchment, the dull shine of the brass dividers. He knuckled his eyes, his exhaustion returning to make water of his muscles. And then he had to sit back and laugh at he knew not what.

THE small change of course he had ordered woke him from a troubled sleep. He climbed out of the swinging cot and pulled on his sodden boots, blinking and yawning. In his dreams he had been terribly thirsty, his tongue swollen in his rasping mouth, and he had been seated before a pitcher of water and one of wine, unable to quench his raging thirst because he could not choose between the two.

He stumped up on deck to find a strained atmosphere and a crowded quarterdeck. Arhuz nodded, checked the traverse board and reported, "Course east-south-east, skipper, wind backing to west-south-west so we have it on the starboard quarter. Do you want to call all hands?"

Hawkwood studied the trim of the sails. They were still drawing well. "What's our speed?"

"Six knots and one fathom, holding steady."

"Then we'll continue thus until the change of the watch, and then get square yards on fore and main. Rouse out the sailmaker, Arhuz, and get it all set in train. Bosun! Open the main hatch and get tackles to the maintop."

The mariners went about their business with a calm competence that pleased Hawkwood greatly. They were not his *Ospreys*, but they knew their craft, and he had nothing more to tell them. He studied the sky over the taffrail. The west was clouding up once more, banners and rags of cloud gathering on the horizon. To the north the air was as clear as ice, the sea empty of every living thing.

"Lookout!" he called. "What's afoot?" On an afternoon like this, with the spring sun warming the deck and the fresh breeze about them, the lookout would be able to survey a great expanse of ocean whose diameter was fifteen leagues wide.

"Not a sail, sir. Nor a bird or scrap of weed neither."

"Very good." Then he noticed that both Isolla and Jemilla were on deck. Isolla was standing by the larboard mizzen shrouds wrapped in a fur cloak with skeins of glorious red-gold hair whipping about her face, and Jemilla was to starboard, staring up into the rigging with a look of anxiety. "Captain," she said with no trace of coquetry, "can you not say something to him, issue some order?"

Hawkwood followed her gaze and saw what seemed to be a trio of master's mates high in the fore topmast shrouds. Frowning, he realised that one of them was Bleyn, and his two companions were beckoning him yet higher.

"Gribbs, Ordio!" he bellowed at once. "On deck, and see master Bleyn down with you!"

The young men halted in their ascent, and then began to retrace their steps with the swiftness of long practice.

"Handsomely, handsomely there, damn you!" and they moderated their pace.

"Thank you, Captain," Jemilla said, honest relief in her face. Then she swallowed and her hand went to her mouth.

"You had best get below, lady." She left the quarterdeck, weaving across the pitching deck as though she were drunk. One of the quartermasters lent her his arm at a nod from Hawkwood and saw her down the companionway. Hawkwood felt a small, unworthy sense of satisfaction as she went. This was his world, where he commanded and she was not much more than baggage. He had seen her a few times at court in recent years, a high-born aristocrat who deemed it charity when she deigned to notice his existence. The tables had been turned, it seemed. She was a refugee dependent on him for the safety of her son and herself. There was satisfaction to be had in her current discomfort, and she was not so alluring with that pasty puking look about her.

She will gain no hold on me, Hawkwood promised himself. Not on this voyage.

The wind was picking up, and the *Seahare* was pitching before it like an excited horse, great showers of spray breaking over her forecastle and travelling as far aft as the waist. Hawkwood grasped the mizzen backstay and felt the tension in the cable. He would have to shorten sail if this kept up, but for now he wanted to wring every ounce of speed he could out of the blessed wind.

"Arhuz, another man to the wheel, and brail up the mizzen course."

"Aye, sir. Prepare to shorten sail! You there, Jorth, get on up that yard and leave the damn landlubber to make his own way. This is not a nursery."

The landlubber in question was Bleyn. He managed a creditable progress up the waist to the quarterdeck until he stood dripping before Hawkwood, his face wind-reddened and beaming.

"Better than a good horse!" he shouted above the wind, and Hawkwood found himself grinning at the boy. He was game, if nothing else.

"Get yourself below, Bleyn, and change your clothes. And look in on your mother. She is taken poorly."

"Aye, sir!" Hawkwood watched him go with an inexplicable ache in his breast.

"He seems a fine young fellow. I wonder he was not presented at court," Isolla said. Hawkwood had momentarily forgotten about her.

"You too might be better below, lady. It's apt to become a trifle boisterous on deck."

"I do not mind. I seem to have become accustomed to the

movement of the ship at last, and the air is like a tonic."

Her eyes sparkled. She was no beauty, but there was a strength, a wholeness about her that informed her features and somehow invited the same openness in return. Only the livid scar down one side of her face jarred. It did not make her ugly in Hawkwood's eyes, but he was reminded of his debt to her every time he saw it.

What am I become, he thought, some kind of moonstruck youngster? There was something in him which responded to all three of his passengers in different ways, but he would sooner jump overboard than try to delve further than that. Thank God for the ceaseless business of the ship to keep his thoughts occupied.

He recalled the chart below to his mind as easily as some men might recall a passage from an oft-read book. If he kept to this course he would, in mariner's terms, shave the south-west tip of Gabrion by some ten or fifteen leagues. That was all very well, but if the southerlies started up out of Calmar he would not have much leeway to play with. And then, to play for more sea room would mean eating up more time. Two days perhaps.

The figures and angles came together in his head. He felt Isolla watching him curiously but ignored her. The crew did not approach him. They knew what he was about, and knew he needed peace to resolve it in his mind.

"Hold this course," he said to Arhuz at last. What Bleyn had said had tipped the scales. They could not be profligate with time. He would have to chance the southerlies and gain leeway by whatever small shifts he could. The decision left his mind clear again, and the tension left the deck. He studied the sail plan. The lateens on fore and main were drawing well for now. He would let them remain until the wind began to veer, if it did at all. No need to call all hands. The watch below might snore on undisturbed in their hammocks.

"Bosun!" he thundered. "Belay the swaying up of the square yards. We'll stick to the lateens for now. Take down those tackles."

He stood there on the quarterdeck as the crew took to the

mizzen shrouds and began to fight for fistful after fistful of the booming mizzen course, tying it up in a loose bunt on the yard. The *Seahare*'s motion grew a little less violent, but as Hawkwood watched the sea and the clouds closely he realised that the weather was about to worsen. A squall was approaching out of the west; he could see the white line of its fury whipping up the already stiffening swell, whilst above the water the cloud bunched and darkened and came on like some purposeful titan, its underside flickering with buried lightning.

He and Arhuz looked at one another. There was something disquieting about the remorseless speed of the line of broken water.

"Where in the world did that come from?" Arhuz asked wonderingly.

"All hands!" Hawkwood bellowed. "All hands on deck! Arhuz, take in fore and main, and make it quick."

The off-duty watch came tumbling up the companionways from below, took one look at the approaching tempest, and began climbing the shrouds, yawning and shaking the sleep out of their heads.

"Is there something the matter, Captain?" Isolla asked.

"Go below, lady." Hawkwood's tone brooked no argument, and she obeyed him without another word.

The mizzen was brailed up and the maincourse was in, but the men were still fighting to tie up the thumping canvas of the forecourse when the squall reached them.

In the space of four minutes it grew dark, a rain-swept, heaving twilight in which the wind howled and the lightnings exploded about their heads. The squall smote the *Seahare* on the starboard quarter and immediately knocked her a point off course. Hawkwood helped the two helmsmen fight the wicked jerking of the wheel and as the thick, warm rain beat on their right cheeks they watched the compass in the binnacle and by main strength turned one point, then two and then three points until the beakhead pointed east-north-east and the ship was running before the wind.

Only then could Hawkwood lift his gaze. He saw that the

forecourse had broken free from the men on the yard and was flying in great, flapping rags, the heavy canvas creating havoc in the forestays, ripping ropes and splintering timber as far forward as the jib boom. Even as he watched, the sailors managed to cut the head of the sail free of the yard, and it took off like some huge pale bird and vanished into the foaming darkness ahead.

The *Seahare* was shipping green water over her forecastle, and it flooded down the waist as the bow rose, knocking men off their feet and smashing through the companion doorway and thus flooding the cabins aft. Hawkwood found himself staring at slate-grey, angry sky over the bowsprit, and then as the ship's stern rose the waves soared up like dark, foam-tipped phantoms and came choking and crashing over the bow again.

Arhuz was setting up lifelines and double-frapping the boats on the booms. Hawkwood shouted in the ear of the senior helmsman, "Thus, very well thus." The man's reply was lost in the roar of wave and wind, but he was nodding his head. Hawkwood made his way down into the waist as carefully as a man negotiating a cliff face in a gale. The turtle deck was shedding the green seas admirably, but they had surmounted the storm-sills of the companionways and he could feel the extra weight of water in the ship, rendering her stiffer and thus more likely to bury her bowsprit. It was a following sea now, and thank God the xebec was not square-sterned like most ships he had sailed and thus the waves which the wind was flinging at them slid under her counter without too much trouble. Hawkwood found himself admiring his sleek vessel, and her winsome eagerness to ride the monstrous swells.

"She swims well!" he shouted in Arhuz's ear. The Merduk grinned, his teeth a white flash in his dark face. "Aye sir, she was always a willing ship."

"We need men on the pumps, though, and those hatchway tarpaulins are working loose. Get Chips on deck to batten them down."

"Aye, sir." Arhuz hauled himself aft with the aid of the just-rigged lifelines.

It was the lack of heavy broadside guns that helped, Hawk-wood realised. The weight of a couple of dozen culverins on deck raised the centre of gravity of a ship and made her that much less seaworthy. It was the difference between a man jogging with a pack on his back, and one running unencum-bered. The xebec was running before the wind with only a brailed-up mizzen course to propel her, but her speed was remarkable. Perhaps too remarkable. A vision of the chart still pinned to his table below decks floated into his mind. They were steering directly for the ironbound western coast of Gabrion now, and there was not a safe landfall to be made there for many leagues in any direction; the promontories of that land loomed out to sea like the unforgiving ravelins of a fortress. They must turn aside if they were not to be flung upon the coast and smashed to matchwood. Hawkwood closed his eyes as the water foamed around his knees. A northerly course was the safer bet. Once they were around that great rocky peninsula known as the Gripe, they would find anchorages aplenty on Gabrion's flatter northern shores. But it would mean giving up on the southern route. They would then be committed to a passage of the Malacar Straits, the one thing he had tried so hard to avoid.

He opened his eyes and stared at the lowering sky again. Sudden squalls such as this were unusual but by no means unknown in the Hebrian Sea. Mostly they were quick to pass, a brief, chaotic maelstrom most dangerous in the first few minutes. But every horizon was dark now, and the sun had disappeared. This squall would blow for a day or two at least. The southern passage was too risky. He cursed silently. They would have to go north as soon as the ship could bear it.

He blinked rain out of his eyes. For a moment—

And then he was sure. He had seen something up there against the dark racing clouds, a shadow or group of shadows moving with the wind. His blood ran cold. He stood staring with wide eyes, but saw nothing more than the galloping clouds, the flicker of the lightning, and the shifting silver curtain of the rain.

His cabin was swimming in at least a foot of water which sloshed back and forth with the pitch of the ship. A hooded lantern set in gimbals still burned feebly and he opened its slot to give himself more light, then bent over the chart and picked up the dividers. Navigating by dead-reckoning, with a rocky shore to leeward and the ship running full tilt towards it before the wind. A mariner's nightmare. He wiped salt water out of his eyes and forced himself to concentrate, estimating the ship's speed and plotting out her course. The results of his calculations made him whistle soundlessly, and he tossed down the dividers with something like anger. There was nothing natural about this squall, of that he was now sure. It had reared up out of a clear sky at just the right moment, and was meant to wreck them on the rocks of Gabrion. It would blow until its work was done.

"Bastards."

He roused out a bottle of brandy and gulped from the neck, feeling the good spirit kindle his innards, wondering if the xebec could stand a change of course to the north. The wind would be square on the larboard beam then, trying to capsize her. The decision had to be made soon. With every passing minute they were running off their leeway, thundering ever closer to that killer coast.

A knock on the door of his cabin. It stood open, swinging back and forth with the pressure of the water that sloshed underfoot. He did not turn around, and was unsurprised to hear Isolla's voice, somewhat hoarse.

"Captain, may I speak to you?"

"By all means." He sucked from the neck of the brandy bottle again as though inspiration might be found therein.

"How long do you suppose this storm will endure? The mariners seem very concerned."

Hawkwood smiled. "I've no doubt they are, lady." The lurch of the ship sent Isolla thumping against the door jamb.

Hawkwood steadied her with one hand. Her cloak was sodden and cold. She was as soaked as he was.

"I believe the Himerians have found us," Hawkwood said at last. "It is they who have conjured up this squall. It's not violent enough to threaten the ship—not yet—but it is making us go where we do not want to go." He gestured to the chart, which was wrinkling with wet. "If I cannot change course very soon we will run full tilt on to the rocks of Gabrion. They timed their weather-working well."

Isolla looked startled. "How can they cast a spell over so great a distance? Hebrion is hundreds of miles behind us."

"I know. There must be another ship out there, somewhere beyond the walls of this storm. Weather-workers can only maintain one spell at a time; I believe they have used sorcery to speed their own vessel and draw within range of us, and then have switched their focus and unleashed this storm, which they think will propel the ship to its doom."

"And will they succeed?"

"Even a preternatural storm can be weathered like any other, given good seamanship and a little luck. We're not beaten yet!" He smiled. Perhaps it was the brandy, or the storm, but he felt a certain sense of licence.

"You're wet through. You must try and keep yourself out of the water. Huddle in your cot under a blanket if you have to."

She shrugged, and gave a wry smile. "It's pouring in the door and down from the ceiling. There's not a dry spot in this ship I believe."

Hawkwood leaned towards her on an impulse and kissed her cold lips.

Isolla jerked back, astonished. Her fingers went to her mouth. "Captain, you forget yourself! Remember who I am."

"I've never forgotten," Hawkwood said recklessly, "Not since that day on the road all those years ago when your horse threw a shoe, and you served me wine in Golophin's tower."

"I am Hebrion's Queen!"

"Hebrion is gone, Isolla, and in a day or two we may all be dead."

He reached for her again, but she backed away. He cornered her by the door and set his hands on the bulkhead on either side of her, the bottle still clenched in one fist. Around them the ship pitched and heaved and groaned and the water swept cold about their legs and the wind howled up on deck like a live thing, a sentient menace. Hawkwood bent his head and kissed her once more, throwing all sense of caution to the ravening wind. This time she did not draw away, but it was like kissing a marble statue, a tang of salt on stone.

He leant his forehead on her damp shoulder with a groan. "I'm sorry." The moment where all had been possible faded like the mirage it had been, burning away with the brandy fumes in his head.

"Forgive me, lady." He was about to leave her when her hands came up and clasped his face. They stared at one another. Hawkwood could not read her eyes.

"You are forgiven, Captain," she said softly, and then she lowered her face into the hollow of his neck and he felt her tremble. He kissed her wet hair, baffled and exhilarated at the same time. Half a minute she remained clinging to him, then she straightened and without looking at him or saying another word, she left, splashing up the companionway towards her own cabin. Hawkwood remained frozen, like a man stunned.

WHEN he finally came back up on deck he felt oddly detached, as though the survival of the ship was not something that was important any longer. There were four men on the wheel now, and the remainder of the crew were huddled in the half-deck under the wheel, sheltering from the wind. Hawkwood roused himself and checked their course by the compass board. They were hurtling east-north-east, and if he was any judge the *Seahare* must be making at least nine knots. Before the squall they had been perhaps fifty leagues to windward of the Gabrionese coast. At their current speed they would run aground in some sixteen hours. There was no time to play with. His mind clear, Hawkwood stood by the wheel, clutched the lifeline, and bellowed at the helmsmen, "Two points to port. I want her brought round to north-north-east, lads. Arhuz!"

"Aye, sir." The first mate looked as dark and drowned as a seal.

"I want a sea anchor veered out from the stern on a five-hundred-fathom length of one-inch cable. Use one of the top-gallant sails. It should cut down on our leeway." Arhuz did not answer, but nodded grimly and left the quarterdeck, calling for a working party to follow him below.

The decision was made. They would try and weather the Gripe and strike out for the northern coast. If the southerlies finally kicked in after they had left this squall behind, then they would have the broad reaches of the Hebrian Sea to manoeuvre in instead of fighting for sea room all along the southern coast of Gabrion. They would have to risk the straits. It could not be helped.

If we make it that far, Hawkwood thought. He kept thinking of Isolla's arms about him, the salt taste of her lips unmoving under his own. He could not puzzle out what it might mean, and he regretted the brandy she must have tasted on his mouth.

The ship came round, and the blast of the wind shifted from the back of his head to his left ear. The xebec began to roll as well as pitch now, a corkscrew motion that shipped even more water forward, whilst the pressure on the rudder sought to tear the spokes of the ship's wheel from the fists of the helmsmen. They hooked on the relieving tackles to aid them, but Hawkwood could almost sense the ropes slipping on the drum below.

"Steer small!" he shouted to the helmsmen. They had too little sea room to work with, and her course must be exact.

Bleyn came up on deck wearing an oilskin jacket too large for him. "What can I do?" he shouted shrilly.

"Go below. Help man one of the pumps." He nodded, grinned like a maniac, and disappeared again. The pumps were sending a fine spout of water out to leeward, but the *Seahare* was making more than they could cope with. As if conjured up by Hawkwood's concern, the ship's carpenter appeared.

"Pieto!" Hawkwood greeted him. "How does she swim?"

"We've three feet of water in the well, Captain, and it's gaining on us. She was always a dry ship, but this course is opening her seams. There's oakum floating about all over the hold. Can't we put her back before the wind?"

"Only if you want to break her back on Gabrion. Keep the pumps going Pieto, and rig hawse bags forward. We have to ride this one out." The carpenter knuckled his forehead and went below looking discontented and afraid.

Hawkwood found himself loving his valiant ship. The *Seahare* shouldered aside the heavy swells manfully—they were breaking over her port quarter as well now—and kept her sharp beakhead on course despite the wrenchings of her rudder. She seemed as stubbornly indomitable as her captain.

This was being alive, this was tasting life. It was better than anything that could be found at the bottom of a bottle. It was the reason he had been born.

Hawkwood kept his station on the windward side of the quarterdeck and felt the spray sting his face and his good ship leap lithe and alive under his feet, and he laughed aloud at the black clouds, the drenching rain, and the malevolent fury of the storm.

FOURTEEN

CORFE had decreed that the funeral should be as magnificent as that of a king's, and in the event Queen Odelia was laid to rest with a sombre pomp and ceremony that had not been seen in Torunn since the death of King Lofantyr almost seventeen years before. Formio's Orphans lined the streets with their pikes at the vertical, and a troop of five thousand Cathedrallers accompanied the funeral carriage to the cathedral where Torunna's Queen was to be interred in the great family vault of the Fantyrs. The High Pontiff himself, Albrec, intoned the funeral oration and the great and the good of the kingdom packed the pews and listened in their sober finery. With Odelia went the last link with an older Torunna, a different world. Many in the crowd cast discreet glances at the brindled head of the King, and wondered if the rumours of an imminent Royal wedding were true. It was common knowledge that the Queen had wanted her husband to be re-wedded before even her corpse was cold, but to whom? What manner of woman would be chosen to fill Odelia's throne, now that they were at open war with

the might of the Second Empire, and Hebrion had already
fallen and Astarac was tottering? The solemnity of those
gathered to bid farewell to their Queen was not assumed.
They knew that Torunna approached one of the most critical
junctures in her history, more dangerous perhaps than even
the climax of the Merduk Wars had been. And there were
rumours that already Gaderion was beset, General Aras hard-
pressed to hold the Torrin Gap. What would Corfe do? For
days thousands of conscripts had been mustering in the capital and were now undergoing their Provenance. Torunn had
become a fortress within which armies mustered. Whither
would they go? No one save the High Command knew, and
they were close-lipped as confessors.

When the funeral was over, and Odelia's body had been
laid in the Royal crypt, the mourners left the cathedral one
by one, and only a lonely pair in the front rank of pews
remained. The King, and standing in the shadows Felorin his
bodyguard, and General Formio. After a brief word Formio
departed, laying his hand on the back of the King's neck and
giving him a gentle shake. They smiled at each other, and
then Corfe bent his head again, the circlet that had been Kaile
Ormann's glinting on his brow. At last the King rose, Felorin
following like a shadow, and knocked on the door of the
cathedral sacristy. A hollow voice said "Enter," and Corfe
pushed the massive ironbound portal open. The Pontiff Albrec stood within flanked by a pair of Inceptines who were
in the process of disrobing him. Behind him gleamed a gal-
lery of chalices and reliquaries and a long rail hung with the
rich ceremonial garments a Pontiff must needs don at times
like this.

"Leave us, Brothers," Albrec said crisply, and the two Inceptines bowed low to King and Pontiff, and departed
through a small side door.

"Corfe—will you give me a hand?" Albrec asked, tugging
at his richly embroidered chasuble.

"Felorin," the King said. "Wait outside and see no one
enters."

The tattooed soldier nodded wordlessly and heaved shut

the great sacristy door behind him with a dull boom.

Corfe helped Albrec out of his ceremonial apparel and hung it up on the rail behind, whilst the little cleric pulled a plain black Inceptine habit over his head and, puffing slightly, kissed his Saint's symbol and settled it about his neck. The air wheezed in and out of the twin holes where his nose had been.

There was a fire burning in a small stone hearth which had been ingeniously hewn out of a single block of Cimbric basalt. They stood before it warming their hands, like two men who have been labouring together out in the cold. It was Albrec who broke the silence.

"Are you still set on this thing?"

"I am. She would have wished it. It was her last wish, in fact. And she was right. The kingdom needs it. The girl is already on the road."

"The kingdom needs it," Albrec repeated. "And what of you, Corfe?"

"What of me? Kings have duties as well as prerogatives. It must be done, and done soon, ere I leave on campaign."

"What of Heria? Is there any word on how she is taking all this?"

Corfe flinched as though he had been struck. "No word," he said. He stood rubbing one hand over the other before the flames as though he were washing them. "It has been eighteen years since last I saw her face, Albrec. The joy we shared so long ago is like a dream now." Something thickened in Corfe's voice and his face grew hard and set as the basalt of the burning hearth before him. "One cannot live by memory, least of all when one is a king."

"There are other women in the world, other alliances which could be sought out," Albrec said gently.

"No. This is the one the country needs. One day, Albrec, I foresee that Torunna and Ostrabar will be one and the same, a united kingdom wherein the war we fought will be but a memory, and this part of the world will know true peace at last. Anything, any sacrifice, any pain, is worth the chance of that happening."

Albrec bowed his head, his eyes fixed on Corfe's tortured face. *And you my friend,* he thought, *what of you?*

"Golophin has been transporting messages swiftly as a hawk's flight. Aurungzeb knows of Odelia's death, and we have both agreed on a small, a—a subdued ceremony, as soon as the girl arrives. There will be no public holiday or grand spectacle, not so soon after . . . after today. The people will be told in time, and I will be able to leave for the war without any more delay. I want you to conduct the ceremony, Albrec." Corfe waved an arm. "In here, away from the gawpers."

"In the sacristy?"

"It's as good a place as any other."

Albrec sighed and rubbed at the stumps where long ago frost had robbed him of his fingers. "Very well. But Corfe, I say this to you. Stop punishing yourself for what fate has visited upon you. It is not your fault, nor is it anything to feel ashamed over. *What's done is done.*" He reached up and set a hand on Corfe's shoulder. The Torunnan King smiled.

"Yes, of course. You sound like Odelia." A strangled attempt at a laugh. "God's blood, Albrec, but I miss her. She was one of the great friends of my life, along with Andruw, and Formio, and others long dead. She was another right hand. Had she been a man, she would have made a fine king." He pushed the palm of his hand into the hollow of one eye. "Perhaps I should have told her. She might not have been so insistent on this thing."

"Odelia? No, she would still have wanted it, though it would have tortured her much as it is tormenting you. It is as well she never knew who Ostrabar's Queen is."

"Ostrabar's Queen . . . I wonder sometimes—even now I wonder—about how it was for her, what nightmares she must have suffered as I fled Aekir with my tail between my legs."

"That's enough," Albrec said sternly. "What's done is done. You cannot change the past, you can only hope to make the future a better place."

Corfe looked at the little cleric, and in his bloodshot fire-glazed eyes Albrec saw something which shook him to the core. Then the King smiled again.

"You are right, of course." He tried to make his voice light. "Do you realise that Mirren will have a step-mother younger than she is? They will be friends, I hope." The word *hope* sounded strange coming out of his mouth. He embraced the disfigured little monk as though they were brothers, and then knelt and kissed the Pontifical ring. "I must away, Holiness. A king's time is not his own. Thank you for yours." Then he spun on his heel and thumped the sacristy door. Felorin opened it for him, and they left together, the King and his shadow. Albrec stared unseeing into the depths of the bright fire before him, not hearing his Inceptine helpers re-enter the room and stand reverently behind him. He was still shaken by the light he had seen in Corfe's eye. The look of a man who cannot find peace in life, and who means to seek it in death.

In the midst of the crowded activity that currently thronged Torunn, few remarked upon the entry into the city of a Merduk caravan several days later. It was some thirty wagons strong, and halfway down their column a curtained palanquin bobbed, borne on the shoulders of eight brawny slaves. They had been given an escort of forty Cathedraller cavalry, and entered the city via the North Gate, where the guards had been told to expect them. Merduk ambassadors and their entourages were a common sight in Torunn these days, and no one remarked as the caravan made its stately way to the hill overlooking the Torrin Estuary on which loomed the granite splendour of the palace, its windows all draped black in mourning for Torunna's dead Queen.

Ensign Baraz was within the palace courtyard as the heavily laden covered wagons rattled through the gates, drawn by camels whose heads bobbed with black and white ostrich feathers. He drew up the ceremonial guard, and at his crisp command they flashed out their sabres in salute. The palanquin came to a halt upon the shoulders of the sweating slaves, and a bevy of silk-veiled Merduk maids lifted back the curtains to reveal a barely discernible form within. This shape was helped out with the aid of a trio of footstools and the ministrations of the maids and stood, slim, and somewhat uncertain, with the cold spring wind tugging at her veil. Baraz stepped forward and bowed. "Lady," he said in Merduk, "you are very welcome in the city of Torunn and kingdom of Torunna."

He got no farther through the flowery speech of welcome which he had devised the night before after the King had peremptorily informed him of his mission. A stout Merduk matron with black eyes flashing above her veil waddled forward and demanded to know who he was and why the King was not here to greet his bride-to-be in person.

"He has been unavoidably detained," Baraz said smoothly. "Preparations for the war—"

"Sibir Baraz! I know you! I served in your uncle's household ere he was transferred to the palace. My brave boy, how you've grown!" The Merduk matron enfolded Baraz in her huge arms and tugged his head down to rest in her heaving, heavily scented cleavage. "Do you not know Haratta, who wiped your nose when you could barely say your name?"

With difficulty Baraz extricated himself from her soft clutch. Behind him, a fit of coughing had spread throughout the men of the honour guard and the eyes of the slim girl who had been in the palanquin were dancing.

"Of course I remember you. Now lady,"—this to the girl—"I have been instructed to guide you and your attendants to your quarters in the palace and make sure that all is as you wish there."

Haratta turned and clapped her hands. In an entirely different tone, a harsh bark, she began to issue orders to the hovering maids, the slaves, the wagoneers. Then she turned back to Baraz, having produced a chaotic turmoil of activity out of what had been stately stillness a moment before, and pinched his burning cheek. "Such a handsome young man, and high in the favour of King Corfe, no doubt. Lead on, master Baraz! The lady Aria and I would follow you anywhere, I'm sure." She winked with a kind of jovial lechery, and when he hesitated shooed him on as though he were a chicken clucking in her path.

The procession had something of the circus about it, Baraz leading, with Haratta beside him chattering incessantly, Aria following with her maids about her, and then an incongruous crocodile of burly, sweating men burdened with trunks, cases, rolled carpets, bulging bags and even a flapping nightingale in a cage. But the sombre mourning hangings which festooned the palace soon put paid to even Haratta's loquaciousness and by the time they reached their destination they were a silent troop, and somewhat subdued.

The palace steward, an old and able quartermaster named Cullen, was waiting for them surrounded by sable-clad courtiers. The Merduk party was installed in a cavernous series of marble-floored rooms which were traditionally reserved for visiting potentates, but which had seen little use since the days of King Minantyr forty years before. Even the braziers, which had been lit in every corner, seemed to have done little to dispel the neglected chill within. Haratta eyed the suite critically, but was courteous, even restrained to Cullen and his subordinates. The Merduk slaves deposited a small hillock of luggage in every room, and then were shown to their own quarters above the kitchen—no doubt warmer and less draughty than the grand desolation their betters occupied.

Baraz turned to go, but Aria laid a hand on his arm. "When will I see the King, Ensign Baraz?"

"I do not know, lady. My orders were to see you comfortably installed here and then to report to him, that was all."

She drew back, nodded. Her eyes were incredibly young and somewhat fearful under the cosmetics which had been painted about them. Baraz smiled at her. "He is a good man," he said kindly, then collected himself and saluted. "A pair of palace maids will be stationed in this wing to see that you have everything you need. Fare well, lady." And he was gone.

Aria's entourage spent the rest of the day converting the

cold chambers into something more befitting a Merduk princess, and by the time evening had rolled in, and with it a chill spring rainstorm out of the heights of the Cimbrics, they had transformed the austere suite into an approximation of the luxurious living spaces they were used to. Rich and colourful carpets had been unrolled to cover the bare marble, hangings had been hooked upon the walls, brass and silver lamps had been lit, incense was burning, and the nightingale sang his drab little heart out from the confines of his golden cage.

Aria and Haratta were in the bedchamber unpacking silken dresses and shawls from one of the larger trunks, Haratta enlarging upon the merits and defects of each garment, when one of the doe-eyed maids rustled in and fell to her knees before them.

"Mistress, mistress! The Torunnan King is here."

"What?" Haratta snapped. "Without a word of warning? You are mistaken."

"No! It is he, all alone but for a tattooed soldier who waits down the passage. He wishes to talk with the Princess!"

Haratta threw down the costly silk she had been examining. "Barbarians! Send him away! No, no, we cannot do that. My sweet, you must receive him—he is a king after all, though now I believe those stories about his peasant upbringing. Unheard of—to force himself upon us unheralded, catching us unawares. Veil yourself, girl! I will speak to him and set him to rights." Haratta rose and, twitching her own veil about her pouting mouth, stalked from the chamber in a shimmer of billowing raiment.

In the main antechamber a man of medium height stood warming his hands at the glowing charcoal of a brazier. He was dressed in black and his close-fitting tunic sat on him as trimly as on the torso of a youth. But when he turned Haratta saw that his hair was three parts grey and his eyes were sunken, though they gleamed brightly in the lamplight. He wore a simple silver circlet about his temples and no other ornament or decoration of any kind. King or no, Haratta had intended to upbraid him politely but icily for his presumption, but something about his eyes stopped her cold. She curtseyed in the Ramusian way.

"You speak Normannic?" the man asked.

"A small piece, mine lord. Not very goods."

"Haratta your name is, I am told."

"Yes, lord."

"I am Corfe. I am here to see the lady Aria. I apologise for my absence at your arrival, but I was detained by matters of state." He paused, and seeing the look of alarm and incomprehension crossing her face his eyes softened. In Merduk he said:

"I wish only to speak with your mistress for a moment. I will wait, if that is necessary."

Her face cleared. "I will ask her to come at once." There was something in this man's gaze, something which even at first meeting made one eager to obey him.

WHEN Aria entered the room a few moments later she was swathed in yards of midnight silk, the finest she possessed, and kohl had been applied to her eyelids, the lashes drawn out at the corners of her eyes with black stibium. Haratta followed her and took an unobtrusive seat in a shadowed corner as her mistress walked steadily towards her future husband, a man old enough to be her father.

The Torunnan King bowed deeply and she inclined her head in answer. He did not look as old as she had feared, and had in fact the bearing of a much younger man. He was not ill-looking either, and the first, absurd, girlish fears she had harboured faded. She was not to share a bed with some pot-bellied bald-headed libertine after all.

They exchanged inconsequential courtesies, all the while taking in every detail of the other. His Merduk was adequate, but not fluent, as though it had lately been studied in a hurry. They switched to Normannic at her request, for she was at home in both, thanks to her mother. He had a stern cast to his face, but when she made him smile she saw a much younger man beneath the Royal solemnity, a glimpse of someone else. She found herself liking his gravity, the sud-

den, unexpected smile which lifted it. His eyes were almost
the same shade as her own.

He asked about her mother, turning away to poke at the
brazier with a fire iron as he did so. She was very well, Aria
told him lightly. She sent her greetings to her future son-in-
law. This last thing she had invented as an empty courtesy,
no more, but as she said it the fire iron went still, and remained poised in the burning red heart of the coals. The King
went silent and she wondered what she had said to offend
him. At last he turned back to her and she could see sweat
glittering on his brow. His eyes seemed to have sunk back
into his head and the firelight raised no gleam from them.

"May I see your face?" he asked.

She was taken aback, and had no idea how to deal with
such a bold request. She glanced at Haratta in the shadows
and almost called the older woman over, then thought better
of it. Why not? He was to marry her, after all. She twitched
aside her veil and drew back her silken hood without speaking.

She heard Haratta gasp with outrage behind her, but had
eyes only for the King's face. The colour had fled from it.
He looked shocked, but mastered himself quickly. His hand
came up as if he were about to caress her cheek, then fell
away without touching her.

"You are the very image of your mother," he said
hoarsely.

"So I have been told, my lord." Their eyes locked and
something indefinable went between them. There was a
great, empty hunger in him, a grieved yearning which
touched her to the quick. She took his hard-planed fingers in
her own, and felt him tremble at her touch.

Haratta had reached them. "My lord King, this is no way
to be behaving. I am here as chaperone for the Princess, and
I say that you overstep the mark. Aria, what are you thinking? Cover yourself, girl. A man does not see his bride's
face until their wedding night. For shame!"

Corfe's eyes did not leave Aria's for a second. "Things
are done differently here in Torunna," he said quietly. "And

besides, we are to be married in the morning."

Aria felt her heart flip. "So soon? But I—"

"I have communicated with your father. He has agreed. Your dowry will be sent on with your brother Nasir and the reinforcements he is leading here."

Haratta seemed to choke. She dabbed at her eyes. "Oh my little girl, oh my poor maid. Are you ashamed of her, my lord, that you rush through this thing like—like a thief in the night?"

Corfe's cold stare shut her mouth. "We are at war, woman, and this kingdom buried its Queen this morning. My wife. It is not how any of us would have wished, but circumstance dictates our actions. I must leave for the war myself very soon. Forgive me, Aria. No disrespect is intended. Your own father recognises this."

Aria bowed her head. "I understand." She still held his fingers in her own and she felt the pressure as he squeezed them, then released her.

"A covered carriage will be waiting for you in the morning, and will convey you to the cathedral where we are to be married. You may bring Haratta and one other maid, but that is all. Are there any questions?" He seemed to think he was briefing a group of soldiers. His voice had become hard and impersonal; the tone of command. Aria and Haratta shook their heads silently.

"Very good. I will see you in the morning then." He raised Aria's hand to his lips and kissed her knuckle, a dry feather touch. "Good night, ladies." Then he turned on his heel and strode away. When the door had closed behind him Aria covered her face with her hands and fought the sudden sobs which threatened to burst free.

THE bells woke her. There had been a late spring snowfall a few days before, probably the last of the year, and Aurungabar's usual clatter and clamour had been muffled by the white tenderness of the snow. But now all over the city this morning the bells of every surviving Ramusian church were toiling, and chief among them the mournful sonorous pealing of Carcasson's great bronze titans. Heria threw aside the piled coverlets and shrugging a fur pelisse about her shoulders she darted to the window and tugged aside the ornate shutters.

The cold air made her gasp and the whiteness was blinding after the gloom of the room. The sun was still rising and was nothing more than a saffron burning glimpsed through thick ribands of grey cloud. Some kind of emergency? But the people trudging through the streets seemed unafraid. The wains heading to market in great clouds of oxen-breath trundled obliviously, their drovers yawning muffled figures unpanicked by any news of war or fire or invasion.

A knock on the door, and immediately after her maids entered bearing hot water and towels and her clothes for the day. She closed the shutters without a word and let them undress her; they might have been deaf for all the notice they took of the tolling bells. When she was naked she stepped into the broad, flat-bottomed basin in which the water steamed and they dabbed at her with scented sponges brought up from the jewel-bright depths of the Levangore. They wrapped warm towels about her white limbs and she stepped out of the basin to peruse the garments they had brought for her to choose from.

The Sultan entered the room without fanfare or ceremony, rubbing his ring-bright fingers together. "Ah! I caught you!"

The maids all went to their knees but Heria remained standing. "My lord, I am at my ablutions."

"Ablute away!" Aurungzeb was grinning white out of the huge darkness of his beard. He settled himself on a creaking chair and arranged his robes about his globular paunch. The curved poniard he wore in his sash jutted forth as though it had been planted there. "It is nothing I have not seen before, I am sure. You are still my wife, after all, and a damned fine figure of a woman. Drop those towels, Ahara; even queens must not stand on their dignity all the time."

She did as she was told and stood like a white, nude statue while the maids cowered at her feet and Aurungzeb eyed her appreciatively, ignoring or unaware of the blazing hatred in her eyes.

"Splendid, still splendid. You hear the bells? Of course you do. I thought I would be the one to tell you. The union I have long sought is concluded. This morning our daughter weds Corfe of Torunna, and our kingdoms are indissolubly linked for posterity. My grandson shall one day rule Torunna. Ha ha!"

Blood coloured her face. "This was not to happen so soon. We were to be at the ceremony. I—I was to give her away. We agreed."

Aurungzeb flapped a hairy-knuckled hand. "It proved impossible in the event—and what is a little ceremony, after all? They have just buried their queen. Corfe wanted a quiet wedding, without fanfare. He is to leave for the war very soon, and had best try and plant a seed in Aria ere he goes."

Heria snatched a dressing robe from one of the frozen maids, wrapping it about her. Her eyes were blazing but vacant, as if they gazed upon some cruelty only she could see. "I was to be there," she repeated in a murmur. "I was to see them. I was . . ."

Aurungzeb was becoming irritated. "Yes yes, we know all that. Matters of state intervened. We cannot have all we wish in this world." He hauled himself out of the chair and padded over to her. "Put it out of your mind. The thing is done." He raised her chin and regarded her face. She stared through him as though he did not exist, and he frowned.

"Queen or no, you are my wife, and you will bend to my will. You think the world will stand still to suit you?" When he released her his fingermarks left red bars on her cheek.

Heria's eyes returned to the room. After a moment, she smiled. "My Sultan, you are in the right of it as always. What do I know of matters of state? I am only a woman." Her hand sought his, raised it, and slipped it inside the loose collar of her robe so that he cupped one of her full breasts. Aurungzeb's face changed.

"Sometimes I must be reminded that I am a woman,"

Heria said, one eyebrow arching up her forehead. Aurungzeb licked his upper lip, wetting his moustache.

"Leave us," he growled at the maids. "The Queen and I desire a private word together."

The maids rose to their slippered feet and backed out of the room with their heads bowed. When the door had shut behind them Aurungzeb smiled. He reached up and twitched Heria's robe aside. It fell to her waist.

"Ah, still beautiful," he whispered, and grinned. "My sweet, you always knew how—"

Her hand, which had been stroking the sash about his voluminous middle, fastened upon the ivory hilt of the poniard tucked away there. She drew it forth with a flash.

"But you never knew," she said. And she stabbed him deep, deep in the belly, twisting the blade and slicing open the flesh so that his innards bulged out and blood flooded with them. Aurungzeb sank to his knees with an astonished gasp, trying vainly to press his lacerated flesh together.

"*Guards,*" but the word came out as little more than a strangled whisper. He fell over on his side in a widening pool of his own blood, his eyes bulging white. His legs twitched and kicked uselessly.

"*Why—?*"

His Queen looked down on him contemptuously, with the bloody knife still gripped in one small fist. "My name is Heria Car-Gwion of the city of Aekir, and my true husband is, and has always been, Corfe Cear-Inaf, one-time officer in the garrison of Aekir, now King of Torunna." Her eyes bored into Aurungzeb's horrified, dying face.

"*Do you understand?*"

Ostabar's Sultan gurgled. His horror-filled eyes seemed to dawn with some awful knowledge. One hand left his terrible wound and reached for her like a claw. She stepped back leaving bare footprints in his blood, and watched in silence as his movements grew feebler. He tried again to shout, but blood filled his mouth and came spitting out. She dropped her robe over his contorted face and stood naked, watching him struggle ineffectually under it. At last he was still. Tears streaked her face, but her features were stiff as those of a caryatid.

She blinked, and seemed to become aware of the weapon still clenched in her hand. Her arm was crimson to the elbow. There was a soft, insistent knocking at the door.

She looked around the room through a blaze of tears, and smiled. Then she thrust the keen blade deep into her own breast.

FIFTEEN

THE Royal bedchamber was something of a forbidding place, the vast four-poster dominating it like a fortress. The bed seemed to have been sturdily built to accommodate duties rather than pleasures. Corfe had slept alone in it for fourteen years.

He stood before a fireplace wide enough to roast a side of pork, and warmed his hands unnecessarily at the towering flames. The same room, the same ring on his finger, but soon a different woman to warm the bed. He reached for the wine glass which glinted discreetly on the tall mantel, and drank half its blood-red contents at a gulp. It might have been water for all he tasted.

A quiet ceremony indeed. Only Formio, Comillan and Haratta had been present as witnesses, and Albrec had been brief and to the point, thank God. Aria had removed her veil and hood, for she was a Torunnan now, and she had bowed her head as the Pontiff placed the delicate filigree of a queen's crown upon her raven tresses.

Corfe rubbed his chest absently. There had been an ache

there since this morning which he could not account for. It had begun during the wedding ceremony and was like the dull throb of a bruise.

"Enter," he said as the door was knocked so softly as to be barely audible.

A miniature procession entered the room. First came a pair of Merduk maids bearing lighted candles, then came Aria, her black hair unbound, a dark cloak about her shoulders, and finally Haratta bearing another candle. Corfe watched bemused as the three women stood around Aria as though shielding her. The cloak was dropped by the bedside, and he caught only a candlelit glimpse of a white shape flitting under the covers before Haratta and the maids had turned again. The maids left like women in a trance, not flinching as the wax of their candles dripped down the back of their hands, but Haratta paused.

"We have delivered her intact my lord, and have fulfilled our duty. We wish you joy of her." The look in Haratta's eye wished him anything but. "I shall be outside, if anything is needed."

"You will not," Corfe snapped. "You will return to your quarters at once. Is that clear?" Haratta bowed soundlessly and left the room.

The chamber seemed very dark as the candles were taken away, lit only by the red light of the fire. Corfe threw back the last of his wine. In the huge bed, Aria's face looked like that of a forgotten child's doll. He tugged off his tunic and sat on the side of the bed to haul off his boots, wishing now that he had not had so much wine. Wishing he had drunk more.

The boots were thrown across the room and his breeches followed. Kaile Ormann's circlet was laid with more reverence on the low table by the bed. Corfe rubbed his fingers over his face, wondering at the absurdity of it all, the twists of fate which had brought himself and this girl into the same bed. Better not to dwell on it.

He burrowed under the covers feeling tired and vinous and old. Aria jumped as he brushed against her. She was cold.

"Come here," he said. "You're like a blasted icicle."

He put his arms about her. He was warm from the fire but she was trembling and chilled. She seemed very slim and fragile in his grasp. He nuzzled her hair and the breath caught in his throat. "That scent you're wearing. Where did you get it?"

"It was a parting gift from my mother."

He lay still, and could almost have laughed. He had bought that perfume as a young man for his young wife. The Aekir bazaars sold it yet it seemed.

He rolled away from the trembling girl in his arms and stared at the flame light dancing on the tall ceiling.

"My lord, have I offended you?" she asked.

"You're my wife now, Aria. Call me Corfe." He pulled her close. She had warmed now and lay in the crook of his arm with her head resting on his shoulder. When he did not move further she began to trace a ridge of raised flesh on his collar bone. "What did this?"

"A Merduk tulwar."

"And this?"

"That was . . . hell, I don't know."

"You have many scars, Corfe."

"I have been all my life a soldier."

She was silent. Corfe found himself drifting off, his eyes struggling to shut. It was very pleasant lying here like this. He laid a hand on Aria's smooth hip and traced the curve of her thigh. At that, something in him kindled. He rolled easily on top of her, supporting his weight on his elbows, his hands cupping her face. Her mouth was set in an O of surprise.

That face within his hands, the dark hair fanning out from it. It smote him with old memories. He bent his head and kissed her mouth. She responded timidly, but then seemed to catch fire from his own urgency and became eager or, at least, eager to please.

He tried not to hurt her but she uttered a sharp, small cry all the same, and her nails dug into his back. It did not take long. When he was spent he rolled off her and stared at the ceiling once again, thinking *it is done*. His eyes stung and in the dimness he found himself blinking, as though he faced the pitiless glare of a noon sun.

"Does it always hurt like that?" Aria asked quietly.

"The first time? Yes, no—I suppose so."

"I must bear you a son. My father told me so," she went on. She took his hand under the covers. "It was not as bad as I thought it would be."

"No?" He smiled wryly. He could not look at her, but was grateful for her warmth and the touch of her hand and her low voice. He tugged her into his arms again, and she was still talking when he drifted off into black, blessed sleep.

A hammering on the door brought him bolt upright in bed, wide awake in an instant. The fire was a volcanic glow in the hearth. The slats of sky beyond the shutters were black as coal; it was not yet dawn.

"Sire," a voice said beyond the door. "News from Ostrabar. Tidings of the utmost urgency." It was Felorin.

"Very well. I'll be a moment." He pulled on his clothes and boots whilst Aria watched him wide-eyed, the sheets pulled up to her chin. He hesitated, and then kissed her on the lips. "Go back to sleep. I will return." He smoothed her hair and found himself smiling at her, then turned away.

The palace was dark yet, with only a few lamps lit in the wall sconces. Felorin bore a candle-lantern and as the two men strode along the echoing passageways it threw their shadows into mocking capers along the walls.

"It is Golophin, sir," Felorin told Corfe. "He is in the Bladehall and refuses to speak to anyone save you. Ensign Baraz brought me word of his return. He has been to Aurungabar, by some magic or other, and something has happened there. I took the liberty of rousing out General Formio also, sir."

"You did well. Lead on."

The Bladehall was a vast cavernous darkness save at one end where a fire had been lit in the massive hearth and a table pulled across upon which a single lamp burned. Golophin stood with his back to the fire, his face a scarred mask impossible to read. At the table sat Formio with parchment, quills and ink, and standing in the shadows was Ensign Baraz.

"Golophin!" Corfe barked. Formio stood up at his approach. "What's this news?"

The wizard looked at Baraz and Felorin questioningly.

"It's all right. Go on."

Golophin's face did not change; still that terrible mask empty of expression. "I have been to Aurungabar, never mind how. It would seem that both the Sultan and his Queen were assassinated this morning."

No one spoke, though even Formio looked stunned. Corfe groped for a chair and sank into it like an old man.

"You're sure?" Baraz blurted.

"Quite sure," the old, mage snapped. "The city is in an uproar, panicked crowds milling in the streets. They managed to keep it quiet for a couple of hours, but then someone blabbed and now it is common knowledge." He faltered, and there was something like disgust in his voice as he added: "It is all wearily familiar."

They looked at Corfe, but the King was sitting with his elbows on his knees, his eyes blank and sightless.

"Aruan?" Formio asked at last.

"That would be my guess. He must have wormed an agent into the household."

She was dead. His Heria was dead. Finally Corfe spoke. "This morning, you say?"

"Yes, sire. Or yesterday as it is now. Around the third hour before noon."

Corfe rubbed his chest. The ache had gone, but something worse was settling inexorably in its place. He cleared his throat, trying to clear his mind.

"Nasir," he said. "How far along the road is he?"

"My familiar is with him now. He is ten leagues east of Khedi Anwar at the head of fifteen thousand men—the army he was to bring here."

"He knows?"

"I told him sire, yes. He has already broken camp and is marching back the way he came."

"We need those men," Formio said in a low voice.

"Ostrabar needs a Sultan," Golophin replied.

"He's a boy, not yet seventeen."

"The army is behind him. And he is Aurungzeb's publicly acknowledged heir. There is no other."

Corfe raised his head. "Golophin is right. Nasir will need those men to restore order in the capital. We must do without them." Heria was dead, truly dead.

He fought the overwhelming wave of hopelessness which was trying to master him.

"Nasir will be five, maybe six days on the road before he re-enters Aurungabar. Golophin, are there any other claimants who could make trouble before he arrives?"

The wizard pondered a moment. "Not that I know of. Aurungzeb has sired other children by concubines, but Nasir is the only son, and he is well-known. I cannot foresee any difficulties with the succession."

"Well and good. Who is in authority in Aurungabar at the moment?"

Golophin nodded at Ensign Baraz who stood forgotten in the shadows. "That young man's kinsman, Shahr Baraz the Younger. He was a bodyguard of the Queen at one time, and remained a confidant. It was he who took charge when the maids discovered the bodies."

"You have spoken to him?"

"Briefly."

Golophin did not relay his own suspicions about Shahr Baraz. The most upright and honourable of men, while he had told the wizard frankly of the assassinations he had nevertheless been holding something back. But, Golophin was convinced, not for his own aggrandisement. Shahr Baraz the Younger was of the old *Hraib*, who held that to tell a lie was to suffer a form of death.

Corfe stood up. "Formio, have fast couriers sent to Aurungabar expressing our support for the new Sultan. Our whole-hearted and if necessary material support. Get one of the scribes to couch it in the necessary language, but get three copies of it on the road by dawn."

Formio nodded, and made a note on his parchment. The scrape of his quill and the crack and spit of the logs in the

hearth were the only sounds in the looming emptiness of the
Bladehall.

"We will be short of troops now," Corfe continued steadily. "I will have to weaken Melf's southern expedition in
order to make up the numbers for the main operations here."
He strode to the fire and, leaning his fists on the stone mantel,
he stared at the burning logs below.

"The enemy will move now, while our ally is temporarily
incapacitated. Formio, another dispatch to Aras at Gaderion.
He should expect a major assault very soon. And get the
courier to repeat the message to Heyd on the road north.
Henceforth he will move by forced marches.

"As for Torunn itself, I want the field army here put on
notice to move at once. We have wasted enough time. I will
lead them out within the week."

Formio's scratching quill went silent at that. "The snows
are still lying deep in the foothills," he said.

"It can't be helped. In my absence you will remain here,
as regent."

"Corfe, I—"

"You will obey orders." The King turned from the fire and
smiled at Formio to soften his words. "You are the only
person I would trust with it."

The Fimbrian subsided. From the tip of his quill the ink
dripped to blot a black circle on the pale parchment. Corfe
turned to Golophin.

"It would ease my mind were you to remain here with
him."

"I cannot do that, sire."

Corfe frowned, then turned away. "I understand. It is not
your responsibility."

"You misunderstand me, sire. I am going with you."

"What? Why in the world—?"

"I promised a dying woman, my lord, that I would remain
by your side in this coming trial." Golophin smiled. "Perhaps
I have just got into the habit of serving kings. In any case,
I go with you on campaign—if you'll have me."

Corfe bowed, and some life came back into his eyes. "I

would be honoured, master mage." As he straightened he turned to Ensign Baraz, who had not moved.

"I would very much like to have you accompany me also, Ensign."

The young man stepped forward, then came stiffly to attention once again. "Yes, sir." His eyes shone.

"There is one more thing." Here Corfe paused, and as they watched him they saw something flicker in his eyes, some instantly hidden agony.

"Mirren must go to Aurungabar at once, to be married."

Formio nodded, but Baraz looked utterly wretched. It was Golophin who spoke up. "Could that not wait a while?" he asked gently. "I have barely begun her tuition."

"No. Were we to delay, it would be seen as uncertainty about Nasir. No. They sent us Aria, we must send them Mirren. When she marries Nasir the whole world will see that the alliance is as strong as ever despite the death of Aurungzeb, the turning back of the Merduk reinforcements."

"It is the clearest signal we can send," Formio agreed.

And it was only right, Corfe thought, for himself to suffer something of what Heria suffered. There was an ironic symmetry about it all, as though this were laid on for the amusement of some scheming god. So be it. He would shoulder this grief along with the others.

"Ensign Baraz," he said, "fetch me the palace steward, if you please. Formio, get those notes off to the scribes and then rouse out the senior staff. We will all meet here in one hour. Felorin, secure the door."

When only he and Golophin remained in the hall's vast emptiness, Corfe leant his forehead against the hot stone of the mantel.

"Golophin, how did she die?"

The old mage was startled. He seemed to take a moment to comprehend the question. "The Merduk Queen? A knife, Shahr Baraz told me. There were maids close by, but they heard nothing. So he says."

Corfe's tears fell invisibly into the flames below, to vanish with not so much as a hiss to note their passing.

"Sire—Corfe—is there something else the matter?"

"This is my wedding night," the King said mechanically. "I have a new wife waiting for me."

Golophin set a hand on his arm. "Perhaps you should return to her for a little while, before she hears the news from someone else."

Dear God, he had almost forgotten. He raised his head with a kind of dulled wonder. "You are right. She should hear it from me. But I must talk to Cullen first."

"Here then. Have a swallow of this." The wizard was offering him a small steel flask. He took it automatically and tipped it to his mouth. Fimbrian brandy. His eyes smarted and ran as he filled his mouth with it and swallowed it down.

"I always keep a mote of something warming about me," Golophin said, drinking in his turn. "Nothing else seems to keep out the cold these days."

Corfe looked at him. The mage was regarding him with a kindly surmise, as though inviting him to speak. For a moment it was all there, crowding on his tongue, and it would have been a blessed relief to let it gush forth, to lean on this old man as other kings had before him. But he bit back the words and swallowed them. It was enough that Albrec alone knew. He could take no sympathy tonight. It would break him. And others would need sympathy ere the night was done.

Footsteps the length of the hall, and Baraz was returning with the grizzled old palace steward. Corfe drew himself up.

"Cullen, you must have the Princess Mirren woken at once. She is to pack for a long journey. Have the stables harness up a dozen light wagons, enough for a suitable entourage. Ensign Baraz, you will, with my authority, pick out a tercio of cuirassiers as escort."

"Where shall I tell the Princess she is going, sire?" Cullen asked, somewhat bewildered.

"She is going to Aurungabar to be married. I will see her before she goes, but she must be ready to leave by daybreak. That is all."

The steward stood irresolute for a second, his mouth opening and closing. Then he bowed and left hurriedly, drawing his night robes closer about him as if the King exuded some baleful chill. Baraz followed him unhappily.

A blessed quiet for a few minutes. Corfe felt an overwhelming urge to go down to the stables, saddle up a horse, and take off alone for the mountains. To run away from this world and its decisions, its complications, its pain. He sighed and drew himself up. His bad leg was aching.

"You had best stay here," he said to Golophin. "I will be back soon." Then he set off to tell his new wife that she was an orphan.

THE troop transports took up four miles of river-frontage. There were over a hundred of the wide-beamed, shallow-draught vessels, each capable of carrying five tercios within its cavernous hold. They had been taking on their cargoes for two days now, and still the wharves of Torunn's waterfront were thronged with men and horses and mules and mountains of provisions and equipment. A dozen horses had been lost, and several tons of supplies, but the worst of the embarkation was over now and the transports would unmoor with the ebb of the evening tide in the estuary, and would begin their slow but sure battle upstream against the current of the Torrin river.

"The day has come at last,"
Formio said with forced lightness.

"Yes. At one time I thought it never would."

Corfe tugged at the hem of his armoured gauntlets. "I'm leaving you three thousand of the regulars," he told Formio. "Along with the conscripts, that will give you a sizeable garrison. With Aras and Heyd at Gaderion, and Melf and Berza in the south, they should not even have to see battle."

"We will miss those Merduk reinforcements ere we're done," Formio said gravely.

"Yes. They would have eased my mind too. But there's no use crying after them now. Formio, I have been over all the paperwork with Albrec. As soon as I step aboard the transports you become regent, and will remain so until I return. I've detached a few hundred of your Orphans to take over the training from the Bodyguard. The rest are already boarded."

"You're taking the cream of the army," Formio said.

"I know. They have a hard road ahead of them, and there's no place for conscripts upon it."

"And the wizard goes too."

Corfe smiled. "He may be useful. And I feel he is a good man."

"I do not trust him, Corfe. He is too close to the enemy. He knows too much about them, and that knowledge he has never explained."

"It's his business to know such things, Formio. I for one shall be glad of his counsel. And besides, we shall face wizardry in battle before we're done. It's as well to be able to reply in kind."

"I would I were going with you," Formio said in a low voice.

"So would I, my friend. It has seemed to me that the more rank one acquires in this world, the less one is able to do as one prefers."

Formio gripped Corfe by the arm. "Do not go." His normally closed face was bright with urgency. "Let me take them out, Corfe. Stay you here."

"I cannot. It's not in me, Formio. You know that."

"Then be careful, my friend. You and I have seen many battlefields, but something in my heart tells me that this one you are setting out for shall be the worst."

"What are you now, a seer?"

Formio smiled, though there was little humour in his face. "Perhaps."

"Look for us in the early summer. If all goes well we shall march back by way of the Torrin Gap."

The two men stood looking at one another for a long moment. They had no need to say more. Finally they embraced like brothers. Formio moved back then and bowed deep.

"Farewell, my King. May God watch over you."

HALF the city came down to the waterfront to see them off, waving and cheering as ship after ship of the transport fleet pulled away from the wharves and nosed out into the middle of the estuary. The fat-bellied vessels set their courses to catch the south-east wind that was blowing in off the Kardian, and in line astern they began the long journey upriver.

Torunna's sole Princess had already left for Aurungabar and her wedding, but the kingdom's new Queen was there in the midst of a cloud of ladies-in-waiting, courtiers and bodyguards. She raised a hand to Corfe, her face white and unsmiling, the eyes red-rimmed within it. He saluted in return, then turned his gaze from the cheering crowds and stared westwards to where the Cimbric Mountains loomed bright in the sunlight, their flanks still deep in snow, clouds streaming from their summits. Somewhere up in those terrible heights the secret pass existed which led all the way down to the Sea of Tor, and that was the path this great army he commanded must take to victory. He felt no trepidation, no apprehension at the thought of that mountain passage or the battles that would follow. His mind was clear at last.

PART THREE

NIGHTFALL

"Men worshipped the dragon, for he had given his authority to the beast, and they worshipped the beast, saying, 'Who is like the beast, and who can fight against it?'"

Revelation ch:13 v. 4

SIXTEEN

THE sun was a long time clearing the Thurian Mountains in the mornings, and down in the Torrin Gap it remained drear and chill long after the surrounding peaks were bright and glowing with the dawn. The sentries paced the walls of Gaderion and cursed and blew into their hands whilst before them the narrow valley between the mountains opened out grey and shadowed, livid with frost, and out in the gloom the campfires of the enemy gleamed in their tens of thousands.

General Aras walked the circuit of the walls with a cluster of aides and couriers, greeting the sentries in a low voice, halting every now and then to look out at the flickering constellations burning below. This he did every morning, and every morning the same view met his eyes.

The defenders of Ormann Dyke must have experienced something like this, back in the old days. The knowledge that there was nothing more to do than to wait for the enemy to move. The nerve-taut tension of that wait. The Himerian general, whoever he was, knew how to bide his time.

Finally the sun reared its head up over the white-frozen Thurians, and a blaze of red-yellow light swept down the flanks of Candorwir in the western arm of the valley. It lit up the blank, pocked cliff face that was the Eyrie, travelled along the length of the curtain wall and kindled the stone of the redoubt, the sharp angles of the fortifications thrown into perfect, vivid relief, and finally it halted at the foot of the donjon walls, leaving that fortress in shadow. Only the tall head of the Spike was lofty enough to catch the sun as it streamed over the white peaks behind it. In the donjon itself Aras heard the iron triangles of the watch clanging, summoning the night watch to breakfast, and sending the day watch out to their posts. Another day had begun at Gaderion.

Aras turned away. His own breakfast would be waiting for him in the donjon. Salt pork and army bread and perhaps an Vapple, washed down with small beer—the same meal his men ate. Corfe had taught him that, long ago. He might eat it off a silver plate, but that was the only indulgence Gaderion's commanding officer would allow himself.

"The last of the wains go south this morning, do they not?" he asked.

His quartermaster, Rusilan of Gebrar, nodded. "Those are the last. When they have gone, it will be nothing but the garrison left, and several thousand fewer mouths to feed, though it's hard on the family men."

"It'll be easier on their minds to know their wives and children are safe in the south, once the real fighting starts," Aras retorted.

"The real fighting," another of the group mused, a square-faced man who wore an old Fimbrian tunic under his half-armour. "We've lost over a thousand men in the last fortnight, and are now penned in here like an old boar in the brush, awaiting the spears of the hunters. Real fighting."

"A cornered boar is a dangerous thing, Colonel Sarius. Let him move within range of our guns and he will find that out."

"Of course, sir. I only wonder why he hesitates. Intelligence suggests that the Finnmarkans and Tarberans are all up now. He has his entire army arrayed and ready, and has had them so for at least four days. His supply lines must be a quartermaster's nightmare."

"They're convoying thousands of tons of rations across the Sea of Tor in fishing boats," Rusilan said. "At Fonterios they have constructed a fair-sized port to accommodate them all now that the ice is almost gone. They can afford to wait for the summer if they choose; the Himerians can call on the tribute of a dozen different countries."

The retort of an artillery piece silenced Rusilan, and the group of officers went stock-still. High up on the side of the Spike, the smoke of the gun was hanging heavy as wool in the air, and before it had drifted a yard from the muzzle of the culverin that had belched it, the alarm triangles were ringing.

Aras and his party ran along the curtain wall to the donjon proper, against a tide of soldiers coming the other way. When they had passed through the small postern that linked the wall with the eastern fortifications they climbed up to the catwalks there and peered out of an embrasure whilst all around them the gun crews were swarming about their weapons.

"Our adversary is on the move, it seems," Colonel Sarius, the keen-eyed Fimbrian, remarked. "I see infantry formations, but nothing else as yet."

"What strength?" Aras asked him.

"Hard to gauge; there are still hordes of them forming up in front of their camps. Two or three grand tercios at the least. A mile of frontage—but that's only the front ranks. I do believe it's a general assault." The Fimbrian's hard eyes sparkled as though some great treat were in store for him.

"Horse teams coming up from the rear—yes, he's bringing forward his guns. That's what it is. He's decided to begin siting his batteries. And in broad daylight! What can he be thinking?"

"Ensign Duwar," Aras barked. "Run up to the signallers. Have them hoist 'General Engagement, Fire at Will'."

"Aye, sir!" The young officer took off at a sprint for the signal station on top of the Spike.

"Gentlemen," Aras said to the more senior officers remaining, "to your posts. You all know what to do. Rusilan and Sarius, remain with me. We shall repair to the upper battlements, I think, and get ourselves a better view. It's apt to grow somewhat busy down here once the action starts."

There was a strange gaiety in the air, Aras realised. Even the common soldiers of the gun crews were grinning and chattering as they loaded their pieces, and their officers seemed afire with anticipation. For days, weeks even, they had been harried and beaten back by the enemy until they had no option but to retreat behind the stout walls of Gaderion. Now that those walls were about to be assaulted, they knew they would be able to wreak a bloody revenge.

On the topmost battlement of the donjon, with the blank stone of the Spike's towering menace at their back, Aras and his remaining colleagues halted, breathless from having run up several flights of stairs. They could see the entire valley spread out below them, the sharp-angled shape of the redoubt, the snaking curtain wall, the sun glinting on the iron barrels of the Eyrie's guns as they were run out of the rock of the very mountain opposite. And all along that intricate and formidable series of defences, thousands of men dressed in Torunnan sable were labouring in the casemates or loading their arquebuses or running here and there in long lines bearing powder and shot and wads for the batteries.

"Here they come," Sarius said dryly.

"I wish I had your eyes, Colonel," Aras told him. "What are they?"

"Rabble from Almark. He won't waste good troops in the first wave. He's got to know we have that entire valley ranged. Look at their dressing! They've never so much as smelled a drill square, this lot."

A mile and a half away Aras could now see that the crowd of men which darkened the face of the land was moving in a broad line. Behind that line there came another, this one more ordered. And behind that, the beetling mass of scores of horse teams hauling guns and limbers and caissons.

The first wave came on very swiftly, keeping no formation beyond that of a broad, ragged line. They were clad in Almarkan blue, some carrying pikes and swords, others jogging along with arquebuses resting on their shoulders. On the valley floor before them, a scattered line of thin saplings had been planted years before with a half-furlong between each tree. This marked the extreme range of the Torunnan guns. Aras held his breath as the host approached them. His men had been trained to hold their fire until the enemy was well beyond the line of trees.

All along the walls of Gaderion's fortresses the crowded activity gave way to an intent stillness. The smell of slowmatch drifted about the valley. "The perfume of war," old soldiers called it.

A puff of smoke from one of the redoubt casemates, followed a second later by the dull boom of the explosion. Right in the middle of the enemy formation a narrow geyser of earth went up, flinging aside the ragged remains of men, tearing a momentary hole in the carpet of tiny figures.

A second later every gun in the entire valley opened up. The air shook, and Aras felt the massive stone of the battlements trembling under the soles of his boots. The noise of that opening salvo was experienced by the entire body rather than just heard by the ears. Waves of hot air and smoke came billowing up from the embrasures like a wind passing the gates of hell.

And hell came to earth instants later for the men of the Himerian vanguard. The valley floor seemed to erupt in bursting fountains of stone and dirt. It reminded Aras of the effect a heavy rainstorm has on bare soil. The lead enemy formations simply disappeared in that tempest of explosions. The Torunnan gunners were using hollow shells packed with powder for the most part. When these detonated they sent wicked showers of red-hot metal spraying in a deadly hail, tearing men apart, maiming them, tossing them through the air. In the lower embrasures, however, the batteries were loaded with solid shot, and these skimmed along at breast height, cutting great swathes of bloody slaughter through the close-packed enemy, each shot felling a dozen or a score of men and sending their sundered fragments flying among their fellows. Aras found he was beating his fist on the stone of the merlon as he watched, and his face had frozen open in a savage grinning rictus. There were perhaps fifteen thousand men in that first wave, and they were being torn to pieces while still a mile from Gaderion's mighty walls. From those walls he could hear a hoarse roaring noise. The gunners were cheering, or baying rather, even as they reloaded and ran out the culverins again. A continuous bellowing thunder rang out, magnified and echoed by the encircling mountains until it was almost unbearable and could hardly be deciphered from the hammering beat of the blood in Aras's own heart. The smoke of the bombardment reared up to blot out the morning sunlight and cast a shadow on the heights of the Cimbrics in the west. It seemed impossible that such a noise and such a shadow could be made by the agency of men.

"They're coming on!" Colonel Sarius shouted in disbelief.

Out of the broken, smoking ground the enemy were struggling onwards, leaving behind them the shattered corpses of hundreds of their comrades; and now the massed roar of their voices could be heard amid the thunder of the guns.

"They're going to make it to the walls," Aras said, incredulous. What could make men move forward under that murderous fire?

The entire valley floor seemed covered with the figures of running men, and among them the shells rained down unceasingly. It could be seen now that many of them carried spades and baulks of wood and others had the wicker cages of empty gabions strapped to their backs. In their midst armoured Inceptines urged them on from the backs of tall horses, waving their maces and shouting furiously.

Back up the valley, a second assault wave started out. This one was heavily armoured, disciplined, and it moved with forbidding alacrity. Tall men in long mail coats with steel cuirasses. They bore two-handed swords or battleaxes, and all had matchlock holsters slung at their backs. Gallowglasses of Finnmark, the shock infantry of the Second Empire.

The men of the first wave had now halted well short of arquebus range, and there they went to ground as if by prior order. The Almarkan soldiers began digging frantically amid the shellbursts, throwing the frozen soil up over their shoulders and shoring up the sides of their scrapes with slats of wood and hastily filled gabions. Hundreds more died, but the shells that killed them broke up the ground and aided them in their digging. As the holes grew deeper, the Torunnan artillery had less effect. The culverins of Gaderion fired on a flat trajectory, so once the enemy was below ground level it was almost impossible to depress the guns low enough to bear.

Aras fumbled in his pouch for pencil and parchment. Leaning on the merlon, he hastily scratched out and signed a note, then turned to one of the couriers who stood waiting, as they had throughout the assault. "Take this along the walls and show it to all the battery commanders. They are to switch fire—do you understand me? They are to switch fire to the second wave. Go quickly."

The young man sped off with the note in one fist and his sword scabbard held high in the other.

"I see it now," Sarius was saying. "The enemy is cleverer than we thought. He's sacrificing the first wave to gain a secure foothold for the second. But it still won't do him any good—they'll just sit there and get plastered by our guns."

"Perhaps not," Aras said. "Look up the valley, beyond the gallowglasses."

Sarius whistled soundlessly. "Horse artillery, going full tilt. He can't mean to bring them all the way up to the front! It's madness."

"I believe he does. Whoever the enemy general is, he is an original thinker. And a gambler too."

As the courier's message went along the walls the guns of Gaderion shifted their aim, and began to seek out the second enemy wave, which was making steady and relatively unhindered progress up the valley. As soon as the first shells began to land in the midst of the gallowglasses their orderly formation scrambled and began to open out. They increased speed from a slow jog to an out-and-out sprint. Aras could see many of them falling, tripped by the broken ground and the weight of their armour. There were perhaps eight thousand of them, and they had half a mile to run before they gained the shelter of the trenches their Almarkan comrades were so frantically digging.

"Sarius," Aras said. "Go down to the redoubt. We will attempt a sortie. Take half the heavy cavalry, no more, and hit the Finnmarkans. They'll be winded by the time they reach you."

"Sir!" Sarius took off, running like a boy.

Aras turned to another of his young aides. "Run along the walls. All battery commanders. We are about to make a sortie. Be prepared to hold fire as soon as our cavalry leaves the gates."

Minutes passed, while Aras stood chafing and the gallowglasses struggled closer to the line of crude trenches. They were taking casualties, but not so many as the first wave had, a tribute to their superior armour and more open ranks. The roar of the battle was a dull thumping in the ear now, for every man in the valley was partially deafened.

The great gates of the redoubt swung open and files of Torunnan cavalry began to ride out and form up beyond the covering redan. The Himerian troops in the southern half of the valley seemed to pause, and then redouble their efforts, though Aras saw many throw aside their spades to pick up arquebuses.

Sarius formed up his men on sloping ground before the redoubt. Four lines of horsemen some half a mile long. As soon as they were in position Aras saw Sarius himself together with a trio of aides and a banner-bearer place themselves square in the front rank. Then there was the flash of a sword blade, the bright gleam of a bugle-call in the smoke-ridden murk, and the first line of four hundred horsemen began to move. When it had gone a few horse lengths the second started out, and then the third, and the fourth. Sixteen hundred heavy cavalry in sable armour with matchlock pistols held cocked and ready at their shoulders.

In the makeshift trenches three furlongs to their front the Almarkans dropped their spades and reached for weapons instead. The guns of the redoubt and the curtain wall had ceased fire, masked by the cavalry, but those up in the Eyrie and the donjon were still pouring a storm of shot and shell into the ranks of the gallowglass infantry who were now almost at their goal. Fully five hundred of them had fallen but the remainder knew their only hope of survival was to gain the shelter of the line of trenches. If they had to retreat the way they had come they would be destroyed.

Aras watched the Torunnan cavalry charge forward. The instant before impact there was a sudden eruption of smoke all along their line as they fired their matchlocks at point-blank range. They were answered by the arquebuses of the Almarkans, and horses began to stumble and fall, men toppling from their saddles.

Into the trenches. Some riders leapt their steeds across the line of earthworks, some halted at the lip, and not a few tumbled cartwheeling into them. The second line reined in and fired their matchlocks where they could. Sarius's banner was waving, but Aras could not make him out in that terrible maelstrom of men and horses and jetting smoke. He had been busy though: the third and fourth ranks of cavalry broke off and wheeled to the flanks before charging home in their turn.

All across the floor of the valley the fighting was savage and hand-to-hand. The Almarkans were no match for the peerless heavy cavalry of Torunna, but what they lacked in training and morale they made up for in numbers. Sarius was outmatched nine to one, and the gallowglasses were forging along that last quarter-mile relentlessly. Once they joined battle the cavalry would be swamped.

Men in blue livery running in one and twos, then by squads and companies out of the killing floor of the trenches. The Almarkans were beginning to break. Too late.

The gallowglasses joined the line, swinging their great swords or two-handed axes. Aras saw a destrier's head cut clean from its neck by a swing from one of the huge blades. Sarius's banner was still waving, pulling out of the scrum. Riderless horses were screaming and galloping everywhere. Faint and far-off in the huge tumult of battle there sounded the silver notes of a bugle. Sarius was sounding the retreat.

The cavalry broke off, firing their second matchlock over the rumps of their steeds as they went. There was little attempt to dress the ranks; the gallowglasses pressed them too closely for that. A formless mob of mounted men streamed away from the mounded dead of the earthworks and began a retreat up the slope to the redan where two hundred arquebusiers of the garrison were waiting to cover their return. Sarius's banner, scarlet and gold, was nowhere to be seen.

The cavalry thundered up the incline, many two to a horse. Other unhorsed troopers hung on to tails or stirrups and were dragged along. The great guns of Gaderion began to thunder out again, the gunners maddened by the slaughter of their comrades in the cavalry. The Himerian earthworks became a shot-torn hell of flying earth and bodies. The gallowglasses and Almarkans broke off the pursuit and cowered in their trenches as the sky turned black above them and the very earth screamed below their feet. But the rage of the Torunnans was impotent. The Almarkans had held on just long enough for the trenches to be reinforced in strength, and the enemy would now be impossible to dislodge. Perhaps fifteen thousand men were now dug in within a half-mile of Gaderion's walls.

Aras ran down the great stairs to the curtain wall, and became enmeshed in the fog of battle smoke. Grimy, sootstained men were still working the guns maniacally and the air in the casemates seemed to scorch his lungs. Finally he made it out to the courtyard in the centre of the redoubt where the cavalry were still streaming in through the tall double gates.

"Where is Sarius?" he demanded of a bloody-browed officer, only to be met with a mad vacancy. The man's mind was still fighting out in the trenches.

"Where is Sarius?" he asked another, but was met with

blankness again. At last he caught sight of Sarius's banner-bearer being carried away and halted the litter-bearers.

"Where is your colonel?"

The man opened his eyes. He had lost his arm at the elbow and the stump spat and dribbled blood like a tap.

"Dead on the field," he croaked.

Aras let the litter-bearers carry him away. The courtyard was a milling crowd of bloody men and lacerated horses. Beyond them, he heard even over the roar of the artillery the gates of Gaderion boom shut as the last of the rearguard came in. He wiped his face, and began to make his way back up to the fuming storm of the battlements.

CARTIGELLA, like many of the Ramusian capitals, had started life as a port. The chief city of the tribal King Astar, it had fallen to the newly combined Fimbrian tribes over eight hundred years before, and Astarac, as the region about it became known, had become the first conquest of what would one day be the Fimbrian Empire. The city rebelled against its northern conquerors within a hundred and fifty years of its fall, but was besieged and crushed by the great Elector Cariabus Narb, who had also founded Charibon. Those rebels who survived the sack scattered southwards for the most part, into the jungles of Macassar, and their descendants became the Corsairs. Some, however, kept together and under a great sea-captain named Gabor they sailed through the Malacar Islands, seeking some place they might live in peace, untroubled by fear of Fimbrian reprisals. They settled a large island to the south-west of Macassar, and that place became Gabrion.

It would be almost four hundred years before Astarac finally threw off the decaying Fimbrian yoke, and in those centuries the Fimbrians made of ruined Cartigella a great city. But they deliberately refused to fortify it, remembering the agonies of the year-long siege it had taken to reduce the place. So Cartigella's walls were later constructs of the Astaran monarchy—for Astar's bloodline had somehow survived the long years of vassalage—and they were perhaps not so high or formidable as they might have been, had they been constructed by the Imperial Engineers.

And now Cartigella was besieged again.

The Himerian army had started out from Vol Ephrir at midwinter, and by the time the first meltwaters were beginning to swell the rivers tumbling out of the Malvennors, they were on the borders of East Astarac, the hotly contested Duchy which King Forno had wrested from the Perigrainians scarcely sixty years before. So well had they hidden their movements with dweomer-kindled snowstorms, and so unexpected was this midwinter march, that King Mark had left with the Fleet for his rendezvous with the rest of the allied Navy off Abrusio unaware that his kingdom was about to be invaded.

The Astaran army, left under the command of Mark's son Cristian, was caught completely by surprise. The Himerians advanced deep into East Astarac before they were challenged, and in a confused battle which took place in a blizzard in the Malvennor foothills they were worsted, and thrown into retreat. Their retreat became a rout as they were harried night and day by Perigrainian cavalry and packs of huge wolves. Most fell back in disorder upon the city of Garmidalan, and there prepared to fight to the last. But the Himerians merely surrounded the city and began casually to starve it into submission.

The main body of the Empire's forces had not joined in the pursuit. Instead, they struck off westwards for the Malvennor passes, which were lightly guarded by an Astaran rearguard. As the first spring meltwaters began to swell the mountain rivers, they marched down from the heights largely unmolested, and carved a bloody swathe across King Mark's kingdom, driving the Astaran troops and their inexperienced Crown Prince before them, until finally they came to a halt before the walls of Cartigella, the capital.

Outnumbered many times over by an army which employed weather-working and legions of beasts, Prince Cristian nonetheless held out some hope. The sea lanes had not yet been closed, and thus Cartigella might yet be saved by reinforcements from her ancient ally Gabrion, or perhaps even the Sea-Merduks. He sent out swift dispatch-runners to every free kingdom of the west, and strengthened his walls, and waited, whilst the Himerians brought up siege artillery and began to bombard the city from the surrounding hills.

On the day of Sultan Aurungzeb's death, the first breach was made in Cartigella's defences, and fighting began to rage in the wall districts of the city. The Astarans, soldiers and civilians alike, fought with savage heroism but were pushed back from the outer fortifications by Inceptine warrior-monks leading companies of werewolves. Thousands died, and Cristian withdrew to the citadel of Cartigella itself. There the Himerian advance was halted, foiled by the impregnable fortress on its high crag which dominated the lower city. From there the Astaran gunners poured a torrent of artillery fire into the ranks of the Himerian beasts that even werewolves could not withstand. The Himerians drew back, and the garrison of the citadel under their young Prince dared to believe that they might hold out.

But the next morning a vast fleet appeared in the bay below, and from the holds of its vessels there issued a foul swarm of flying creatures. These descended upon the citadel like a cloud of locusts, and overwhelmed the defenders. Cristian was slain and his bodyguard died in ranks around him. Cartigella was sacked with a brutality which surpassed even the legendary excesses of the Fimbrians, and the smoke of its burning climbed up in a black pillar which could be seen for many miles in the clear spring air.

Within three days, Astarac had capitulated, and was incorporated into the Second Empire.

SEVENTEEN

> " *'And now is Hell come to earth,*
> *And in the ashes of its burning will totter*
> *All the schemes of greedy men.*
> *The Beast, in coming, will*
> *Tread the cinders of their dreams'* "

"THUS spake Honorius the Mad, four and a half centuries ago, and he was never wrong in his predictions—though he was cursed in that they were fated to be dismissed in his lifetime as the ravings of an insane anchorite. My friends, we are tools of history, instruments in the hands of God. What we have done, and what we will do in the time to come is but a fulfilment of His vision for the good of the world. So set your minds at rest. Out of blood and fire and smoke shall dawn a new sunrise, and a second beginning for the scattered peoples of the earth."

Aruan did not seem to raise his voice, but every man in the vast host which stood listening heard his words, and as they did, something about their hearts kindled and uplifted them, and each one straightened his shoulders as if the Vicar-General were speaking to him alone.

On the waterfronts they listened, and in the rigging of the ships, and all through the streets of ancient Kemminovol, capital of Candelaria. As he spoke, the night drew back from the margins of the horizon and the sun sprang up above the grey silhouette of the promontory to the east, touching the mastheads of the tallest ships with gold.

"So go now about your work, and know that it is the work of God you do. His blessing is upon you this day."

Aruan raised a hand in benediction, and the listening crowds bent their heads as one. Then he left the rough dais which had been cobbled together out of old fish boxes, and the men who had been listening sprang into a swarm of activity, and the ships moored there were thick with their sweating and hauling companies.

Bardolin supported the arch-mage as he climbed down from his wooden podium. Aruan was white-faced and perspiring. "I'll not do that again for a while. I believe I misjudged the effort required. What a task it is, to lift men's hearts!"

"There were many thousands listening to you—you are not telling me you touched every one," Bardolin said gruffly.

"Oh yes. I can bend the will of armies, but it takes an effort. I must sit down, Bardolin. See me to the carriage, will you?"

They climbed inside the closed box of the four-wheeler and in its padded leather confines Aruan threw his head back and closed his eyes. "Better, much better.

"With Almarkans and Perigrainians it is easier. They have traditional antagonisms with Astarans and Torunnans—a matter of history, you understand. But the Candelarians have been a nation of merchants for centuries, opening their doors to whatever conqueror comes along and then going on with business as usual. I had to fire them up a little, you might say."

"They will be the first wave then?"

"Yes. The main host of the Perigrainians will follow up

the seaborne assault with an advance on Rone, crossing the Candelan river up in the southern foothills. Southern Torunna is lightly defended; it will fall quickly. Our intelligence reports that the Torunnan King is finally on the move with his main army. He is going north by ship, to the gap. All that is left in the capital are a scattering of regulars and a mob of conscripts. By the time the great Corfe realises what we're at, we'll be sitting in Torunn and he will be caught between two fires."

"And Gaderion? How hard do you want the Torunnans pressed there?"

"Very hard, Bardolin. Corfe must be persuaded that his presence at the gap is essential to prevent its fall, so the assault must be pressed home with the utmost ferocity. If it falls, so much the better. But it does not have to fall; its role is to suck in the main Torunnan armies and keep them occupied."

Bardolin nodded grimly. "It shall be so."

"What of Golophin? Have you had any more words with him?"

"He has disappeared. He has cloaked his mind and cut himself off. He may not even be in Torunna any longer."

"Our friend Golophin is running out of time," Aruan said tartly, mopping his bald pate. "Track him down, Bardolin."

"I will. You may count on it."

"Good. I must rest now. I will need all my strength in the days to come. Four of the Five Kingdoms are ours now, Bardolin, but the fifth, that will prove the hardest. When it falls we will be close to matching the Fimbrian Empire of old."

"And the Fimbrians, what of them?" Bardolin asked. "We've heard no word since their embassy left Charibon, weeks ago now."

"They're waiting to see how Torunna fares. Oh, I have plans for Fimbria also, make no mistake. The Electors have stood aloof too long; they think their homeland is inviolable. I may have to prove them wrong." Aruan smiled, his eyes gazing upon a vision of a single authority that spanned the continent. Firm, but benign, harsh at times, but always fair.

"You shall be Presbyter of Torunna, once it falls," he told Bardolin. Then his eyes narrowed. He pursed his full lips. "As for master Golophin, I shall give him one last chance. Find him, speak with him. Tell him that if he comes over to us with a full heart and a clear conscience, he shall have Hebrion to govern in my name. I cannot say fairer than that."

Bardolin's eyes shone. "That will do it; I'm sure of it. It will be enough to tip the scales in our favour."

"Yes. We will have to disappoint Murad, of course, but I am sure we will find something else for him to do, once he has slain the Hebrian Queen and her mariner. Good! Things are progressing, my friend. Orkh is already installing himself in Astarac and our armies are poised for the final campaign. You must go back to Gaderion and begin hammering on those walls again." He gripped Bardolin by the hand. "My Mage-General. Get me Golophin's loyalty, and the three of us will together set this unhappy world to rights."

THE vast foam-flecked and moonlit expanse of the Levangore, stirred into a stiff swell by an inconstant wind blustering out of the south-south-east. Above it a sky empty of cloud, the stars brilliant pinpoints in that black vault, the moon as bright as a silver lantern.

Richard Hawkwood fixed his eye on the North Star and stared through the two tiny sights on his quadrant. The plumb line of the instrument hung free and he swayed easily with the ship, compensating without conscious effort for the pitch and roll. When he was satisfied, he caught the plumb line and read off the numbers on the scale. The ship was six degrees south of Abrusio's latitude. Those six degrees of latitude corresponded to over a hundred leagues. By his dead-reckoning, they had made some two hundred leagues of easting in the past eleven days. They were south of Candelaria, not far off the latitude of Garmidalan, and two thirds of their journey was behind them.

Hawkwood checked the pegs of the traverse board. They were headed north-north-east, and the wind was on the star-

board quarter. He had sent up the square yards on fore and
main at last, retaining the lateen only on the mizzen, and the
Seahare rode the swells easily under courses and topsails,
making perhaps five knots. Sprightly though her progress
might be, an experienced observer would note that much of
the rigging had been knotted and spliced several times over,
and her foremast had been fished with beams of oak and line
after line of woolding to hold together the crack which ran
through it from top to bottom.

They had outpaced the storm, and had run through the
Malacar Straits at a fearsome clip, Hawkwood on deck day
and night, the leadsman in the forechains continually calling
out the depth. The wind had backed round after that, and had
slowly become a natural thing once more, the seasonal airs
of the Hebrian Sea replacing the Dweomer-birthed gale. But
that had not ended the hard labour on board. The Seahare
had taken a severe battering in her race with the squall and
while she could neither pause in her voyage nor put in to
shore, her crew were able to start the work of restoring her
to full seaworthiness.

The repairs had taken the better part of a week, and even
now the ship was making more water than Hawkwood liked,
and the pumps had to be manned for half a glass in every
watch. But they were still afloat, and they seemed to have
outrun their pursuers with a mixture of luck, good seamanship, and the valour of a swift-sailing ship. The ship's company were a crowd of whey-faced ghosts who dropped off
to sleep as soon as they were off their feet, but they were
alive. The worst was over.

Hawkwood put the traverse board away in the binnacle-
housing, noted the ship's position in the crowded chart that
was his mind, and yawned mightily. His belt hung slack
about his waist; he would have to make another hole in it
soon. But at least he had hair on his head once more, a salt-
and-pepper crop which stood up like the bristles of a brush
on his scalp.

Ordio, one of the more capable master's mates, had the
watch. He was scanning the brilliant night sky with studied

nonchalance, standing by the larboard rail. They were two glasses into the morning watch, and it would be dawn in another hour. When they had finally made landfall, Hawkwood promised himself, he would sleep the clock around. He had not had more than an hour or two's uninterrupted rest in weeks.

"Call me if the wind changes," he told Ordio automatically, and went below, staggering a little with the everpresent tiredness. The blankets in his swinging cot were damp and smelled of mould, but he could not have cared less. He drew off his sodden clothes and crawled under them gratefully and was asleep in moments.

He woke some time later, instantly alert. The sun had come up by now despite the darkness in the cabin, and the *Seahare* was still on her course, though by the tone of the water running past the hull she had picked up a knot or so. But it was not that which had woken him. There was someone else in the cabin.

He sat up, throwing the blankets aside in the closed darkness, but two hands on his shoulders stopped him from getting to his feet. He flinched as a pair of cold lips were placed on his own, and then the warm tongue came questing over his teeth. His hands came up to cup the face of the one who kissed him, and he felt under his fingers the ridged scar tissue on the otherwise smooth cheek.

"Isolla."

But she said no word, only pushed him back down into the cot. There were rustlings and the click of buttons, and she climbed in beside him, shivering at the touch of the fetid blankets on her skin. Her hair was down and covered both their faces with its feather-touch as they sought each other in the darkness. The cot swung and the ropes which supported it creaked and groaned in time with their own smothered sounds. When they were done her skin was hot and moist under his hands and their bodies were glued together by sweat. He started to speak, but her hand covered his mouth and she kissed him into silence. She climbed off the cot and he heard her bare feet padding on the wood of the

deck as she dressed. He raised himself up on one elbow and
saw her slim silhouette in the cracks of light which slipped
under the cabin door.

"Why?" he asked.

She was tying up her hair, and paused, letting it tumble
once more about her shoulders. "Even queens need a little
comfort now and again."

"Would you still need it, if you were not a queen of a lost
kingdom?"

"If I were not a queen, Captain, I would not be here—nor
you either."

"If you were not a queen I would marry you, and you
would be happy."

She hesitated, and then said quietly, "I know." Then she
gathered her things and slipped out of the door as silently as
she must have arrived.

Two more days passed in the bright spring blue of the
sea, and the routine of the ship became a way of life for
all of them, ruled by bells, punctuated by unremarkable
meals. As the *Seahare* sailed steadily onwards it became their
entire world, self-contained and ordered. They had a fair
wind, a sky uncluttered save by a little high cloud, and no
sight of any other ship, though the lookouts were kept at the
masthead day and night. It seemed strange to Hawkwood.
The Levangore, especially the western Levangore, was
crossed by the busiest sea lanes in the world, and yet in all
their passage of it thus far they had sighted not a single sail.

The wind kept backing round until it was east-south-east,
and in order to preserve some of their speed, Hawkwood
altered course to north-north-east so it was on the beam. To
larboard they could see now the blue shapes of the Malvennor Mountains that formed the backbone of Astarac, Isolla's
birthplace. She spent hours standing at the leeward rail,
watching the land of her childhood drift past. The lookouts
kept their gaze fixed on the open sea, and thus it was she
who came to Hawkwood in the afternoon watch, and pointed
at the south-western horizon.

"What do you make of that, Captain?"

Hawkwood stared, and saw dark against the blue shadows of the mountains a sombre stain on the air, a high column rising blackly against the sky.

"Smoke," he said. "It's some great, far-off fire."

"It is Garmidalan," Isolla whispered. "I know it. They are burning the city."

All day she remained on deck staring over the larboard quarter at the distant smoke, and as the daylight faded it was possible for all to see the red glow on the western horizon which had nothing to do with sunset.

Bleyn appeared on deck at dusk, having stayed dutifully by his sea-sick mother all day, and joined Isolla at the rail. An unlikely friendship had grown up between the two, and when Hawkwood saw the both of them standing together at his ship's side with the swell of the sea rising and falling behind them he felt an almost physical ache in his heart, and knew not why.

"Sail ho!" the lookout called down from the masthead.

"Where away?"

"Fine off the port quarter, skipper. She's hull down and with not too much canvas abroad, but I do believe she's ship-rigged."

Hawkwood dashed up the starboard shrouds, then the futtock shrouds into the maintop. The lookout was on the cross-yards above him. He peered back along their wake, slightly phosphorescent in the gathering starlight, and caught the nick on the red and yellow glimmer of the horizon. He wiped his watering eyes but could make out nothing more. The strange ship, if ship it were, was on almost the same course as they, but it must have no more than reefed courses up or he'd have seen them pale against the sky. Not in a hurry then.

He did not like it all the same, and began bellowing orders from the maintop.

"All hands! All hands to make sail! Arhuz, send up top-gallants and main and mizzen staysails."

"Aye, sir. Rouse out, rouse out, you sluggards! Get up that rigging before I knot me a rope's end."

In minutes the rigging was full of men, and a crowd of them climbed past Hawkwood on the way to loose the top-gallant sail. As the extra canvas was sheeted home and the yards braced round he felt the ship give a quiver, and the dip of her bow became more pronounced. Her wake grew even brighter with turbulence and he could feel the masts creaking and straining. The *Seahare* picked up speed like a spurred thoroughbred. Hawkwood stared aft again.

There—the pale shapes of sails being unfurled. Despite their extra speed, the stranger was hull up now. She must be a swift sailer indeed, and have a large crew to cram on so much extra sail in so little time. Fore and aft sails on main and mizzen—so she was a barquentine then. God almighty, she was fast. Hawkwood felt a momentary chill settle in his stomach.

He looked down at the deck below. They were lighting the stern lanterns at the taffrail.

"Belay there! Douse those lights!"

The mood on board changed instantly. He saw pale faces looking up into the rigging at him, and then over the stern to where the strange ship was visible even from the quarter-deck she was coming up so fast.

Hawkwood swallowed, cursing the sudden dryness in his mouth. A row of lights appeared along the barquentine's sides. She was opening her gun-ports. He hung his head a moment and then called out hoarsely:

"Master-at-arms, beat to quarters. Prepare for battle."

He climbed slowly down from the maintop whilst the deck exploded into a crowded, frantic activity below him. The enemy had caught up with them once more.

EIGHTEEN

THE last of the wagons had been abandoned and now the men of the army were bent under the weight of their packs, while at the rear of their immense column a clanking, braying cavalcade of heavily burdened mules were cursed forward by their drovers. They had left behind the last paved road and were now forging upwards along a single stony mountain track whilst above them the Cimbrics reared up in peak on peak, and the snow blew in streaming banners from their summits.

They were ten days out of Torunn, and the first, easy stage of their journey was behind them. They had been three days on the river, and after the interminable disembarkation had been five days more marching across the quiet farmland of northern Torunna, cheered to the echo at every village and town and freely given all the food supplies they needed. A thousand mules and seven thousand horses had cropped the new spring grass of every pasture in their path down to the roots, and the Torunnan King had every evening summoned the local landowners about him and had compensated them in gold coin from his own hand.

But the kindly plains were behind them now, and so were the lower foothills. They were on the knees of the Cimbric Mountains, highest in the western world, and their sweating faces were set towards the snows and glaciers of the high places. And the battle which would be fought on their other side.

CORFE sat his horse on the brow of a tall, crag-faced hillock, and watched as his army streamed past. Beside him were Felorin, General Comillan of the Bodyguard, Ensign Baraz, and a sable-clad man on foot, Marshal Kyne, commander of the Orphans now that Formio was left behind in the capital.

The Cathedrallers were in the van, five thousand of them leading their warhorses by the bridle, most of them natives of these very hills. Next came ten thousand picked Torunnans armed with arquebuses and sabres, then the Orphans, ten thousand Fimbrian exiles with their pikes balanced on their shoulders, and then the straggling length of the mule train. Bringing up the rear would be the five hundred heavy cavalry of Corfe's Bodyguard in their black *Ferinai* armour.

In the midst of both the Torunnan infantry and the Orphans, light guns were being manhandled along, sometimes lifted bodily over deep-running streams and broken boulders which had tumbled from the heights above. They were six-pounder horse-artillery, three batteries" worth in total. All that Corfe dared try and take across the mountains.

All told, more than twenty-six thousand men were trekking westwards into the fastnesses of the Cimbrics this bright spring morning, and their column stretched along the inadequate track which bore them for almost four miles. It was not the largest army Torunna had ever sent forth to war, but Corfe felt that it must surely be one of the most formidable. The best fighting men of four disparate peoples were represented in that long column: Torunnans, Fimbrians, Cimbric tribesmen, and Merduks. If they succeeded in making their way through the mountains, they would find themselves alone and unsupported on the far side, and arrayed against them would be armies from all over the remainder of the world. They would have to take Charibon then, or they would be destroyed, and with them the last, best hope of this earth.

The end was very close now—the climax of the last and greatest war that men would fight in this age of the world. Hebrion was gone, and Astarac, and Almark and Perigraine were subjugated. Of all the Monarchies of God, Torunna alone now stood free.

I will raze Charibon to the ground, Corfe thought as he sat his horse and watched his army march past. I will slaughter every wizard and shape-shifter and witch I find. I will make of Aruan's fall a terrible lesson for all the future generations of the world. And his Inceptine Order I shall wipe from the face of the earth.

A gyrfalcon wheeled in a wide circle about his head, as though looking for him. Finally it came to earth as swiftly as though it were stooping on prey, and perched on the withered branch of a rowan tree to one side. Corfe rode away from his officers so that he might speak without being overheard.

"Well, Golophin?"

"Your path exists Corfe, though perhaps 'path' is an optimistic word. The sky is clear halfway through the Cimbrics, but on their western flanks a last spring blizzard rages, and the snow there is deepening fast."

Corfe nodded. "I expected no less. We have it from the Felimbri that winter lies longest on the western side of the divide; but the going is easier there all the same." He gestured to where the army marched before him, like a barbed serpent intent on worming its way into the heart of the mountains. "Once we leave the foothills behind us and get above the snowline we will meet with the tail of the glacier the tribes name Gelkarak, the 'Cold-Killer.' It will be our road through the peaks."

"It is a dangerous road. I have seen this glacier. It is pitted and creviced like a pumice stone, and avalanches roar down on it from the mountains about."

"Beggars would ride, if wishes were horses," Corfe said with a wry smile. "I would we all might sprout wings and fly across the mountains, but since we cannot, we must take whichever way we can." He paused, and then asked, "How go things where—where you are now, Golophin?"

"Aurungabar has been cowed by the return of Nasir with his host, and he has been recognised by all as the Sultan of Ostrabar. He will combine his coronation and his wedding in one ceremony, as soon as Mirren enters the city."

Corfe's breath clicked in his throat. "And how far has she to go?"

"Another five days will see her within the gates. She has left the wagons behind and has been making her way very swiftly with a small entourage on horseback."

Corfe smiled at that. "Of course she has. And you, Golophin—when do you return to the army?"

"Tonight I hope, when you camp. I meet this evening with Shahr Baraz the Younger. He has something on his mind, I believe. After that, I will remain with the army until the end. It seems to me you will need my help ere you are done with the Cimbric Mountains, sire. Fare well."

And with that the gyrfalcon took off from its perch, leaving the wizened rowan shaking behind it, and disappeared into the low cloud that hung over the peaks of the nearest mountains. Corfe nudged his mount back to where his officers stood patiently.

"Tomorrow, gentlemen," he said, his eyes following the bird's flight, "we will enter the snows."

BUT the snows came to them first. As they were pitching camp that evening a chill gale of wind came roaring down from the heights, and in its train whirled a swift, blinding blizzard of hard snow, dry as sand and almost as fine. Many men were caught unawares, and saw their leather tents ripped out of their hands to billow high in the air and vanish. Cloaks were plucked out of packs and sent flying, and the campfires were flattened and quenched. The mules kicked and panicked and some broke free from their drovers and galloped back down the way they had come, while a few, crazed by the impact of a flapping tent which had come tumbling out of the snow at them like a fiend, jumped over a low cliff and landed in broken agony on the rocks below, their packs smashing open and spraying black gunpowder upon the snow.

The blizzard created a wall about the huddled thousands who darkened the face of the hills, and it was several hours before some kind of order was restored, tents made fast to crags and weighted down with stones, mules hobbled and picketed into immobility, and the troops wolfing down cold rations about the smoking embers of their campfires.

The wind eased off with the rising of the moon, and Corfe, standing outside his skewed tent, looked up to see that the sky was clearing, and the stars were out in their millions, flickering with far-off flames of red and blue and casting faint shadows on the drifts of deep, fine snow that now crunched underfoot. They had been somehow transported to a different world it seemed, one of blank, twinkling greyness lit up by the moon so that the drifts seemed strewn with tiny diamonds, and men were black silhouettes in the moonlight whose breath steamed and clouded about them.

In the morning the troops were up well before the dawn, and the tent-sheets were stiff as boards under their numb fingers. The water in their canteens had thickened to a slush that made the teeth ache, and if bare metal touched naked skin it clutched it in a frozen grip painful to break free of.

Comillan trudged through the snow to the King's tent. Corfe was blowing on his gauntleted hands and looking up at the way ahead through the narrow passes whilst behind him the dawn was a pale blueness in the sky, and the stars still twinkled coldly above.

"Eleven mules lost, and one hapless lad who went out for a piss in the night and was found this morning. Aside from that, we seem to be in one piece." When the King did not respond Comillan ventured: "It will be heavy going today, I'm thinking."

"Aye, it will," Corfe said at last. "Comillan, I want you

to pick thirty good men and send them forward on foot—
they can leave their armour behind. We need a trail blazed
for the main body. Tribesmen like yourself for preference."

"Yes, sir."

"Are these sudden blizzards usual this late in the foothills?"

"In spring? No. But they are not unknown. Last night was
just a taster. But it sharpened up the men at least. The winter
gear is being dug out of packs, and they're gathering wood
while they can. I'll load as much as I can on the mules. We'll
need it in the high passes."

"Very good,"

"I take it the wizard did not return, sire?"

"No, he did not. Perhaps mages are as blinded by blizzards
as the rest of us."

An hour later the sun was over the horizon and rising fast
into an unclouded blue sky which seemed as brittle and transparent as glass. The world was a white, glaring brightness
and the soldiers smudged the hollows of their eyes with mud
or soot to reduce the glare while some held leaves between
their teeth to prevent the blistering of their lower lips. Comillan's trailblazers forged ahead with the easy pace of men
who are in familiar country, while behind them the great
column grew strung out and disjointed as the rest of the army
trudged wearily upwards, even the cavalry afoot and leading
their snorting mounts by the bridle. Entire tercios were assigned to each of the artillery pieces, and dragged them up
the steep, snowbound track by main force.

When Corfe paused, gasping, to look back, he could see
the green land of Torunna blooming out below him like some
kindlier world forgotten by winter, and sunlight shining off
the Kardian Sea in a half-guessed glitter on the edge of the
horizon. The Torrin river snaked and meandered across his
kingdom, bright as a sword-blade, and here and there were
the dun stains of towns leaking plumes of smoke to bar the
cerulean vault which overhung them.

The sky held clear for two more days, and while no more
snow fell, and the wind remained light and fitful from the

south-east, the temperature plummeted so that men walked with their cloaks frosted white by frozen breath, and icicles hung from the bits of the horses. The snow became hard as rock underfoot, which made for better going, but on the steeper stretches men had to go ahead of the main column and hack rude stairs out of the ice with mattocks, or else there would have been no purchase for the thousands of booted and hoofed feet following.

They were high up in the mountains now, and far enough within their winding flanks so that the view of the land below was cut off, and they were surrounded on all sides by spires of frozen rock, blinding snowfields, and hoar-white slopes of scree and boulder. In the dark, freezing nights Corfe halved the length of sentry duty, for an hour at a time was as much as the men could bear out of their blankets, and few fires were lit, for they were trying to conserve their meagre store of wood for some future emergency.

So, they came to the end of all man-made tracks, and found themselves at the foot of the Gelkarak glacier, and stared in wonder at what seemed to be a broken and tumbled cliff of pale grey, translucent rock. Except that it was not stone, but ancient ice which had come oozing down from the mountainsides in millennia of winters to form a vast, solid river fully half a mile wide, and many fathoms deep.

"We'll have to rig ropes and pulleys at the top to haul up the animals and the guns," Corfe said to Comillan and Kyne, who stood swathed in furs beside him. "We'll work through the night; there's no time to play with. Comillan, you handle the horses; Kyne, give Colonel Rilke a hand with his guns." The King stared at a sky which was still largely clear, but ahead of them there were sullen clouds gathering on the peaks, heavy with snow.

They were two days and a night hauling up the horses and mules and artillery pieces one by one to the top of the glacier. There was little engineering skill about it. Instead, the commanders had teams of up to three hundred men hauling on a cat's cradle of ropes at the lip of the glacier, and even the most recalcitrant mule could not argue with that amount of brute force.

On the second day of this rough portage the clouds arrived above them and snow started again. Not the wicked blizzard of before, but a heavy silence of fat white flakes which accumulated with amazing speed, until the teams at the top of the glacier were labouring thigh-deep, and the ropes were buried. Yet more men were put to clearing the snow from the bivouacs, and half a dozen fell into hidden crevasses and were lost. A company of Felimbric tribesmen from the Cathedrallers then explored up the glacier for several miles, roped together and feeling their way step by step. They marked each crevasse with an upright pike thrust into the snow, a dark rag flying from the tip, and thus blazed a safe road for the army to follow. And still it grew colder, and the men's lungs began to labour in the thinning air.

They lost a field piece and six mules as a whole series of rime-stiff ropes snapped in the same instant and they tumbled down the cliff of the glacier's end, but at the end of their fifth day in the mountains proper, the army was united on the back of Gelkarak itself, and the advance went on.

The glacier wound like a vast, flat-backed snake through the heights of the surrounding mountains. A wide, safe highway it seemed with its concealing blanket of snow, but below that snow it was pitted and fissured and cracked and in the dark, windless nights they could hear it groaning and creaking under their feet, so that it seemed they were crawling like ants atop the spine of some enormous, unquiet beast. Its course ran roughly westwards, and every now and then a lesser ice tributary would creep down from the high surrounding valleys to join it. In three more days of travel Corfe lost fifteen men staking out the trail for the main body. Even the tribes had never come this deep into the Cimbrics.

GOLOPHIN returned at last, appearing at the door of the King's tent late one icy night and entering with a nod to Felorin, who stood stamping his feet nearby. The wizard's gyrfalcon was perched like a grey frosted sculpture on his forearm, and his face was livid with tiredness.

Corfe was alone, poring by candlelight over the ancient, inadequate text which Albrec had discovered in Torunn. A small charcoal brazier burned in a corner of the tent, but it did little to heat the frigid air within. He looked up as Golophin entered, and frowned. "You're late," he said shortly.

The wizard sat down on a camp stool and let his familiar hop to the foot of Corfe's cot. He took off his wide-brimmed hat, letting fall a glittering shower of unmelted snow.

"My apologies." Corfe handed him a leather bottle and he gulped from the neck before wiping his mouth and replacing the cork. "Ah, better. Thank you, sire. Yes, I am late. I have travelled far since last you saw me, farther than I had intended. The Eighth Discipline is a great gift, but it sometimes tempts one to overdo things, such is the thirst for news in men."

"What news?"

"Your daughter reached Aurungabar today, and is to be married in the morning. The new Sultan of Ostrabar will be crowned and wed in the same ceremony. After it is done Nasir will ride forth with the men promised you by his father. Fifteen thousand, mostly heavy cavalry."

"Good," Corfe said, though he looked anything but relieved.

"Colonel Heyd has reached Gaderion, and the Himerians there are gearing up for a second assault. I bring General Aras's compliments. He will hold as long as he can, but his losses are high, while the Himerians seem to multiply daily. They have breached the curtain wall in three places but have not yet established a foothold beyond it. Communications with the south are still open. For the moment."

Corfe nodded silently. His face was gaunt and grey with cold. "Is that all?"

"No. I save the most startling news for last. In Aurungabar I talked again to Shahr Baraz the Younger. The Sultan and his consort are in their tomb and Ostrabar's succession is now established, but still he is a haunted man."

Corfe stared at the old wizard but said nothing. His eyes glittered redly in the light of the brazier.

"He is convinced—and much persuading it took for him to admit it—that Aurungzeb died not at the hand of an assassin." Golophin hesitated. "But at the hand of his own queen."

Corfe went very still.

"Not only that, but he then believes she turned the knife on herself. This Ramusian lady, the mother of his children, his wife of seventeen years. She must have harboured an enduring hatred in secret all that time. What finally made her act on it no man can say. Shahr Baraz loved her like a daughter. It is he who put about the story of foreign assassins in the pay of Himerius, and the court and harem believed him. Why should they not? Not even Nasir suspects the truth, and it is perhaps best left that way. But I thought you would like to know."

The King had turned his face and it was in shadow. Golophin watched him closely, wondering.

"Sire, I cannot help thinking there was something between you and the Merduk Queen. Something . . ." Golophin tailed off.

The King did not move or speak, and the old mage rubbed his chin. "Forgive me, Corfe. I am like a woman fishing for gossip. It's a besetting fault of old age that when you start a hare you feel you must run it to ground. My mind has become over-subtle with the passing years. I see connections and conspiracies where there are none."

"She was my wife," Corfe said quietly.

"What?"

The King was staring into the red gledes at the heart of the brazier, unblinking. "Her name was Heria Car-Gwion, a silk merchant's daughter of Aekir. And she was my wife. I thought her dead in the fall of the city. But she lived. She lived, Golophin, and was taken by Ostrabar's Sultan and made his queen. Her own daughter I took to wife. Because it was the right thing to do for the kingdom. And now you tell me that when she died it was by her own hand. On the day I wed the girl who should by rights have been my own daughter. My child.

"She was my *wife*."

Golophin rose to his feet hurriedly, knocking over the camp stool. Corfe had turned to stare at him through bright, fire-filled eyes, and in that moment the wizard was mortally afraid. He had never seen such torment, such naked violence in another man's face.

Corfe laughed. "She is at peace, dead at last. I wished her dead over the years, because I could not forget. I wished myself dead also. I might rest, I think, if I were laid in the tomb beside her. But even in death we will never be together again. Once I would have torn every Merduk city in the world brick from brick to get her back. But I am a king now, and must not think only of myself."

His smile was terrible, and in that moment he radiated more menace than any great mage or shifter that Golophin had ever known. The air seemed to crackle about him.

Corfe rose, and Golophin backed away. His familiar flew to his shoulder with a harsh, terrified screech. The King smiled again, but there was some humanity in his face now, and the terrible light had left his eyes.

"It's all right. I am not a madman or a monster. Sit down, Golophin. You look as though you had seen a ghost."

Golophin did as he was bidden, soothing his frightened familiar with automatic caresses. He could not get past the stunning realisation which was flooding his mind.

There was Dweomer in this man.

No, that was not correct. It was something else. An adamantine strength greater than the craft of mages, an *anti-*Dweomer perhaps. He could not fully explain it, even to himself, but he realised that here was a man whose will would never be tamed, whom no spell would ever subdue. And this also: Odelia's dying instincts had been correct. In victory, this man might well revel in an enormous bloodletting. His wife's fate had kindled an unassuageable pain in him which sought outlet in violence. And Golophin, in ignorance, had just stoked the fires of his torment higher.

•   •   •

THREE more days the army laboured painfully and slowly up the Gelkarak glacier. They were struck by a series of brief, vicious snowstorms which cost them dearly in horses and mules, and they lost another artillery piece to a crevasse, as well as the two dozen men who were roped to it. There was a crack like a gunshot, and it sank through the crust of snow and ice and dragged them screaming to their deaths like a series of fish snared on a many-hooked line. The troops were warier after that, and their speed decreased as they realised that it was to some extent a matter of luck whether a man put his foot in the wrong place or not. Pack mules were unladen and harnessed to the guns in the place of men, but this meant that the army marched more heavily burdened than ever. They were making at best two and a half leagues a day, and often much less, and Corfe estimated that no more than half their journey was behind them.

The air grew thin and piercing, and even the fittest of the men gasped for breath as he marched. Mercifully though, the weather cleared again, and though the raging, intense cold was a torture in the star-bright nights, the days remained fine and sunlit. Many of the animals became lame as the surface crust of the snow gashed their legs, and the cavalry quickly learned to bind wrappings about the hocks of their mounts. But the cold was wearing down both animals and men. Soon there were many cases of frostbite and snow blindness, mostly among the Torunnans, and after a meeting of the senior officers it was decided that those so afflicted would be left behind with a small guard to make their way back eastwards as soon as they were able. With them stayed scores of worn-out animals that might yet bear the weight of men, and a good store of rations.

But they were over the highest point of their passage, and had left the glacier road behind. There was a narrow pass leading off to the west-south-west and this they took, following the ancient trail described in Corfe's text. It was a harder road than the glacier, being much littered and broken with boulders and shattered stones, but it was less treacherous, and the men's spirit's rose.

And at last there came the evening, twenty-four days out of Torunn, when the army paused on the opening of a great glen between two buttresses of rock, and looked down to see the vast expanse of the Torian Plains darkling below under the sunset, and closer by, almost at their feet it seemed, there glittered red as blood the Sea of Tor.

The army was fewer by over a thousand men and several hundred mules and horses, but it had accomplished the crossing of the Cimbrics and there were now only thirty leagues of easy marching between it and Charibon.

NINETEEN

AURUNGABAR had seen a sultan and his queen buried, and a new sultan and his queen wed and crowned, all in the same month. The city was still unsettled and volatile, but the presence within its walls of a host of soldiery entirely loyal to Sultan Nasir had a considerable soothing effect. The harem had been purged of all those who had fomented intrigue in the brief interregnum and Ostrabar's absolute ruler had proved his mettle, acting swiftly and without mercy. A youth he might be, but he had an able vizier in the shape of Shahr Baraz the Younger, and it was rumoured that his new Ramusian wife was a great aid to him in the consolidation of his position. A sorceress of power she was reputed to be, even mightier than her witch of a mother. Unruly Aurungabar had been swiftly cowed therefore, and it was rumoured throughout the city that the Sultan already felt sure enough of his position to wish to set out immediately for the wars of the west.

He was closeted with his new vizier in one of the smaller suites off the Royal Bedchamber. He sat at a desk leafing through a pile of papers whilst Shahr Baraz stood looking over his shoulder, pointing something out now and again, and the spring rain lashed at the windows and the firelight sprang up yellow in the hearth to one side. A set of Merduk half-armour stood on a wooden stand by the door, and a scabbarded tulwar had been set on the mantelpiece. At last Nasir rubbed his eyes and straightened back from the desk with a mighty yawn. He was slim and dark, with olive skin and grey eyes, and he was dressed in a robe of black silk which shimmered in the firelight.

"All this can wait, Baraz. It's frivolous stuff, this granting of offices and remission of taxes."

"It is not, Nasir," the older man said forcefully. "Through such little boons you buy men's loyalty."

"If it must be bought it is not worth having."

Shahr Baraz gave a twisted smile. "That sounds like your mother speaking."

Nasir bowed his head, and his clear eyes darkened. "Yes. I never thought I would get it this way, Baraz. Not this way."

The vizier laid a hand on his shoulder. "I know, my Sultan. But it rests on your shoulders now. You will grow into it in time. And you have made a fair beginning."

Nasir's face lit up again, and he turned round. "Only fair?" They both laughed.

The door was knocked, and without further ceremony the Queen entered, also clad in midnight silk. Her golden hair was down and her marmoset clung to her shoulder chittering gently, its eyes bright as jewels.

"Nasir, are you ever coming to bed? It's hours past the middle of the—" She saw Shahr Baraz and folded her arms.

Nasir rose and went to her. The vizier watched them as they looked upon each other, half shy still, but an eagerness in their eyes. That, at least, had turned out well, he thought. One must be thankful for small mercies. And those not so small.

"I'm being drowned in dusty details," Nasir told his wife, "when all I want is to get on the road with the army."

"Are you sure that is all you want, my lord?" They grinned

at one another like two mischievous children, and indeed they were neither of them yet eighteen years of age.

"The army marches in the morning, my Queen," Shahr Baraz said, his deep old voice bringing them up short.

"I knew that," Mirren said with the laughter gone from her face. "Golophin spoke to me. He has been in and out of here for days. If Nasir is to be up before the dawn he must have some rest at least."

"I quite agree," Shahr Baraz said. "Now the Sultan and I have some last business to attend to, lady, and the night is passing."

Mirren's eyes narrowed, and the marmoset hissed at Shahr Baraz. The rebellion in her face faded however, seeing the vizier's implacable eyes. She kissed Nasir on the mouth and left. When the Sultan turned around with a sigh he found the old man shaking his head and smiling.

"You make a handsome pair, the dark and the gold. Your children will be fair indeed, Nasir. You have found yourself a fine queen, but she is as strong-willed and stubborn as an army mule." When Nasir's mouth opened in outrage Shahr Baraz laughed, and bowed. "So says Golophin. For he has spoken to me also, the old meddler. She is her father's daughter in more ways than one. And in truth she reminds me somewhat of—" And then he stopped, though they both knew what he had been about to say.

THE Merduk army marched out before sunrise, when the streets were as quiet as they ever became in the capital. They formed up in Glory of God Square where once the statue of Myrnius Kuln had frowned, and then led off in long files by prearranged streets to the West Gate. It was a cold, clear night with the sun not yet begun to glimmer over the Jafrar in the east, and King Corfe of Torunna, who had once fled through this very gate as Aekir burned about him, was not yet in the high foothills of the Cimbrics. Nasir was leading fifteen thousand heavily armoured cavalry westwards to the aid of the kingdom which had once been his people's bitterest foe. But he was young, and dwelt seldom on such ironies. Besides, half of his own blood belonged to that people. As did his new wife, whom he already knew he loved.

THAT same dawn found two ships coursing swift as cantering horses across the eastern Levangore. Their masts were rigid with almost every sail they possessed and their decks were black with men. All through the previous evening and the night they had been hurtling north-north-east with the freshening wind on their larboard quarters, and now to port loomed the purple shapes of the southern Cimbric Mountains as they marched down to the sea east of the Candelan river. Torunna, last free Kingdom of the West, rising up in the dawn light with the snow on the summits of the mountains catching the sun first, so that they tinted scarlet and pink and seemed to be disembodied shapes floating over the darker hills below.

Murad stared at that sunrise briefly and then focused once more on the ship ahead. The xebec had tried to lose them in the night, but the moonlight had been too bright and the eyes of the pursuers too keen. She was little more than four cables ahead now, almost within gunshot, and the *Revenant* was closing the gap.

The thing which had once been the Lord of Galiapeno glanced aft to see a man in the black of an Inceptine habit standing before the mainmast, solid and unyielding as a stone gargoyle despite the pitch and roll of the barquentine. From him there seemed to hum a silent vibration which could be felt underfoot in the wood of the decks. A soundless thrumming which, Murad knew, was responsible for the present speed, or part of it.

For Richard Hawkwood was too canny a sailor to be caught by conventional seamanship. He had survived the storm sent to sink him and they had almost lost him in the vast sea wastes of the Levangore, until one of Murad's homunculi had glimpsed him by chance as it flew high and far beyond its master in search of news. There would be no second storm—such tactics were obviously inadequate. No, to Murad's great joy Aruan had given him leave to capture the *Seahare* intact if he chose, and dispose of her crew in any way he wished—provided Hebrion's Queen met her end in the process. What a pleasure it would be to meet his old shipmate and comrade again, and to preside over his unhurried death.

Murad knew much of death. On the night of the fleet's destruction he had become lost in the fog on his way back from the flagship, and thus had watched from his longboat as that great armada was reduced to matchwood all about him. He remembered prising the fingers of desperate drowning survivors from the gunwales of his little craft less they swamp it in their panic. He had bade his men row them out, far out into the fog, and there they had leant on their oars and watched the ships burning through the mist, listening to the screams. They had escaped that slaughter, or so he had thought.

Then the mage had come in a furious storm of black flame which incinerated Murad's companions in a flashing second and seemed like to do the same to himself. But a curious thing had happened.

I know you, a voice had said. Murad had lain in the smoking bottom of the longboat with the swells washing around his charred body, and the thing had hovered over him like a great bat. He felt he were being turned this way and that for inspection, though he had not been touched.

Kill him, another voice said, a familiar voice. But the first laughed.

I think not. He may well prove useful.

Kill him!

No. Put aside your past hates and prejudices. You and he are more similar than you think. He is mine.

And thus had Murad of Galiapeno been taken into the service of the Second Empire.

And he had been willing to serve. All his life he had hated mages and witches and the workings of the Dweomer, but more than that Murad had chafed at his subordination to men he deemed less able than himself, even Hebrion's last King. Now he took orders from one he acknowledged to be his superior, and there was a strange comfort in it. He was at last glad to merely do as he was told, and if the orders he received chimed with his own inclinations, so much the better. As for the Dweomer, well he had become reconciled to it, for was it not now a part of him?

And what was more, he would be ruler of Hebrion once this woman he pursued was dead. It had been promised, and Aruan always kept his promises.

"Run out the bow-chasers," he said, and his crew jumped to do his bidding. A few of them were ordinary mercenaries, sailors of many navies, but most were tall, gleaming black men of the Zantu. They had cast aside their horn carapaces and now teams of them hauled sweating on the cables which trundled out the forward-aimed guns of the ship until they came to bear on the stern of their prey.

"Usunei!"

"Yes, lord."

"Let us see if we cannot scratch his paintwork. Fire when ready."

The grunting gun crews levered the two culverins round with handspikes while the gun captains sighted along the bronze barrels with smoking slow-match grasped in their fists. At last they were content and held up their free hands. As the bow of the ship rose they whipped the match across the touch-holes, springing aside with the grace of panthers as the culverins went off as one and leapt inboard, squealing on their trucks. A cloud of smoke went up and was quickly winnowed into nothing by the wind and the speed of the ship's passage. Watching intently, Murad saw two splashes just short of the *Seahare*'s stern.

"Good practice! More elevation there, and we shall have her."

The next shots could be followed by those with quick eyes: two dark blurs which punched holes in the xebec's mizzen course and then sent splinters flying from something in her waist. Murad laughed and clapped his hands, and the gun crew's faces split in wide, fanged grins.

A minute later the xebec's wounded mizzen course split from top to bottom and flapped madly from the yard. Spray struck Murad in the mouth and he licked the salt tang of it away, his eyes shining. The *Seahare* lost speed. The next pair of shots went home in the mizzen rigging and he saw a small, wriggling figure blown off the yard and flung into the sea.

"More speed!" Murad screamed. "You there, give us another two knots and we'll have them before breakfast!"

The hooded Inceptine to whom he spoke did not answer, but he seemed to hunch over within his robe, and the tone of the vibration which filled the ship rose by an octave. The *Revenant* dipped deeply and water came flooding in the chaser gunports, green and cold. The masts creaked and complained and the backstays were wringing taut, but nothing gave away. The weather-worker was not moving the ship, but the water within which it travelled, and spreading out all around the ship's hull was a violent turbulence of broken, foaming spray which was at odds with the natural swell of the sea about them. The ship trembled and shook as though it were being rattled in the grip of some undersea giant, and several of the crew were knocked off their feet, but Murad stood on the wave-swept forecastle gripping one of the foremast shrouds, and the light in his eyes grew to a yellow fire. They drew nearer to their prey. Now only a cable and a half—three hundred yards—separated the tip of the barquentine's bowsprit and the *Seahare*'s taffrail. In half a glass they would be abreast. Murad raised his voice. "All hands, prepare for boarding," and an homunculus wheeled out of the rigging and settled on his shoulder. About him on the forecastle clustered a great mob of the Zantu, now clad again in their black horn armour and clicking their pincers impatiently. The armour began as a natural construct of horn and leather, but when a man donned it, he became somehow part of it, and it augmented his strength as well as protecting his flesh. The Zantu were fearsome warriors in their own right, but when wearing their black harness they were well-nigh invincible.

"Remember!" Murad yelled. "The Captain is to be taken

alive, and the woman's body I must see with my own eyes. The rest are yours."

The Zantu had fasted for days in preparation of this hour, and from the depths of their shining masks their eyes glittered with hunger and anticipation.

Murad could actually recognise Hawkwood now. He stood at the stern of his ship with an oddly familiar dark-haired boy beside him, and shouted orders that were lost in the wind and the foaming tumult of the waves. The *Seahare* suddenly yawed hard a port so that she revealed her full broadside, such as it was. Six gun-ports gaping, and then the side of the ship disappeared in a bank of smoke, and a heartbeat later came the roar of the retorts. Murad felt the wind of one shot pass his head, and it staggered him. The rest smashed down the full length of the *Revenant*, leaving chaos in their wake. Blocks and fragments of rigging were hurled through the air and the close-packed boarding party was blasted to pieces, so that the scuppers ran with blood and fragments of men were blown as far aft as the quarterdeck.

The humming tremble of the ship's hull ceased, and looking aft Murad saw that one cannonball had cut his weather-working Inceptine in two. The *Revenant* lost speed and the foaming water about her began to settle into a more rational wake.

"Get me back my speed!" he shrieked at the ship's master, a renegade Gabrionese who stood white-faced by the wheel. "Shoot them! Catch them, sink them for the love of God!"

The master put the wheel about and the barquentine yawed in her turn, exposing her much heavier metal. "Fire!" he shouted, and the gun crews collected their wits and sent off a ragged broadside.

But the Zantu were not the well-trained sailors of Hawkwood's crew. Murad saw three of the balls strike home amidships, and a hail of wood splinters went flying as the *Seahare*'s larboard rail was demolished, but most went high, slicing cables in the rigging but doing little serious damage.

Both ships had lost speed now, and both were turning back to starboard, into the wind. An arquebus ball zipped past

Murad's ear and he ducked instinctively. Hawkwood had several sailors with small arms firing from his stern. There was a series of splashes in the xebec's wake; they were throwing their dead overboard. Murad beat his fist on the forecastle rail in his frustration and his homunculus jumped up and down on his shoulder, screeching.

"More sail!" he shouted to the master. "If they escape then your life is forfeit, master mariner."

The crew raced up the shrouds and began piling on every scrap of canvas the barquentine possessed. Staysails and jibs were flashed out and the *Revenant* began to accelerate through the water at something approaching her previous rate. The xebec still had not sent up a new mizzen course, and they were gaining again. Murad ignored the arquebus balls that whined and snicked about him, and helped the deplcted chaser crews run out their guns once more. They fired on the rise and this time the shots smashed square into the *Seahare*'s stern, sending timbers flying through the air and tossing one of the arquebusiers into the sea. Murad laughed again, and called for more men to come forward.

Another party of Zantu joined him by the chasers. Aboard the *Seahare* a party of men were busy on the quarterdeck and the odd ball came hissing overhead from their arquebusiers. Barely fifty yards separated the two ships now. Murad could see Hawkwood clearly; he was manning the ship's wheel himself, watching the barquentine as it came up hand over fist. That dark boy was helping him, and to one side of them was Isolla herself. She was aiming an arquebus. Murad, startled, saw the smoke spurt from its muzzle, and something thumped the side of his head. He went down and the homunculus squawked harshly. Labouring back to his feet he realised he was deaf on one side, and when he put up a hand it came away wet. Isolla had shot off half his ear.

Furious, he opened his mouth, but at that moment the *Seahare* made a sharp turn to port, going directly before the wind. As she turned her guns went off in measured sequence, and the *Revenant* was raked again, the cannonballs passing the full length of the ship.

Her sails shivered, then banged taut, and she fell away before the wind. Looking aft, Murad saw that the ship's wheel had been splintered into pieces and the master lay dead beside it along with the helmsman. The decks were slimy and slick with blood and everywhere fragments of jagged wood and scraps of flesh lay piled amid sliced cables and shattered blocks. Murad dashed aft to the companionway and shouted at the Zantu who staggered there, dazed and bewildered. "Get below to the tiller and steer her from there! You others, get back to your guns and commence firing!"

He climbed to the quarterdeck, slipping in blood and cursing, his hand held to the ragged meat where his ear had been. The two vessels were sailing directly before the wind now, on parallel courses less than a cable's length apart. They were pointed at the long inlet which housed the Torunnan port of Rone; Hawkwood was making a run for shore.

Both ships began firing again, broadside to broadside. The *Revenant* had heavier guns and more of them, but the *Seahare*'s were better served, and more accurate. She was slower in the water, though, and her pumps were sending thick jets of water out to port. Murad must have holed her below the waterline.

The lean nobleman's spirits rose. His crew had taken severe casualties, but there were still enough of them to board the enemy. He shouted down the hatch to the tiller deck below: "Hard a starboard!"

The *Revenant* made the turn sluggishly, but managed two points into the wind until her beakhead pointed square at the xebec's larboard forechains. The gap closed frighteningly quickly, and before Murad could even shout a warning the ships had collided with a massive jolt that knocked everyone aboard them both from their feet. The *Revenant*'s bowsprit splintered with a sickening crash and tore loose to rake down the xebec's side, only to be halted again by the mainchains. There it stuck in a fearsome snarl of broken wood and cordage and iron frapping, and the two ships continued before the wind hopelessly entangled, both out of command.

Murad recovered his wits and his feet quickly, and drew

his rapier. "Boarders away!" he shrieked, and ran down the length of his ship to where the wreckage of the bow joined her to the enemy xebec. Two dozen unarmoured Zantu gunners followed him clutching boarding axes and cutlasses and roaring like beasts. They crossed the perilous bridge of wrecked spars with the sea foaming below them and charged down on to the waist of the xebec. The *Seahare* was low in the water now; they had indeed breached her hull with their gunfire, and she was sinking under them.

Three or four gunshots met the invaders, and one of Murad's followers was blown off the side to plunge into the sea. Then Hawkwood was there—*Hawkwood, at last*—with a cutlass in one hand and a pistol in the other, and the two were glaring naked hate at one another while all about them their ship's companies engaged in a savage hand-to-hand fight in the waist and along the gangways of the *Seahare*.

Hawkwood's pistol misfired, a flash in the pan and no more. Murad laughed and closed with him, darting in the flicker of the rapier whilst his homunculus went for the mariner's eyes.

The pair were in the midst of a murderous mob of fighting men, but they might have been alone in the world for all the notice they took. Hawkwood drew his dirk and stabbed at the flapping homunculus even while clashing Murad's blade aside. The little creature screamed and fastened itself on the back of his neck, biting, reaching round for his eyes with its needle claws, flapping its wings. Murad lunged forward, still laughing, and the tip of the rapier pierced the mariner's thigh a full three inches. He twisted the blade as he withdrew and Hawkwood fell to one knee. The homunculus had clawed out one of his eyes, but he dropped the dirk and seized the little beast in his fist. He clenched his fingers about it and popped its tiny ribs, then threw it dying at Murad.

Murad batted it aside. It was not a familiar, merely a messenger, and thus no loss to him. He sprang forward again, a great joy rising in him, and drew back his sword for the kill.

But he was buffeted by the mêlée which raged about them, and thrown off-balance. Cursing, he reached forward again but something struck him in the side, a blunt blow that knocked the breath out of him. He hissed in pain. A woman stood over Hawkwood—*it was Isolla*. Her face was scarred by fire but he knew her at once, though she wore a seaman's jacket over her skirts. Her face was white and resolute, fearless. She fired the arquebus at point-blank range.

And missed. In the push and shove of the scrum the barrel was knocked aside. The muzzle blast scorched Murad's hair and half blinded him. He grabbed the barrel with his free hand and stabbed at her with his rapier. His blade caught her below the collar bone and sank deep, deep through her heart. She crumpled and slid off the bloody steel to lie on top of Hawkwood. Murad grinned and raised the rapier to finish the job.

But there was a sudden, savage blow to the side of his neck. It numbed his left arm and made him stumble in astonishment and pain. His lemon yellow eyes flickered as the Dweomer which bound his burned limbs together faltered. He turned, and the rapier slipped from his nerveless fingers.

Bleyn stood there, his own stepson. And in his hand Hawkwood's dirk, bloody to the hilt. The boy's face was livid and glaring, though his cheeks were running with tears. Murad reached out his good hand towards him, utterly baffled. *"What—?"* he began.

But Bleyn darted forward and punched the dirk into his chest. It stuck there, grating through his breastbone, and Murad sank to his knees.

"How . . . ?"

Hawkwood was staring at him, his remaining eye glittering, Isolla's body cradled in his arms. The inhuman light in Murad's own eyes winked out, and for a few seconds his old dark gaze met Hawkwood's maimed stare in startled disbelief. "I didn't know—"

Hawkwood simply gazed on him, without hatred or anger, and watched the life flit from Murad's face. The nobleman's chin sank on his breast and he toppled over on to the bloody deck, mere burnt carrion. Around him his followers saw their leader's death and faltered, and were beaten back into the sea.

THEY abandoned the *Seahare* and tossed flaming torches up on to the decks of the *Revenant* as they took to the boats. In the gathering dusk the waves were full of dark faces and others were diving off the sides of the barquentine and swimming out to them. They shot them in the water or hacked their hands from the sides of the boats as they tried to climb on board. Finally they drew clear, their wake lit by the blazing ship behind them, and landed the ship's boats on the shelving shore east of Rone, and stood a while with the surf beating about their knees and watched the *Revenant* burning against the evening sky. At last the fire reached the powder room, and the barquentine vanished in a bright explosion that echoed and re-echoed in a sharp, brief thunder about the hills of the inlet. For a long while afterwards the wreckage tumbled and splashed down in the quiet waters of the bay, and the evening darkened into night upon the waters.

Richard Hawkwood had fulfilled his mission and had brought Hebrion's Queen to Torunna, and they buried her on a hilltop overlooking the sea and set a cairn of stones upon her grave.

TWENTY

THE couriers arrived in Torunn in the red light of dawn, their mounts near foundering, streaked with foam and slathered with mud. The men slid from their saddles in the courtyard of the palace and then half staggered, half ran to the great doors. The gate guards there took their dispatches and after a quick, urgent word, ran pelting to the Bladehall.

Formio, Regent of Torunna, stood before the blazing hearth therein and behind him on the massive mantel there was a lighter space where once the Answerer had hung. But it was gone to war in the hands of the King, and who knew if it would ever hang there again? The Fimbrian was rubbing his hands together absently at the fire and when the guards burst in with the dispatch cases he did not seem much surprised. He looked at the seals, nodded grimly, and spoke to the panting soldiers who had brought them.

"Rouse out his majesty the Sultan and bid him come here—humbly, mind. And then relay to Colonel Gribben my compliments, and he is to stand to the entire garrison at once, and then join me here also."

As the men left him alone again, Formio snapped open the dispatch cases and read their uncurled contents, frowning.

Rone, 20th Forialon

The Himerians have struck here in the south. We knew they might, but they have arrived in much greater strength than we had expected and have incorporated the host of Candelan into their ranks. My command was worsted in a battle five miles east of the Candelan river and we have fallen back on Rone, where Admiral Berza's ships are based. Most of his vessels are in dock, being refitted, and he has agreed to turn over his marines to my command. I shall hold as long as I can, but I need reinforcements. The Perigrainians alone muster some twenty-five thousands. The enemy are infantry in the main, but they have also some of these accursed Hounds in their ranks, and the fear of them is out of all proportion to their numbers.

I believe that this is no mere raid, but a full-scale invasion. The enemy intends to overrun the entire kingdom from the south while our forces are engaged far to the north. I need men, quickly.

> *Yours in haste,*
> *Steynar Melf,*
> *Officer Commanding Army South*

Formio's lips moved in silent oaths as he read the dispatch. There came attached a muster and casualty list and a rough map of operations. Melf was a professional if nothing else, but he was no military phoenix. And even with Berza's marines he had less than five thousand men left to withstand this huge Himerian army.

Formio looked up as the Merduk Sultan strode down the hall flanked by two bodyguards. With him came Colonel Gribben, second in command of the garrison of Torunn, and a pair of aides. All of them had that bleared, dull look of men who have been roused out of sleep.

"My lord Regent," Nasir said, "I hope that this is—"

"How soon can you put your men back on the road, Sultan?" Formio asked harshly.

Nasir's mouth snapped shut. His eyes opened wide. "What has happened?"

"How soon?"

The young man blinked. "Not today. We have just made a long march. The horses need more rest. Tomorrow morning, I suppose." Nasir rubbed his unlined forehead, his eyes darting to left and right under his hand.

"Good. Gribben, I want you to pick out ten thousand of the best men of the garrison. They must be fit also, capable of a long forced march."

"Sir!" Gribben saluted, though his face was a picture of alarm and perplexity.

"This combined force will move out at dawn tomorrow, and it will travel light. No mules or wagons. The men will carry their rations on their backs. No artillery either."

"Where are we going?" the Sultan asked, sounding for a moment very like the boy he had so lately been.

"South. The Himerians have invaded there and defeated our forces. They have stolen a march on us, it seems."

"Who will command, sir?" Gribben asked.

Formio hesitated. He looked at Nasir and gauged his words carefully.

"Majesty, you have not yet commanded an army in war, and this is not the time to learn. I—I beg you to let a more experienced man lead this combined army." And here Formio nodded at Gribben, who had fought in all the Torunnan army's battles since Berrona, seventeen years before, and had been lately promoted by Corfe himself.

Nasir flushed. "That is out of the question. I cannot turn over the cream of Ostrabar's armies for you to do with as you will, not while I am here with them. I shall command them, no other."

Formio watched the young man steadily. "Sultan, this is not a game, or a manoeuvre on the practice fields. The army that goes south cannot afford to lose. I do not doubt your valour—"

"I will not stand aside for a mere colonel. I could not do so, and still look my men in the face. But do not mistake me, my lord Regent. I am not some foolish boy dreaming of glory. If anyone takes overall command, it must be you, the Regent of Torunna, the great Formio himself. You, they will obey." Nasir smiled. "As will I, sultan or no."

Formio was taken aback, but made his decision at once. "Very well, I shall command. Gribben, you will remain here in the capital. Majesty, I salute your forbearance. We have much to do, gentlemen, and only one day to do it in. By this time tomorrow we must be on the road south."

In the night the wind dropped and the sky was entirely free of cloud. The little group of castaways huddled around their campfire in a dark, silent ring, but one of them, a broad-shouldered young man with sea-grey eyes, stood apart on a small rise some distance away and peered towards the horizon with the waning moon carving shadows out of his face.

"Another city burns," Bleyn said wearily. "Which one might that be?"

Hawkwood stared south and west with his good eye, shivering. "That would be Rone, the southernmost city of Torunna. As well we never reached it."

"The world is gone mad," Jemilla said. "All the old seers were right. We are at the end of days."

Hawkwood cocked his head towards her. Bleyn's mother was sitting upon a folded blanket hugging her knees to her breasts and her hair hung about her face in a rat-tailed hood. She had lost weight during the voyage, for seasickness had prostrated her the greater part of it, and there were lines running from the corners of her mouth and nose that had not been so noticeable before. Age had claimed Jemilla at last, and she no longer held any allure for Richard Hawkwood.

She seemed to know this, and was almost diffident in his company. She had gathered wildflowers to set atop Isolla's cairn, something the old Jemilla would have scorned, and when she spoke her voice held none of its former ringing bite. But Hawkwood sensed something about her, some secret knowledge which was gnawing at her soul. When he had been supported by Bleyn in their limping stumble inland, he had found her watching the pair of them with an odd expression on her face. It held almost a note of regret.

He dropped his head again and continued to work on the rude crutch he was fashioning from a broken oar, then paused. His dirk still had some of Murad's blood on it. He wiped the cold-running perspiration from his face.

Jemilla was right, perhaps. The world had indeed run mad, or else those unseen powers which fashioned its courses were possessed of a bitter humour. Well, this particular race was almost run.

For a moment the light of the fire was a broken dazzle in Hawkwood's remaining eye. He had been loved by a queen, only to lose her almost as soon as he found her. And Murad was dead at last. Oddly, he could take no joy in the nobleman's end. There had been something in his dying eyes which inspired not triumph but pity. A baffled surprise, maybe. Hawkwood had seen that look in the faces of many dying men. No doubt he would one day wear it himself.

"I know nothing of this part of the world," Bleyn said. "Whither shall we go now?"

"North," Hawkwood told him, fighting himself upright and trying out the crutch for size. His breath came in raw, ragged gasps. "We are in the country of friends, for now at any rate. We must stay ahead of the Himerians and get to Torunn."

"And what then?"

Hawkwood hobbled unsteadily over to him. Then it'll be time to get drunk." He clapped the boy on the shoulder, unbalancing himself, and Bleyn helped him keep his feet.

"We'll need horses and a cart. You won't get far on that."

Jemilla watched them as they stood together beyond the firelight, so alike, and yet so unalike. Father and son. She wiped her eyes angrily, covertly. That knowledge would remain sealed in her heart until the day she died.

"Bleyn is now the rightful king of Hebrion," she said

aloud, and the sailors about the fire looked at her. "He is the last of the Hibrusid Royal house, whether born on the wrong side of the blanket or no. You all owe him your allegiance, and must aid him in any way you can."

"Mother—" Bleyn began.

"Do not forget that, any of you. When we get to Torunn his heritage will be made public. The wizard Golophin already knows of it. That is why we were told to take ship with you."

"So the rumours were true," Arhuz said. "He is Abeleyn's son."

"The rumours were true. He is all that is left of the Hebrian nobility."

Hawkwood nudged Bleyn, who stood wordless and uncertain. "I beg leave for leaning on the Royal shoulder, majesty. Do you think you could stir the Royal legs and go hunt us up some more firewood?" And both Bleyn and the mariners about the fire laughed, though Jemilla's thin face darkened. The boy left Hawkwood and went out into the moonlit darkness on his errand, while the mariner stumped back to the fire.

"Jemilla," he said sharply, and she glared at him, ready for argument. But Hawkwood only smiled gently at her, his eyes fever-bright.

"He'll make a good king."

T HE next morning the early sunlight rose over the world to reveal bars of smoke rising up from the south-western horizon. The nearest was scarcely ten miles away. The castaways climbed out of their blankets, shivering, and stamped their feet, staring at the besmirched sky. There was little talk, and less to eat, and so they started off at once, hoping to come across some friendly village or farm that would speed them on their journey.

Villages and farms they found in plenty, but they were all deserted. The inhabitants of the surrounding countryside had seen the smoke on the air also, and had decided not to await its coming. Bleyn and Arhuz ranged far ahead of the rest of

them and procured food in plenty, and extra blankets for the
chill nights, but all manner of steed and vehicle had left with
their fleeing owners, and so they must needs limp along on
foot, their faces always set towards the north, and Hawkwood
the slowest of them all, the dressing on his eye weeping a
thin continual stream of yellow fluid.

Four days they proceeded in this manner, sleeping in
empty farmhouses at night and starting their daily marches
before dawn. On the fifth day, however, they finally caught
up with the streams of other refugees heading north and
joined a straggling column of the dispossessed that choked
the road for as far as the eye could see. The crutch-wielding
Hawkwood was found space on the back of a laden wagon,
and Jemilla joined him, for the mariner's fever had risen
inexorably over the past few days, and she kept him well
wrapped and wiped the sweat and the pus from his burning
face.

The days were becoming warmer as late spring edged into
an early summer, and the crowds of people which choked
the roads sent up a lofty cloud of dust that hung in the air
to match the palls of smoke that pursued them. Talking to
the fleeing Torunnans, Bleyn learned that Rone had fallen
after a bitter assault, and its defenders had been massacred
to a man. The ships docked in the harbour had been burned
and the land about laid waste. The Torunnan commander,
Melf, and Admiral Berza of the fleet were both dead, but
their stand had bought time for the general population to get
away from the jubilant Perigrainians and Candelarians who
were on the roads behind. But ordered companies of disciplined men will always make better time than mobs of panicked civilians, and the enemy were gaining. What would
happen when the Himerian forces caught up with the refugees no one would speculate upon, though many of them had
lived through the Merduk Wars and had seen it all before.
Where is the King? they asked. Where is the army? Can they
all be up in Gaderion, or have they given any thought to the
south at all? And they trudged along the dusty roads in their
tens of thousands, holding their children in their arms and

hauling hand carts piled high with their possessions, or urging along slow-moving ox wagons with a frantic cracking of whips.

"HELP me get him off the wagon," Jemilla told her son, and together the two of them lifted the delirious Hawkwood from the bed of the overburdened vehicle as it trundled forward relentlessly in the heat and the dust. The mariner jerked and kicked in their arms and mumbled incoherently. The heat of his body could be felt even through the sodden blanket in which he was wrapped.

The other sailors had long deserted them, even Arhuz, becoming lost in the trudging crowds and teeming roadsides. So it was with some difficulty that Jemilla and Bleyn carried their mumbling burden off the road and through the ranks of refugees, until they were clear of the exodus and could lay the mariner down on a grassy bank not far from the eaves of a green-tipped beech wood. Jemilla laid her palm on his hot brow and thought she could almost feel the poison boiling within his skull.

"His wound has gone bad," she said. "I don't know what we can do." She took the mariner's hand and his brown fingers clenched about her slender pale ones, crushing the blood out of them. But she said no word.

Bleyn knuckled his eyes, looking very young and lost. "Will he die, Mother?"

"Yes. Yes, he will. We will stay with him." And then Jemilla shocked her son by bowing her head and weeping silently, the tears coursing down her pale, proud face. He had never in his short life seen his mother cry. And she clung to this man as though he were dear to her, though during the voyage she had treated him haughtily, as a noblewoman would any commoner.

"Who was he?" he asked her, amazed.

She dried her eyes quickly. "He was the greatest mariner of the age. He made a voyage which has passed already into legend, though small reward he received for it, for he was of low blood. He was a good man, and I—I loved him once.

I think perhaps he loved me, back in the years when the world was a sane place." The tears came again, though her face remained unchanged. More than anything she wanted to tell Bleyn who this man really was, but she could not. He must never know, not if he were to make his claim to Hebrion with any conviction.

Even to herself, Jemilla's reasoning seemed hollow. The Five Kingdoms were gone, their last hope, Torunna, falling to pieces in front of her eyes. There would soon be no room in the world for herself and her son and the old order of things. But she had come too far to relinquish hope now. She remained silent.

The day passed around them unnoticed as they sat on the grass, a trio of lost people to one side of a great concourse of the lost and the fearful and the fleeing. Hawkwood's eye opened once ere the end, and he gripped Jemilla's hand until the bones creaked under his strong fingers.

"Clew up, clew up there," he whispered in a cracked dry voice. "Billerand, set courses and topsails. Steer due west with the wind on the quarter."

Then he sighed, and the pressure of his fingers relaxed. The light faded from his eye. Richard Hawkwood's long voyaging was over.

TWENTY-ONE

Aruan woke out of sleep with the knowledge that something had changed in the black hours of the night, some balance had shifted. He was a master of soothsaying as he was of every other Discipline, but this feeling had nothing to do with the Dweomer. It was more akin to an old man's aches before a storm.

He rose and called for his valet and was quickly washed and robed in the austere splendour of the Pontifical apartments, for he resided there now though Himerius and not he was Pontiff in the eyes of the world. He looked out of the high window upon the cloisters of Charibon below and saw that the dawn had not yet come and the last hours of the night still hung heavy above the horns of the cathedral and the Library of St. Garaso.

He clenched and unclenched one blue-veined fist and stared at it darkly. He had overtired himself in his travels, bending the wills and raising the hearts of men up and down the length of the continent. But now Rone had fallen and southern Torunna was being invaded with little resistance, while at Gaderion Bardolin had laid the curtain wall in ruins and the Torunnans there were besieged within their three great fortresses, relief column and all. Hebrion and Astarac and Almark and Perigraine were conquered, their peoples his to command, their nobility extinguished. Only Fimbria now stood alone and aloof from the convulsions of the world, for the Electorates had sent no word since the departure of their embassy months before. Well, they would be dealt with in time.

But still he was afflicted by a restless uneasiness. He felt that he had overlooked some piece of his opponent's upon the gaming board of war, and it troubled him.

As dawn finally broke open the sky in bands of scarlet behind the white peaks of the Cimbrics, King Corfe Cear-Inaf brought his army down from the foothills to the shores of the Sea of Tor, and where the land levelled out into the first wolds of the Torian Plains, he set his men into line of battle, a scant four miles from the outskirts of Charibon itself. It was the eleventh day of Enderialon in the Year of the Saint 567, and it was thirty-one days since he had set out from Torunn.

The army he led was a good deal smaller than that which had taken ship on the Torrin river those weeks before. Many had died in the unforgiving mountains, and over two thousand men, Fimbrians and Torunnans and tribesmen, had been detached while still high up in the foothills, their mission to destroy the Himerian transports docked at the eastern shore of the Sea of Tor, and thus cut the supply lines of the army which was entrenched in the Thurian Line and before Gaderion.

So it was with less than twenty-two thousand troops that Corfe descended from the high places to give battle to the forces of the Second Empire before the very gates of their capital. It was still dark as he set his men into line, and despite their depleted numbers their ranks stretched for over two and a half miles.

He rested his right flank on the shore of the sea itself, and there three thousand Torunnan arquebusiers were placed in four ranks, each half a mile long. To their left was the main body of the Orphans, eight thousand Fimbrian pikemen under Marshal Kyne, with a thousand more arquebusiers mingled in their files. The pike phalanx bristled nine ranks deep and had a frontage of a thousand yards. Next to them stood another three thousand arquebusiers, and out on the far left was the main body of the Cathedraller cavalry, four thousand heavy horsemen in four ranks, armed with lance and sabre and matchlock pistols, their lacquered armour gleaming red as blood in the morning light. Comillan had been newly made their commander, for their previous leader had died in the snows. Hidden in their midst were three batteries of horse-artillery and their teams, awaiting the signal to unlimber and begin firing.

Behind this first wave, and closer to the left of the line than its centre, rode the Torunnan King himself at the head of his five-hundred-strong Bodyguard. He kept back with him a mixed formation of some two thousand Fimbrians and Torunnans to act as a general reserve, and also to bolster the open flank. For off on that flank, on the higher ground leading down to Charibon, the citadel of the Knights squatted, a grey low-built fortress around which were the tents and baggage of a small army. As the Torunnans advanced towards Charibon proper, they would have this fortress and encampment in their left rear. Not only that, but the fast-riding Cathedraller scouts which had been scouring the land about the army for days had only yesterday reported seeing a large body of infantry bivouacked some fifteen miles to the west of Charibon, square upon the Narian Road. They had not drawn close enough to this force to ascertain its nationality, but there was little doubt that it consisted of more levies on their way to swell the ranks of the Empire. And so Corfe had hurried his men through the night, to attack Charibon before this fresh army came up.

He had no illusions about the slimness of the thread from which his men's survival hung, and he knew that even if they were victorious before the monastery-city, there was little hope of their ever returning to Torunna. But this was the head of the snake here before him, and if it were destroyed, the west might yet rise again and throw off the yoke. That chance was worth the sacrifice of this army. And as for his own life, he knew that it had been twisted beyond hope of happiness, and he would be content to lay it down here.

Ahead of the Torunnans and Fimbrians as they formed up on the plain more tent encampments sprawled amid a web of gravel roads, and beyond them the tricorne tower of the Cathedral of the Saint loomed tall and stark, matched in height by the Library of Saint Garaso and the Pontiff's Palace close by, all connected by the Long Cloisters. That was the heart of Charibon, and of the Second Empire itself. Those buildings must all be laid in ruin and their inhabitants destroyed if the head of this snake were to be cut off.

Albrec had passionately disagreed when Corfe had told him of his intentions back in Torunn, but Albrec was not a soldier, and he was not here, staring at the vast factory of war that Charibon had become. Corfe would rather a thousand books burn than he needlessly lose a single one of his men, and he would see the history of ages go up in smoke rather than let one scion of Aruan's evil brood escape. This he had impressed upon his officers and his men in a council of war held up in the hills, though Golophin, who had attended, had said nothing.

"They have no pickets out," Ensign—Haptman rather—Baraz said incredulously. "Sir, I believe they're all asleep."

"Let us hope so, Haptman." Corfe looked up and down at the line which stretched out of sight in the raw dawn light. Then he breathed in deep. "Alarin, signal the advance."

Corfe's colour-bearer was a Cimbric tribesman, a close kinsman of Felorin's. He now stood up in his stirrups and waved the sable and scarlet banner of Torunna forward and back, for no bugle calls were to be used until the army had joined battle. The signal was taken up all down the line, and slowly and in silence that huge ordered crowd of men began to move, and became a muffled creeping darkness which edged closer to the tents of the enemy, bristling with barbed

menace. Anyone looking closely at the war harness of the
army's soldiers would have rubbed their eyes and stared, for
every man had welded to his armour short spikes of iron
nails, and even the horses' chamfrons and breastplates were
similarly adorned, whilst the spear points of the Fimbrians
and lanceheads of the Cathedrallers were not bright winking
steel, but black iron also. Save for the scarlet of the Cathedrallers, the appearance of the army was sombre as a
shadow, with hardly a gleam of bright metal to be seen.

When they had advanced two miles Corfe ordered the reserve to edge farther out on the left, for they were passing
the camps of the Knights Militant about their citadel. There
was activity there now where there had been none before,
and he could see squadrons of cavalry mounting their horses.
And then a bright series of horn calls split the morning and
from the summit of the citadel's tower a grey smoke went
up.

"It would seem the enemy has clambered out of bed at
last," he said mildly. "Baraz, ride to Colonel Olba with the
reserve and tell him to drop back farther and cover our left
rear. He is to go into square if necessary, but he is to be
prepared to ward off the Knights Militant from the main
body."

"Sir!" Baraz galloped off.

"Ensign Roche."

"Yes, sir." The young officer's horse was dancing under
him and his eyes were bright as glass. He was about to see
a real battle at last.

"Go to Marshal Kyne in the middle of the phalanx, and
tell him that he is to keep advancing for Charibon itself, even
if he loses contact with the arquebusiers on his left. He has
my leave to detach a flank guard if he sees fit, but he must
keep moving regardless. Clear?"

"Yes, sir!" Clods of turf flew through the air like birds as
Roche wheeled his horse away in turn.

Yes, the enemy was awake all right. A mile in front of
the army men were tumbling out of their tents and forming
up with confused haste. They were in Almarkan blue, ar-

quebusiers and sword-and-buckler men. Many thousands of them were now preparing to bar the way into Charibon. As they milled about, the bells of the Cathedral of the Saint, and those of every other church in the monastery-city began to peal the alarm, and Corfe could see that the streets of Charibon were clogging with troops rushing south and east to meet him. Out to the west of the city he could see other formations moving on the plain, Finnmarkan gallowglasses according to the word of his scouts. They had vast camps out there, but had two miles to march before they would be on his flank. Corfe drew the Answerer, and the ancient pattern-welded iron of John Mogen's sword glittered darkly as it left the scabbard. He raised it in the air and led the Bodyguard out to the left rear of the Cathedrallers. The Torunnan army was eating up the yards to Charibon at pace, and was now deployed in a great L-shape with the base of the L facing west. Not a single battlecry or shout came from the ranks; the only sound was the dull thunder of all those thousands of hoofs and feet.

"Ensign Brascian," said Corfe to another of his young staff who clustered about him. "Go to Colonel Rilke of the artillery. You will find him with the Cathedrallers. Tell him to deploy his guns to the west at once and commence to engage the Knights Militant. Then find Comillan and say he is to charge the Knights at his own discretion, but he is not to pursue. He is not to pursue, is that clear?"

"Very clear, sir."

"He is to pull back as soon as the enemy is halted and in disorder, and the guns will cover his withdrawal. Then he is to hold himself in readiness for further orders."

Seven or eight thousand of the Knights Militant had now formed up in a long line facing east, in front of their citadel and the tents that were pitched at its foot. They would advance very soon, and must be neutralised. Corfe watched Brascian pelt off, slapping his horse's rump with the flat of his sabre. He disappeared into the sea of red-armoured horsemen that was the Cathedrallers, and scant minutes later the ranks of the cavalry parted and the gun teams began to

emerge and set up before them. The Cathedrallers halted behind the line of six-pounders and dressed their ranks. For all
that they were composed mainly of the Cimbric tribes, they
were as well disciplined as Torunnan regulars now, and
Corfe's heart swelled at the sight of them. What had once
been a motley band of ill-armed galley slaves had over the
years become the most feared body of cavalry in the world.

The Knights Militant began to advance, a tonsured Presbyter out to their front and waving them on with his mace.
They too were heavily armoured, with the Saint's Symbol
picked out in white upon their breastplates, and their faces
were hidden behind their closed helms. Their horses were of
the fine, long-limbed strain which had been bred as hunters
and palfreys on the Torian Plains for centuries by the aristocracy of Almark, but they were smaller in stature than the
massive destriers of the Cathedrallers. The horses of Corfe's
mounted arm were descended from those brought east by the
Fimbrians, back in the ancient days when some of their
troops still went mounted, and the best of these had been
stolen and raided by the tribesmen of the Cimbrics over the
years, and for centuries after had been selected and bred
purely for size and courage. For war.

The startling boom of a gun as the first six-pounder went
off, followed by a close-spaced salvo from all three batteries.
Rilke had trained his gun teams well. Hardly had the cannons
jumped back on their carriages than his men were levering
them forward again, worming and sponging them out, and
reloading. They were using canister, hollow metal shells
filled with scores of arquebus balls, and as the smoke cleared
the carnage they produced was awesome to see. All along
the front of the Knights' line horses were tumbling screaming
to their sides, crushing their riders, or rearing up with their
bowels exposed or backing frantically away from the deadly
hail to crash into their fellows behind them. The Knights'
advance stalled in bloody confusion. The horse of their Presbyter was galloping riderless about the field with gore
streaming from its holed neck and flanks, and its owner

lay motionless in the grass behind it, his tonsure pale as a porcelain bowl on the trampled turf.

"Now," Corfe whispered, banging his gauntleted hand on his knee. *"Go now."*

Comillan seemed to have read his thought, for as soon as the artillery had fired their second salvo he spurred out to the front of his men with his colour-bearer in tow, and with a wordless cry ordered them forward. The hunting horns of the Cimbrics sounded full and clear over the screams of maimed horses and men, and that huge line of armoured cavalry began to move, like some monstrous titan whose leash had been slipped. Corfe's heart went there with them as they quickened into a trot, a canter, and then the lances came down in a full-blooded charge to contact. The earth trembled under them and the tribesmen began to sing the terrible battle paean of their native hills, and still singing they ploughed into the enemy formations like the blade of a hot knife sinking into butter. The first and second lines of Cathedrallers made a deep scarlet wedge in the ranks of the Knights Militant, and the smaller horses of the Himerians were knocked off their feet by the impact of that charge. The Cathedrallers discarded their broken and bloody lances and fired a volley of matchlock pistols at point-blank range, adding to the carnage and the panic. Then the silver horn calls signalled the withdrawal, and the first two lines turned about and fell back, covered by the advance of the third and fourth ranks, who rode through their files, formed up neatly and fired a rolling pistol volley in their turn. Comillan's command trotted back across the field unmolested and seemingly unscathed, though Corfe could see the scarlet bodies which littered the plain they left behind them. But these were as nothing compared to the great wreckage of carcasses and steel-clad carrion which had once been the proud ranks of the Knights Militant.

The survivors of the charge, many now on foot, streamed back across the plain through the trampled debris of their tented camp, and sought sanctuary about the walls of their citadel. The Torunnan advance continued.

• • •

ARUAN, aghast, watched the ruin of his Knights from the high tower of the Pontifical Palace. Inceptine clerks and errand-runners clustered about him like black flies settling on a wound, but none dared meet their master's blazing eyes. As his gaze went hither and thither across the wide battlefield, he saw the Almarkan troops south of Charibon stand to fire a volley of ragged arquebus fire. The oncoming Torunnans were not even checked, but closed up their ranks and marched over the bodies of their dead. Even as he watched, the pikes of the Orphans came down from the vertical and became a bristling fence of bitter points which reflected no light. The Almarkans could not withstand that fearsome sight, and began to fall back to the dubious shelter of their encampment, pausing to fire as they went. The Torunnan phalanx paused, and the thousand arquebusiers within its ranks fired in their turn. Then out of the smoke the Orphans marched on once more. They did not seem to be men, but rather minute cogs in some great, terrible engine of war, as unstoppable as a force of nature.

Aruan's eyes rolled back in his head and a great snarling came from his throat. His aides backed away, but he was utterly indifferent to them. He gathered his strength and launched a bolt of pure, focussed power into the east, like a puissant broadhead propelled by a bow of immense force. This lightning-swift Dweomer scrap carried the message of his mind's demand.

Bardolin, to me.

He came back to himself and snapped at his aides without looking at them, his eyes still fixed on the vast panorama of the smoking battlefield below.

"Loose the Hounds," he said.

THE Torunnan line opened out. As the main body of the infantry advanced, the Cathedrallers turned north and covered their open flank, and with them came Rilke's guns. But in the gap left by the departure of the red horsemen, Colonel Olba's reserve formation shook out from column into line of battle, and faced west to guard against any fresh attack by the remnants of the Knights. Near the apex of these two lines the Torunnan King, his standard rippling sable and scarlet above him, took up position surrounded by his Bodyguard.

From the north-west the long columns of glittering mailclad gallowglasses, the storms troops of the Second Empire, approached, while from their camps along the shores of the Torian Sea trotted fresh contingents of Almarkans and Perigrainians and Finnmarkans. The blue sky was dotted with the tiny flapping shapes of homunculi running their master's errands. Aruan was recalling every tercio that remained between the Cimbrics and the Narian Hills to the defence of Charibon. And still the bells tolled madly in the churches, and the Torunnans came on like a wave of black iron.

It was Golophin who sensed their coming first. He stiffened in the saddle of the army mule which was his preferred mount and seemed almost to sniff the air.

"Corfe," he cried. "The Hounds!"

The King looked at him, and nodded. He turned to Astan his bugler. "Sound me the 'halt'."

Clear and cold over the tumult of the battle the horn call rang out. As soon as the notes had died the buglers of other companies and formations took it up, and in seconds the entire battle-line had stopped moving, and the Orphans grounded their pikes. Those two miles and more of armed men and stamping horses paused as though waiting, and the field became almost quiet except for stray spatters of gunshots here and there and the neighing of impatient destriers. To the north the bells of Charibon had fallen silent.

Golophin seemed to be listening. He stood up tense and stiff in his stirrups while his mule shifted uneasily under him. Soon all the men of the army could hear it. The mad, cacophonous chorus of a wolf pack in full cry, but magnified so that it rose up over the trampled and bloodstained and scorched grass of the battlefield and seemed to issue from the very air about their heads.

"Arquebusiers, stand by!" Corfe shouted, raising the Answerer, and down through the army the order was repeated, while the Cathedrallers clicked open their saddle-holsters and reached for their matchlocks.

They came in a huge pack, hundreds, thousands of them. From the centre of Charibon they poured along the streets in a fanged, hairy torrent, their eyes glaring madly and their claws clicking and sliding on the cobbles. The human troops of Aruan made way for them in terror, shrinking against walls and ducking into doorways. But the Hounds ignored them. Running now on four legs, now on two, they burst out of the narrow streets and formed up vast as a cloud on the plain before Charibon, marshalled by mail-clad Inceptines. Lycanthropes of every shape and variety imaginable milled there, yapping and snarling and hissing their hatred at the silent ranks of the Torunnans, a tableau from some primeval nightmare.

The Almarkans, who were caught between the two lines, streamed west in utter panic, collapsing the last of their tents behind them, some dropping their weapons as they ran. They were not professionals but shepherds of the Narian Hills, fishermen from the shores of the Hardic Sea, and they wanted no part of the slaughter to come.

Corfe stared narrowly at the mobs of shifters who snapped and spat by the thousand before his men, but yet obeyed the commands of their Inceptine leaders and remained in place. He shaded his eyes and looked up at the high buildings of Charibon itself, less than a mile away now, and wondered if perhaps one of the figures he saw standing there was the architect of these monstrosities. A small group of men was watching from the tower next to the cathedral—one of them must be Aruan, surely. And even as he watched the air seemed to shimmer about them, and ere he looked away, rubbing his watering eyes, he was sure their number had increased by one.

In that moment, the Hounds of God sprang forward. They loped through the ruined camp of the Almarkans looking from afar like a tide of rats, and the roaring, howling and snarling they made as they came on made the horses rear up and fight their bridles in fear. Corfe gave no order, for his men knew what to do. The Hounds ran straight up to his line in a boiling mass, and with them came an overpowering, awful stink, heavy as smoke.

With forty yards to go the Orphans levelled their pikes once more, and every firearm in the entire army was discharged in one long, stertorous volley that seemed to go on for ever. The front of the army was hidden in a solid wall of smoke and a moment later hundreds and hundreds of werewolves and shifters of all shapes and misshapes came hurtling out of it and threw themselves upon the Torunnan front rank.

The army seemed to shudder at the impact, and was at once engaged in hand-to-hand combat all along its length, and Corfe could see soldiers being flung through the air and smashed and clawed off their feet. But every time a shifter struck one of Corfe's men, no matter how glancing the blow, it shrieked and at once collapsed. Soon at the feet of the Orphans and the Torunnans of the front line a horrible tide-mark built up, a barricade of nude bodies. For when the shifters were so much as grazed by the spiked iron of the Torunnan armour, the Dweomer left them, and their beast-bodies melted away.

As the smoke of the initial volley cleared and drifted in rent patches out to sea, it was possible to perceive the carnage that the arquebusiers had wrought. Thousands of naked corpses littered the plain, in places lying piled in mounds three and four deep. The grass was dark and slimy with their blood.

The attack of the Hounds faltered. Even through the blood rage that impelled them they finally realised their mistake, and began to pull back from that deadly line of iron-clad men. They streamed away in their hundreds, trampling their Inceptine officers or, snarling, beating them aside. But there was to be no chance even in retreat. As soon as they broke off the army's arquebuses were levelled again, and Corfe heard the voices of his officers bellowing out. Another volley, and another. Every round his men fired was made not

of lead, but of pure iron, and the heavy bullets snicked and
whined and scythed across the battlefield so that the surviving Hounds were cut down in swathes as they withdrew.
When the smoke finally cleared again the plain was empty
of life, and the corpses of Aruan's most feared troops littered
it like a ghastly windfall. They had been utterly destroyed.
An eerie silence fell over the field, as though all men were
astounded by the sight.

Corfe turned to Astan his bugler and simply nodded. The
tribesman put his horn to his lips and blew. The Torunnan
advance began again.

"GOLOPHIN has betrayed us," Aruan said, his voice harsh
as stone. "He has told the Torunnans how to kill us."

Bardolin stood with the last shifting threads of the Dweomer dwindling about him. His clothes smelled slightly
scorched and his face was wan with fatigue. "Any hedge
witch could have told them the same."

"There are none left in Torunna. No, it was Golophin. He
has chosen his side at last. A pity. I thought he would see
sense in the end." Aruan's eyes seemed slightly out of focus,
as if they could not quite take in the enormity of the spectacle
before them.

"Their infantry are entering the city," he said. "Bardolin,
in God's name what kind of men are these? Does nothing
daunt them?"

The Hebrian mage did not answer his question. "The
Hounds have failed us, for the moment. There are others we
can call on when the time is right. But for now we must fight
the enemy sword to sword. Reinforcements are on their way
from the north, and the south. Corfe has made a brave fight
of it, but he cannot win, not against the numbers we will
bring to bear on him."

Aruan clapped him on the shoulder. "That is what I like
to hear. I am glad you came, Bardolin. I have need of your
good sense. A man must be a stone not to lose a little of his
equilibrium at a time like this."

"Then I had best give you my news before you lose any

more. Yesterday an army of Torunnans and Merduks under Formio defeated our forces in a battle near the town of Staed in southern Torunna. The invasion has failed."

Aruan did not move or speak, but a muscle clenched and unclenched like a restless worm under the skin of his jaw. "Is that all?"

"No. Our spies tell me that after the battle Formio received a young man at his headquarters who claims to be heir to the throne of Torunna, Abeleyn's illegitimate son by his one-time mistress. He told the Fimbrian Regent that Queen Isolla is dead. Murad killed her in the Levangore before being slain himself." Bardolin looked down, and his voice changed. "Richard Hawkwood is dead also."

"Well, we must be thankful for what we are given, I suppose. Our plans have gone awry, Bardolin my old friend, but the setback is temporary. We have fresh forces on the way which will weigh heavy in the scales, as you say." He smiled, and the perilous lupine light burned in his eyes, gloating with secret knowledge.

An Inceptine who was leaning over the tower parapet with his fellows threw back his hood and pointed south. His voice quavered. "Lord, the Torunnans are advancing up the very streets. They are approaching the cathedral!"

"Let them," Aruan said. "Let the doomed have their hour of glory."

THE battlefield had grown, so that now the monastery-city itself had been swallowed by it. Corfe had wheeled the Orphans westwards once more so that their right flank was resting on the complex of timber buildings that constituted the southern suburb of Charibon. Those arquebusiers who had been positioned on the shore of the Sea of Tor now advanced northwards and began pushing towards the Great Square at the heart of the city while the Cathedrallers formed up south of the Orphans to protect their open flank, and Olba's reserve began moving at the double northward to join in the taking of the city. Buildings were burning here and there already, and the Himerian troops who were trying to

hold back the Torunnan advance were confused and leader-
less. The hard-bitten Torunnan professionals herded them
like sheep, advancing tercio by tercio so that the once tranquil cloisters of Charibon rang with the thunderous din of
volley fire and the screams of desperate men. No quarter was
given by the iron-clad invaders, and they cut down every
man, woman and black-garbed cleric in their path so that the
gutters ran with blood.

But the Second Empire had not yet committed all its
strength. From the west the glittering ranks of mail-clad gallowglasses advanced in unbroken lines with their two-handed
swords resting on their shoulders and their faces hidden
behind tall, masked helms. And beyond them more regiments
of Almarkans and Perigrainians were forming up on the
plain, preparing to push the Torunnans into the sea.

A wind off the Torian carried the smoke and stink of the
battle inland and the sun came lancing in banner-bright
beams through the curling battle reek, making of the armed
formations brindled silhouettes. For three square miles south
of Charibon the wreck and smirch of war covered the earth,
as though the battle were some dark flaming brush fire which
left blackened carrion in its wake. And it was not yet mid-
morning.

Rilke's artillery began to bark out once again and create
flowers of red ruin among the ranks of the advancing gallowglasses. However, these Finnmarkans were not the frightened boys that the Almarkan conscripts had been, but the
household warriors of King Skarp-Hethin himself. Their advance continued, and they closed their gaps as they came so
that Corfe could not help but admire them.

He studied the battlefield as though it were some puzzle
to which he must find the answer. Huge masses of men had
almost completed the dressing of their lines behind the gallowglasses; the foremost had already begun to advance in
their wake. He was outnumbered several times over, and it
would not be long before someone in the enemy high command had the wit to move round his left and outflank him.

He could either pull his men back now and await the enemy onslaught, or he could throw caution aside.

He looked north. The outskirts of Charibon were on fire and his men were fighting their way street by bloody street into the heart of the city. That was where the battle would be decided: in the very midst of the hallowed cloisters and churches of the Inceptines. He must make a deliberate choice. Battlefield victory was impossible; he knew that. He must either fight this battle conventionally, harbouring his men's lives and hoping that they could stage a fighting withdrawal through the hordes pitted against them. Or deliberately send the thing he loved to its destruction, throw away the tactics manual and chance everything on one throw of the dice. All to accomplish the death of a single man.

If he failed here; if Aruan and his cohorts survived this day, then the west would become a continent of slaves and the magicians and their beasts would rule it for untold years to come.

Corfe looked at Golophin, and the old wizard met his eyes squarely. He knew.

Corfe turned to Ensign Roche, who was wide-eyed and sweating beside him again.

"Go to Comillan. He is to charge the gallowglasses, and follow up until they break. Then go to Kyne. The Orphans must advance. They will keep advancing as long as they are able."

The young officer took off with a hurried salute.

And as easily as that: it was done, and the fate of the world thrown into the balance. Corfe felt as though a great weight had been raised off his shoulders. He spoke to Haptman Baraz.

"I am taking the Bodyguard into the city. Tell Olba to follow up with his command." And when the young officer had gone he turned to Golophin again.

"Will you be there with me at the death?" he asked lightly.

The old wizard bowed in the saddle, his scarred face as grim as that of a cathedral gargoyle. "I will be with you, Corfe. Until the end."

TWENTY-TWO

BARDOLIN watched the charge of the Cathedrallers from the roof of a building off the Great Square. In all the houses around he had gathered together what he could of the retreating Almarkans and had stationed them at windows and on balconies, ready to fire down on the Torunnan invaders as they came. More reinforcements were still flooding through the city from the north, and while the Torunnans were burning and killing their way forward he and Aruan had set in place many thousands of fresh troops to bar their way, rearing up barricades across every street and positioning arquebusiers at every corner.

But out on the plains beyond the city the red horsemen of Torunna were advancing side by side with a Fimbrian pike phalanx, eight or nine thousand strong, to meet the gallow-glasses of Finnmark. Something in Bardolin stirred at the sight, some strange grief. He watched as the Cathedrallers charged forward, a scarlet wave, and the terrible pikes of the Orphans were lowered as they followed up. Scarlet and black upon the field, the colours of Torunna. He heard faintly over the roar of the battle the battle paean of the Cimbric tribes come drifting back to the city, fearsome and beautiful as a summer storm. And he watched as the gallowglasses were shunted backwards and the lines intermingled silver and red as the Cathedrallers' legendary charge struck home. The Finnmarkans fought stubbornly, but they were no match for the army that Corfe Cear-Inaf had created, and eventually their line broke, and splintered, and fell apart. And the Orphans came up to finish the bloody work, their pikes as perfect as though they were being wielded in a parade-ground review.

A nudge, a subtle spike in his brain.

Now, do it now.

Bardolin rose with tears in his eyes. He raised hands to heaven and called out in Old Normannic. Words of summoning and power which shook to its foundations the building whereon he stood. And he was answered. For out of the south there came a dark cloud which sullied the spring sky. It drew closer while the battle below it opened out heedlessly below and the smoke of Charibon's burning rose to meet it. At last other men saw the looming darkness, and cried out around him in fear. In a vast flock of many thousands, the Flyers of Aruan came shrieking down out of the sun and swarmed upon the advancing armies of Torunna like a cloud of locusts. Even the destriers of the Cathedrallers could not withstand the sudden terror of that attack from above, and they reared and threw their riders and screamed and milled in confusion. The scarlet armour of the tribesmen was hidden as by a black thunderhead and in the midst of it, dismounted, buffeted by their panicked steeds, they began a savage fight for survival. The remnants of the gallowglasses, and the regiments of Himerians behind them, took heart, and began to advance. The Orphans moved to meet them, and Corfe's Fimbrians fell under the cloud also, and all that part of the battlefield became a whirlwind of shadow and darkness within which a holocaust of slaughter was kindled.

●   ●   ●

THE sunlight had gone, and a premature twilight had
fallen upon the world. Great tumbling clouds had come
galloping up from the south propelled by wizened smatter-
ings of lightning and a chill had entered the air. It began to
rain, and with the rain fell long slivers of ice which scored
men's flesh and rattled like knives off their armour. The battle plain began to soften, and the churned footfalls of soldiers
and horses sank into mud below them so that a vast quagmire
was created, and within it heavily burdened men swung their
weapons at each other and battled with the unthinking ferocity of animals.

Such was the press and congestion in the streets of the
city that Corfe and his Bodyguard had to dismount and leave
their horses behind. Armed with sabres and pistols, the five
hundred men in raven-black *Ferinai* armour picked their way
forward on foot, the rain dripping from their fearsome helms.
They were tribesman and Torunnan, Fimbrian and Merduk;
the cream of the army. As the regular Torunnans fighting
there in the shadow of the burning houses saw them they set
up a great shout. "The King is come!"

The Bodyguard walked on until they came to the first of
the street barriers behind which Almarkan arquebusiers were
firing and reloading frantically. There came a sound like
heavy hail rattling off a tin roof, and several of the Bodyguard staggered as arquebus bullets slammed into them. But
their armour was proof against such missiles. They walked
on, shielding the match in their pistols from the rain, and
delivered a volley at point-blank range. Then they discarded
their firearms and drew their sabres and began climbing over
the barricades. The Almarkans ran.

The Torunnans marched on. Men were still firing at them
here and there from upper windows but for the most part the
Himerians had fallen back to the Great Square before the
cathedral and the Library of St. Garaso. They gathered there
and were placed in order by Bardolin and Aruan and dozens
of Inceptines. A few surviving Hounds squatted snarling on
the cobbles and homunculi wheeled overhead like vultures.

Corfe and his men burst out of the streets and into the

square itself. The rain had quenched every scrap of slow-match between both armies and the arquebusiers had thrown aside their useless firearms and drawn their swords. The tall helms of the Bodyguard as they formed up in the square made them seem like black towers alongside their more lightly armoured comrades, and behind them in the streets Olba's reserve, a thousand of whom were Orphans, were coming up at the double, their pikes resting on their shoulders, the sharpshooters felling them by the dozen as they advanced.

Charibon's Great Square was almost half a mile to a side. At its north end stood the Library of St. Garaso, greatest in the world since the sack of Aekir. To the west loomed the towers of the Pontifical Palace, a newer construction much expanded in the last decade. And to the east was the triple-horned Cathedral of the Saint. The square, for all its size, was hemmed in by tall buildings on all sides and resembled nothing so much as a huge amphitheatre. Across it Corfe could see two glittering figures who must be Aruan and Bardolin. They wore antique half-armour worked with gold, and it flashed and gleamed in the rain. Even as he watched, the Torunnan King saw one of these two straighten before his troops, heedless of the invaders, and lift his arms to the lowering sky and the ice-mingled rain. He was saying something in a strangely beguiling chant, and as he did his troops straightened and lifted their heads and looked at the fearsome Torunnans across the short distance of the square and were no longer afraid. They began to cheer and howl and beat sword-blade against breastplate so that a deafening din of clattering metal rose up under the rain.

Corfe's Torunnans had dressed their lines, and stood motionless and silent. The Bodyguard formed the front rank, with a thicker knot of them about the King. Behind them came a thousand Orphans, their pikes projecting over their shoulders, and behind them two thousand more Torunnan arquebusiers, fighting with sabres alone.

Golophin stood beside the King, the only man in all that densely packed square who wore no harness and carried no weapon. Corfe looked at him. "Which one is which?"

"Aruan is the bald one with the hawk nose. Bardolin's nose is broken and he looks like a soldier. That is him, on the right."

"And Himerius, where is he do you think?"

"Himerius is near eighty now. I doubt he'll take to the field."

Golophin was not far off that age himself, Corfe realised. He set a gauntleted hand on the wizard's shoulder. "Maybe you'd best go to the rear, Golophin."

The wizard shook his head, and his smile was not altogether pleasant. "No weapon will bite me today, sire. And I am not without weapons of my own."

Corfe raised his voice to be heard over the clamour of the Himerians and the hissing rain.

"Then help me kill him."

Golophin nodded, but said no word. He turned so that his wide-brimmed hat hid his eyes.

At that moment the Himerian troops in the square charged, screaming like fiends. They came on in a frenzied rush and, crashing into the tall armoured line of the Bodyguard, began to hammer upon the Torunnans like men possessed.

Corfe's line bent but did not break. The Orphans of the reserve came forward and leant their weight to the mêlée, some stabbing blind with their pikes, others drawing their short, broad-bladed swords and pitching in where a falling Bodyguard left a gap.

The discipline of the Torunnans mastered even the Himerians' Dweomer-fed rage, and indeed that rage caused many of the enemy to leave themselves open as they neglected to defend themselves in their haste to kill. They pulled down many of the tall Torunnans, three and four of them attacking a single soldier at a time, but Olba's Fimbrians strode forward to fill the gaps and the line remained unbroken.

Corfe felt the moment when all was poised, and the initiative began its slip away from the enemy, like the moment when a wave crests the beach and must begin to ebb.

"Sound the advance!" he shouted at Astan, and the horn

call blew loud and clear over the tumult of battle. A hoarse
animal roar came from the throats of the Torunnans, and they
surged forward. The spell broke under the strain, and the
Himerians began to fall back.

"Come with me," Corfe said to those around him, and a
group of men clustered under his banner and began cutting
a path through the retreating enemy to where Aruan and Bardolin stood on the steps of the Library of St. Garaso with a
crowd of soldiery about them. Baraz was with Corfe, and
Felorin, and Golophin, and Astan and Alarin and two dozen
more. They held together with the compact might of a mailed
fist and when their foes saw the light in Corfe's eye they
blenched and fell back.

The Torunnans poured across the square in the wake of
their King. Before them the enemy retreat degenerated into
a rout. The Himerians had fought Hebrians and Astarans;
they had cowed the petty kingdoms and principalities of the
north and they had set their stamp across two thirds of the
known world. But faced by the elite of Torunna's warriors
and their soldier-king, they were hopelessly outmatched, and
not even the wizardry of Aruan could make them stand fast.

Corfe and his followers strode across the corpse-choked
square until they were scant yards from Aruan and Bardolin
and their last bodyguards crowded on the library steps. Aruan
looked like a man exhausted, but there was a deadly light in
his eyes and he stood straight and arrogant. At his shoulder
was Bardolin, his armour covered in other men's gore, a
short-bladed broadsword in his fist. The darkness of the day
was deepening, for Charibon was on fire all about them now,
and shrouds of smoke hid the sky. The rain poured down in
shining rods and leapt up bloody from the cobbles. Across
the square a quiet fell, though all around them in the distance
they could hear the battle raging on beyond, as though Charibon were groaning in its death throes.

Corfe pointed at Aruan with the tip of the Answerer's
blade.

"It ends here."

Astonishingly, the Arch-Mage laughed. "Does it, indeed?

Thank you for the warning, but I fear, little King, that you are misinformed. Golophin, be a good fellow and tell him. You know the truth of it. You have seen it with your far-sight."

Golophin frowned, and Corfe spun on him. "What does he mean?"

"Sire, the Cathedrallers and the Orphans are defeated and surrounded upon the field. They are gathering for a last stand. This thing's flying legions have broken their lines, and more troops are on their way from the west, a great army. The battle is lost."

Corfe turned to Aruan again, and to the astonishment of all, he smiled. "So be it. They have done their job, and now I must do mine."

He raised the Answerer and kissed the dark blade, then began to march forward.

His men came with him, and the tribesmen among them began singing. Not a battle paean this time, but the mournful song raised by hunters at the place of the kill.

Aruan's mouth opened and closed. Then he shut his eyes and his body shimmered and appeased to grow transparent. Just when it seemed he would disappear entirely, a bolt of blue light came lancing across the heads of his men and smote him to the ground. He grew solid again in the blink of an eye and fell to his hands and knees, gasping.

Golophin lowered his still-smoking fist. "No one runs away," he said. "Not today."

A last, bitter fight took place on the steps of Charibon's ancient library, wherein long before Albrec had once discovered the document which united the great religions of the world. The Himerians fought with a savagery hitherto unseen, the Torunnans like dreadful machines of slaughter. The bodies tumbled down the steps and built up at their foot, but all the while Corfe cut his way ever closer to Aruan and Bardolin. As the last of their defenders fell, the doors of the library opened behind them, and a fresh wave of their troops poured out, yelling madly. But they could not drown out the sombre death hymn of the tribes, and these too were pushed

back by a black hedge of flailing iron blades, until the mêlée
had moved and retreated into the tall dimness of the library
itself. There it opened out, and by lamplight and torchlight
amid the tall shelves and stacks of books and the ash-grey
pillars of the building the fighting went on, and men scattered
trying to flee or trying to kill. But Corfe and his companions
held together and followed the gleam of Aruan's bright armour, and pursued him back through the shadows of the
library until he stood at bay with few about him, his eyes
glaring hatred and a kind of madness, and the stench of the
beast rising in him.

Bardolin strode forward then and clashed swords with
Corfe himself, but the Torunnan King seemed to have grown
in the shadows of the ancient building until he loomed like
some giant warrior out of legend. He knocked Bardolin aside
with one mailed fist, and kept going with his eyes fixed on
Aruan.

The beast erupted out of the Arch-Mage, uncontrollable
and baying. The armour it wore burst its straps and fell from
its body and it became a huge monolithic darkness within
which two yellow eyes gleamed and long fangs clashed in
its slavering muzzle. It lunged forward and careered into a
tall shelf full of books, sending it tumbling over. The heavy
wood caught Corfe on his left side and knocked him off his
feet. The Answerer skittered across the stone floor. The wolf
Aruan towered over him, and then bent to bite out his throat.

But two more shapes sprang forwards, their swords stabbing out above their prone King. Baraz and Felorin, charging
like champions at the huge shifter, yelling defiance. The wolf
leaped back with preternatural speed and ripped free a heavy
shelf from the wall. This it swung in a great arc that caught
Baraz across the side of the head and broke his neck. It raised
the heavy wood again, but Felorin ducked under the swing
and stabbed upwards. He missed, but the wolf fell back
swiftly, holding the shelf before it like a shield. Then Felorin's mouth opened and he dropped his sword to the floor
with a clatter. He half turned but something smote him deep
once again, and he sank to his knees.

Bardolin pulled his sword free and stepped back as Felorin collapsed face up on the floor. There was a haziness to his outline, as if he possessed more than one shadow, and indeed as he turned back to the King it could be seen that a second shadow detached itself from him and left to be lost in the gloom of the library. He strode forward, and behind him the wolf followed.

Corfe's left arm was broken, and the ribs on that side had been cracked and displaced. He tasted blood in his mouth and a harsh gasp of pain left his lips as he struggled to his feet, then bent to retrieve his sword. His bugler and colour-bearer were dead behind him, at whose hand he knew not, and though fighting could be heard all through the library, here at this end he stood alone.

Bardolin faced him while the wolf padded off to one side, circling. Corfe stood swaying and the Answerer seemed impossibly heavy in his good fist. He pointed the sword into the floor like a staff to steady himself and stared at the man who had been Golophin's protégé, his apprentice, his friend. He had, as the wizard had said, a soldier's face, and Corfe knew looking at him that at another time or in another world they would have been friends. He smiled. That other world awaited him now, and was not so far away.

Bardolin nodded as if he had spoken his thought aloud, but there was something else in his eye. It looked beyond Corfe, behind him—

The wolf attacked. Corfe, warned by the movement of Bardolin's eye, wheeled round forgetting his pain. The Answerer jumped up light as a bird again in his hand and as the great beast's paws came raking down he stabbed inwards, felt the point break flesh and sink half a handspan, no more. The claws raked the flesh from his face and then fell away. There was a shrieking bellow, like the sound of an animal caught in a trap, and the wolf tumbled to the ground stiffly as a felled tree. Before it hit the flags of the floor it was no longer an animal, but a naked man in old age. And Aruan lay there with blood trickling from a wound over his heart, and he lifted up his head, hatred burning out of his eyes. He

aged as Corfe stood there, his face becoming lined and withered, his muscles melting away, his skin darkening like old
leather. He dwindled to bare, sinew-frapped bone and his
stare was lost in the twin orbits of an empty skull.

Corfe staggered. His flesh hung in rags below his eyes and
the blood was pouring in a black stream down his breastplate.
Now Bardolin strode forward, and his broadsword came up.
His expression had not changed, and his face wore still a
mask of gentle grief.

Corfe managed to clang aside his first lunge. The second
smote his breastplate and knocked him backwards. He came
up against a scribe's angled desk and knocked aside a third.

"No!"

There was a sudden blazing radiance, and Golophin
stepped between them with the werelight spilling out of his
eyes and burning around his fists. He was breathing heavily,
and even his breath seemed luminous. Bardolin retreated before him though there was no fear in his eyes. "Get back,
Golophin," he said calmly.

"We did not agree to this!"

"No matter. It is necessary. He must die, or else it has all
been for nothing."

"I will not let you do it, Bardolin."

"Do not try to stop me. Not now, when we are so close.
Aruan is gone—that was the bargain. But he must go too."

"No," Golophin said steadily, and the light in him increased.

Bardolin's cheeks were wet with tears. "So be it, master."
He dropped his sword and out of him a light flooded to match
Golophin's.

Corfe shielded his eyes. It seemed to him that there was
stroke and counter-stroke in the midst of a storm of whirling
and leaping brilliances. Books caught fire and blazed to
ashes, the stone floor was blackened, but he felt no heat. The
ground under him trembled and shook.

The light winked out, and when Corfe had blinked away
the searing after-images he saw that Golophin was standing

over a prostrate but conscious Bardolin, his chest moving in
great heaves.

"I'm sorry, Bard," he said, and cocked one fist upon which
a globe of blue werelight shimmered like a broadhead trembling at full draw.

But then a shadow flew out of the gloom of the wrecked
library, and as it approached it took on shape and definition
until it seemed to Corfe to be a young girl with a head of
heavy bronze-coloured hair. He shouted at Golophin but his
voice was no more than a harsh croak in his throat. The girl
shadow sprang upon the old wizard's back and his head came
back and he screamed shrilly. She seemed to melt into his
body, and his werelight was sucked into a growing darkness
near his heart. For a moment he metamorphosed into a writh-
ing, grotesque pillar of wildly gyrating limbs and faces, and
then there was a last, blinding flash of light, and the pillar
crumpled to the floor like a bundle of tortured rags.

THE only sound was the cutting rasp of Corfe's breathing.
The air was heavy with the stink of the wolf and another
reek, like old burning. Corfe grasped his sword and crawled
one-handed over to Golophin's body, but there was nothing
there except a shredded robe. The fighting in the library
seemed to have ended, and though men's voices could be
heard far down the aisle of book stacks none but the dead
seemed to remain around him.

He crawled on, until he came across Bardolin's body in
the gloom, and there he halted, utterly spent. It was done. It
was over.

But Bardolin stirred beside him. He raised his head and
Corfe saw his eyes glitter in the darkness, though no other
part of him moved.

"Golophin?"

"He is dead."

Bardolin's head fell back and Corfe heard him weeping.
Moved by some feeling he could not explain, he released his
grip on the Answerer and took the wizard's hand.

"He could not do it, in the end," Bardolin whispered. "He

could not betray you." Corfe said nothing, and Bardolin's fingers tightened about his own.

"There should have been a better way," he said in the same, racked whisper. His eyes met Corfe's again. "There must be a better way. It cannot always be like this."

He turned his head, and Corfe thought he could almost feel the life slipping out of him. It was growing lighter. The darkness outside the tall windows of the library was clearing. Lifting his eyes, Corfe saw a shard of blue sky breaking through the clouds far above. From farther down the library came the sound of men approaching, Torunnans by their speech.

"It will be different now," he told Bardolin. But the wizard was already dead.

Out on the fuming expanse of the battlefield, the remnants of the Torunnan army had come together in a great circle, and were beleaguered there by a sea of foes while behind them Charibon burned unchecked, its smoke hiding the light of the sun. Around them there piled up a monstrous mound of corpses, and the teeming regiments of the Himerians attacked with merciless persistence, men clambering over the bodies of the dead to come at each other. The Torunnan circle shrank inexorably as thousands upon thousands more of the enemy came up on all sides, and within it men cast away hope, and resolved to sell their lives dearly, and their discipline held firm despite their shrinking numbers. They would make an end worth a song, if nothing else.

Another army came marching over the horizon out of the west, and the Torunnans watched its advance with black despair while the Himerians were inspired to fresh heights of violence. But the keen-eyed on the battlefield paused as they watched it, and suddenly a rumour and a strange hope swept the struggling tercios and regiments that battled there.

The approaching army opened out and shook into battle-line with the smooth efficiency of a machine. And now all on the western edge of the field could see that it was clad in

black, and its soldiers carried pikes on their shoulders. As
they drew near, the Himerian attack faltered, and the rumours
grew until they were being shouted from man to man, and
the Torunnans lifted their heads in wonder.

Thus the Fimbrian army, fifty thousand strong, came
marching to the aid of their old foes the Torunnans, and the
forces of the Second Empire took one look at that sable jug-
gernaut, and began to flee.

EPILOGUE

THE dreaming heights of the Jafrar Mountains were wrapped in everlasting snow, but down on their knees a summer evening was blue with the approaching dusk, and the first stars had begun to burn bright and clear in an empty sky.

About the campfire two old men sat warming their hands while behind them their mounts nosed at the fresh grass, one a common mule, the other a fine-limbed grey gelding such as the Merduks had bred upon the eastern steppes for generations. The two men said nothing, but watched the approach of a third rider as he made his way up into the empty hills towards them. He was clad in a black cloak, and a circlet of silver was set on his head. He carried a sword of great lineage, and yet his face was ridged and scarred as by the claws of some beast. He halted at the limit of the firelight and dismounted, and as he walked towards them they saw that he was lame in one leg.

"I saw your fire, and thought I might join you," he said and, wrapping his cloak about himself, he sat close to the embers of the wind-flapping flames.

"You are weary," one of the others told him, a kind-eyed man with a monk's tonsure and a grey beard.

"I have come a long way."

Then you shall stay with us and have peace," the second said, and he was a white-haired old man with the face of a Merduk.

"I would like that."

The three sat companionably enough about the fire as the night swooped in around them and the mountains became vast black shadows against the stars. Finally the scarred man stirred, rubbing his leg.

"I almost lost my way, back down there. I almost took the wrong path."

"But you did not," the tonsured one said, smiling, and there was a great compassion in his eyes. "And now perhaps, all will be well at last. And you may rest."

The scarred man sighed and nodded. But it seemed that some last thing troubled him. "Who are you, lord?" he asked in a low voice.

"Men called me Ramusio, when I dwelled among them. And my friend here was named Shahr Baraz. If you wish, you shall stay with us."

"I would like that," the man said, and he seemed to slump, as though a last burden had been taken from him.

"And what may we call you?" Shahr Baraz asked gently.

The man raised his head, and it seemed a much younger face now looked out at them, and the scars thereon had disappeared.

"My name is Corfe. I was once a king," he said.

His two companions nodded as though it were something they already knew, and then the trio sat quiet in the night staring into the firelight whilst above them the great vault of the night sky glittered and under their feet the dark heart of the earth turned on in its endless gyre amid the stars.